Deadly Reunion

(A Grace Holliday Cozy Mystery)

Elisabeth Crabtree

First Printing, December 2012
V9/22/13

AUTHOR'S NOTE

This is a work of fiction. Names, characters and situations are completely fictional and a work of the author's imagination. Any resemblance to any person, living or dead is purely coincidental.

OTHER BOOKS IN THE GRACE HOLLIDAY SERIES

Deadly Magic
Deadly Reunion
Death Takes a Holiday

CHAPTER ONE

"OH, JUST COME inside. You look fine," Hope Holliday encouraged.

Grace Holliday glared at her sister. "I do not and you know it! I look like a giant, fluffy, pink cupcake."

Inadvertently catching a glimpse of herself in the school's glass door, Grace quickly shut her eyes. Calling the pink monstrosity currently swallowing her body, 'a fluffy, pink cupcake' could actually be considered a compliment. Grace opened her eyes and pulled at the pink taffeta wrapped around her waist, hoping that by some magic, she could twist the dress into a more flattering shape. She had already removed the puffed, lilac colored rear bustle with matching blue and purple taffeta rosettes, but surprisingly, there was little improvement.

Hope released a long-suffering sigh. "You look very nice," she said, adopting the dulcet tones of a used car salesman. "Elegant . . . regal . . . and if you don't stop, you're going to rip it."

Grace felt her normally pretty features twist into an ugly scowl. Knowing Hope, she did this on purpose. She could never stand to be in anyone's shadow. Grace didn't know why Hope worried. Very few people could outshine Hope. Not even her own, albeit fraternal, twin.

Especially right now, Grace thought, looking at her own reflection in the glass and back again at her sister. Hope was sporting the latest in haute couture, a purple silk dress that complimented her long wavy red hair and lithe body. In Grace's opinion, it was cut far too low down the bust and far too high up the thigh. No doubt worth more than what most people make in a month, but it certainly grabbed your attention.

Grace's dress was also designed to grab one's attention, just not in quite the same way. The pink nightmare she was wearing had far more in common with an eighties bridal party than with haute couture. "You know I don't look good in pink and when was the last time you saw a hoop skirt? Just where did you find this dress, Hope?"

"Would you stop complaining? It's not my fault the invitation insisted on semi-formal attire. Whatever that means. I have one rule—never be underdressed."

Grace decided to let that statement pass without comment, since she was far more interested in removing the large silk flower sitting on her hip, than shattering any delusions her sister might have at the moment.

"Besides, it's the best I could find on such short notice." Hope swatted at her sister's hands. "You're going to ruin it."

Grace reluctantly looked at her reflection in the window and sighed. "That isn't possible. There is no way I could possibly make this dress worse."

"You knew the reunion was tonight. Why didn't you bring something appropriate to wear? I made sure to have two back up dresses just in case something went wrong with this one," Hope said, smoothing the purple silk dress down her thigh.

"First of all, I did not know the reunion was tonight. I thought it was last night. Had I known it was tonight I would have made sure not to come home 'till tomorrow. You told me it was last night, Hope."

"Did I? How strange. I'm usually so careful with dates," Hope said innocently.

"Secondly, the airline lost my luggage and all of my clothes—"

"You mean the clothes you stole from me?" Hope said sweetly.

"Borrowed," Grace said, convinced that her sister put her in this getup as a form of revenge. "Even if I had an appropriate dress, I couldn't have worn it."

"Oh well, the important thing is that you didn't miss the reunion. Don't you want to see our old friends? You know, see who got married, who is still married, who made it big, who is going to be crowned Reunion Queen. I've been looking forward to this for weeks."

Grace suddenly stopped adjusting her dress and asked incredulously, "Is that what all of this is about? Reunion Queen? You can't be serious."

Hope raised an eyebrow. "Serious? Of course, I'm serious. I should be Reunion Queen. I was Prom Queen. Homecoming Queen. I was even—"

"What are you doing, going for the trifecta?" Grace interrupted.

"As I was saying, I was even the Orange Blossom Queen of Overlook County. It's only natural that I should be crowned Reunion Queen, as well."

"Who's your competition?"

Hope walked up the remaining steps and pulled open the door. "It doesn't make any difference."

"Let me take a wild guess. It wouldn't be Crystal, would it? I heard through the grapevine that she has been calling around trying to drum up support. In fact, I heard about it a few weeks ago. About the same time you suddenly decided what fun it would be to go to our high school reunion."

Hope smirked. "I couldn't care less about Crystal."

"You won, Hope. You're successful. World famous. I can't pass a supermarket without seeing your face on the cover of a magazine. Let her have this."

Hope, open mouthed, just stared at her sister as if the very idea of letting Crystal win was unfathomable. "I am not leaving this high school without that crown. Now come inside," Hope growled, grabbing Grace's hand and dragging her across the threshold.

♛ ♛ ♛

Grace walked into her old high school and looked around. The gym had been completely transformed. Well, not completely. A gym, in the end, always looked exactly like a gym, except with streamers and balloons. Nevertheless, as far as gyms went, the planning committee had done a rather good job of camouflage.

Gold and red balloons covered every available surface of the gym floor, while streamers, party lights and a sparkling disco ball hung from the ceiling. Even the ugly bleachers had been folded up and hidden behind gold curtains. Several red and gold covered round tables, each one decorated with centerpieces of white lilies and tiny candles, were placed along the sides of the gym. And in the center of the gym, multi-colored lighted floor tiles shined from beneath the multitude of balloons. To Grace's eye, it looked more like a wedding reception than a reunion.

Grace cautiously walked into the room, her dress inadvertently sweeping balloons out of the way, and turned around. Except for the band setting up their equipment on a makeshift stage at the far end of the gym, and one or two school volunteers, the place was virtually deserted.

No chance of getting lost in the crowd here, at least not right now, Grace thought, while trying to affix the nametag to her chest.

Grace sighed. This was the last place she wanted to be. A year ago, she had been looking forward to the reunion. In fact, she had been thrilled at the very thought of it. And why not? She had just been given a promotion, which had been accompanied by a very nice raise in salary, a new office with a view, and a much-needed assistant to help her with her new duties. She had also begun dating the very handsome attorney who worked in the building next door. Everything in her life was going better than planned, and she couldn't wait to return home and see all of her old friends. Absolutely thrilled. Of course, that was before Allen Madison, the bane of her existence, married the new boss and was subsequently promoted to Vice President of the toy company where they worked. Now, she's returning home, alone and unemployed, and just in time for her ten-year reunion, too.

She had hoped she could ease back into town with very little fanfare. Just slowly re-emerge and re-establish herself. But now she's back, and worse, attending her high school reunion wearing a dress Scarlett O'Hara's maiden aunt wouldn't have been caught dead in. Grace shook her head. And to think, she had been voted *Best Dressed* her senior year.

She had used every trick in the book to get out of attending the reunion: sickness, the weather, jet lag, the fact that she deplaned no more than thirty minutes before, but in the end, she was no match for Hope's secret weapon, a five-foot-four whirling dervish they affectionately referred to as mom. Before she knew what was happening, she had been trussed up and pushed into the family car with "maybe you'll meet a nice man" echoing in her ears.

Grace quietly swore as she began to collect balloons under her dress. Kicking them out from under the hoop skirt only seemed to cause more to gather. Giving up, she let the skirt slide back down to the floor. The trick to surviving this night with her dignity and reputation intact, she decided, was to draw as little attention to herself as possible. Considering the circumference of her dress could hide a small car, Grace knew she faced an uphill battle on that front.

Grace carefully looked around the room as more and more people began to filter in through the gymnasium doors. A nice secluded dark corner table is what she needed. One in the back. Preferably, close to a door.

Eyeing a particular out of the way spot, Grace carefully lifted her skirt a few inches off the floor and dashed across the gym, a streak of pink and purple taffeta. The only evidence of her mad dash was the small wake of balloons floating behind her.

Arriving safely at her hiding spot, she happily sank into a chair facing away from the dance floor. With any luck, she'll be able to spend the rest of the evening in absolute anonymity.

"Grace, is that you?"

Grace quietly swore to herself. She had immediately recognized that voice. Beth Gragson. Beth, while never a close friend, was one of those girls from high school who seemed to be friends with everyone. She never met anyone with whom she wouldn't immediately have a lengthy and heavily one-sided conversation with: the star quarterback, the weird kid who kept to himself and drew pictures of maniacal clowns, even the store clerk who was just trying to check her out. No one was safe.

Grace reluctantly turned in her seat and froze. The smile that had been forming, quickly transformed into a panicked, horrified grimace.

It wasn't the sight of Beth, which caused Grace to unconsciously mimic the bride of Frankenstein. After all, Beth hadn't really changed much since high school. Her black hair was still cut in a pixie style with red spiked tips, which in turn, matched her always-present red framed glasses, ruby-red lipstick, and matching fingernails. Sometime during elementary school, Beth had decided that red would, forever more, be her signature color. She was nothing if not committed.

No, it wasn't the sight of Beth, which made her freeze. It was what was in Beth's hands and pointed directly at Grace—a shiny, brand new, digital recorder.

"It is you! I almost didn't recognize you. It's been so long," Beth said, throwing her arms around Grace, and rocking her back and forth.

Unprepared, Grace grasped at the edge of the table to keep from tipping over.

Beth quickly straightened, and physically pulled Grace up. "Look at you! Oh my, I absolutely love your dress," she said, slowly panning the camera up and down. "You just don't see those types of dresses anymore. Twirl around, so I can get a good look."

"Oh, this old thing," Grace said, her mind furiously trying to think of a way to get the camera away from Beth.

"Why haven't you come to visit more often?"

"Well, I—"

"I know. You are just like your sister; couldn't wait to get away. I don't know why. I never wanted to leave," Beth interrupted, proving that people never really change.

Grace could count all the words she spoke to Beth, from kindergarten through high school, on one hand. It seemed like no one could get a few words out, before Beth jumped in and would carry on the rest of the conversation. Hope once attempted to time Beth in order to see how long she could talk without anyone else saying a word. The experiment, unfortunately, had to be postponed. According to Hope, she had a life and couldn't wait that long.

"What have you been up to since graduation? Are you married? Any kids? I have four. Do you want to see their pictures?" she asked, thrusting her wallet into Grace's hands.

Grace nodded, dutifully opening the wallet, looking at each picture, and making the appropriate cooing sounds when necessary.

"Beatrix, Sophia, Darryl and Marty. Don't you think they look just like their father?"

Grace gave her a puzzled look.

"Mark Lewis. Remember? He was in our senior art class."

"Wasn't he the kid who drew those . . ." Grace hesitated, deciding that adding a descriptive adjective such as disturbing, might be considered insulting, "clowns?"

"Yes! You do remember him! He'll be so pleased," Beth said. "He was afraid no one would remember. He is a cartoonist now. Do you know the *Clown Family on Parade* comic strip? That's his!"

Still distracted by the video camera pointed her way, Grace asked, "What are you doing with that?"

"It's my new camcorder." Beth proudly held out the camera and twisted it around so that Grace could see from all angles. "I'm helping Melodie and Crystal with the reunion. Crystal wants to do a video montage and set it up on the website. She's going to send a link to everyone after the reunion. Isn't that a good idea?"

"Reunion montage," Grace repeated, a shudder creeping up her spine. "Are you filming right now?"

"Of course! I haven't turned this off since I got here. I'm not going to miss a moment." Grace wondered what type of montage they would be able to get, considering that Beth tended to talk with her hands. Perhaps, she should advise Crystal to add a warning to the video. Something like 'Warning: anti-nausea medication should be taken before viewing'.

Better yet, Grace thought, she could volunteer to edit the montage herself. After all, it would be such a shame if a recording of her dress ended up on the editing floor. "I would love to help. Are you part of the committee?"

Beth solemnly shook her head. "I volunteered. I felt so bad for Melodie. I just think this reunion is too much for her."

"Melodie?" Grace asked in surprise. "She's the queen of organization. I remember—"

"It's too soon. I mean Larry just died a couple of months ago. Well, give or take a few weeks."

"Larry's dead?" Grace asked, in disbelief, slowly sinking back down into her seat. She couldn't believe it. Why had no one told her? Anytime someone sneezes in town, her mother is immediately on the phone describing the who, what, when and where of the event in nauseating detail. How could she have missed this?

"Didn't you know? He was driving down McGraw Parkway when a deer dashed in front of him. He swerved and ended up hitting a tree. He died instantly."

"Poor Melodie," Grace said, her heart breaking for her old friend.

"Yeah. There's going to be a memorial slide set up to honor all the graduates who've died since graduation. It's a nice thought and all, but I hope Melodie can handle it. Oh, I don't want to talk about this. Today is a happy day. Let's talk about you. What have you been up to? I want to hear everything."

"Well, I've been living and working in New York, but recently, I've been thinking of moving back home." Grace decided it wasn't necessary to mention it was really her employer's pink slip that triggered her sudden desire to move back home. Her employer and the eviction notice taped to her door last week. "I was working at the Straker Toy—"

"You might be moving back? That's wonderful! Oh, everyone will be so excited. What will they do at the agency without you?"

"The company," she said, automatically correcting Beth. "I'm sure they'll manage."

"You know, your little brother was in my comic book store last January. I overheard him talking about your work. It just sounds so exciting."

"Thank you!" Grace smiled, pleased that someone found her work interesting. Working at a company that manufactured games and toys wasn't as thrilling as being a model like Hope or a doctor like her younger sister, but Grace still found the work interesting.

"Please, tell me all about it." Beth's eyes lit up in excitement. "Your brother walked out before I could hear how everything ended."

Grace thought back to last winter. She had been working on developing board games for kids, ages fourteen and above, and had used her fifteen-year old brother, Jeff, as a guinea pig. Jeff must have been describing one of them to his friends. But, which one? She had five in various stages of development when she had been summarily fired. Was it the game involving dragons? The numbers game? Or maybe it was the one about magicians. Jeff had seemed particularly interested in that one.

"I always knew you would end up doing something exciting. My father did that sort of thing at his company. He was really good at it."

Grace shook her head, vaguely recalling Beth's dad working as a security guard at the mall.

"Oh, look, there's Crystal." Beth waived the camera in the air, trying to get the other woman's attention. "She wanted me to let her know if I saw Hope tonight. Is your sister here?"

"She—"

"I bet she didn't come. I told Crystal that she wouldn't come. I mean, why would Hope come back? She hates it here. Oh, wait, isn't that Hope over there?" Grace turned to see her sister talking to a member of the band. "Grace, why did you say she wasn't here?

"I didn't. I—"

"Oh, never mind," Beth said smiling. "You're so funny. I see you haven't lost your sense of humor. You haven't changed a bit. I am just going to run over there and say hi. I will be right back, and then you can finish telling me all about your job." Beth patted Grace's hand and then just as quickly as she appeared, she dashed off into the crowd; her recorder placed protectively out in front of her, sure to capture everyone's chins or chests depending on their height.

"Finally! I thought she would never leave," a voice whispered into Grace's ear.

Turning in her seat, Grace smiled and stood up. "Melodie!" she said, reaching out to hug the other woman. "It's so wonderful to see you. You look beautiful."

Which was true. Melodie had made a dramatic transformation in the ten years since Grace last saw her. Gone was the awkward, gangly, baby-faced teenager in oversized shirts and jeans. Tonight, she looked sophisticated and elegant in a light blue evening dress, which complemented her unusual bright blue eyes. Even her usually unruly, curly auburn hair had been carefully swept up into a French twist. She looked stunning.

Melodie smiled at the compliment, tucking an errant strand of hair into the French twist at the back of her head.

"Are you okay? I'm so sorry to hear about Larry. I had no idea. Beth just told me."

"Thank you," she said, taking the empty seat opposite of Grace. "It hasn't been easy, but I've been doing better the last few weeks. Organizing the reunion has really helped me."

"Everything looks beautiful. You can't even tell this is a gym."

Melodie made a face. "I wanted to have the reunion at the country club, but it was going to be too expensive. We had to decide between an absolutely beautiful location and finger food or here . . .," Melodie said with a small grimace, "and a catered three course meal. The committee chose food."

Good choice, Grace thought. "Well, maybe the next reunion."

Melodie nodded. "I am so glad you came. I absolutely love your dress. It's just so—" Melodie halted, struggling to come up with an appropriate description.

Sparing her friend, Grace quickly said, "It's not mine. Hope found it for me at the last minute."

Melodie laughed. "Oh thank goodness, I didn't think I would be able to come up with a convincing compliment for that thing. You should know better than to let Hope pick out your outfits. I learned that lesson in fifth grade when she tried to convince me that I looked cute in baggy overalls and flannel shirts."

Grace laughed.

"I was afraid I wasn't ever going to see you or your sister again. What have you been up to lately?"

"Oh, there's not much to tell. I've just been working." Well, except for the last couple of weeks, Grace thought. "Trying to stay busy and pay the bills. You know how it goes." Not exactly feeling up to discussing her life, Grace decided to change the subject. "How's your sister?"

"Oh, I'm sure Crystal is sharpening her claws, waiting for Hope to appear."

Grace raised an eyebrow, surprised by the bitterness in Melodie's voice, as well as the expression of utter disdain. Growing up, Melodie had always adored Crystal. Being only ten months apart, Melodie had looked up to her older sister, often taking Crystal's side in her many battles with Hope. "Is something wrong?"

Melodie paused, before slowly shaking her head. Smiling, she insisted everything was fine.

Feeling the sudden tension in the air, Grace turned her head. The band had started playing, as more people began filling the room. In the corner of the room, she spotted her former next-door neighbor and childhood crush. "Is that Adam Phelps over there? I had no idea he was going to be here. I didn't think I would ever see him again." Suddenly, the night was looking up.

"Oh, he wasn't about to miss tonight."

Grace was too distracted to recognize the cynicism in Melodie's voice. "I heard he was filming a movie in Spain." Grace began waving frantically, trying to get Adam's attention.

"No, he finished that six months ago. For some reason he's been hanging around here for the last month. You can stop waving, here he comes."

Grace dropped her hand, pleased to see Adam walk up to their table.

"Grace. I can't believe it's been ten years since I last saw you," he said, reaching down to warmly embrace her. "You look absolutely wonderful. I can't tell you how glad I am to see you. In fact, I've been meaning to call you up and ask you to be in one of my films."

Grace laughed. Ten years ago, she might have gladly jumped at the chance to follow him to Hollywood. Unfortunately, he hadn't asked her. To everyone's surprise, Adam left the day after graduation on route to Hollywood, determined to make a name for himself. He had succeeded beyond everyone's wildest imaginations. Using his quite considerable inheritance, he had turned a screenplay he had written into a somewhat acclaimed, if not popular, independent movie. He eventually turned that success into another and another.

According to the gossip magazines, he was one of Hollywood's most sought after directors, as well as one of its most notorious womanizers. With his dark brown curly hair, lopsided grin, and easy manner, he would be hard for any woman to resist. Nevertheless, for some reason, Grace had always been able to resist him. Staring up into his handsome face, she had a hard time remembering why.

"Is your sister here?"

Grace nodded, suddenly remembering why she was able to resist him so easily. It wasn't difficult, considering Adam had spent all four years of high school lusting after Hope and only Hope.

"Here she comes," Melodie said, her head nodding to the right. "And here comes Crystal."

Adam looked over his shoulder and grinned. "Well, this should be fun."

CHAPTER TWO

"HOPE! DIDN'T YOU hear me?" Crystal asked. "I called your name back there."

Hope's normally serene face hardened, as she pivoted to face the other woman. "Oh my, Crys, is that you? I had no idea. I would never have recognized you. I didn't realize ten little years could change someone so much. You look really . . ." Hope's features twisted into a sneer. "Well, you look so much better than you did."

Grace sighed. Actually, Crystal hadn't changed at all in the ten years they had last seen her. Her hair was the same shade of bleached-blonde it had been in high school. She still wore the same self-satisfied smirk. The same tight clothing. The same bubble-gum pink fingernails. The same tacky blue eye shadow. It was like going back in time. The only thing missing was the chewing gum she usually had in her mouth.

"Hope, you haven't changed at all." Crystal smiled, her eyes lighting up like a Christmas tree. "I just wanted to let you know how sorry I was to hear about your job. I felt so bad when I heard you were fired from Madam Dupis. It is a shame," she said, clucking her tongue. "But that's the modeling business for you. You get a few wrinkles, gain a pesky ten pounds—or is it thirty? Oh well, it doesn't matter. You hide it well—and it's all over. Life's just so unfair." Crystal shook her head in pity.

Hope smirked. "You're so lucky you've never had to worry about such things. I mean, obviously, you can gain as much weight as you want. It's not like anyone cares what you look like."

Crystal smirked. If Hope's comment bothered her, she didn't show it. "I'm the same size I was in high school."

Hope scrunched up her face. "I know."

Crystal drew in a breath before releasing it slowly. "Well, at least you have your education to fall back on. Oh wait, I'd forgotten, you left for Paris after graduation, didn't you? You know the community college has several great degree programs. I know the Dean of Admissions at OCC. I would be happy to give you a recommendation."

Hope tossed her long red hair over her shoulder. "That is so sweet of you, but I'd think you'd be so busy what with recovering from your recent divorce. My goodness, my heart just broke for you when I heard. Was it another woman? Now, don't let it get you down. That's just the way some men are. Always wanting to trade up. You know, find a younger, prettier, thinner, nicer woman. It's just awful."

Grace winced, instinctively knowing how Crystal would respond.

Crystal's smile grew wider. "Well, I'm sure you're an expert on that subject, by now."

Hope stiffened. Grace had to admit, Hope walked right into that one.

"But I'm afraid you've been listening to some bad gossip. I'm not getting a divorce. Thomas and I have never been happier. In fact, we are renewing our wedding vows soon. I do hope you can attend. Especially, since you missed our wedding. Don't worry; I'll make sure to add you to our invitation list."

Noticing her sister's stunned face, Grace forced a smile and said, "I guess congratulations are in order," briefly wondering what the etiquette actually was on renewals. Do you even issue congratulations?

"Yes," Hope said, looking over Crystal's shoulder. "Why, there's the groom. I think I'll go over and offer my condolences." Grace quickly put out a restraining hand. The last thing that this party needed was her sister and Tom Lake to make a scene.

Sensing blood in the water, Crystal stepped closer to Hope. "Did you hear, Thomas is the Assistant District Attorney. Assistant District Attorney today and Senator tomorrow. Where's your husband, Hope? Oh, that's right. You've never been married. Didn't I hear that you were engaged, though?" Crystal looked up at the ceiling. "Oh wait; no, that's not right. The last thing I read said he broke it off." She shook her head sadly. "Pity. So, how many times has it been for you? Five or has it been six engagements, so far?"

Hope flushed angrily. "Just the three, Crystal."

"Were you able to bring a date, at least?"

"No. I didn't see any reason to. Now, if you will excuse me," Hope said, sliding past Crystal and heading straight for Tom.

Before she could get very far, Grace slipped her hand into Hope's and pulled her in the opposite direction.

"So, do I have your vote for Reunion Queen?" Crystal yelled, as Grace dragged Hope towards the hallway.

"What are you doing? You are not going to talk to Tom, are you?"

"Why not?" Hope asked, digging in her heels and looking back over her shoulder. "We are both adults. I'm sure we can have a pleasant conversation with one another."

"Hope, I don't think that is a good idea. Why don't you just try to enjoy the night?"

Hope sighed in frustration.

"What?"

"I've lost him. He's disappeared," she said, her eyes scanning the room. "Why don't you go sit down? I'll be there in a minute. I'm just going to go to the ladies' room to freshen up."

"You've been in there since we arrived."

"Don't worry. I won't cause any problems," Hope promised as she walked away.

Not fully believing her sister, but not knowing what else to do, Grace slowly made her way back to her table.

She was surprised to see it had filled up in her brief absence. Beth was back with her recorder, making sure to capture the momentous event of Grace wading through the crowd on her way to her seat. To Beth's left, sat her husband Mark who was busy doodling a picture of what looked like a clown eating a bus, on the back of one of the reunion invitations. To Beth's right, sat Melodie and then Crystal, the former, apparently trying to convince the latter, to behave herself. And just sitting down next to Crystal was her husband Tom, looking like he would rather be anywhere else.

Grace couldn't blame him. He looked absolutely miserable. That should make Hope happy. Grace remembered how handsome he had been in high school. Long, thick, dark hair; green eyes; athletic build. He had been the poster child for tall, dark, and handsome. Now he looked like the poster child for the overworked, alcoholic attorney. He was still handsome, but his appearance was starting to look haggard. His black hair was cropped close to his head and prematurely graying at the temples and his once clear green eyes were bloodshot and sunken in. Life as the Assistant District Attorney was clearly not agreeing with him. Well, that's what happens when you marry Lucifer's handmaiden, or, as she's known here on Earth, Crystal Hogan.

Rounding out the rest of the table was Adam Phelps and Grace's former history professor, Eric Collins.

"Grace, come and sit down, we saved you a seat," Beth said, using the camera to gesture to the empty chair between Eric and Adam.

Grace sat down and turned to her former teacher. "Hi, Mr. Collins."

Eric Collins smiled brightly. "You're out of school now Grace, please call me Eric."

"Just what are you doing here? Last time I spoke to you, you were planning to retire as soon as we graduated. Something about how we wore you out."

Eric laughed. "I don't know. I just couldn't get away. But this year I'm going to do it. I'm going to finally break free. This year is it. I can feel it."

"Now, don't listen to him. He loves it here. Always has." Grace turned to see Diana Collins walk up to the table and place a hand on her ex-husband's shoulder. Her ruby wedding ring flashing in the light. Eric smiled as he reached up to pat Diana's hand.

Realizing her mouth was hanging open Grace snapped it shut. She had never seen the battling Collins in the same room together, at least, not without one of them hurling insults or on one occasion, knives. Granted, they were plastic knives from the cafeteria, but still, the sentiment was there.

Diana squeezed his shoulder. "If he didn't, he wouldn't have taken the principal's job this year."

Tom stood up. Picking up an empty chair from a neighboring table, he moved his own chair to the side and set the extra chair down next to Crystal.

"It's so good to see everyone again," Diana said, moving to the other side of the table. "Grace, it's so nice seeing you. We have missed you and your sister."

Crystal gave a less than lady-like snort.

Grace ignored Crystal, smiled, and asked if Diana was still the school nurse, vaguely recalling Diana's plans to move out east after their senior year.

Diana nodded her head. "I moved back in January, actually. Luckily, my old job became available during the summer," she said, smiling at Eric. "I can't tell you how happy I am to be home." Diana turned to Melodie. Leaning down, she gave Melodie a quick hug. "Sweetie, I'm sorry I couldn't be here to help, earlier."

"I was here Aunt Diana. Wasn't I, Melodie?" Crystal asked, drawing attention back to herself. When Melodie didn't answer, Crystal addressed the rest of the table, "Wait 'till you see what I have planned. I want to do a Graduate Retrospective."

"We're going to have a few fun games to play tonight," Melodie said, quickly changing the topic.

"Games! I came at the right time, then." Grace looked over her shoulder to see Steve Mattingly walk up to the table, wearing a checkered jacket, much too long for him and mustard yellow pants, much too short. Still, Grace had to admit, he was dressed better than she had ever seen him.

"Where have you been?" Crystal demanded rudely. "You were supposed to be here an hour ago."

"Sorry! I was tied up. I'm here now, so just relax."

"Did you bring your camera?"

"No." Steve held out the black bag in his hand. "I just carry an empty camera case around for fun."

"What'd you hire him for?" Adam said, jerking a thumb in Steve's direction.

"I didn't hire him," Crystal said. "He volunteered. Didn't you, Stevie?"

Steve opened his mouth to answer, but shut it and closed his eyes when Crystal answered for him. "He was happy to volunteer. He's going to take pictures of all the fun we're going to have tonight. We have a special web page devoted to the reunion. Isn't that wonderful?" Crystal glanced around the table. No one seemed the slightest bit interested.

Adam snorted. "Terrific."

"I thought it would be a wonderful idea to have a before and after page. You know, tie it into our yearbook. We would place everyone's high school picture next to what they look like now."

"Crystal, we talked about this," Melodie said in a low tone, clearly embarrassed.

Ignoring her, Crystal continued. "We're also going to add a biography section. See what everyone has accomplished since graduation and then compare it to what everyone said they were going to do when they were in high school. We're going to really go into depth. You know, look into why, exactly, they didn't accomplish everything they thought they were going to do."

Grace glanced at the other horrified expressions around the table.

"I would have had it already set up, but we ran out of time." Crystal looked accusingly across the table at Adam. "Don't worry, I'll send everyone the link after the reunion."

Steve smiled. "I personally think that's a great idea, Crystal. In fact, if you want, I could help you interview everyone." Steve slapped a hand on Adam's shoulder, causing the other man to wince. "Let's start with Adam. I've always wanted to ask you, where do you get your ideas from?"

Adam's expression darkened. "Thanks Steve, but I wouldn't want to bore everyone. Besides, I think I answered that during my last award speech." Adam turned around into his seat and faced Steve. "Why don't we start with you? Tell me, how did your life turn out? Crack that last case, did you?"

"I heard your last movie flopped. How does one recover from such personal failure?"

"I don't know, you tell me."

Grace glanced at the people sitting at the table. Their expressions ranged from embarrassment to amusement. Steve and Adam had never been close, but she couldn't remember such animosity between them before.

"Bite me."

Eric Collins interrupted. "That's enough, guys. This is supposed to be fun, remember."

"That's right," Crystal said, seizing the spotlight once again. "Thank you, Eric. Melodie has worked very hard on tonight, and I think she deserves some recognition." Crystal pointed to the left side of the gym. "I want everyone here to pay special attention to the Remembrance slide show. I spent a long time working on it. It's going to include some pictures of classmates that are, unfortunately, no longer with us. Such as my wonderful brother-in-law, Larry . . ." Crystal gently patted Melodie's hand. Grace watched as Melodie slowly pulled her hand away, and laid it in her lap. Without missing a beat, Crystal continued, "as well as, Sam Baxter, Nora Fuller, Sarah Col—"

Steve turned to Grace. "So Grace, what about you? What have you been up to?"

"I was speaking," Crystal said icily.

"I'm helping, Crystal. You want me to get all the juicy details, don't you? For your web page, right?"

Not interested in sharing just yet, Grace decided to turn the question back on Steve. "I haven't heard anything about you, Steve? What have you been up to since graduation?"

Adam leaned forward. "Haven't you heard? He's our resident 'private dick'."

Sneering Steve said, "No one says that anymore, Hollywood. I'm a licensed private investigator."

"You're only a private investigator because you couldn't pass the entrance exam for the police academy," Adam countered.

Steve's naturally ruddy complexion flushed even more. "I never intended to be a cop. I just wanted to take the test. I didn't fail by the way. But if you want to talk about failure, let's talk about your last movie. I hear that you lost so much money on it that you can't get a picture deal out of Hollywood. The studios won't even return your calls anymore. I also heard that you're in debt up to your curly little head."

Adam's eyes narrowed. "Why are you here? You've been telling me for the last month how you're a big detective in Denver. So, why have you been hanging around our small little town?"

Steve shrugged. "Why has a big time Hollywood director been hanging around our small little town?"

Adam shrugged. "I grew up here."

"So did I. In fact, I've decided to move back. I plan on moving my business here."

"Oh my gosh! Isn't that exciting?" Beth asked, reaching across the table to get Grace's attention. "Oh, Grace, isn't that just the most perfect timing. You were just saying how you wanted to move back here. Think about it, you two could work together."

Grace looked at Beth in confusion, silently praying that Beth wasn't thinking of playing matchmaker, not with her and Steve Mattingly. Steve and Grace had never gotten along. He had always had an annoying habit of attaching himself to any group outing or activity, usually without having been invited. His manners were atrocious. He was arrogant, rude, generally unpleasant and had a tendency to behave like a sexist lout. As far as Grace was concerned Steve was not romance material, for anyone.

Making a face, Steve turned to Grace. "Yeah . . . Thanks. I hate to disappoint you, but I've got a secretary."

"Oh, that's just too bad," Grace said sarcastically.

"If you want, you can submit a resume. You know, in case anything opens up," he said with a shrug.

"Yeah, like anyone in their right mind would work for you." Adam reached for Grace's hand. "How would you like to dance with me?"

Grace quickly accepted his invitation. There was no sense in hiding any longer. Most of her friends had already seen her dress. Might as well try to enjoy the rest of the night, she thought, as she followed Adam to the dance floor.

� ♟ ♟

Grace laid her head on Adam's shoulder, sighing contentedly as his arms encircled her waist. The last two dances had been fast. She had been out of breath by the end of the first song, and was ready to pass out by the end of the second one. She was relieved when the band switched to a slow song.

"I was afraid you weren't going to show up tonight," Adam whispered into her ear.

She leaned back so she could look up into his hazel eyes. "I almost didn't, but I'm really glad I did."

He smiled. His eyes crinkling up in the process.

"I've never seen a show quite like that before. It was very entertaining. Have you two been fighting like that very long?"

Adam smirked. "I never did like him. He's such a blowhard."

"You could have fooled me. I remember you two hanging out at one time."

"Only because we were in the drama club together. We had no choice."

Grace tilted her head. Standing directly under one of the overhead lights, she could make out a rather large bruise on Adam's temple. "Have you been in a fight?"

Adam smiled at her. "No. Why?"

"Your head's bruised." Bringing her gaze down, she noticed a black smudge on his collar. "What have you been up to?"

Adam reached up and gingerly touched his face. "I don't know why it would be bruised. I haven't hit my head on anything," he said, confused.

Grace shrugged and told him he might want to take a look at it in the bathroom.

Promising her he would, he asked, "You aren't going to work with Steve, are you?"

Grace shook her head. "Of course not! Why would I?"

"Good. I wouldn't hire you if you were working with him."

"Hire me? Are you serious? You really want me to be in one of your movies?"

Adam laughed. "No. I need your help on another project. I spoke to Beth last week, and we got around to talking about you. She told me what you've been doing up in New York. I could really use your help."

"Oh?" she asked skeptically. "How can I possibly help you?"

Adam looked over his shoulder. "We'll work out all the details tomorrow. Let's just enjoy tonight."

Shrugging, Grace laid her head back down on his chest as he led her across the dance floor. A few moments passed while her mind wandered peacefully until a sudden tearing sound shattered the mood.

Grace giggled. "Kyle, you're stepping on my dress."

"Adam."

"What?" Distracted, Grace carefully lifted the edge of her dress off the floor. She bent over and ran her fingers across the six-inch tear running along the hem and up a seam. She straightened quickly when she felt her inner slip begin to slide down her hips.

"My name is Adam."

Dropping the hem back to the floor, Grace smiled in confusion. "I know that, Adam. Come on. We'd better go back to the table. I think my hoop is about to come undone."

Grace weaved passed the other dancers, gripping her skirt tightly, as she felt the inner slip start to sag to the floor.

Temporarily averting embarrassment, she gratefully sank back down into her seat, wondering how she was going to make it to the bathroom in order to remove the dress' slip without tripping over it. Grace smiled at Adam as he took the seat next to her.

"See, this is what happens when someone watches too much TV. When Thomas and I have children, they are not going to be allowed to watch TV. I don't want them getting ridiculous notions." Speaking directly to Grace, Crystal said, "At least, you finally came to your senses and decided to come home."

"Eventually," Grace said sarcastically, wondering what Crystal was babbling about.

"About time you two finally got back," Steve said. "We've been waiting here for the last thirty minutes while you and Hitchcock have been tripping the light fantastic."

Grace looked at the table of expectant faces.

"Well?" Steve demanded rudely.

"Well, what?" she asked irritated. It was clear that they all had been talking about her in her absence. With the way she was dressed, she rather expected that, but she couldn't understand the hostility that was coming from Steve.

"Is it true? Are you planning on staying here?"

She leaned back in her chair, wondering why he seemed to care. "Yeah, for a little while."

Grace watched as beads of sweat formed on his brow. "Are you going to open up your own business? Look, sweetheart, I don't think that's a good idea. This is a small town—"

"What's the matter, Steve," Adam asked, "you afraid of a little competition?"

"I don't understand this." Crystal pushed her hair back away from her face, her large sapphire and diamond heart wedding ring catching the light. "Weren't you selling toys or something?" Her tone of voice making it clear what she thought of such an occupation.

Grace shook her head. "No, not exactly."

"That's what I thought, too," Melodie said.

Beth shook her head, clearly upset. "Grace, tell them. They won't believe me."

Frustrated, Grace asked, "About what, Beth? What are you all talking about?"

Beth, clearly exasperated, dropped the camera she had been holding onto the table. "That you're a detective, of course."

"Ah," Grace said, shaking her head. So that was it. Last December Grace had jokingly told her little brother about her new job duties as the toy company in-house detective tasked with the responsibility of discovering the boss' wife's killer. Beth must have overheard Jeff discussing her predicament with his friends. It also occurred to her that must have been what Adam had been alluding to out on the dance floor.

Crystal rolled her eyes. "Here comes Hope. Maybe she can straighten this out."

Tom, who had been alternatively looking down at the table or glaring at Adam and Steve, suddenly stood up at the mention of Hope's name. "I'm going to make myself a drink."

Before Tom could completely stand up, Crystal said, "Excellent idea, honey, get me some punch."

"I would love some, too. That is, if you're offering?" Hope asked as Tom walked away.

It didn't escape Grace's or anyone else's notice that Tom took the long way around the table to get to the drink area. "Was it something I said?" Hope asked.

Grace sighed. Well, that wasn't too painful.

"Hope, isn't Grace a private detective?" Beth asked.

"A private detective?" Hope's lips started to curve up.

"I knew it," Steve gloated. "I knew you weren't a detective. A trained professional can spot a fake a mile away."

"Is that why you were sweating over her setting up shop just a few minutes ago," Adam pointed out.

"Really, Grace." Crystal's voice became pitying. "I knew someone at this reunion would pretend to be something that they're not, but I didn't expect it to be you."

Laughing, Grace shook her head. "Listen. There's been a mis—"

"Would all of you leave her alone? If she says she is a detective, then she is. I've always known Grace to be truthful," Mr. Collins said, sweetly smiling at Grace.

"Here." Steve reached into his wallet, pulled out twenty dollars, and laid it on the table. "I will bet you she is not a detective."

"Fine, I'll take that bet," Adam said, turning to look up at Hope. "Is it true?"

Grace looked up at her sister. To her surprise, Hope answered in the affirmative.

Adam smiled as he pocketed the twenty, while Grace raised a hand to her suddenly pounding head.

Diana, apparently having enough of the show, stood up. "All right, everyone. You got your answer. Now leave her alone. Why don't you guys go get some food?"

"Yeah, that's right. You should see the feast I had prepared just for my wonderful classmates," Melodie said, getting up from the table and dragging Crystal with her. As everyone left the table for the buffet located at the front of the gym, Hope sat down next to her sister.

"What are you doing? I know this is your first time lying, but let me give you some advice. If you are going to lie, start small. Let it be something within the realm of reality. Like you could have pretended you had just been promoted head doll maker, or whatever it is that you do."

"Just exactly how is my being a detective beyond the realm of possibility? Besides, I didn't tell them I was a detective. Beth got the idea into her head and ran with it."

"All right, I'll go along with you on this. Just tone it down. Try to make the story a bit more believable," Hope whispered as she stood up.

"There's no reason to go along with me on this. As soon as everyone gets back to the table, I'm going to explain to them that it's all a big misunderstanding."

"Oh, please, don't embarrass me tonight," Hope whined. "You'll just look foolish if you go back on your lie now. Besides, what harm is it going to do? You're not the only one embellishing their life here tonight. Sabrina Matthews has been running around, telling everyone she is a doctor, but I have it on good authority she dropped out of med school and is working at a restaurant somewhere in Virginia. Just stick with the story for a little longer."

Grace groaned. "Fine. Are you going to get something to eat?"

"No, I've lost my appetite." Hope stood up and looked around the room. "I see some of my cheerleading squad. I think I'll go visit with them for a while."

"I'll go with you."

"No, you stay here. I want to know everything that Crystal and Tom say."

"I'm a fake detective, not a fake spy, Hope. Get someone else," Grace whispered as Hope turned and walked to the other side of the room.

Grace debated between following her sister anyway, or going to the buffet. The reunion was in full swing now. Couples were swaying to the music. Almost every table was full, and people were just starting to line up at the buffet table. The food did look excellent, and smelled even better. Melodie spared no expense on tonight: stuffed mushrooms, beef wellington, herb roasted chicken, and garlic-mashed potatoes lined the tables. Grace took a deep breath, and felt one of her back buttons pop off.

Well, this is just great, she thought. Grace carefully turned around in her seat. With one hand, she felt around her back. Please don't be a top button. Her hand reached the middle of her back and continued down. There, near the ribbon. Good. Hopefully, it's not too noticeable. She twisted around and looked on the floor behind her. With any luck, the button can be reattached. Where is it? Grace turned back around, and carefully looked under the table. Spotting the button a few inches away, Grace leaned under the table and reached out a hand.

"Grace, what are you doing?" Adam asked from somewhere above her.

Startled, Grace banged her head on the table. Seconds later, she felt Adam's hand wrap around her arm and pull her up.

"Clearly living up to her name." Grace heard Crystal say.

Everyone was slowly returning to the table, plates full of food in hand.

"I'm sorry, Grace. I was just having some fun earlier." Steve said, appropriately conciliatory. He must have gotten an earful from one of the others. "Who knows maybe we can work together in the future."

Beth sat down, holding a drink with a plate balanced on top with one hand, and the video camera in the other. Well, at least this time the video camera was pointed at Beth and away from everyone else, Grace thought happily.

Beth placed the camera on the table, taking care to point it directly at Grace. "Grace, you still haven't told me about what happened with your case? Was Mr. Bankcroft Moneypenny really murdered while skydiving and was it his wife or his nephew who killed him? And which one had the gambling problem?"

"Moneypenny?" Grace chuckled. So, it wasn't Lily Straker's death Jeff had been discussing with his friends; it was the mystery board game Grace had been developing. She shook her head. None of the board game suspects had a gambling problem. Now, Louisa Straker had a gambling problem, she thought, becoming more confused by the minute. "I'm not sure—"

Beth nodded, "I didn't quite understand what Jeff was talking about. He kept saying something about someone rolling the dice over and over again."

Thankfully, Melodie interrupted Beth. "No one has said anything about all of my wonderful decorations. I'll have you know, this didn't happen overnight. I struggled over picking the right color of gold streamers for weeks now."

"It's beautiful, Melodie," Diana said warmly. "You did a great job!"

"Thank you, but I didn't do this alone. I had a wonderful reunion committee, and I had a lot of help from my favorite Aunt." Melodie pulled Diana into a hug.

"Don't forget your favorite sister," Crystal reminded Melodie, placing her hand over Melodie's trembling hand.

Melodie's smiled faltered. "How could I forget you Crystal?" Melodie slid her hand from underneath Crystal's and picked up her cup. "You were a big help, too," she added. Grace felt Adam's knee brush against her own and wondered if he was picking up the sudden tension around the table, as well.

"We have a lot of fun things planned for tonight," Crystal said, tapping a black binder she had picked up off the floor and set on the table.

Grace felt Adam shift in his seat next to her. She slightly turned her head to see what had captured his attention. To her surprise, Adam's face was turning red.

"What is that?" Steve asked.

"This?" Crystal asked, pointing to the binder in front of her. "Just the schedule for tonight."

"Can I see it?" Adam asked, holding out his hand.

Eyes fixated on the gym door, Melodie suddenly asked in a breathless whisper, "Who is that?"

Crystal placed the binder down on the ground at her feet and looked toward the gym door. "Who?"

"That man standing there," Melodie said, biting her lower lip.

Crystal sat up straighter in her seat, craning her neck to see whom Melodie was referring to. Suddenly, her eyes lit up. "Wasn't he in our calculus class?"

"No," Melodie said. "You're thinking of Travis Shaw. I saw him a few minutes ago dancing with Becky. No, I don't remember graduating with this guy."

Grace turned to look, but a large group heading to the buffet table blocked her view.

"You think he may be a party crasher?" Steve pushed his chair back and stood up. "You want me to bounce him?"

Adam rolled his eyes. "Yeah, tough guy, go try to bounce this guy. Just who do you think would want to crash our reunion?"

"Excuse me for a moment. He looks lost, and as head of the reunion committee, I should probably help him." Melodie pushed back her chair and adjusted her dress. Grace watched as she deftly navigated her way around the dance floor, sashaying lightly as she headed towards the entrance, with Steve following close behind her.

Adam smiled ruefully. "There goes our class president. Always there to help." To Grace, he whispered, "Larry's not even cold, yet."

CHAPTER THREE

GRACE RIPPED ANOTHER rose from her dress. She had managed to make it to the bathroom without tripping over her skirt, which she decided was nothing short of a miracle. It had taken her thirty minutes to remove the rest of the slip and finally, the hoop. After she had stuffed the remnants in the trashcan, she started removing the tulle, only stopping when the dress began to come apart at the seams. Now, she was busy removing the little roses attached across the bust. Staring at herself in the bathroom mirror, Grace sighed. No matter, how much tulle, roses, or ribbons she removed, there still seemed to be plenty left. Maybe if she made her hair bigger, the dress would stand out less, she thought, reaching for her purse.

"Oh my God! Isn't he gorgeous?"

Grace looked up as two women she barely recognized walked into the room and stood next to Grace. Both were laughing, clearly enjoying themselves. Obviously freaks. The taller woman, she recognized from Hope's cheerleading squad. Janet something or other, she thought, as she dumped the contents of her purse onto the counter.

They nodded politely at Grace, who was still staring at her reflection, wondering if she could get away with taking the dress completely off and running around in her slip. It worked for rock stars. Besides, it couldn't be any worse than what she was wearing right now, she reasoned.

"I'd still be out there if it weren't for Dennis, glaring at me. He can be so jealous sometimes."

Grace reached for her fingernail clippers. If she could get the straps off, perhaps it wouldn't look so bad.

"I really wanted to stay and listen to him," Janet said, pulling out a compact and lipstick. "He's just so fascinating."

"I know. I was seriously considering hiring him."

"What do you need a detective for?"

Startled, Grace stopped what she was doing. They were talking about Steve? Fascinating? Gorgeous? Sure, physically Steve had improved since high school. His face had cleared up; he had lost around seventy pounds; he was no longer wearing novelty t-shirts depicting comic book characters (usually scantily clad females), but gorgeous?

Grace, realizing she was making a face, smoothed her features out and went back to hacking away at her straps.

"I figured I could use him to check up on Dennis. Make sure he isn't cheating."

Janet put her lipstick down. "He's not—"

"No! But that doesn't mean I can't do a little checking up on him."

They both laughed.

"Why didn't you stay and listen? Your husband doesn't seem like the jealous type?"

"He isn't. I just can't stand *him,*" Janet said grimacing.

At her friend's questioning glance, she clarified, "Adam Phelps. He's just so sleazy. My husband says he's been running around town trying to dig up dirt on people."

Grace finally managed to tear one strap off, which she threw in the trashcan. What was Adam up to? she wondered.

Both women stopped to stare.

Smiling at them, Grace began working on the second strap.

Shrugging their shoulders the women went back to refreshing their makeup. "I heard that rumor. I don't believe it. What's there to dig up? Nothing ever happens here."

Grace silently nodded her head as she tore off the second strap. She had to agree with Janet, what could Adam hope to find here? Dropping the nail clippers back into her purse, Grace reached for her lipstick.

The smaller woman sighed and looked pityingly over at Grace. Catching Grace's eye, she said, "Pretty dress," while shoving her makeup back into her purse. "Come on, let's go back out. I want to make Dennis crazily jealous tonight. Where did he say he was from?"

Janet opened the restroom door. "New York. I think he said he worked for the Straker Detective Agency in New York City."

Grace dropped the lipstick.

"No, I thought he said he left that agency and created his own. I really wished he had brought a business card with him," the other woman said as the door closed behind her and her friend.

Grace glanced at her reflection in the mirror. A streak of red now stained the front of her dress. Uncaring, she shoved the lipstick into her purse and headed for the bathroom door.

🏆 🏆 🏆

The Straker Detective Agency? In New York? Grace opened the door to the gym, her heart beating faster with each second. She had never heard of the Straker Detective Agency. She shook her head. Of course, she wasn't familiar with every detective agency in New York, she thought, trying to shake the gnawing feeling of dread forming in her stomach. The only Straker she knew was her old boss, Franklin Straker, and the only business he was in was the toy business. It's probably just a strange coincidence, she told herself, hoping that she was right.

She passed by the buffet tables and made her way to the back of the room, dodging classmates left and right. She noticed that most of her classmates had left their tables, and were now on the dance floor or milling around reconnecting with old friends. With any luck, her table will be empty, and she'll be able to eat in peace.

Unfortunately, Grace's luck had run out. As she came closer to her table, she noticed that her friends were back in their seats. She also noticed that her seat was now occupied.

Her heart dropped. She'd recognize that blond, wavy hair and broad shoulders anywhere. It can't be, she thought. He wouldn't come all this way. Why would he be here? Why right now? Why, when she looks like a reject from *Gone With the Wind* set?

Grace wondered if she had enough time to run away and hide. She could call him from the parking lot. Better to threaten him with bodily harm over the phone. No witnesses that way.

He turned in his seat suddenly. A happy grin spreading over his face when he saw her standing behind him. "Ms. Holliday! I have been looking for you all day."

Grace walked forward and squeaked out, "What are you doing here?"

Standing up, he ushered her to her seat. "Well, I needed to talk to you about one of our clients. I'm afraid, *Her Majesty*," he said in a stage whisper, "is in desperate need of our help. Those jewels aren't going to find themselves."

Grace groaned. He can't be serious. "Uh huh." She reached for his hand. "Let's talk about it outside," she said not giving him a chance to object.

"Grace, don't be rude, Mr. Drake was just telling us about his last case," Crystal snapped.

Grace glared at her former assistant.

Melodie, completely enthralled by whatever lies Kyle had been telling, reached out her hand and touched the edge of his sleeve. Smiling seductively, she asked, "How did you find out the murderer was hiding in the old clock?"

"Who cares about that?" Crystal asked annoyed. "How in the world did you get off the ship in time?"

"Well, let me tell you, it wasn't easy, but luckily Ms. Holliday was here to save me at the last minute," he said, pulling another chair up to the table.

Before he could sit down, Grace hopped up and grabbed him by the arm, knocking over several cups in the process.

"What about the twins?" Beth asked, as she helped pick up the empty cups that had turned over onto the table. "Were you able to free them?"

"Yes, of course," Grace said, as she dragged Kyle away from her friends. "They're free. Everyone's free."

"Sorry all, I will be right back," he shouted, as Grace propelled him past the dancers and toward the gym door. "We just have some important business to attend to. I promise we won't be long."

As soon as they were out and away from everyone, Grace said, "What are you doing here?"

"I came to apologize for getting you fired."

"What was all of that?" she said, angrily pointing back to the gym.

"I was helping. When I told your friend that I worked with you, she asked me if I was a detective too. Naturally, I said yes."

"Naturally." Grace rubbed her hands across her face. "What was that story you were telling in there?"

"Have you ever read *The Mystery of Mary Price*?" When she shook her head, he added, "Neither have your friends. It's an old mystery book I read when I was a kid."

"You were describing a book?"

"Don't worry. I changed things around. There weren't any twins in the book. They're from an old movie."

"Are you crazy? Wait," she said holding up her hand. "I already know the answer to that. What exactly did you tell them?"

"I kept it real simple. I'm a private detective from New York."

"The Straker Detective Agency?"

"Well, I wasn't sure what you had told them. I started out telling them that I was with the Straker Detective Agency but then when I realized that you hadn't told them much, I changed the story. I told Melodie that I left Straker, branched out, and created my own agency. It was only natural. I mean, after I saved the President and all," he said chuckling.

"Oh, of course," Grace said, shaking her head. "What did you tell them about me?"

"Not much."

Grace sighed in relief. "Good."

"Just that you joined my agency a few months ago."

"I work for you?"

He shrugged. "I thought it would be a nice change of pace."

"And that's it?"

Kyle nodded.

Grace briefly considered her options. "Well, that's not too bad." She could tell her friends Kyle was just joking or perhaps she won't have to say anything. If Kyle left now, her friends might forget about the whole thing. After all, if Kyle just told them that she worked for him briefly then they might lose interest and move on to another topic.

Kyle smiled proudly at her. "I also told them that you were my best detective and the Mayor of New York was planning a parade in your honor after you foiled a plot on his life a couple of weeks ago."

Realizing her mouth was hanging open, she snapped it shut. "What? Why? What? How?" she asked, momentarily incapable of forming complete sentences.

He lifted his hands up. "Calm down. It's okay. You're supposed to exaggerate at reunions."

"You're not exaggerating, Kyle. You're flat out lying."

His smile fell from his face. "I didn't start it," he said defensively. "You're the one who told them you were a detective. I'm actually surprised at you. Telling a lie like that. After all of your lectures on honesty." Kyle shook his head in mock disappointment. "Why did you tell them that?"

"I didn't!" Grace caught the eye of a few classmates walking down the hall. She took a deep breath. He did have a point. He didn't actually start this misunderstanding. He's just gleefully keeping it going, she thought ruefully. She couldn't blame him. This situation is far too tempting for a born performer like Kyle. Which is more than enough reason to get him out of here, she decided. "It's a long story," she said, leading him out the door and to the parking lot. "How in the world did you find me, anyway?"

"I'm a detective, remember?"

"Funny."

"Why did you leave without saying good-bye?" Kyle asked, suspiciously sounding hurt.

"I did say good-bye. The day we were fired. There was no point in sticking around there any longer." Grace said, as she dragged Kyle across the parking lot, narrowly avoiding tripping over her dress. When she finally realized that she had no idea where he was parked, she stopped and faced him. "Why are you here? I thought you had some sort of show lined up?" In addition to being her former assistant, Kyle had a somewhat lucrative career as a performing magician. Somewhat being the operative word.

Kyle hung his head. "It didn't quite pan out."

"What happened?"

"People really take their magic seriously today."

"What did you do?"

"I accidentally set one of the tables on fire. They freaked out," he said. "There's always a bit of danger. That's what makes magic so much fun."

Grace nodded sympathetically, remembering the time he set the office copier on fire. The microwave. The paper wastebasket. His coat. "You really need to take fire out of your act."

"You sound like my father," he accused.

"Speaking of whom, have you taken him up on his offer?"

Kyle shook his head. "I don't need his help. I'm doing fine, all on my own."

So far Kyle had stubbornly refused his famous father's offer to join his magic show currently touring through Europe. Grace wondered how long that would last. "Tell your dad hi for me," she said, turning back towards the school.

"No, wait! Why do they think you are a detective, and what are you wearing?" Kyle asked, grabbing a fistful of taffeta, and pulling her back.

"It's a horrible misunderstanding. Beth overheard my brother talking about the plot to the mystery game we were working on. She thought it was real, and that I was a detective."

Kyle laughed.

"I don't know what Jeff was saying, but somehow Beth is convinced I'm a detective. She's been in there," she said, pointing towards the school, "desperately trying to convince everyone else. I tried to tell everyone the truth, but I couldn't get a word in edgewise."

"Oh, don't tell them. Let's have some fun," he cajoled, grinning. "It's harmless fun. No one will know."

His grin was infectious. Despite her annoyance, Grace felt herself smiling back at him. "I don't want to lie to my friends."

"It's not really lying. Straker did ask you to find out who killed his wife last year. Which you did." He looked down at her affectionately. "I think that makes you a detective. A very good one. Besides, we can tell them the truth later. Let's just have fun for tonight." He turned around and took a step toward the school.

Grace reached out and grabbed his jacket before he could get very far. She still wasn't convinced that it was a good idea to set him loose among her friends.

Reluctantly turning back, Kyle asked, "Aren't you glad to see me?"

"Of course, I'm glad you showed up," Grace said, realizing that she was telling the truth. She was glad to see him. She didn't want to admit it, but she had been missing him a little since she left New York this morning. "It's just, other than Beth, they don't really think I'm a detective."

His eyes lit up. "No problem, by the time I am through, everyone in that gym will believe you are the best detective in the world."

Well that feeling didn't last long. "No, no, no! Kyle, please don't help. I mean, you don't have to help. I mean, honesty is the best policy. I'll just go and explain that it was a joke. I'll tell them that I just wanted to see how far I could go. Something like that. I'm sure they will understand."

"Grace," Hope shouted from the door, "I need your help."

Kyle gave a low whistle. "Who's that?"

"My twin sister, Hope."

"Is your sister trying to look like Veronica Lake?"

Grace nodded sadly. "I think it's because of the last name."

"You know, you two don't look alike at all."

"Yes, I am aware, thank you." Grace briefly touched his arm. "I have to go. Why don't we get breakfast before you leave for New York? Call me on my cell tomorrow morning," she said, as she walked back to the school.

CHAPTER FOUR

"IF YOU'RE DONE playing with your imaginary friend, I could use some help."

"He's not imaginary, Hope. You can see him, can't you?"

"I can't believe the amount of work you have put into this story of yours. First, you get Jeff to plant the idea in Beth's head. Then you pass the rumor around the school, and you top it off by hiring, what is obviously an actor, and not a very good one by the way, to play the part of—"

"I did not plant any story with Jeff, pass any rumor, or hire an actor. He is not an actor." When Grace realized that Hope didn't believe her, she insisted, "I'm telling the truth. He—is—not—an—actor."

"Well, where did you find him?" Hope stopped and looked at her sister with growing horror. "Oh no! You didn't. Please tell me, you didn't. He's not one of those is he?" Hope whispered aghast.

"One of what?" Grace asked, not knowing what her sister was implying, but insulted on Kyle's behalf just the same.

Hope's face was a mixture of pity, disgust, and horror. "You didn't hire him off the street, did you?"

"No! Of course not!" Grace shrieked, unable to believe her own sister would accuse her of such a thing.

"Do you know what Mom and Dad will say when they find out?"

"I did not hire him off of the street, and what do you mean *when* they find out? They are not going to find anything out, because you are not going to mention this to them," Grace growled. "Didn't you say you needed my help, Hope? Well, what do you want?"

Hope pointed towards the gym. "I want you to go in there and talk to our classmates. I need to know who is voting for me and who is still voting for Crystal. Now, I have managed to change some votes, and I have no doubt that I will win, but I want to make sure it is a bloodbath. Go in there and start canvassing the voters. You help me Grace, and perhaps, I will forget to mention this to Mom and Dad."

🏆 🏆 🏆

Kyle watched Grace walk into the school. He frowned slightly. This wasn't the welcome he was hoping for. He had considered her more than just his supervisor, and if it hadn't been for that no-fraternization policy, which she held up like a shield between them for the last six months, their relationship might have progressed beyond the employer/employee stage. At the very least, he had hoped Grace would be happy to see him.

Granted, he was partially responsible for her firing. Which was so unusual. Usually, he was getting her out of trouble, not into it. He still couldn't understand how she survived until he came on the picture. If anyone needed an assistant, it was her, and it had quickly turned out to be a full-time job.

He almost panicked when he went to her apartment this morning, and was told by her neighbor she had packed up and moved.

He had the devil of a time finding her. Luckily, he ran into Mina, from personnel, and was able to convince her to have lunch with him. An hour later, he had the address where Grace's final check was to be sent. A few minutes after that, he had her mother's phone number.

Now here he was, at her old school, watching her walk away again. Kyle's frown deepened. She didn't seem too happy when he arrived. He didn't like the idea of these people laughing at her. Though, he had to admit, this whole detective thing was pretty funny.

Kyle smiled. It's so unlike her. She'll never be able to pull it off. At least not by herself, he thought.

Kyle ran his hand through his hair, considering. How hard would it be to pretend to be a detective? It would just be for the night. In fact, this would be a good way to apologize to her for getting her fired. Decided, Kyle walked up the steps to the school and opened the door.

🏆 🏆 🏆

"This is my five-year old, Aaron. Isn't he cute? He's been accepted into the Caine Academy. That's for gifted children, you know," Laura Talbot drawled.

Grace dutifully nodded at the pictures presented to her. For the last thirty minutes, she had chatted with various classmates, trying to win votes for her sister. So far, all she had succeeded in doing was verifying that almost everyone in her class had brought along their photo albums to offer visual proof to the world that their children were obviously smarter and prettier than anyone else's children.

As far as the Reunion King and Queen went, Tom Lake had a lock on Reunion King, which, considering his good looks, popularity in school, and success after school wasn't that surprising. Reunion Queen, however, was very much in the air.

There were three contestants: Hope Holliday, Crystal Lake, and Chloe Bell. The two main contenders, however, were Hope and Crystal. Almost half the class (mostly the men) intended to vote for Hope, simply based on her popularity while in school and her successful modeling career after. The other half (mostly the women) considered her celebrity status negatively, and were planning on voting for Crystal, the 'home-town girl', who was actively involved in several local charities.

"Your children are so beautiful. They look like they could be models. Speaking of models," Grace said, desperately trying to find a way to steer the conversation into the real reason she was here, "did you know my sister is in the running for Reunion Queen?"

"Oh, yes. I absolutely love, Hope!"

Grace smiled. Another vote.

"I was planning on voting for her, but I've decided to go with Crystal."

Grace's smiled faltered. "Why, did Hope do something?"

"No, not at all. It just wouldn't be right for Tom to be the King and his wife to lose."

"Oh, I'm sure Crystal wouldn't mind," Grace lied.

"You've met Crystal, haven't you?" Laura asked, before taking back her pictures and moving on to another classmate.

Surprisingly enough, there was a small contingent of voters, who were voting for Crystal simply based on whether they thought her husband would be King.

It was going to be close. Too close for Grace's comfort.

Grace just hoped that whatever happened, Hope would be a gracious winner or loser, as the case may be.

"Hello everyone! Can I have everyone's attention?" Grace looked up to see her sister standing in the middle of the stage holding a microphone. Grace had forgotten that 'gracious' wasn't in Hope's vocabulary.

"I hope everyone remembers me, but just in case you've forgotten, I am Hope Holliday," she said, as modestly as she could over the crowd's cheers. "I just wanted to say how happy I am to be back home." More cheers. "I have missed you all. No place I have been, and I have been everywhere, compares to home."

Grace felt a cold hand touch the small of her back. "How does she say these things with a straight face? I really should have her in my next movie."

Grace laughed. "Adam, I doubt you could afford her."

"You're probably right. So, where did you disappear to?"

"I didn't disappear. I have been right here getting to know my old classmates."

"Oh no! I know what you have been up to. Hope roped you into getting her votes."

"How did you guess?" she said, looking up into his handsome face. Tilting her head, she noticed the bruise she had seen earlier was now missing.

"She gave me the same marching orders. It's not looking good. I think Crystal has a small majority. What will Hope do to us if we fail?"

"I have no idea, but I am going to be standing right by the door when they make the announcement."

"All right, if they announce Crystal's name, I'll be right behind you." Adam laughed. "Hey, I'm sorry for all the trouble Steve and the others were giving you at the table. Steve was always a jerk."

"Let's forget about what happened at the table." Grace desperately wished everyone could forget about what happened at the table.

"Your boss is . . . interesting. He seems rather young to be a detective." Grace nodded, as she tried to think of a way to casually steer the conversation away from Kyle. "He has led a rather fascinating life. You too, apparently. I am still having trouble believing everything he has been saying about you. With all that you've done, when did you have time to become an expert in Brazilian Jiu-Jitsu and cage fighting?"

"Weekends," she lied automatically, while thinking Kyle had better pray she never does take up Jiu-Jitsu.

Adam looked at her doubtfully. "Hmm. I'm still thinking of hiring you two, or actually, just you. I need help."

Grace quickly shook her head. "Sorry, Adam. I don't work alone, and I'm afraid Mr. Drake's already on his way back to New York."

"No, he's not. He's over there." Adam pointed to a table, near the entrance, surrounded by people.

Grace turned her head in time to see Kyle pull brightly colored-scarves out of his coat. Feeling the nerve behind her left eye twitch, Grace reached a hand up to her head.

"Uh oh. Crystal just got on the stage. This looks interesting. I think I'll go watch. Coming?"

Grace was torn between wanting to support her sister, and wanting to strangle Kyle. Finally, self-preservation won out over loyalty, as Grace turned towards Kyle and his groupies. "No. I think I should talk to my . . . my . . ." Grace gestured hopelessly, trying to think of what she should call him.

"Your boss?" Adam supplied helpfully.

"Yeah, my boss. He's going to miss his flight if he doesn't leave. I'd better get him on his way. See you later," she said, trying to weave through the crowd.

Everything's going to be all right, she thought, trying to console herself. There's nothing to worry about. In a few minutes, Kyle will be out the door, and far far away from her friends. Grace vowed to make sure he would be far far away, even if she had to buy a plane ticket, and personally escort him back to New York tonight. Hopefully, he's just been talking about the school, or the weather, or New York.

"That's when I discovered the murderer was actually the police detective investigating the case," she overheard Kyle telling the crowd that had gathered around the table. Feeling nauseous, Grace pushed her way past the group to reach Kyle's side.

"What did you do? How were you able to prove the astronaut was the one who killed the old man?" a man Grace recognized from her eleventh grade science class asked animatedly.

Kyle, noticing Grace was now standing next to him, smiled up at her. "Well luckily my able assistant, Ms. Holliday, was there. She found the proof and—"

"And that was it. I'm sorry to interrupt, but could I speak to you? Please, sir?" Grace grabbed one of Kyle's arms. Wrapping her other arm around his waist, she pulled him out of his chair, and back toward the gym doors behind them. She had always heard that fear can cause people to exhibit almost superhuman strength, such as mothers lifting cars off their children. She didn't believe it, but now she felt that if she had to she could have picked Kyle up in her arms and carried him back to New York.

As soon as they were back outside and away from others, she wheeled around. "Have you lost your mind? What are you doing?"

"You should have been there. They were eating it up. They loved it." Kyle leaned back against a lamppost. "You know, your friends are really nice."

"Go home, Kyle."

"I can't. My plane doesn't leave for another week. Don't worry," Kyle added, as Grace paced in front of him, massaging her temples, and talking to herself. "I have this all under control."

Grace stopped her pacing. "I'm going to kill you. I have to live here, you know. I'll be seeing some of these people every day. Hopefully, I'll find a job soon. What am I going to tell them if they ask me about some of these stories you are telling? I don't know anything about being a detective."

"Shh. Someone's coming," Kyle hissed.

They both watched as Melodie opened the door. "Hey, you guys aren't leaving, are you? Please don't go." Melodie reached out to grab Grace's hand and drag her back inside.

Grace watched in surprise as Melodie's eyes began filling up with tears. "I need your help. We have to keep Hope and Crystal away from each other. I have such a bad feeling about tonight. I worked so hard to make our reunion wonderful, and now it's being destroyed."

Grace quickly reassured her friend that she would be happy to help her.

Melodie smiled in relief before turning shiny blue eyes towards Kyle. "You'll be able to stay too, won't you?"

Before Kyle could answer, Grace said soothingly, "Don't worry, Melodie, I won't go, but Mr. Drake, unfortunately, has to leave."

"Oh no!" Melodie turned to Kyle. Smiling shyly, she said, "Everyone is so interested in you. Please, can't you stay a little while longer?"

Grace glared at Kyle over the top of Melodie's head.

"Of course, I can stay. In fact, I can stay all night," Kyle promised, taking Melodie's elbow and escorting her back to the gym. "You know, I once investigated a murder at a high school reunion."

🏆 🏆 🏆

Once back inside, Grace headed straight for the buffet tables. "Chocolate, where is the chocolate?" she muttered to herself, as she scanned the tables set up in the corner of the gym. Spotting the dessert table at the far end, she quickly navigated her way through the various stragglers congregated around the food: the hopelessly lost, the still undecided, and the clueless. It was the last group that usually provides the most trouble.

There were five of them. They were grouped together in front of the desserts, carrying on a full conversation and effectively blocking access to the table directly behind them. They were a formidable group, seemingly unable to sense that they were in the way, despite the fact there was one woman attempting to contort her body around one member of the group, in a vain attempt to reach a piece of pie. These unfortunate people seemed oblivious to the fact they could just as easily talk to one another three feet away from the table. Well, Grace was here to help.

"Excuse me! Do you mind?" she asked as sweetly as she was capable of at the moment. They appeared confused by her request. One of the more self-aware of the group glanced behind his shoulder, obviously just noticing the table of dessert a couple of inches behind him. Realizing what she wanted, he helpfully turned to the side, giving her three inches of space in which to reach a part of the table.

Luckily, reinforcement came in the form of another, larger group who also felt the need to feed their sweet tooth.

Outnumbered, the clueless moved to another part of the gym where they were sure to converse without interruption: the drink station. Grace was confident she would see them again later in the night, more than likely in front of the door leading to the parking lot.

Once the table was clear of stragglers, Grace looked in satisfaction at the spread laid out before her. Melodie certainly out did herself on the dessert cart. There were yellow and red iced cupcakes, cherry-covered cheesecake, chocolate torte, brownies, and her favorite, chocolate-covered strawberries. Grace filled up her plate and walked back to her table.

The band was playing and most everyone was in the center of the gym, line dancing. Everyone, except for Hope, who sat at the table, alone, her eyes fixated on Crystal and Tom who were standing close together near the stage.

Grace placed her plate on the table and sat down. "Hope, let's go home."

Hope tore her eyes away from Tom and Crystal. "No."

"I really don't think you're going to win tonight. It will be close, but not close enough."

Hope merely smiled. "Just watch, sister dear. I told you, I have no intention of losing to that backstabbing, bleach-blonde, bimbo. Why would anyone vote for her over me?"

"She's become rather popular since school, Hope. I've heard that she's involved in several charities. She helps out at the hospital. Here at the school. She organized—"

"You know why she does all of that, don't you? It's not out of the goodness of her heart. She's wants to be a Senator's wife someday. She's doing all of that for attention. For the connections. Not because she cares," she said matter-of-factly.

"You don't know that."

Hope looked down at her sister's plate. "What are you eating?" Hope picked up Grace's plate to examine it and dropped it back on the table in disgust. "Do you have any idea how many calories are on that plate?"

"Yes I do, and I don't care," Grace said, moving her plate out of harm's way. "I'm not having a very good time, and admit it, you aren't either."

"Not yet, but I will be very soon. Look at them, standing there," Hope jerked her head toward Tom and Crystal. "They've been standing there arguing for quite some time."

Grace looked over at the couple. Crystal had her hand on Tom's arm, smiling as her husband whispered into her ear. She looked happy and serene. "They don't look like they're arguing."

Hope's voice was sharp. "They are. Tom's playing with his championship ring. He always does that when he's angry." Picking up her silk wrap and purse, Hope stood up. "I'm going to take a walk. I'll be back in a few minutes."

Grace pushed her plate away. The soap opera that was her sister's life stopped being entertaining years ago.

She glanced over to the stage. Crystal was still standing there, but Tom was gone. In his place stood Adam, looking none too happy.

"What are you staring at?" a familiar voice whispered in her ear, making her jump. "I'm sorry. I didn't mean to scare you," Kyle said, placing a warm hand on her shoulder to steady her.

"I was just wishing I could read minds."

"Anyone's in particular?"

Grace nodded and pointed in Adam's direction.

Kyle sat down next to Grace, took a chocolate-covered strawberry off her plate, and popped it in his mouth. Swallowing, he asked, "Is that Adam Phelps the director? I thought he looked familiar. I absolutely loved his last movie. What's he doing here?"

"Hogan High is renowned for three things in this community: the Rabid Rabbits, the best high school football team in the state, and having produced two celebrities, my sister and Adam Phelps.

"Why don't you introduce me?" Kyle stood up, holding out his hand.

Grace sat for a second, considering, but in the end decided against it. "How would you like a tour of my old high school instead?" Grace asked, taking his hand.

Kyle smiled, recognizing the diversion. "Okay, sounds like a plan."

♛ ♛ ♛

Kyle stood staring at the life-size wall mural of a grizzled, old cowboy shooting down another grizzled, old cowboy. "This is nice."

"Yeah, it is. It wasn't here when I went to school." She bent down to read the artist's name. "David Hart, July 2002," she read. "This was painted a few months after I graduated. David Hart? Why does that name sound so familiar?"

Kyle shrugged. "Why is your school named Hogan High?"

"It's named after Marshal Benton Hogan. He cleaned up this little gold-mining town in the late 1880s." Grace pointed to the mural. "I'm going to hazard a guess that the man standing in the center street looking heroic and menacing is supposed to be Marshal Hogan and the red-headed man, hiding and shooting from behind the rather dour looking woman pictured here, is more than likely my ancestor, Jeptha Holliday."

At Kyle's surprised look, she smiled and said, "Huge travesty of justice. Jeptha was a law-abiding citizen struck down in his prime. Our family swears to this day he was just an innocent bystander in that bank robbery in 1886."

"I'm sure," Kyle said.

"And in the train robbery of '87."

"Of course."

"And '88. I'll let you in on a town secret. Marshal Hogan wasn't as good and noble as everyone here likes to pretend. He had a second wife. He married my great aunt, Elizabeth Holliday. Jeptha's younger sister."

"What's wrong with that?"

"His first wife, Maddie, was still alive and still married to him at the time. She went crazy when she found out. So, one night she killed him and his new bride with an axe. Cut their heads clean off, but you won't find that in the town history books. They tried to place the blame on Jeptha's kin. Claimed it was revenge for killing Jeptha, but my family knows the truth. No one in the family would have hurt one of our own. It was Maddie. The town didn't want to accuse her, on account of her family owning the mine and most of the town. Scandal, you know. So, they ended up hanging two of my great uncles, instead."

"What a charming little town," he said, following her down a flight of stairs. "Are your family and the Hogan's still feuding? Sort of like the Hatfields and McCoys."

Grace smiled, "No. Melodie is a Hogan, and we've been friends since kindergarten." She stopped. "Actually, that's not really true. Hope and Crystal have been feuding for years. I guess they're trying to keep the animosity alive and well between our two families."

Turning the corner, they came across a row of trophy cases.

"And last on our tour," Grace said, pointing out a large trophy case set inside the wall.

"Ah, very beautiful." Kyle noticed Grace was rhythmically tapping on one portion of the glass, trying and failing to look innocent. To the right of the case was a rather large first place trophy with Grace's name etched at the bottom. "You were a runner?"

"Yep," Grace watched as Kyle examined the lock on the trophy case with far too much interest. "Oh no you don't," she said, pulling at his arm.

"Oh come on. I want to see it. It'll only take a few minutes to pick the lock. I won't break anything," he promised, sticking a hand in his pocket and pulling out a small black case.

Grace laughed as she took the case out of his hand. "No, leave it alone. That trophy is going to stay in there forever, you know. Fastest in the county. So far, no one has beaten my record."

"I doubt anyone ever will."

Grace and Kyle turned around to see Tom Lake strolling up to them. "Hello, Tom."

"Hello, Tom? That's it. No hug for your old friend," he said, clumsily spilling the drink in his hand.

"Do you expect me to greet you with open arms? After what you did to my sister?"

"Speaking of your sister, why is she back here?"

"It's our reunion. This is our home. We haven't seen our friends in ten years." Grace felt there were plenty of explanations for her and her sister to come to their high school reunion.

Tom shook his head, as though none of the reasons Grace were giving were good enough. "Why don't you do her a favor and take her home?"

Kyle straightened his back. "Listen, I don't know what's going on, but Ms. Holliday and her sister has just as much right to be here as you do, so why don't you go back to the party?" He smiled at the other man. "Have a few more drinks."

"Are you implying that I'm drunk? I'm far from drunk. I haven't—" Tom stopped himself and looked up towards the staircase. They all heard the sound of high heels click-clacking across the ceiling.

"Thomas? Thomas Anthony Lake, where are you?" Crystal called from upstairs.

"I'm down here Crystal. Next to the trophy case." Tom downed the rest of his drink.

"Her name's Crystal Lake? Really?" Kyle whispered in Grace's ear.

"I think that's one of the reasons she married him," she whispered back.

"Would you get up here? They're going to start counting the votes soon, and I want you—" Crystal immediately stopped speaking when she reached the bottom of the stairs and saw that Tom wasn't alone. She stood staring at Kyle for several seconds, before rushing forward and pulling Grace into an awkward hug.

"I'm so glad you're still here. I was afraid you had left. I hope you know, I was only kidding upstairs. I never doubted that you were a detective. Not one minute. Steve is such an idiot."

Crystal released Grace when she accidentally dropped the binder she was carrying.

"How clumsy," Crystal said, somehow making it sound like it was Grace's fault Crystal dropped the binder. Stooping to pick it up, she said, "I am so sorry, I didn't get a chance to properly apologize to you sooner. You know what happens when your sister and I get in the same room. She just causes me to lose all my manners. I hope that this unpleasantness between Hope and me hasn't spoiled our friendship. It hasn't, has it?" she asked, turning to gaze up at Kyle.

"Hello, Crystal." Grace said, redirecting the other woman's attention.

Crystal spared a glance at Grace before turning back to Kyle. "So, you and our Grace are detectives? That's so exciting. You seem a bit young to be a detective."

"Looks can be deceiving, Crystal." Grace said before Kyle could answer. Realizing she was approaching dangerous waters, Grace quickly changed the subject. "Did I hear correctly? You're thinking of having children?"

Crystal's smile faltered slightly. "Yes, very soon. We've just been waiting for the perfect time. We wanted to wait until after Thomas finished law school, passed the bar, and started to work. Now there's nothing left to stop us, right honey?"

"Absolutely nothing, dear," Tom drawled, looking down at his empty cup.

"But enough about us, let's talk about you. Last I heard you were selling toys, when did you become a detective?"

Before Grace could reply, Tom grabbed his wife's arm and pulled her back against him. "Leave Grace alone. Why don't we go upstairs? You don't want to miss the coronation, do you?" he asked dryly.

"Of course not. You're right, darling. Grace, are you and Mr. Drake coming?"

"We'll be there in just a second," Grace said, relieved they were finally leaving.

When the other couple had finally disappeared upstairs, and the sound of Crystal's footsteps could no longer be heard, Kyle turned to Grace and said, "Wow. That was uncomfortable. What was all of that about?"

"That was the reason my sister and I haven't been back home since graduation." Grace sighed. Hope would be upstairs expecting her. "Come on, we don't want to miss the big event, do we?" Grace asked sarcastically.

Grace slowly climbed the stairs and led Kyle down the main hallway towards the gym.

She was about to push the door open when she heard Kyle laughing behind her. She turned and saw Kyle smiling at one of the poster boards. "What are you laughing at?"

"This 'Most Likely To' board. It's pretty funny."

"You have a strange sense of humor, Kyle."

"Come over here and read this."

"I read it a few hours ago."

"You didn't think it was funny?"

"No, it's just the typical most likely to be popular all their life, most likely to succeed, most likely to—"

"Be a porn star."

"What?"

"That's what it says."

"No, it doesn't. Where does it say that?"

Kyle pointed to Thomas Lake's name on the board. Someone had written over the original awards with a red magic marker.

"Where's yours?" Kyle asked, while scanning through the names on the board.

Grace held up a hand to her mouth. "I don't believe this. Look at Crystal's. 'Most likely to die of a sexually transmitted disease'."

"Oh boy," Kyle said, stepping in front of the poster board and holding up his hands. "Now, don't get excited."

"Why? What does mine say?" Grace pushed Kyle aside and gasped. "Most likely to lie about your life at all future reunions."

"I'm sure it doesn't mean anything."

"Hope!"

"What about her?"

"She did this."

"Are you sure?"

"Of course I am. Read Hope's. 'Most likely to leave and pretend she was never here'. That's not nearly as bad as the others. Also, not everyone's has been changed, only the people in our little group of friends. See there's Tom, Crystal, Steve, Adam, Melodie, and even Beth."

Kyle turned around and faced the opposite wall. "Uh oh. Someone has been busy tonight."

Grace followed his gaze. On the opposite wall were four framed pictures of Hogan High. Each one, a drawing or painting of the high school during the four seasons. The first one was a colored pencil drawing of the school during the summer. The second one was an oil painting of the school during the fall.

It was the third frame that caused Grace to gasp. Someone had torn the charcoal drawing entitled A BIRD'S EYE VIEW FROM THE BELL TOWER DH - JAN '02 into pieces.

"Someone was certainly a critic," Kyle said.

"Who would do such a thing?" Grace asked, bending down to pick up a rather large piece lying on the floor. She carefully placed the piece back into the frame. It was just a simple drawing of the back of the school.

Kyle stood over her shoulder. "Is that writing?"

Grace nodded. At the top of the drawing was only one word 'who'. "The rest of it is missing."

Grace placed her hands on her hips. She had a good idea who defaced the 'Most likely to' boards, but she couldn't believe Hope would go this far.

"SPRINGTIME IS FUN TIME AT HOGAN HIGH is still here," Kyle said, pointing to the last frame, a watercolor of the school.

Rubbing her eyes, Grace turned to the gym doors.

"Where are you going?"

"I'm going to go inside and have a chat with my sister."

"You might want to wash your hands first."

Grace threw a quizzical look over her shoulder. Kyle was still standing next to the charcoal drawing, a grin slowly spreading his face as he looked at her. "After that, you might want to wash your face. Clean your dress."

Grace looked down at her hands. Her fingertips were stained with charcoal dust. Looking past her hands, she noticed tiny smudges on her dress as well. Sighing she said, "This night can't possibly get any worse."

♔ ♔ ♔

Ten minutes later Grace emerged from the bathroom and scanned the gym. Kyle was standing off to the side of the gym doors speaking to a group of people, mostly women. Grace could just make out the words 'secret government mission' and 'nuclear weapons'. Shaking her head, she walked up to the group.

"Ah and here is my esteemed colleague, Ms. Holliday. If it wasn't for her, I would still be locked up in that Turkish military installation. She was the first one to figure out that the Senator was actually a double agent."

"Wow! How did you do that, Grace?" a rather large man she recognized from homeroom asked in awe.

Grace glared at a grinning Kyle. "He had a slight accent. Excuse us for a moment," she said, grabbing Kyle's elbow and pulling him away.

"We're supposed to be detectives, not spies," she hissed into his ear.

Still smiling, he said, "We've diversified."

"Have you seen, Hope?"

"No. But they must be getting ready to start." Kyle pointed towards the stage.

Crystal was standing on the stage, smiling at the crowd in front of her. Tom was standing behind her with his arms wrapped around her waist, staring off to the side. Standing next to them were Scott Younts, Max Wellington, and Chloe Bell, the other contenders to the crowns. Hope was missing. Grace stood on her tiptoes trying to locate her in the crowd. Even with the three-inch heels, she borrowed from her sister, she still couldn't see over everyone's heads.

She looked up at Kyle. "Do you see Hope anywhere?"

Kyle shook his head. "Your friend Melodie is bringing out the crowns. Pretty."

Grace didn't ask whether he was referring to Melodie or the crowns. "Can you hear what she's saying?" she said, straining to listen.

"I think the microphone is broken. Something about . . ." Kyle leaned forward and shook his head. "I think they're waiting on your sister. Let's try to get closer." Kyle placed one hand on the small of Grace's back and the other on her elbow. "Did you lose a button?"

"This isn't my dress," Grace said by way of explaining.

"Oh."

Kyle and Grace managed to push and pry their way to the stage without stepping on too many toes in time for Melodie to announce the winner of Reunion King. "The results have been counted by our reunion committee, and our King is . . ." Melodie paused to open up the envelope in her hand, "Thomas Lake." The crowd erupted in whoops and cheers. Grace winced at the level of noise her class was making.

Melodie held out the crown, but was intercepted by Crystal, who took it off the pillow and placed it on her husband's head, before pulling him into an indecently long kiss. The crowd's cheers turned into catcalls. Crystal only pulled back when she inadvertently knocked the crown off of Tom's head, sending it crashing to the floor as everyone laughed. Smiling, Tom reached down, picked up the crown, pulled his wife back against him, and gently kissed her shoulder.

Melodie turned back to the table on the stage and picked up another envelope. "We're still waiting for Hope so we can announce the results of Reunion Queen."

"I'm here," Hope said, walking onto the stage. "I'm sorry I'm late."

"Finally," Grace whispered to Kyle. "I wonder where she's been."

"Okay! Now that we finally have all of our nominees with us," Melodie said, pointedly looking at Hope, "we can get started."

Melodie opened up the envelope and pulled out a sheet of paper. "This one was very close. After careful counting our Reunion Queen is . . ." Melodie turned and smiled at Crystal. "Hope Holliday!"

The crowd cheered. Grace let out a little yell, happy for her sister.

"Congratulations, Hope!" Melodie said, placing the crown on Hope's head and kissing her cheek. The crowd started chanting "Speech! Speech!" Hope caught Grace's eye and winked. After the crown was sufficiently secured, Melodie turned to Tom and motioned for him to stand next to her. Grace caught the look that passed between Tom and Crystal. Neither one was happy.

Melodie, tiring of waiting for Tom, reached out and grabbed his hand, dragging him to his place next to Hope, while Steve moved up to the stage to take their picture. "Well, this looks familiar," Melodie said to the crowd. "Let's congratulate our Reunion King and Queen."

The crowd cheered. "Okay, they're going to start us off on a dance, and then we are going to get this party started."

Smiling, Hope walked down the steps to stand on the dance floor. When Hope reached the center of the floor, under the disco ball, she turned around, her arms outstretched as the band played *My Heart Will Go On.* Her smile faltered, when she realized Tom was still standing on the stairs.

"What's he waiting for?" Kyle asked. "He can't leave her standing there."

Grace agreed, but was afraid that's exactly what Thomas Lake would do. She wouldn't blame Tom for walking out. Why is the band playing that song of all songs? Grace watched as Tom looked back at his wife who was standing on the stage, her arms crossed. Some silent communication must have passed between them, because Tom suddenly turned around, walked up to Hope, took her in his arms, and began to slowly sway to the music. Grace let out a relieved breath.

"Are you going to tell me what all that is about?" Kyle asked.

"Tom is my sister's ex-fiancé. He left her after graduation for Crystal. That was their song. *Titanic* had a major impact on their lives. Her engagement ring was a blue sapphire heart. They were supposed to dance to that song at their wedding. They even booked an Atlantic cruise for their honeymoon."

"Did they happen to notice how that movie ended?"

"I doubt it. While Melodie and I were sobbing our little hearts out, Hope and Tom were making out in the seat next to us. To this day, I become nauseous whenever I see the ocean."

CHAPTER FIVE

GRACE SURVEYED THE buffet table. She hadn't had anything to eat today except for the salted pretzels provided by the airline. Well, that, and the chocolate-covered strawberries she shared with Kyle an hour ago. Darn it. Everything had been picked through.

"This is all pretty exciting! I've never been to a reunion before," Kyle said, picking up a plate at the buffet table. "Mine's not for another couple of years."

"Great. Just great." Grace disliked being reminded that he was not only younger, but a world apart from her. How can he possibly be having a good time? He doesn't even know these people. She couldn't help but smile at his enthusiasm, though. Kyle was always happy which was one of the things she liked best about him. Never worried or stressed. Just pleasantly happy with life. Weird.

"Who were your friends in school? I think we can count out Crystal and Tom." Kyle examined the garlic potatoes, trying to decide whether to add it to his growing plate of food.

"No, they were friends of mine in school. Tom was one of my best friends. Well, actually, he was Hope's best friend, but we were all close. We were like the three musketeers growing up."

"What about Crystal?" Kyle asked.

"Her sister, Melodie, is my friend, so Crystal was naturally included."

"You three graduated together? So, are Crystal and Melodie twins, too?"

"No, they're a year apart. Crystal was left behind in junior high. She got in some trouble and failed her classes."

"What about your director friend?"

"He was my next-door neighbor," Grace said, heading back to the dessert table.

"Are you talking about me?" Adam asked, coming up behind her and wrapping his arm around her shoulder. "Talking about me behind my back. You ought to be ashamed, Holliday."

Grace smiled. "Adam. There you are. Where have you been?"

"Consoling Crystal. She's convinced she was robbed."

"She's handling her loss gracefully, is she?"

"As only Crystal can." Adam reached out and grabbed a brownie from the table, nearly bumping into Kyle.

Kyle held out his hand. "I'm sorry. I don't think we've actually been introduced, yet. I'm Kyle Drake. Sorry, I must have forgotten my business cards," he said, patting his coat pockets.

Grace rolled her eyes.

"That's all right," Adam said. "I didn't ask for one."

"I loved your last movie."

"Everyone did." Adam turned back around and eyed Grace up and down. "I have missed you. What say you and I take a turn on the dance floor? Here, you don't mind holding this, do you?" Adam asked, as he took Grace's plate from her hand, and passed it to Kyle.

"No, not at all," Kyle said testily.

Grace found herself being pulled onto the dance floor. "That was kind of rude, wasn't it?"

"I'm sorry." Adam sighed and shook his head. "I've had a bad day, and I have a feeling it's about to get worse."

"What happened?"

"Crystal is insisting on a recount."

Grace was incredulous. "For Reunion Queen?"

"She apparently took a poll before the reunion, and knows how many were voting for her and how many for Hope. She suspects Hope rigged the vote somehow."

"That's ridiculous!" Even as the words left Grace's mouth, she knew it wasn't so ridiculous. Hope was bound and determined to win tonight. She must have been the one to bribe the band to play that song, but would she rig the vote and take a chance on being caught, just so she could dance with Tom? "What does Tom think about it?"

"He thinks it's ridiculous, too."

Grace glanced over Adam's shoulder. "Do you know where Hope is?" She ought to warn her sister that Crystal was going to try to make trouble tonight.

"I don't know, but take a look over there," he said, jerking his head to the left.

Grace followed his gaze. Eric and Diana Collins were dancing in the corner of the room. They were both laughing, as Eric attempted to dip her. "Amazing. How long has this been going on?"

"I have no idea. It's rather spooky. I keep expecting one of them to go for the other's throat at any moment."

Grace frowned. Crystal was standing a few feet away from the dancing couple, her arms folded across her chest. A scowl twisted her features.

Grinning, Adam said, "Maybe there's hope left for Tom and, well, Hope."

"I wish, but I doubt it. Speaking of my sister, do you see her yet?"

Adam stood on his tiptoes. "There she is. She's holding court at the table next to the stage."

"I'd better go talk to her. You want to come?"

Adam nodded. Grace could hear laughter and her sister's voice as they approached the table. Adam wasn't kidding when he said she was holding court. Hope sat on top of the table with the silly crown sitting on her head. A throng of admirers, mostly men, stood around her, hanging on her every word. "I once did this photo shoot on the Riviera. Completely naked. The sand was carefully arranged so that you couldn't see anything, but it was such a thrilling experience."

"What was the shoot for?" Steve asked, practically salivating.

"Oh who knows, perfume, jeans, something. That's not important. All I know is that I looked good." Everyone except Grace laughed.

"Where are you going next, Hope?" a man Grace didn't recognize asked.

"I've decided to take a break and stay home for a while," Hope said, surprising all, including her sister.

Grace decided now was as good a time as any to drag Hope away from her entourage. "Hope, can I speak to you privately?" Suddenly, the table erupted in cries of denial, as if Grace had suggested taking Hope out back and hanging her. "It's all right; I'll bring her back," Grace quickly reassured the group.

Smiling, Hope promised the table that she would in fact be back, before following her sister to the ladies' restroom. "You want to try on my crown?" Hope teased her sister, once they were in the restroom.

"No. Have you heard the latest? Crystal is asking for a recount. She thinks you cheated."

"This is what you dragged me in here for?" Hope turned to walk back out.

Grace grabbed her arm to stop her. "Well, don't you have anything to say?"

"Say? Yes, I have plenty to say, but I think I will save it for Crystal."

Grace leaned down and checked under the stalls before she asked, "Did you cheat, Hope?" Grace looked up from the last stall to see that her sister had already walked out.

♀ ♀ ♀

Kyle looked around the sea of faces. Where did Grace disappear to? Last time he saw her, she was waltzing around the dance floor with that hack director.

He felt a hand touch his elbow and turned to see Melodie looking up at him. "You look lost," Melodie said, smiling seductively.

"No, I was just looking for Grace."

"Oh, I haven't seen her for a while. Don't worry she's probably with Adam. She had quite the crush on him in high school. They're probably making up for lost time." Melodie looked at the two plates in his hand. "Come, let's sit down."

Kyle followed her to an empty table, his eyes scanning the room trying to locate Grace.

Sitting down at a table, he said, "You seem happier than you did an hour ago."

Melodie blushed. "I'm sorry about that. I guess I have been under a great deal of stress. When I agreed to plan this reunion, I didn't know how much work it would be. Thankfully, it's almost over. There are only a few things left to do, and then we can go home and relax." Melodie leaned forward, brushing her knee against his. "Do you have a place to stay tonight?"

"Yes, I found a little motel just a few miles away. I'm actually hoping to stay here for a few weeks. I've never been to Colorado."

"Well, I would be happy to show you around. And you know, you don't have to stay at a motel."

Before Kyle could answer, Melodie looked up and sighed loudly. Annoyed she asked, "What's wrong now?"

Kyle turned to watch a slightly older version of Melodie rush forward, a worried look across her face.

"I'm sorry to interrupt. We have one small problem and one large problem."

Melodie put her head in her hands and groaned. "All right, Aunt Diana, give me the small problem first."

"The Remembrance slideshow is gone. Someone stole the flash drive."

"What? Why would anyone steal a flash drive? The only thing on it was pictures." Melodie shook her head. "Never mind. I don't want to know. Tonight's been a complete disaster."

"Were the pictures saved to the hard drive?" Kyle asked.

Diana shook her head. "I looked. They're not there. Do you know whether Crystal made a backup, Melodie?"

"I think so. I probably have a copy in my folders at home. It doesn't matter, Aunt Diana. No one was really paying attention to it, anyways," she snapped. "Now, what's the big problem?"

"Crystal is not happy. Melodie, can you please go talk to her? I can't do it anymore. She is being completely unreasonable. Tom can't even calm her down. She's in my office."

Melodie sighed and looked at Kyle regretfully. "I have to go. You're not leaving, are you?"

"No, not yet. I'll let you know when I do, though."

Melodie smiled and walked out of the gym. Diana sat down next to Kyle. "Tonight is turning into such a mess. I'm sorry. I didn't mean to interrupt you and Melodie."

"No, it's quite all right. You're Melodie's aunt?" Kyle asked, holding out his hand.

Nodding, Diana smiled and shook his hand. "Are you enjoying yourself?"

"Yes, I think tonight has gone quite well. Well, except for the theft. You just can't trust anyone nowadays. I guess if you could, I would be out of a job."

Diana threw up her hands and shook her head. "Why would anyone steal a flash drive?"

Kyle shook his head. "Hmm. Did you see what happened to the pictures out in the hall?"

Diana's face flushed angrily. "I can't believe one of our students would do such a thing. This was such a good class. Never had any trouble out of any of them. It's just unbelievable. I had Eric remove the boards. Hopefully, no one else saw them. It's such a shame. I know Melodie spent a lot of time on them. And the drawing . . . I just can't believe it."

"Did you see what someone wrote across the drawing?"

Diana shook her head. "No, I just saw the ripped up pieces. Someone wrote on it? What did it say?"

"Only one word. *Who.* The rest was missing."

"Who would write on a piece of artwork? It's been laying under a glass covering, untouched, for years and now all of a sudden . . ." Diana stopped and flashed Kyle a small smile. "Maybe we should hire you and Grace to find our vandal."

"Speaking of Grace, you wouldn't happen to know where she is, do you?"

"No, but there's her sister." Diana pointed behind his head. Kyle turned to see Hope heading straight for them.

"Diana, where's Crystal?" Hope demanded when she reached their table.

Diana shook her head. "Hope, you don't need to see Crystal right now. Why don't you just go and have fun? Go dance. I'm sure Mr. Drake would be happy to dance with you."

Kyle was a bit surprised to find himself pressed into service, but politeness forced him out of his chair. "Sure, I would be happy to—"

"I don't want to dance. I want to talk to Crystal. She's making accusations, and she needs to stop."

"Hope, I know. Crystal is just upset. She'll calm down soon. For Melodie's sake, please don't cause trouble tonight," Diana pleaded. "Look, here comes Grace. I'm sure she will agree with me."

Grace walked up to the table in time to hear Diana's last statement. "I completely agree, Hope." Diana was obviously trying to play peacemaker, and Grace was willing to agree to anything to help her.

Grace smiled at Kyle, who was holding her plate out for her. "I added some more chocolate-covered strawberries for you."

Smiling, Grace took the plate. "Thanks, Kyle. I don't know how I missed those."

Diana smiled. "So, how long have you two worked together?"

"Since last Christmas," Grace replied, quickly realizing her mistake when she saw Kyle wince.

Hope smirked. "Hmm. Strange." She looked down at Kyle. "I thought you said that she came to work at your agency just a few months ago, Mr. Drake."

Grace resisted the urge to kick her sister.

"We met about a year ago," Kyle said smoothly. "I didn't hire her until just recently, though."

Hope sat down next to Kyle, pushing Grace into the next chair. She leaned in and tapped Kyle on the back of the hand. "Not that I need your services, you understand, but I just was curious; how much do you charge an hour?"

"An hour? I don't really charge by the hour." Kyle glanced at Grace, who was rubbing her eyes. "Usually my going rate is around five hundred a day plus expenses." He'd never hired a detective before, but vaguely recalled a fictional one quoting that price on a TV show before.

"Expenses?" Hope smiled. "Oh . . . you mean the hotel and dinner, something like that."

"Sure, that would count—"

"Five hundred dollars? That seems pretty high. Is that a normal price, Grace?" Hope asked, turning to her sister.

Realizing what Hope was implying, Grace asked, "How in the world would I know?"

Diana looked at Grace curiously. "Why wouldn't you know how much your agency charges for services?"

Grace glared at her sister. "I don't really handle the agency's finances."

"No, Ms. Holliday isn't really involved in that aspect of our work," Kyle confirmed, wondering what the two sisters were really talking about.

Hope patted her sister on the shoulder as she stood up. "I would certainly hope not."

🏆 🏆 🏆

Grace carefully opened the door to her old science room. "Okay. It's safe in here." She turned, as Kyle walked in and reached for the light. "No!" Grace shrieked. "Don't turn on the lights."

"Why? What are we doing in here?"

"Hiding. We're going to stay in here, until it's all over."

"We're going to stay in here all night?"

"All night?" Grace scoffed. "Not all night. Just the next hour and half."

"Not that I mind spending any amount of time with you anywhere, why can't we be with the others?"

"Don't be ridiculous. Did you see how close we came to making a mistake out there?" Grace asked, trying to slide into one of the school chairs.

"We? I didn't make a mistake out there. As far as I'm concerned, I am a detective. You are the one that messed up back there."

"Fine. I made a mistake. Happy now?" Grace asked, still trying to fit herself and her dress into the chair. "The point is we, I mean I—" Grace corrected herself before Kyle could do it for her, "am liable to make another mistake. So, we, are safer here."

Kyle slid into a chair next to Grace. "Why don't we just leave? I rented a car. We could leave right now. The night's still young," he cajoled. "You could show me around. We could catch a late movie. We could—"

Grace was on the verge of agreeing when she felt her phone vibrate. "Hold that thought," she said, reaching into her purse and pulling out her phone. "It's Hope."

"Are you going to answer it?"

Grace looked up at the ceiling. "I know I'm going to regret this," she said, flipping open the phone. "Hello, Hope."

"Where are you?" Hope asked, sounding annoyed.

"I'm in the lab. What do you want?"

"They're doing a re-vote. I need you to come up here and vote. Now!"

"Okay! Okay! Calm down. I'll be right there." Grace closed the phone. "I have to go back to the gym. They're re-voting."

"Wow, you people take your reunions seriously around here."

"You have no idea." Grace stood up. "Do me a favor. Stay here. I promise, I will be right back, and then we can leave."

CHAPTER SIX

THE GYM WAS a mad house. Everyone was gathered around the stage, talking at once. Melodie was standing in the center of the stage, along with the Reunion Queen nominees, Hope, Crystal, and Chloe. Once the crowd had quieted down, Melodie explained that they did a recount, and discovered that there were more votes than people who actually graduated with the class. Apparently, Crystal had insisted on a head count vote.

"Everyone who wants to vote for Crystal, please move to the right of the stage. Your right, people. Not mine. Everyone who wants to vote for Hope, please move to the left. Everyone who wants to vote for Chloe, please move to the front of the stage. The committee is going to walk around and do a count, so please stay where you are. Remember, only classmates can vote. Guests, please move out into the hall."

Grace dutifully moved to the left side. Despite some grumbling, mostly about how idiotic this was, the crowd was pretty orderly. Everyone neatly lined up on each side.

From Grace's count it was going to be close. About twenty percent of the class voted for Chloe. The other eighty percent seemed to be equally divided between Crystal and Hope.

Grace looked around to see which of her friends were voting for Hope, and which ones were voting for Crystal. On Hope's side, she saw Beth and Mark. To her surprise, Adam and Steve were on Crystal's side. Odd, considering how much Adam lusted after Hope, and how much Steve disliked Crystal.

"Okay, can I have everyone's attention?" Melodie stood in the center of the stage. "We have the new numbers. It was very close. By a win of only twenty votes, the crown goes to Crystal Lake."

"Great, can we go back to dancing now?" someone shouted. The crowd erupted in laughter. Everyone was clearly tired of this game, and wanted to go on to other things. Grace couldn't blame them.

Melodie turned to Hope and gestured helplessly. Hope merely shrugged, smiled, and removed the crown from her head. She walked over to Crystal, placed the crown on her head, and whispered something in her ear. Grace watched as Crystal's face turned a deep red.

♛ ♛ ♛

Kyle put away the microscope. Grace had been gone for over forty minutes, and since that time, he had looked at every slide he could find, reviewed the periodic table, and had even broken into the teacher's desk to see what sort of confiscated goods he could find. He was disappointed to discover it only contained a few rubber balls, one broken pair of glasses, some gum, and a worn mystery novel.

Kyle suddenly felt a slight vibration under his feet. Tilting his head he could just make out the sound of a drum beat in the distance. The band was playing again. He glanced at his watch. Hopefully, that meant Grace would be back soon.

He was about to open the mystery novel, when he heard movement outside, and a woman angrily say, "Let go of my arm. Come in here. I'm not going to talk to you about this out in the middle of the hallway."

Curious, he put down the book, quietly closed the drawer, and walked to the lab door. He opened the door in time to see the door across the hall swing shut. Concerned, he crossed the hall and stood next to the door. He could just make out a woman's voice from the other side. It wasn't very clear, and he had to strain to hear her. "Would you please calm down? I haven't told anyone . . . No, I haven't!" she shouted.

Kyle leaned closer to the door, but couldn't make out what the other person was saying.

"Relax, he's just guessing."

There were a few minutes of silence before he heard, "I have no idea. He's just shooting in the dark . . . I don't have any idea how he found out! I swear, I didn't tell him anything. He just showed up asking questions . . . He'd get suspicious if I did that . . . I told him, he's crazy . . . Yes, I said, I had no idea . . . I don't know why he came to me. Probably, because I was the first person that found . . . Why are you suddenly doubting me? . . . So what? It's just a picture. No one is going to realize it's you, and even if they do, what does it prove? I promise you, I didn't do it intentionally. I didn't even think anything about—"

Kyle's head snapped back. Something had hit the door. Kyle took a few steps back. He could only make out what one person was saying, but it was clear she was making whomever she was speaking to angry. When no one left the room, Kyle crept back to the door.

"No one is going to guess. I doubt if anyone's paying attention . . . I didn't go to the police then, and I'm not going to now. I would think, after all of this time, you would trust me. I never once asked anything from you, and I never will . . . I am not blackmailing you! . . . I don't know. I haven't told anyone . . . I'm telling you, he's just guessing. What would I possibly get from betraying you? . . . That's right. Do you know what he would do to me if he found out I lied to him? No way. He'd kill me if he found out. Trust me. You're safe . . . So what? As long as we both keep our mouths shut, no one will ever know . . . Yeah, big deal! He threatened me. I'm not afraid of him. You let me worry about him . . . I know something about him that he doesn't want people to know. He'll keep his mouth shut, if I tell him to . . . All we need to do is keep calm. He'll eventually go away. Come on; let's go back to the gym. I think we both need a drink."

Kyle stepped back and silently crept back to the lab. Leaving the door slightly open, he waited for the door across the hall to open. When several minutes passed and no one walked out, he walked back out into the hallway. The only sound he could hear was the distant sound of drums coming from the gym.

Nervously, he opened the door, half-expecting to find a dead body in the room. As he opened the door, he heard something scrape against the floor.

Carefully walking into the classroom, he quickly noticed that it was empty, and there was another door on the other side of the room. The only thing out of place was a textbook, which was lying on the floor behind the door.

Kyle bent down and picked up the book. Laying it on the table, he walked to the opposite door and into another hallway.

♈ ♈ ♈

Grace took the steps two at a time. All she wanted to do was to find Kyle and Hope, and go home. When she reached the upstairs, she spotted Diana walking ahead of her.

"Mrs. Collins," she called.

Diana turned, a smile crossing her face. "Hello, again. What are you doing over here by yourself?"

"I'm looking for my boss and Hope. You?"

"I've lost Eric and Melodie. I turned a corner, looked back, and they were gone. I don't suppose you've seen either one of them?"

"I thought I saw Mr. Collins a few seconds ago. I think he was heading to the administration offices and the last time I saw Melodie was in the gym. I'm sorry, Mrs. Collins—"

Diana laughed. "It's Mrs. Baggins now, but please, call me Diana."

"Baggins?" Grace asked in surprise.

"Well, until the divorce is finalized. After that I'll be Mrs. Collins again—" she suddenly stopped, blushing furiously. "I mean, well . . . it will either be Collins again, or I may take my maiden name back. I haven't quite decided, yet."

"I'm so sorry."

Diana patted Grace's arm. "Please don't. I'm not sorry. I'm just glad it's over, and I'm home again. I should never have remarried. Hopefully, Eric and—" she stopped herself suddenly again.

Grace smiled knowingly, which caused the other woman to blush even more. "I'm so happy you and Eric are . . . in a better place."

"Me too. You know, there was a time . . ." Diana stopped and cocked her head to one side. "I think I hear Crystal." Her eyes lost focus as she strained to hear.

Grace looked down the hallway. She could just make out Crystal's voice, as well.

Without warning, Diana gasped, whirled around, and strode down the hall. Grace followed close behind. She could just hear Eric say, "I understand your concern, but I have no intention of hurting Diana. Not ever again."

Grace turned the corner and found Eric and Crystal facing the doors to the library. Crystal had one hand on Eric's shoulder, steadying herself as she kicked off her shoes. The Reunion Queen crown perched on the top of her head.

"Eric, I like you. Really, I do, but I want you to stay away from my aunt."

Diana stepped in front of Grace. "Crystal!"

Eric and Crystal spun around. Crystal looked guiltily from Eric to Diana. "Aunt Diana—"

"This doesn't concern you." Diana took Eric's hand. "Eric and I are adults and I most certainly do not need your protection. Stay out of it," she said coolly, before turning and striding back down the hallway, pulling Eric along behind her.

Bending down, Crystal picked up her shoes, balancing them on the black binder she was still carrying. "You just can't save some people." Glancing at Grace, she smiled sweetly. "Do me a favor and find your sister. I'm thinking of asking her to be one of my bridesmaids. You can have bridesmaids at a renewal, can't you?" she asked, before turning around and entering the library. "If not a bridesmaid, then maybe I can have her give me away. I think that would be rather poetic, don't you?"

♈ ♈ ♈

Kyle turned down another empty hallway. There was no doubt about it. He was lost. He wished he had paid more attention to where they were going, and a little less attention to Grace. Maybe if he had, he would be with her now, dancing the rest of the night away.

Kyle sighed. Every hallway looked the same as the other.

He scanned the walls. There had to be something that would tell him where he was and how to get back to the gym.

Kyle turned down another hallway and walked past two double doors labeled 'Library' in big gold letters. On the opposite side of the door, he noticed a framed map.

Kyle quickened his steps. Standing in front of the map he read, "'You are here'. Great, now where is the gym?"

"On the other side of the building."

Kyle jumped in surprise. Turning, he found Crystal standing in front of the library doors, high heels in one hand, and the Reunion Queen crown on top of her head.

"I see congratulations are in order."

"Oh, this silly little thing." Crystal reached up, and removed the crown from her head. "To tell you the truth, I'm a bit embarrassed to be wearing it," she said, twirling it around her hand. "I mean, it's just an honor to be nominated." Crystal smiled, as she threw her red high heels on top of the trashcan. "I hate these things," she said, referring to her shoes.

"Are you going to go barefoot the rest of the night?"

"Why not? I am the queen, after all," she said, placing the crown back on her head. "Besides, I have no choice. I can't wear them anymore. The heel's coming off on one of them. I almost broke my ankle a few minutes ago. Luckily, I caught myself before I fell down the stairs." Crystal took a few steps towards Kyle. "You wouldn't want me to fall, would you?"

Kyle smiled. "I'm a bit lost. Are you heading to the gym?"

Crystal looked Kyle up and down. "Absolutely gorgeous," she said, running her hand down his arm and across his chest. "You know, you remind me a lot of my husband."

Kyle laid his hand on hers, stopping her from further exploration of his body. "Where is your husband?"

Crystal smiled. "Don't worry about him." Surprising Kyle, Crystal reached up and pulled his head down for a kiss. She pulled away just as suddenly when she heard a noise behind her.

They turned to see Hope standing a few feet behind them, holding out her phone. "Now hold still you two. Smile pretty for the camera." Crystal took three steps away from Kyle and crossed her arms. Hope lowered the phone. "Well, well, Crys. Why am I not surprised?"

"Haven't you been humiliated enough tonight, Hope? Why are you still here?"

"Me, humiliated? Oh, you should talk. What is everyone going to say when they find out you've been cheating on your husband with a prostitute?"

"What?" Kyle and Crystal shouted in unison.

Shocked, Kyle said, "I'm not—"

"Shut up!" Crystal shouted at Kyle. "This is entrapment. You set me up. Get away from me," she said, stepping as far away from him as she could. "Hope, give me your phone. Now!" she demanded, holding out her hand.

"No, but don't worry. I will make sure you get a copy."

"Maybe we can come to some agreement? Name your price," Crystal growled.

"The only thing I want is for Tom to finally see what you're really like." Hope snapped the phone shut and turned away.

Crystal took a step forward.

Fearing the worst, Kyle grabbed Crystal's arm. "Let's calm down. Don't do anything that you will regret."

Crystal sneered up at him. "Get your filthy hands off of me." Kyle held her arm tighter, not quite sure what to do next.

Enraged, Crystal reached down and bit his hand causing him to release her. Once free, Crystal charged after Hope, tackling her to the ground.

Kyle watched, horrified, as both women fell to the ground and then went over the stairs. He rushed forward shouting their names. In the second it took him to reach the stairs, the fight was over. Crystal had only fallen part of the way. She had a hold of the bannister and was already pulling herself into a standing position.

Hope was a few steps below Crystal. Like Crystal, she had broken her fall by grabbing ahold of the bannister. However, unlike Crystal, she was making no attempt to stand up.

Kyle dashed down the stairs and past Crystal, who was slowly climbing back up. By the time Kyle reached Hope, she was sitting up, holding her head in her hands, and moaning. He gently pulled her hands away to see blood pouring out of a large gash on her head. She was going to need stiches. Hopefully, that was all she was going to need, Kyle thought, as he reached for his phone.

"What are you doing?"

"I'm going to call an ambulance." Hope tried to grab his arm. "Stay still, Hope."

"I don't need an ambulance. I'm fine. It's just a little cut," she insisted. "Where's my phone?"

"Hope, that's not important. I think you should be checked out by a doctor."

"I'm fine. Let's just go back to the gym. We'll find Diana and she can patch me up," Hope said, trying to appease him. "I'm sure it looks worse than what it is." Hope looked down at her dress and groaned. "Can you do me a favor first?" she asked, smiling up at him.

Kyle nodded, reluctantly.

"Go into the ladies' room and get me some paper towels. I'm getting blood all over my dress."

Women. Kyle ran his hand through his hair, deciding it would be best to do as she asked. "Where's the restroom?"

"Down the stairs, next to the trophy case," Hope directed.

"Don't move. I will be right back." Kyle ran down the stairs and into the closest restroom. He collected a handful of paper towels, and ran back out and up to the stairs only to discover Hope was already gone.

🏆 🏆 🏆

Kyle closed his cell phone and walked around the perimeter of the gym again. No sign of Hope or Crystal. In fact, he hadn't seen any of Grace's friends since he walked into the gym.

He was starting to get desperate when he noticed Tom Lake walk across the stage, and disappear behind a black curtain.

Kyle followed him. When he reached the curtain, he found Melodie pacing back in forth in front of Diana and Tom, who were seated at a small table.

Diana was pleading with Melodie to sit down. Tom was slouched in a chair with his arms crossed at his chest. Melodie was obviously agitated and angry. As Kyle approached, he overheard her say, "I'm sick of Crystal and her diva attitude. She needs—"

Kyle would have liked to hear the rest of what she was going to say, but Melodie stopped speaking when she heard him approach.

"Have any of you seen Crystal or Hope?"

Tom was the first to speak. "What's wrong?" he asked anxiously.

Kyle explained what had happened, purposely leaving out what the two women had fought about. While Kyle was talking, Tom took out his cell phone, and held it to his ear. "She's not answering," he said, snapping his phone shut.

Diana stood up, shaking. "I'll run to my office and grab my first-aid kit." Turning to Melodie, she said, "I have my phone. As soon as you find either one of them, call me on my cell. I'll find Eric and let him know what's going on, too. I'm sure he'll help us search."

Melodie nodded her head. "I'll check the restrooms," she said, following the older woman out into the gym.

Tom stood up. "I'll check outside. Crystal had said something about needing to go to her car earlier."

"Wait!" Kyle said. "Someone needs to wait here for the ambulance, and to let us know if Crystal or Hope turns up."

"You do it," Tom said, running out before Kyle could protest.

♛ ♛ ♛

Grace closed the door to the lab. Where could he have gone and why was his phone going to voice mail? She told him to stay right here, but since when did he ever do anything he was told. This night was turning into an unmitigated disaster, and she couldn't help but worry that it was going to get worse.

No, she cautioned herself, be optimistic. There is only about an hour left and the reunion will be over. What more can happen in an hour? Everything is going to be fine. Just need a plan. First, find Kyle. Then, find Hope. Go straight home. Go to sleep, and then do everything possible to convince yourself this night was just a bad dream. Good plan. Excellent plan, she thought.

Grace walked by the library. As she was passing a trashcan, she noticed that someone had thrown away a pair of high heels. Grace picked up the bright red shoes. They looked new. Why in the world would anyone throw away new shoes?

Grace checked the size, sighed in disappointment, and laid them on the floor next to the can. No sense in throwing them away, she thought. Maybe someone else could use them.

She looked down the hallway, and then back towards the lab. Just as she did, she caught a flash of purple, turning down the opposite hall.

"Hope, is that you? Hope?"

She was about to race after her, when she felt her cell phone vibrate. Recognizing Kyle's number, she quickly answered.

"Do you know where your sister is?"

"I think I just saw her, why?"

Kyle hurriedly described what happened between Hope and Crystal. "I went ahead and called for an ambulance, just in case. They should be here any minute."

"She may have headed to the administrative offices for a first-aid kit. I'm going to check there first."

After agreeing to meet up by the trophy case, Grace said good-bye and closed the phone. This night was definitely getting worse.

🏆 🏆 🏆

Kyle walked back to the central hallway. He was finally learning his way around. He just needed to go down this hallway, make a right, and then a left, and then walk down the staircase. Make another right, and Grace should be waiting for him at the trophy case.

Kyle found the staircase and started down the steps, when he paused. Someone had turned the lights off downstairs.

Why aren't the emergency lights on, he wondered.

Cautiously, he continued down the stairs and looked around. The only light was coming from a streetlight, shining through a glass door at the end of the lower hallway.

There's no reason to wait down here for Grace, he thought, as he climbed back up the stairs.

Kyle stood up straighter, and looked back down the staircase. He thought he heard a noise from downstairs. Like something falling.

He waited. Maybe it was nothing. It was probably nothing. Still, if Hope is down there, she could be hurt. He walked back downstairs. Walking up to the girls' bathroom, he rapped on the door. When no one answered, he opened the door slightly, and took a step inside. It was pitch black. He couldn't see anything. Deftly feeling around the wall, he made contact with the light switch.

Nothing.

A breaker must have been thrown downstairs. He called out Hope's name again, sighing when he received no answer.

"Kyle? Kyle, where are you?"

Grace. He could hear her calling from upstairs. She sounded upset. Kyle quickly stepped out of the restroom and dashed upstairs. "I'm here."

"Hope wasn't at Diana's office. Have you seen her, yet?" Grace asked, running up to him.

"No, not yet."

"Diana told me that the ambulance is here. Mr. Collins is organizing a search."

"I just don't understand why we haven't found either one of them, yet," Kyle said, running a hand through his hair. "Do you know where we could find a flashlight? The lights are off downstairs."

"They were on earlier," Grace said, taking hold of his hand and leading him down the hall. "Let's go back to the administrative offices. Melodie could probably find one for us."

"Melodie is in the gym. She promised me she would call if Hope or Crystal showed up."

"No, I just saw her in the offices a few minutes ago."

Both jumped when they heard a loud banging noise. They both looked around confused.

"I think it's coming from downstairs," Kyle said. Grace dropped his hand and ran back down the hall to the staircase. "Grace, wait!"

"It might be Hope," she yelled back.

She made it to the staircase with Kyle right behind her. He pulled her back before she could dash down the steps. "Wait. Would you be careful? You could trip on the dress and break your neck." Kyle peered closely at the bottom of the stairs. The bottom was completely dark, but he could just make out a foot lying on the bottom stair.

"Grace, please wait here for me," he said gently.

Grace could tell by the tone of his voice, and the expression on his face that there was something wrong. She turned to look down the stairs, gripping the bannister tight to prevent him from dragging her back up the stairs. "Oh God, Hope," she cried, as soon as she saw the foot. Grace sank to the ground.

As soon as Grace sat down, Kyle ran down the rest of the stairs. There wasn't much light, but he was able to find a hand.

No pulse.

He took out his phone and opened it up, using the light from the phone to take a better look at the body.

"Grace, it's Crystal!"

CHAPTER SEVEN

GRACE STOOD AT the top of the stairs, holding Diana, who was sobbing on her shoulder. Emergency technicians were at the bottom of the stairs, working on Crystal's body.

Pandemonium had broken out. The upper hallway and bottom floor were flooded with former students, significant others, and teachers. Everyone was talking at once.

Eric Collins was at the top of the stairs, trying to take control and get everyone to go back to the gym. Unfortunately, they hadn't listened to him when they were his students, and it was clear they weren't going to start tonight, either.

Grace looked over Diana's shoulder, and saw Beth standing nearby, twisting her camera strap into knots. "Beth? Have you seen Tom or Melodie?"

For once Beth was speechless. She just wordlessly shook her head.

Grace turned to Beth. "Someone needs to find them."

"I'll do it," Diana said, pulling away from Grace. Grace was about to object, but Diana insisted that she should be the one that told Melodie.

Grace nodded her head. Beth recovered from her shock enough to say that she would go with Diana.

Grace turned and made her way through the growing crowd to walk down the stairs and stand next to Mr. Collins. The lights were still out downstairs, but the emergency workers had set up some lighting, so that they could see better. "Can't someone turn on the lights downstairs?"

"No. The breaker isn't working. I've called maintenance. They should be here soon." Eric Collins turned back to the crowd. Exasperated he shouted, "Would everyone stand back, stay off the stairs, and let the emergency workers do their job."

"My friend was the first one who found the body. He's still downstairs. Do you mind if I go and bring him up here?"

Mr. Collins grunted and turned back to the crowd.

Grace quickly walked down the far side of the stairs, trying to stay out of the way. As soon as she got to the bottom step, she skirted away from the body, and over to the wall. It took a few minutes for her eyes to adjust. Several people had gathered downstairs and were lined up against the wall.

All eyes were on the emergency technicians and Crystal. Everyone's but Kyle's. Kyle was rooted to the spot, staring at the girl's bathroom.

It only took a few steps for Grace to reach his side. She lightly touched his elbow and called his name. On a normal day, he would have immediately smiled, and turned his full attention to her. Today was not a normal day.

Worried at his lack of response. She gripped his arm harder. "Kyle, look at me," she demanded.

"I can't. I think someone is hiding in the girl's bathroom. I'm waiting for the lights to turn on, and then I'm going to go in there and see who it is."

"Did you see someone go in there?"

"No."

"Then why—"

"Just a feeling, but I know someone's in there," he whispered back.

"I want everyone's attention," an authoritative voice shouted from the stairs. A big man in a police's uniform stood on the stairs. "Everyone and I mean everyone, who does not belong here needs to go to the gym now. Everyone upstairs needs to leave through the central hallway. Everyone downstairs needs to go through the back entrance and up the sidewalk back into the school. There is a deputy opening the door now to help you make it back to the gym. No one is to leave the area. Does everyone understand? Good. Get going."

Grace grabbed Kyle's hand to lead him away, but he stood firm. "When we get outside, we'll tell the deputy to check the bathroom," Grace reasoned.

Kyle looked ready to argue, when Grace and he were pushed from behind. "Would you two get out of the way? I don't need any more trouble with the law."

Kyle and Grace turned to see a six-foot-two, three hundred-pound man, with a snake tattoo running up the side of his neck, glaring at them. Grace vaguely recognized the man from her tenth grade Home Economics and wondered what happened to the scrawny boy from class. She was about to say something when she felt Kyle's arm encircle her waist, and physically move her out of the man's way.

Kyle let out a whoosh of air. "Quick Grace, look around. Do you see anyone you recognize?"

Grace wanted to point out that this was her high school reunion. The place was full of people she recognized. "Kyle, I can barely see you. Who am I supposed to be looking for?"

"I don't know, but when I turned back to the bathroom, the door was just closing. Whoever was in there just ducked out."

ᛏ ᛏ ᛏ

The atmosphere of the gym had completely changed. The band sat quietly on the stage. No one was dancing, laughing, or telling outrageous stories. Everyone sat somberly at their tables waiting for the police to let them go.

Grace and Kyle walked quietly through the gym. To Grace's relief, she found Hope sitting at the table, next to Beth and Mark. She was holding an ice pack to her head, and quietly whispering to Beth. She smiled and held out her hand when she saw Grace rushing forward.

Grace leaned down to hug her sister. "Where have you been?"

"Right here. Where have you been?"

Grace didn't bother answering her. "Here, let me see your head." Grace moved Hope's hand away to inspect her injury. "You look just awful."

"Thanks a lot," Hope said sarcastically, while looking around her chair. "Have you seen my wrap?"

Grace shook her head.

Hope placed the ice pack against her forehead and shivered. "I've lost it. I know I had it with me earlier. Can you find it for me? I think I left it in one of the labs."

Kyle took off his jacket and draped it around Hope's shoulders. "Don't worry about it. I'm sure it will turn up later."

Hope smiled at Grace. "I see your Ken doll is still with you."

"Ken doll?" Beth asked, looking from Hope to Kyle.

Grace laughed nervously. "Hope, you must have really whacked your head. You know this is my boss, don't you?" she said, digging the heel of her shoe into Hope's foot.

Hope grunted in pain.

"Oh dear. Poor thing. Maybe you should just sit here quietly." Grace removed her foot when she saw her sister nod in agreement.

Kyle sat down next to Grace. "Where are all of your friends?" he asked Hope. Hope just smiled at her sister and shrugged her shoulders.

Unable to keep quiet any longer, Beth happily answered. Mr. Collins was still trying to find out why the lights weren't working downstairs. Steve offered to lend his expertise to one of the deputies. Diana took Melodie to her office to lie down and "Tom's over there," she said, pointing to another table.

Grace looked in the direction Beth was pointing and saw Tom sitting at a table with his hands covering his face. An older man was kneeling next to Tom with one hand on his neck, speaking softly in his ear.

"Who is the man with Tom?" Grace asked.

"That's James Simpson, the District Attorney. Tom must have called him when he found out about . . ." Beth trailed off and shook her head. "Poor Crystal. Breaking her neck like that. It's just awful."

"They haven't said how she died, yet. What makes you think she broke her neck?" Grace asked.

"She fell down the stairs," Beth explained slowly. "Everyone who falls down the stairs breaks their neck."

Grace was happy that Beth's manners prevented her from adding "duh" to the end of her statement.

Beth twisted her camera strap around her fingers. "Poor Crystal. Poor Melodie. It's just awful. Think of it. Losing half your family in one year." She looked at Mark, who simply nodded his head. "First, her husband and now her sister. It's just so sad. Well, at least, she has Diana and Tom left." Beth suddenly shook her head. "Well, I guess not Tom."

"Why do you say that?" Kyle asked.

Beth looked back at her husband and shrugged. "They're not really blood related, and I don't think they're that close," she whispered.

Grace looked around the room. "Where's Adam?"

Beth shrugged. "I haven't seen him in hours."

Kyle tapped Grace's wrist. "There he is and he's bringing the police with him," he announced.

Grace turned to see Adam and two police officers striding to their table. At the same time, she noticed Tom stand up, and shake off his boss, who had a hold of his arm.

The large police officer, who had ushered everyone away from the hallway earlier, walked in front of Adam, and stood next to Hope's chair. "Ms. Holliday, my name is Sheriff Beauford Bellamy, I would like a few minutes to speak to you," he said gruffly, as he pulled out Hope's chair.

Grace's protective instincts kicked in. "Now wait a second. My sister has a head injury and should be at the hospital." She started to rise out of her seat, when she felt Adam place a cautioning hand on her shoulder.

"Be quiet, Grace. I keep telling you, I'm perfectly fine." Hope stood up, tilted her head to the side, causing her long hair to spill over her shoulder, and looked up at the officer through her lashes. "It's just a little bump. How can I help . . . you?" she asked breathlessly.

Grace wanted to tell her sister that she wasn't on a photo shoot or a catwalk. Batting her eyes and lowering her voice seductively, wasn't going to work on the police.

"Aw, miss, please sit down. There's no need to get up." Smiling like a schoolboy, Bellamy gently pushed Hope back into her chair, and kneeled down to speak to her. Grace shook her head, muttering "unbelievable" under her breath.

"Now, I understand from Mr. Lake, there was some kind of altercation earlier, is that right?" Sheriff Bellamy asked gently.

Grace glared at Tom. She knew she was being unreasonable. Of course, he would mention what happened between Hope and Crystal, but she still felt like he was betraying her sister once again.

"Yes," Hope's eyes filled up with tears. Grace was pretty sure they were of the crocodile variety. "Crystal was angry with me. She attacked me, and pushed me down the stairs."

"Now, why did she want to do something like that to you?"

"I don't really know. I think she may have been unhappy with a picture I took of her. It's so silly. Mr. Drake was there and can confirm that," she said, glancing at Kyle, who automatically nodded his head.

"What time was that?"

"A little after 9:30." Hope scrunched up her face as if trying to remember. "I was disoriented and went into the bathroom, near the gym, where I tried to clean myself up. I think I may have passed out. When I came to, Beth was outside crying, and saying something had happened to Crystal."

Beth confirmed that she saw Hope, "leave the little girls' room."

"That's a lie," Tom growled, causing Hope's face to flush. "She didn't spend the whole time in the bathroom. About 9:35, I saw Hope sitting at this table, holding her head in her hand. I asked her what was wrong, but she just told me to go to hell. About the same time, I saw Melodie walk across the stage, and I went into the back to tell her that as soon as Crystal showed up, we were leaving. It wasn't but a few seconds later that Drake here," Tom pointed to Kyle, "said there was a fight, and we needed to find Crystal."

Kyle shook his head and started to speak when he caught the other man's eyes. If looks could kill.

Kyle snapped his mouth shut.

"I went to find Crystal," Tom said. "I saw her outside in the parking lot about 9:40. She was heading back into the school with Adam Phelps."

Bellamy turned to Adam. "Funny, I don't remember you mentioning that, Mr. Phelps."

Adam's eyes widened. "I wasn't with her. I saw her in the parking lot, but we didn't speak or anything. We just both went into the school at the same time. I swear. We weren't together. She went towards the offices, and I went back into the gym."

Bellamy continued to stare at Adam. "What did you do after that, Mr. Lake?"

"By the time I got to the door, Adam and Crystal had disappeared. I went into the gym—"

"I don't remember seeing you there," Adam said.

"I don't remember seeing you there, either," Tom snapped. "Hope was there, and she saw me."

All eyes turned to Hope, who nodded silently.

"Hope was still sitting at this table. We argued again. I asked her what had happened between her and Crystal, but she wouldn't answer me. Instead, she stood up, and walked out of the gym. I followed her out into the hallway and saw her walk into the girl's restroom. I decided to wait at the gym door. I figured Crystal would have to pass that way, eventually. A couple of minutes later Hope came out, and Beth rushed up to her. When I saw Beth's face . . . I . . . ." Tom trailed off.

"I didn't see you here," Beth said.

"No. I saw you crying and knew . . ." Tom lowered his head. "I just knew something had happened. I felt sick and walked back into the gym and sat down."

Sheriff Bellamy turned to Hope. "Is that true, miss? Do you remember speaking to Mr. Lake here?"

Hope looked at Tom with a quizzical expression on her face. "Yes, I think so. I remember telling him to go to hell. I definitely remember that. I also remember seeing him when I came out of the ladies' room. Beth's back was to him, that's why she didn't see him. I'm sorry. Everything is such a blur." Hope brought her hand up to her head. "I think I may need to see a doctor   after   all."

🏆 🏆 🏆

Grace stood outside next to the ambulance. She wasn't quite sure what to do. She wanted to go to the hospital to keep an eye on her sister, but she also wanted to be in the gym to keep an eye on Kyle. After Hope said she wanted to see a doctor, Grace had immediately insisted the police stop questioning her, and asked that she be transported to the hospital. The police called the emergency personnel to come into the gym. After that, the police then turned their attention to Kyle.

"Hope, I've called Mom and Dad. They are going to be at the hospital when you get there. I will be along after I find . . . my . . ." Grace sighed and patted her sister's foot. "I'll see you soon."

"You aren't going to ride with me?" Hope asked, shocked that her sister was abandoning her.

"You're going to be fine. Don't worry." Grace waived as the emergency technician closed the door.

There's nothing to worry about. Sure, when Kyle admits that they aren't detectives, she'll be embarrassed in front of her friends, but no one is going to really care after Crystal's terrible accident tonight.

Grace looked back at the retreating ambulance. Was it really an accident, though? The police weren't treating it as an accident. Grace shook her head. This is silly. Of course, it was an accident. The lights went off. Crystal couldn't see where she was going, and she tripped. The police are just being thorough. Once Kyle gives his statement. They can go home.

Don't worry, she consoled herself. He's telling the truth. Of course, he's telling the truth. He's in there right now. He's being very cooperative, and saying, "My real name is Aleksis Dragovich. I'm a magician and part time—recently out of work—administrative assistant for the Straker Toy Company. I often go by my stage name, Kyle Drake. I am not now nor have I ever been a detective." He wouldn't lie. Not to the police. No, not Kyle. Absolutely not.

♟ ♟ ♟

"All right, Mr. Drake, let me get this straight. You flew in from New York this morning. You needed to speak to your assistant, Ms. Holliday . . ."

Kyle smiled and vigorously nodded his head.

"About a client."

"Yes, she is a good detective, but absolutely horrible at paperwork."

Sheriff Bellamy sighed. "For the last time, please don't interrupt."

"Sorry."

"You ate and drank a little. Ms. Holliday took you on a tour. When she went back for this re-count, you started to explore the school. You overheard two people arguing."

"Definitely."

"But you didn't see who was speaking."

Kyle shook his head. "I'm pretty sure one of them was Crystal . . . or maybe her sister, Melodie. They both sound alike."

"Right, but you didn't actually see Mrs. Lake go into that classroom or Mrs. Baker, for that matter."

"Well, no, but—"

"But you can't say for certain it was either one of them."

"No," Kyle said slowly, "whoever it was, was whispering, but it sounded like her. Kind of . . . or maybe their Aunt Diana. They all three sound very similar."

"Uh huh. And you didn't see or hear the other person, either."

"No."

"And you don't really know what they were talking about."

"Not really. No. But it did sound suspicious. The person I could hear obviously knew something they shouldn't know."

"Such as?"

Kyle hesitated. "I'm not really sure. I think one was accusing the other of blackmail."

"Blackmail? Over what?"

Kyle shrugged his shoulders. "I'm not really sure."

The Sheriff sighed heavily. "Right. So, after that, you ran into Mrs. Lake in front of the library, and spoke with her for a few minutes. Right?"

Kyle nodded.

"Great. Now, what did you talk about?"

"Well, we weren't really talking. More like chatting, you know. You see what we are doing here," Kyle said, motioning between the two of them, "is talking, but chatting is really a wholly different—"

"Fine!" Bellamy shouted. "What were you chatting about?"

"Her crown and her shoes mostly. It was really a quite pleasant chat. But that isn't important. Her shoes—"

"I'll decide what's important," Bellamy snapped. "How long did you two *chat*?"

"A few minutes. Not long. She mentioned winning the recount, and then she placed her shoes in the trash can." Kyle sat back smiling.

"Is that when Hope Holliday arrived?" At Kyle's nod, Bellamy continued. "What did she and Mrs. Lake *chat* about?"

"Mainly photography."

"Photography?" Bellamy asked doubtfully. "Is that what started the fight?"

"Yes. Hope took a picture. Apparently, Crystal didn't think it was very flattering and wanted it back. Hope didn't want to give it back. So Crystal lunged at Hope, and they both went down the stairs."

"A lot of fuss over a picture, don't you think?"

Kyle nodded and leaned in conspiratorially. "I think they're both rather vain." Kyle sighed at Bellamy's lack of reaction. "Anyway, the fight only lasted a second. Neither one had fallen very far. By the time I got to them, they were both hanging on to the bannister. Crystal got up first and walked away. I ran down the stairs to check on Hope. The right side of her head was bleeding pretty bad, so I went into the restroom to get some paper towels. When I came out, she was gone. I eventually found Crystal's family in the gym and told them what happened."

"Did you see Adam Phelps when you went back to the gym?"

Kyle shook his head.

"What did you do then?"

"Well, Grace and I decided to meet up at the trophy case."

Bellamy sat up straighter. "Why there?"

"Because that was the one place I knew how to get to," Kyle explained. "I went downstairs, but it was dark, so I started back up the stairs."

"Did you see anyone?"

Kyle hesitated. A murder had been committed. He was certain Crystal had been killed. He didn't know these people. He didn't really care about any of them, but Grace did, and he cared about Grace. He wished he had time to speak to Grace and Hope before the police questioned him. Knowing Grace, she would want him to cooperate and Hope did have a pretty solid alibi. After all, she was arguing with the assistant DA at the time. Maybe.

"Did you see anyone?" Bellamy repeated louder.

"No." Kyle rubbed his hands across his eyes. "I didn't see anyone, but I think there may have been someone hiding in the girl's bathroom next to the trophy case."

"Why do you think that?"

"I heard a noise. It sounded like something fell, but I didn't see anyone. I don't know what made the noise, but I am pretty sure it came from downstairs near the bathroom."

"Did you see the trophy case?"

Why would they be asking about the trophy case? "Earlier, but not at that time. It was too dark. Why?"

"What did you do then?" Bellamy asked, ignoring Kyle's question.

"I heard Grace calling and I went back upstairs. We walked down the hallway, but stopped when we heard three loud banging noises that sounded like it came from downstairs. We ran back down the hallway, and that's when I saw Crystal's foot at the bottom of the stairs."

"How long did it take you and Grace to leave the staircase, walk down the hallway, and back again?"

"Less than a minute, but more than enough time for someone to push Crystal down the stairs."

"What makes you think she was pushed?"

"Her shoes. She took them off because she said the heel was coming off. I watched her place them in the trash can. When I found her body, she was wearing those exact same shoes."

"So what? She must've changed her mind and went back to get them."

Kyle shook his head. "She said the heel was broken. But that's not all. Someone was hiding in the bathroom."

"Before?"

"And again, after I found the body."

Bellamy leaned forward. "Did you see who it was? Did you actually see someone go into or leave the bathroom?"

Kyle shook his head. "No."

"Then what makes you think she was murdered, and she didn't just fall?"

"I'm a detective and my many years of experience in this business are telling me that she was murdered."

🏆 🏆 🏆

Grace paced the hallway in front of the administrative offices. She had been standing there for thirty-five minutes. Ever since she discovered that the police had set up shop in the principal's office and was still questioning Kyle.

Grace stopped and stared through the glass doors leading to the administrative suite. What is taking so long? What else could Kyle have to say to them? He didn't see her fall. He doesn't know how she fell. So, why is he still in there?

Grace leaned back against the stone wall and looked at her watch again. Forty-five minutes now. That's it. She opened up the door to the main office.

She had never been much of a troublemaker, so she wasn't really familiar with this part of the school. She looked around the main room. The front of the room was taken up by a large imposing desk, where old Mrs. Andrews always sat. Behind the desk sat the secretary's offices with a hallway on either side leading to other offices.

Diana's office, she remembered, was towards the right, down the hallway, and at the end. Whereas, the principal's office was down the left hallway.

Grace walked through the little door, past Mrs. Andrews's desk and made a left. As she turned, she ran into Adam, who was coming out of one of the rooms. "What are you doing here?" she asked, surprised to see him.

Adam stared at her for a moment before speaking. He looked behind him and softly closed the door. "I was looking for the police. I wanted to know what happened to Crystal." Grace tilted her head. She had never seen anyone look so guilty.

"They're not in the vice principal's office, Adam," Grace said, automatically knowing that he already knew that.

Adam shrugged. "Principal. Vice Principal. I knew it was one of their offices. What are you doing here?"

"The same."

"How's Hope?"

"Mom called a few minutes ago. The doctors want to keep her overnight, but they think she is going to be okay."

Adam grinned.

"What's so funny?"

"Hope, that's what's so funny. You saw that performance she put on for the police."

Grace grabbed his arm and shushed him. She motioned for him to follow her back out. The last thing she wanted was for the police to believe Hope was being anything less than truthful. Not that it mattered. Crystal fell. It was an accident.

As soon as they were back in the hallway, Adam started laughing. "My favorite part was when she allowed one tear drop to slide down that pretty face of hers, as she whispered, 'I don't know why Crystal was angry with me'. My second favorite part was when she did her Camille act." Adam lifted the back of his hand to his head and mocked 'I think I may need to see a doctor now.' Seriously, I need to get her in my next movie."

"Would you stop it," Grace said, without much force. Adam was right. Hope was putting on a show, and it was hard to pretend otherwise.

"Oh relax, it's not like you have to worry. She has an alibi. Sort of. Not that she really needs one. She had that cop eating out of her hands back there."

Grace turned to Adam in surprise. "She doesn't need an alibi. You don't think Crystal was murdered, do you?" She shook her head. "It was dark. She couldn't see that well and tripped on her way down the stairs. It's just a horrible accident."

"Then why have they been questioning your boss for the last hour?"

The door opened and Kyle and Sheriff Bellamy walked out.

Kyle froze when he saw Grace. Everything was going so well. The last thing he needed was her telling the police that he wasn't a detective. Not after he spent the last hour convincing them that he was. "Ms. Holliday, there you are. Sheriff, have you met my faithful assistant, Grace Holliday? One of my best detectives. She once—"

Bellamy, ignoring Kyle, smiled at Adam. "Mr. Phelps. There you are. We've been looking for you. May I have a word with you for a moment?"

Adam waved good-bye and followed Bellamy back into the office.

Kyle let out a relieved gust of air, but drew it back in when he saw the look on Grace's face. "I can explain."

"Apparently, there's going to be two funerals this week."

CHAPTER EIGHT

KYLE STOOD IN the doorway of his hotel room, yawning. He glanced past Grace, who was busy stuffing his clothes back in his suitcase, and looked at the clock on the nightstand. Seven-thirty in the morning. How could anyone be up at this obscene time? He knew he shouldn't have opened the door this morning.

"Grace, I can't leave! If I leave, they're going to think I had something to do with her murder. They'll waste their time looking for me when they should be concentrating on catching her killer."

Grace walked into the bathroom. "Why did you bring so much stuff? Hope travels lighter than you," Grace complained, as she walked out of the bathroom carrying the clothes he was wearing the night before. She quickly folded his suit and placed it in his suitcase.

"It's going to look suspicious if I leave so suddenly!"

Grace dropped to her knees and looked under the bed. "Did you bring Abry with you?"

"Grace, you're not listening!"

"Did you?" she asked, worried. That rabbit tended to disappear and reappear at the most awkward moments. The last thing she wanted was to spend the rest of the morning trying to find him.

Kyle shook his head. "I left him with my cousin, Felix. Grace, please listen to me."

Grace sat on her heels and looked up at him. "I am listening. Crystal was not murdered."

"I'm pretty sure she was blackmailing someone or at least the killer thought she was blackmailing them."

"Crystal had more money than she knew what to do with, why would she blackmail anyone?"

"I don't know, but she was."

"You told the police, right?"

Kyle sleepily nodded his head.

"Good. I'm sure the police will look into it."

"I shouldn't leave. I think you're going to need me here, Grace. Your sister—"

"Let's pretend for a moment that you're right and someone pushed her down the steps. The moment the police find out that you lied to them last night, you my friend, are going to jump to the top of their suspect list. Did you think of that?" she asked worriedly.

"They're not going to find out. I promise." At her dubious look, Kyle added, "Besides, I got the impression last night that they already had a suspect in mind."

That got her attention. Grace sat down on the bed and looked at him expectantly.

"They asked a lot of questions about your friend Adam. I don't think they're a fan."

"Adam? That's crazy! Why would Adam kill Crystal?"

"I don't know." Kyle reached down and pulled her up to her feet. Smiling he asked, "Why don't we go into town? Get some breakfast. See what the town gossip—"

"Oh no! No, you are leaving. Your detective days are over Mr. Drake," she said, turning around and zipping up his suitcase.

☙ ☙ ☙

Grace lifted her fork to her mouth. Absolutely delicious. She had forgotten how good the omelets were at the Rabbit Falls Theater and Saloon, a renovated old west saloon.

Walking into the saloon was like walking back into time. Visitors walked through a pair of bat wing doors, entered a large dusty lobby, and were visually assaulted by a gigantic oil painting of a rather well-endowed, but otherwise, quite unfortunate woman with the head of a rabbit hanging on the wall behind a large reception desk. Slightly to the right of the desk were stairs, leading to the upstairs guest rooms. More oil paintings of near naked showgirls hung from the wall leading up the stairs.

One side of the lobby contained the poker, faro, and dice tables. Next to the gambling tables, used for show nowadays, sat a stage where the showgirls used to entertain the locals.

On the other side of the lobby was a restaurant. Twenty wooden tables sat in front of a worn bar, complete with spittoons on either end. The mirror behind the bar looked like it hadn't been cleaned since Billy the Kid swept through town.

Grace smiled as she took another bite. It was good to be home. She looked up at Kyle and back down at his still full plate of food. "I thought you said you were hungry?"

"My eggs are overdone." Kyle picked up his fork, leaned over, and took a bite of Grace's omelet. Grace watched as his handsome face grimaced.

"Aw, Grace, this is awful. How can you eat this stuff," he said, dropping his fork in disgust.

"You wanted to come here, despite my better judgment, I might add. If you want the local gossip you come to the Rabbit Falls Saloon."

Kyle looked around the empty room.

Grace smiled. "Eat up. Next stop, the airport, tovarish."

♛ ♛ ♛

Grace stood a step behind Kyle, glaring at his back. One minute they're on their way to the airport; the next, they're standing on Melodie's doorstep. She knew she shouldn't have let him drive.

"It will only take a second. It would be rude to leave without saying good-bye."

Kyle risked a quick look behind him. Grace had her arms crossed, and one foot was tapping the ground impatiently. She was definitely not happy. He flashed his most charming smile.

It didn't work.

Sighing, he looked up to admire the three-story Tudor style building. "Your friend certainly has done well for herself."

"Her great-great grandfather discovered a gold mine back in the 1870s. Her family's been well off ever since."

Kyle reached out and rang the doorbell again.

"Maybe she's gone. Preparing for the funeral," Grace said hopefully.

Kyle leaned forward. He could hear the sound of footsteps on the other side of the door. "No, I hear someone." Kyle rang the bell again.

Grace groaned and looked up towards the heavens. "Well, she obviously doesn't want visitors, so let's go," she said, grabbing his hand and dragging him away from the door.

Grace led Kyle back to the car, just in time to watch Melodie and Diana drive up. "Five minutes," she warned Kyle.

As soon as Melodie stepped out of the car, she walked up to Grace, crying. Grace held out her arms, and quickly embraced her friend. "I just can't believe it," Melodie sobbed. "It doesn't seem real. She was just here yesterday. She was so excited about last night. It's all my fault."

Grace leaned back and looked into Melodie's tear filled eyes. "It's not your fault. It was an accident."

"She fell because of those stupid shoes. She complained about those shoes all night. The police said the heel had broken off. That's why she fell."

"How is that your fault?"

"I bought her those shoes," Melodie wailed. "I was at the mall, and she said she needed new shoes for her dress and asked if I would pick some up for her. I know it's stupid. I was irritated and picked up the cheapest pair I could find."

Grace patted her back, and told her it wasn't her fault. Diana and Kyle echoed their agreement.

Melodie, suddenly noticing Kyle, reached out her hand and took his in a death grip. "I'm so glad you could come," she said, leading him to the front door.

♈ ♈ ♈

Grace looked around Melodie's magnificent kitchen. It was absolutely beautiful. There were cherry wood cabinets, black granite countertops, a gigantic center island, as well as, a large glass kitchen table sitting in a magnificent bay window. Grace's whole apartment could fit inside Melodie's kitchen. Diana stood at the farm sink rinsing out the coffee pot.

"Are you sure you wouldn't like some coffee?" Diana asked.

"Diana, please sit down. Is there anything I can do to help?" Diana sadly shook her head.

"I'm so sorry to intrude. My family was planning to come by and pay our respects this afternoon, but . . ." Grace trailed off, suddenly not sure how her family, or more specifically, her sister, would be welcomed.

"Oh, I'm so sorry, Grace. I completely forgot about your sister. Is she all right?"

Grace nodded. "They released her from the hospital this morning."

"I wish Crystal and she could have mended their rift. They used to be such good friends. It's a shame they let Tom ruin their friendship." Grace wanted to ask 'since when', but decided now was not the time to shatter Diana's illusions.

"This is going to be so hard for Melodie. For both of us. For the first time, I'm glad my brother isn't around to have seen this. He absolutely doted on Crystal. She was his little princess." Her eyes welled with tears. "Well, it's just Melodie and me now. The rest of the family is long gone."

"I'm sure Tom will still be there for you."

"Tom isn't family," Diana said, angrily echoing Beth's sentiments from the night before. "If there is one good thing that comes from last night, it's that I'll never have to be near Tom Lake ever again."

"I hope you don't mind me saying, but I thought you were happy when Crystal and Tom got together. What happened?"

"I was only happy because I thought Tom would make Crystal happy." Diana sat down at the table across from Grace. "He didn't turn out to be the man we thought he was going to be. Of course, we should have realized that, what with the disgraceful way he treated your sister. Crystal loved him, though." Diana wiped a tear from her eye. "She was so excited about last night. It turned out to be such a mess. First the fight with Adam and then with your sister."

"She fought with Adam?"

"Yes, it was horrible. Tom said he found them outside screaming at each other at one point. He intervened when Adam began shaking her."

Grace was surprised. The Adam she had known was always so laid back and easy going. She couldn't image him becoming violent. "Are you sure?"

"Believe me, when Tom says something I've learned to have it verified before I believe it. I didn't believe it, at first. Adam was such a sweet boy, but then I once thought the same of Tom. After Tom told me, I went to Crystal and asked her about it. She showed me the handprints he had left on her arms. They were just starting to bruise."

"Did she say why he was angry with her?"

"No, not really. She said he had been pestering her for the last month, ever since he came back to town." Diana stood up, but suddenly dizzy, she sat back down with a thud.

"Are you sure there isn't anything I can do?" Grace asked worried, wishing she had thought to bring some food with her.

Diana smiled sadly. "I'm so glad you came. It's been such a terrible night. Neither one of us has slept all night. I'm so tired, but I'm afraid to leave Melodie alone. I hate to ask, but I would really appreciate it if you could stay."

"Of course I can stay," Grace said reassuringly.

♟ ♟ ♟

"Of course I can stay," Kyle said reassuringly, placing his arm around Melodie's shoulders.

"It's all my fault," she said, as she wrapped her arms around Kyle's waist and pressed her face into his chest.

"No, don't say that. I don't believe it's your fault," he said, patting her arms and leading her to the leather couch in the living room.

Sitting down next to him, she said, "That's what Aunt Diana keeps saying. She said we should sue the shoe's manufacturer."

"Well, I don't think that's what . . ." Kyle stopped, suddenly remembering his promise to Grace not to say anything to Melodie about his suspicions.

"What don't you think? You don't think we should sue?"

Kyle looked towards the hallway wondering what Grace would do to him if he told Melodie what he thought. Really, he should. After all, it wouldn't be fair to Crystal to let her murder be ruled an accident. It also wouldn't be fair to her sister or even the poor shoe manufacturers.

"I don't think it was an accident," he whispered looking over his shoulder.

Melodie reacted as though he had reached out and struck her. "Of course it was an accident!" She stood up and walked around the coffee table. "How could you think otherwise?"

"I don't think your sister was wearing those shoes when she died. I think whoever killed her, placed them on her feet afterward. They wanted it to look like an accident." Kyle went on to describe his suspicion that someone was hiding in the bathroom, before and after her sister died.

Melodie sat back down, staring off into space, considering. "If what you are telling me is true, then . . ." Melodie sighed and placed her hand on Kyle's knee. "I would like to hire you. I'll pay you whatever you want. Just name your price."

"I can't," Kyle shook his head regretfully. "I just thought you should know."

"Please, you must help me."

"I'm sorry. I'm not even licensed to practice in Colorado," Kyle said, wondering if he even needed a license to act as a private investigator.

"That's no problem. I can get you a license." Melodie smiled at his shocked look. "My husband's—my late husband's—

brother is a state senator. Let's just say he owes me a rather large favor."

Melodie stood up and walked over to a large ornate credenza. Opening a drawer she pulled out a small pad of paper and began writing. "Here's my cell phone and my brother-in-law's number. You fill out whatever application or paperwork you need to, and we'll make sure it goes through without a hitch."

Kyle was tempted. Very tempted, but also scared to death of Grace. He could just imagine her reaction. She'd kill him. There's no way she would go along with this. He shook his head. "I'm sorry, Melodie. I can't—"

"I'll pay you $10,000 up front."

"I'll have the application to you by the end of the day. Just do me one favor. Don't tell Grace about this just yet."

"Don't tell me what?" Grace asked, as she walked into the room.

"We are . . ." he began, looking at Melodie, who stared at him blankly, "being honored for an award back in New York. Best Detective Agency in the Greater Manhattan area. I wanted it to be a surprise, but oh well, I guess the cat is out of the bag, as they say. Oh my, look at the time," he said looking toward the grandfather clock in the hall. "I'd better be on my way. I don't want to miss my plane."

Grace watched in confusion as Kyle hurriedly walked to the door, almost running over her in his haste to get out of the room.

After telling Melodie she would be right back, she dashed out the door after him. "Kyle," she called, as she hopped down the steps, "what are you up to?"

"Don't worry about a thing," he yelled back. "I'll just drop the rental car off at the airport."

Grace stood at the bottom of the stone stairs, and watched him drive away. He didn't even say good-bye, Grace thought sadly, as she walked up the stairs and back into the house.

CHAPTER NINE

GRACE GRIPPED THE armrest next to her and sent a little prayer above that she, and her newly licensed brother would get home safely. She closed her eyes and took a deep breath, as she felt the right side of the car briefly leave the pavement, and then just as quickly swing back onto the road.

This isn't how she wanted to die. Speeding along in Jeff's used, rusted, extremely old, yellow Volkswagen with hand painted black racing stripes. "Jeff, I really appreciate your picking me up, but I thought Mom was going to come and get me," Grace yelled over the music blaring over the radio.

"Mom's at the store. Hope wanted some special type of seaweed, wheat grass, or something disgusting. What is wrong with her?"

"I have no idea. Are you watching the road?" Grace asked, feeling her stomach do somersaults.

"Yes," he sighed, "of course, I'm watching the road." Jeff turned his head to look at his older sister. "Would you open your eyes? I'm a good driver. I've been driving for two months now, and I've only had one ticket, which wasn't even my fault. It was my friend Cameron's fault. He should have been the one who got the ticket. After all, he was the one driving."

"That's great, Jeff. Look we need to talk about—" Grace stopped herself and opened her eyes. "Why would you get the ticket if he was driving?"

"Because, technically, I was the one in the driver's seat."

Grace opened her mouth to ask how that was possible, when Jeff made a sudden stop throwing Grace forward against her seatbelt. "That's it! Jeff, I want to drive."

"Look," Jeff said, pointing to a small brick house on the corner of the street. Grace stared at the house wondering what she was supposed to be looking at. It was a charming house, but Grace doubted her brother had suddenly developed an interest in architecture.

Grace threw up her hands annoyed. "What am I supposed to be looking at?"

"That's Principal Collins house." Jeff said giggling.

"No, it's not. Mr. Collins lives on Franklin Street. In a giant two story." Grace looked at the house. As cute as the bungalow was, it couldn't possibly compare to the house on Franklin Street.

"He doesn't live on Franklin Street. I did some yard work for him a few years ago. This is his house."

"Fine. I'll take your word for it." Grace leaned her head back against the headrest, wondering why he would have sold his family's gorgeous Victorian with those pretty gingerbread features to move to this little place. "Why are we still sitting here?"

"Didn't you see who walked in there? Whatshername? She's an English teacher. She just walked in there wearing a leather skirt and boots up to her thighs."

"Unless I'm mistaken, Mr. Collins is single. He can do as he pleases." Grace felt a monetary pang of sorrow. Poor Diana.

Jeff just shook his head. "Uh uh, not after she got my girlfriend in trouble last month. Portia was in her third period English class. Whatshername told her she wasn't *dressed appropriately*. Whatever that means. The principal made Portia go home and change. She was dressed better than whatshername is now. What a freak. Portia would love this. Look, here they come," he said, taking out his phone and pointing it at the couple.

Grace reached for the phone before he could take their picture. By the time she was able to wrestle the phone away, Mr.

Collins and whatshername had gotten into a rather dilapidated truck and driven away.

Handing him back his phone, Grace tried to explain the difference between appropriate school wear and appropriate date wear.

"Whatever," he said dismissively, as he pressed on the accelerator barely missing the car parked on the side of the road. "Besides, whatshername isn't single, she's married."

♈ ♈ ♈

"Mom, tell Grace that I'm a good driver," Jeff yelled, as he ran into the house ahead of his sister.

Grace closed the door behind her, suppressing the urge to bend down and kiss the floor. It's only a ten-minute drive from Melodie's home to Grace's parents' home. The way Jeff drove, it took less than three. Three minutes of mind numbing, pure terror. What idiot gave him a license? "Dad," Grace shouted turning toward the family room. "Have you driven with Jeff?"

Grace walked in the family room. An infomercial for wrinkle cream was playing on the fifty-foot television. All the lights were off and the lone occupant of the room, her father, Will Holliday, was sprawled out in the worn leather chair, which had strategically been placed in front of the TV for optimal viewing, remote control in hand and sound asleep.

Grace smiled. Despite the events of yesterday and today, it finally felt like she was home. She had liked living in New York. She had never been lonely. New York was exciting. There was always something to do, and somewhere to go. But this was home and she suddenly realized how much she had missed it.

Grace gently took the remote control out of her father's hand and turned off the TV.

"I was watching that." Grace's father suddenly sat up and looked around. "Oh Gracie, you're home. It's about time. Where've you been all day?"

"Melodie's"

"I'spect she's pretty tore up."

"She's handling it well, I guess," Grace couldn't imagine what she would do if something happened to one of her siblings. "She's thrown herself into the funeral arrangements. We spent the day picking out the casket, flowers, and tombstone. We were just about to go to Crystal's and pick out the outfit she would be buried in when Diana insisted Melodie go to bed. I'm exhausted."

"Hmm, your mother and I have been waiting to talk to you all day," he said, reaching out a hand to stop her from going upstairs. "What's all this detective business about? Who is this detective you work for? Hope said something about him working mainly on street corners. What, exactly, does that mean?"

Grace gritted her teeth. Hope! "Daddy, you know Hope has a wild sense of humor."

"No, she doesn't." Her father countered.

Grace sighed. "I mean, she likes to exaggerate." Surely, her father couldn't deny that. "Oh my gosh, look at the time." Grace yawned loudly. "It is way past my bedtime." Grace leaned down and kissed her father on the cheek. "Night, Dad. See you in the morning."

Grace patted her father on the shoulder and turned towards the doorway, only to find her mother blocking the only exit out of the room. "Oh no, you don't. I want to know who Kyle Drake is, too. I thought he was your assistant at the toy company. I've been talking to Hope and—"

"Mom, Hope doesn't even know him. She had never met him before last night. Now, I really need to go to bed. I have to get up early tomorrow. I promised Melodie that I would go with her to Crystal's house in the morning," Grace reached out and kissed her mother on the cheek while sliding past her. "Is Hope still awake? I just want to check on her before I go to bed. I've been so worried about her all day."

🏆 🏆 🏆

Grace stood in front of the full-length mirror that hung in Crystal's bedroom. She had to admit, she looked pretty good. She was wearing a lavender cashmere sweater and a flowing white and purple floral silk skirt. Purple was always a good color on her. Grace reached up to admire her new princess cut, diamond earrings with matching pendant. Her sister maybe a pain sometimes, but she did have exquisite taste. It's just a shame the sweater was a couple of sizes too small. Well, that's easy enough to fix, Grace thought, as she reached up and pulled the sweater out from her chest, stretching the material out as far as it would go.

Happy with the results, Grace turned around to admire Crystal's bedroom. Crystal certainly had been living the high life. Grace had never seen a headboard decorated with crystals before. She reached out and touched the duvet cover. Pure silk. Everywhere she looked, she saw examples of lavish wealth. Silk, crystals, and furs decorated the room. On the opposite side of the bed, sitting over an ornate fireplace, hung a huge oil painting of Crystal.

Grace looked around the room and noticed the many pictures of Crystal and only Crystal. Crystal playing tennis. Crystal dancing. Crystal winning some type of award. Grace tried to remember whether she saw any pictures of anyone else as she walked through the house this morning, but she couldn't recall any. She walked up to the giant oil painting.

Melodie, seeing Grace's expression, smiled. "Crystal loved that painting. Of course, she tended to love any picture of her."

Not according to Kyle, Grace thought. "It's very beautiful."

Melodie laughed. "You should have been here when she had the thing done. She drove Aunt Diana and me crazy. She couldn't decide on the pose, the background, what she should wear. It was a nightmare. I don't know how Aunt Diana did it, but she did a good job. I keep telling her she should quit and become a full-time artist, but she won't listen," she said, turning and opening up the French door next to the full-length mirror.

Grace followed her into the large dressing room, complete with a giant chandelier and lounging chair. "I told you the same thing in art class. Do you still paint?"

"No, I gave that up. I lost interest in it after we graduated." Melodie stood in the center of the room holding up two dresses. "What do you think, Grace? The blue or the white? She loved this blue dress, but I thought she always looked best in the white one."

"They're both lovely."

"I think . . . the white." Melodie dropped the blue dress onto the chaise, picked up a pair of white high heels and walked out of the room.

Grace looked around the dressing room once again. Dresses, skirts, fur coats. Hundreds of high heels neatly packed away behind glass drawers. Crystal's dressing room had everything. The only thing missing was her husband's clothes. In fact, there was no sign of Tom, anywhere.

Grace walked out of the dressing room and found Melodie sitting on the bed with a box in her lap, reading a letter on orange stationary. "Melodie, where are Tom's things?"

Startled, Melodie jumped up and dropped the box, scattering its contents over the floor. She looked sheepishly at Grace. "I'm sorry. My nerves are just shattered."

"It's all right. Here, let me help you." Grace bent down to gather up the letters and various trinkets that had fallen onto the floor. She carefully placed them back into the box. Out of the corner of her eye she noticed Melodie wad up the letter she had been reading and stuff it into her pocket.

"They're in the bedroom down the hall."

"What?" Grace asked, still wondering what was in the letter.

"Tom's things. Crystal likes to—" Melodie corrected herself, "liked to shop. He sort of, got crowded out. So, he moved his clothes into the other bedroom." At Grace's skeptical look, she added, "The same thing happened at my house. Except, I was the one who got crowded out. My husband was just as much of a clotheshorse as Crystal."

"Where is Tom today?"

"I don't know. Probably with James Simpson." Scowling, she added, "He's always around. Anyway, Tom left a message with Aunt Diana this morning. He said anything we decide about the funeral would be fine with him."

Grace frowned. Clearly, the grieving husband.

"Have you spoken to your boss today?" Melodie asked.

Straker? Grace thought. "No, not today. Why?"

"I was just hoping you had heard from Kyle, that's all. I wanted to see if he was going to be at the funeral."

"Oh, my boss. Yes, sorry, I spoke to him briefly last night." Grace had tried to get in touch with him several times the day before, finally succeeding late last night. Surprisingly, Kyle had not wanted to talk. He hung up, promising he would get back in touch with her in a few days. "He's back in New York, Mel. I don't think he will be able to make it to the funeral."

"Why, did he say that?" Melodie asked sharply.

"Well, no."

"Good," Melodie said smiling.

"Why are you so concerned about Kyle?"

"Oh, I was hoping he could be a pallbearer. Speaking of which, have you heard from Adam? I've been trying to get ahold of him and haven't been able to reach him."

"Are you sure you want Adam to be a pallbearer, after what happened at the reunion?"

"Nothing happened at the reunion," Melodie chided. "They just had a little argument. Crystal, being a natural drama queen, made it out to be bigger than what it was. She was always good at pushing people's buttons. Besides, I'm sure Crystal would have wanted him there. You know, a Hollywood director at the funeral. She would have loved that."

"Has Crystal been pushing many people's button lately?" Grace asked, remembering Kyle's suspicions that Crystal's fall was not an accident.

Melodie walked to the window and pulled back the curtain. Light flooded the room. "No more than usual."

"Do you think it's possible that—" Grace wasn't sure how to finish. How do you ask a grieving friend whether someone hated their sister enough to kill her? Besides, applying Occam's razor, it's more likely that Crystal tripped and fell.

Melodie looked back at Grace, sensing her unspoken question. "Do I think someone pushed Crystal?" Melodie shrugged. "I don't know. I loved my sister, but I'm not naive. Crystal had her faults. She enjoyed causing drama. She couldn't wait for Hope to arrive last night. She was practically giddy with delight when she saw her. I don't know. Maybe Crystal pushed Hope too far, maybe—"

Outraged Grace stepped forward to stand next to Melodie. "Now wait a minute. My sister did not push Crystal. First of all, Hope wouldn't harm a fly. Secondly, it was your sister who tackled Hope, practically throwing them both down the stairs. Not to mention, Hope was in the restroom when Crystal fell. Crystal's own husband can vouch for Hope's whereabouts."

"Grace, I'm sorry," Melodie said, reaching out to touch her friend's arm. "I don't know what I'm saying. I don't believe Hope did anything to Crystal. I only meant, maybe Crystal pushed someone too far. You're right. Hope wasn't the only one angry with her."

Grace shook her head. "I'm sorry, too. Diana mentioned something about Adam pestering her in the last month?"

Melodie smirked. "She seemed happy enough to see him to me. In fact, when we were calling everyone, trying to encourage people to attend, Crystal insisted on calling him herself. She even met him at the airport and invited him to stay here."

"Adam's been staying here?" At Melodie's nod, she added, "For how long?"

"Since he arrived."

"Do you know what they were fighting about at the reunion?"

"No." Melodie turned back to the window. "Crystal had a tendency to cause even the most law abiding, peaceful person to become a raging lunatic. Maybe the police know. Why don't we go ask them?" she said, turning from the window and walking out of the room.

Grace walked to the window. Sheriff Bellamy was just getting out of his police cruiser.

♟ ♟ ♟

Grace pressed herself against the hallway wall. Almost there. Another ten feet and she would be out the back door. From there, she only had to go down the walkway, past the pool and into the neighbor's yard. She looked both ways and strained her ears. She was prepared to slide back into the downstairs bathroom at the first sound of a footfall. She clutched her purse to her chest and tightened her muscles as she stepped away from the wall.

One step.

She looked behind her. No sound. Another step, then another and then another.

Finally, her hand was on the doorknob. She looked out the back door window. All clear. She turned her hand and pressed. Locked. She lifted her other hand to turn the deadbolt when she heard her cellphone ring.

Grace jumped three feet in the air. Panicking, heart thudding, she stepped back into the hallway and opened the first door she came to. The linen closet.

"Do you hear something?"

Grace squeezed into the closet while simultaneously sliding open her phone and pressing it to her chest.

"I think it's coming from down the hall, Sheriff."

At the sound of footsteps passing in front of the door, Grace pressed herself against the shelves.

"Is anyone else here with you, Mrs. Baker?"

"Yes . . ." Melodie's voice sounded strained, ". . . my friend Grace, but she said she was going to walk to my house. I live just down the street."

"We need to speak to her, too. Can you check upstairs to see if she's still here? If so, ask her to meet us in the living room."

Grace breathed a sigh of relief when she heard Melodie and Sheriff Bellamy walk back to the main hallway.

She steadied her heartbeat, and brought her phone to her ear.

"Can't talk. I'll call you back later," she whispered.

"Where are you? What are you doing?" Kyle whispered back, amused.

"I'm in a linen closet hiding from the police." Grace opened the door and peeked around the corner, before sliding out into the hallway.

"Why? What did you do?"

Annoyed Grace snapped, "I didn't do anything. I'm hiding here because I don't want them to ask me any awkward questions. Namely about you."

"Why do they want to question you?"

"I don't know. I'm at Crystal's house. The police suddenly dropped by to pay a visit. They're talking to Melodie right now."

"Good. Can you hear what they are saying?"

"No, I can't hear what they are saying, and before you even ask I am not going to eavesdrop. I do not want to end up in jail for lying to the police, or obstructing justice, or whatever else they could charge me with." Grace could feel Kyle's frustration through the phone. "I'm staying as far away from the police as I possibly can."

🏆 🏆 🏆

Grace crept along the hallway. She could hear Melodie softly crying, and Sheriff Bellamy trying to console her.

Grace passed the hallway table, making sure not to make any noise. If she could make it to the kitchen she would be able to hear what was being said without being seen. She knew she would have to talk to the police, eventually, but she still wasn't sure what she would say if they started asking her about her phony job.

She hated to admit it, but in this case, Kyle was right. She needed to know what was being said. If Crystal was murdered, then Hope could be a possible suspect. Her alibi wasn't exactly iron clad. Especially, considering it came from Hope's former lover and the—possible—murder victim's husband.

She slid around the corner and entered the butler's pantry. Pressing herself against the wall, she could hear everything that was being said.

"Mrs. Baker, if you have any information on who would want to harm your sister you need to tell us."

"I have told you. I just don't know," Melodie said. "Sure, she had arguments and disagreements, just like everyone else, but I can't think of anyone who would *actually* want to kill her."

"How was her relationship with Mr. Lake?"

Grace pressed her ear closer. All she could hear was Melodie's sniffling.

"Mrs. Baker?"

"They have been arguing recently. All couples have rough patches. My husband and I went through a rough patch."

"What were they arguing about?"

"Crystal wanted to start a family, but Tom didn't. Couples fight, but that doesn't mean one of them is going to bash the other's head in with a trophy."

"Can you think of anyone who hated your sister enough to kill her?"

"No. Crystal wasn't easy to get along with, but I can't believe anyone would want to kill her. There is something that I should mention. I didn't think about it . . . I mean, it didn't really mean anything at the time. The day after the reunion, I noticed, or at least I think, someone had been in my house."

"What makes you think that? Was something missing?"

"No. I couldn't find that anything had been taken, and I can't really say for sure, but . . . I think some things had been moved. Not taken, just moved around."

"Why didn't you call us?"

"I thought it was the stress. That my mind was playing tricks on me. Now that I know my sister was murdered, I'm not so sure."

"All right," Grace could hear rustling sounds as someone stood up, "if you can think of anything else, please contact us immediately."

Grace waited in the pantry until she heard the sound of car doors slamming and a car pull away from the house. Once she was sure Bellamy was gone, she left the pantry and entered the dining room. Melodie was still sitting at the table, staring off into space.

"There you are. I was afraid you had left." Before Grace could respond, Melodie stood up and began pacing. Running her hands through her auburn curls, she said, "Grace, they think she was murdered. They said, she didn't fall, but someone had hit her on the back of the head. They asked me a bunch of questions. They're trying to check alibis." She stopped pacing and stood directly in front of Grace. "Can you call Kyle? I really need to speak to him."

"Just calm down." Grace pulled out a dining room chair and sat down. "Why don't we—"

Grace jumped when she heard a door slam and running footsteps. "Melodie? Melodie? Where are you?" Diana's voice sounded strained.

"I'm right here, Aunt Diana. What's wrong?"

"That's what I want to know. Becky from next door called me and said there was a police car parked outside. I was afraid something had happened."

Melodie quickly filled her in on the sheriff's suspicions.

"Murdered?" Diana brought her hand to her mouth. Her face flushed angrily. "I told you, Melodie. I told Crystal, too. I told her he would kill her one of these days."

"Aunt Diana, we don't know what happened. Don't go jumping at conclusions," Melodie snapped. "Grace doesn't want to hear this."

Before Grace's better manners could take over, she found herself blurting out, "Do you know who killed her?"

"No, she doesn't!" Melodie snapped.

Shocked, Diana turned to Melodie. "You're going to let him get away with this? He murdered your own sister. How could you?"

"Aunt Diana," Melodie said, measuring out each word, "we don't know any such thing, and I am not about to start accusing people. We should let the experts handle this."

Diana sat down in a huff. Clearly upset and hurt by her niece's words.

Melodie continued her agitated pacing until she reached the window. "Oh great! It's Sherlock Holmes. I wish he would go back to Denver."

Swiveling around in her chair, Grace saw Steve Mattingly hop out of his car and walk to the front door. Wondering why he was here, Grace asked, "Does he still have a crush on you?"

Melodie made a face and rolled her eyes. Grace smiled. Steve had always been a thorn in Melodie's side. Making no secret of his crush, he had spent every free moment from elementary to high school trying to get Melodie to notice him. He never seemed to accept the fact she just wasn't interested in him. Melodie definitely had a type and unfortunately for Steve, he was not it.

"He's probably already heard the good news and wants me to hire him," she said bitterly. "I'll go talk to him."

Grace and Diana sat in awkward silence until they heard the sound of Melodie opening and closing the front door.

Grace could no longer contain her curiosity. She reached out and gripped Diana's arm. "Who do you think killed Crystal?"

For a second, Grace feared the older woman was going to follow her niece's harsh command, but Diana wiped her watering eyes and blurted out, "Tom! Melodie's protecting him for some reason, but I know it's him."

"How do you know that? Did you see him do it?"

Diana shook her head. "No, but it has to be him. Who's the first person the police automatically suspect when someone dies? The spouse, that's who. But they're not going to look at him. Oh no. Not the Assistant District Attorney. No, they'll try to pin it on someone else, while he walks free. Just watch Grace, they will try to blame someone else."

"But why do you think it's Tom?"

"They fought all of the time. The way he would look at her sometimes. It was just chilling. He didn't really care for her. He never did." Diana started crying harder. Grace slipped her arm around the older woman's shoulders. Her grief palpable. "He just wanted her money, and once he got that . . . If only Crystal had listened to me. I had tried to convince her to leave him, but she wouldn't. "

Both women turned their heads at the sound of the front door opening. Diana squeezed Grace's hand, stood up and walked out of the room.

Grace stood up and walked to the front entrance.

Melodie was standing in the doorway. Her arms folded across her middle and her back to Grace.

"Come on, *Mellow-D*, it was just a question," Steve said smirking.

"Ugh. It was not just a question, Steve. I know exactly what you were implying, and I refuse to answer such demeaning accusations. Besides, you're the last person I would ask for help. For all I know you may have killed her. After all, we both know what you're capable of, so I wouldn't go around throwing accusations around. You know the old saying about people in glass houses, don't you?"

"Are you threatening me?" Steve's voice lowered. "I think the police might be interested in hearing that."

Melodie sneered. "I'm sure the police would be very interested in what I know, particularly about you, so I doubt you're dumb enough to actually say anything to them," she said, slamming the door in his face.

Melodie turned around and froze when she saw Grace. "The vultures," she said, referring to Steve, "are circling. He wanted to know if I would like him to solve Crystal's murder. For a fee of course. I told him to get lost."

Grace looked towards the dining room. "Diana is pretty upset."

"I know. I shouldn't have yelled at her. Not after all she has done for us over the years. I'll go and talk to her." Melodie walked past Grace. "The police have released Crystal's . . . body, so we can set the funeral for the day after tomorrow. Could you call Beth and ask her to come by and help, please?"

CHAPTER TEN

"I THINK SHE looks just lovely. It's like she's just sleeping, and at any minute, she'll wake up. Don't you think so, Grace?" Beth asked, sniffling.

Grace automatically nodded. Actually, she didn't agree at all, but she would never say, 'why no, Beth, I think she looks quite dead'. "Yes, she looks—"

"I'm surprised they're going to bury her in this dress. Crystal disliked wearing white. She said it washed her out and made her look hippy. I remember Diana and Melodie had to talk her out of wearing a red wedding dress. I didn't even wear red and it's my favorite color. Can you believe it? A red wedding dress."

"Shocking!" Grace said with fake horror. Crystal was right. She really didn't look good in white.

"You should have seen my dress. I wish you could have been there." Beth eyes suddenly lit up, as she clapped her hands. All thoughts of Crystal promptly forgotten. "Oh my gosh! I completely forgot—my wedding video. You must come home with me. Then you'll be able to watch me get married! It was so beautiful. We taped the whole thing."

"Oh my—" Grace said, startled, her mind thrown into a sudden panic.

"You must! You absolutely must! I'll call Mark right now and tell him to make sure the video is ready. We'll leave right after the funeral. I can't wait! No one will watch it with me anymore."

"But . . ." Grace snapped her mouth shut as Beth hurried off accidentally knocking into a couple of flower arrangements standing next to the coffin.

"You are in for a real treat," Adam said, as he reached an arm around Grace's shoulders and drew her into a hug. "After the wedding video, which is five hours long, comes the first child's videos. Her birth video. I recommend not eating, by the way. Then the first birthday, second and so on. Then there are the sequels and all of their milestones."

"I take it you've already had the pleasure."

Adam hung his head. "The day after I arrived and then the next day. Luckily, Crystal took pity on me and rescued me."

Grace laughed. "So, what you're saying is that you would like a second viewing."

"You're on your own, Holliday. Speaking of Hollidays, is your sister, actually, going to show her face this afternoon?"

Bristling Grace said, "Yes, why wouldn't she?"

"Come on Grace. Don't pretend. Crystal and Hope have a knock down drag out fight, and then Crystal is murdered just minutes later. If Hope shows up then she has more guts than I would."

"Really! Then I'm surprised to see you here."

"What do you mean?" Adam dropped his arm and stepped away from her.

"I heard you and Crystal fought that night, too."

"We had a simple disagreement, out in the hallway, in front of witnesses," Adam said, picking his words carefully. "We handled it like mature adults. We did not wrestle each other to the ground and then tumble down the stairs."

"A disagreement? About what?"

"Grace, I don't really think now is the time."

"If it was such a simple disagreement, then you should be able to say what it was about?"

"You sound like the police," Adam snapped. "I'm sorry, Grace. I'm just really stressed right now." Adam motioned for Grace to follow him.

They walked past the other mourners and out into the funeral home's hallway.

"The truth is . . . I'm worried. Scared actually. I think the police suspect me." Adam ran his hand through his curly chestnut hair. "It's crazy. I didn't kill her. I wouldn't kill her. I needed her. There are so many more suspects out there Grace, but they're not looking at them." Adam gripped her arm tightly. "I tried to tell them, but they don't believe me."

"Adam, slow down. Who do you think killed her?"

"You mean besides your sister?"

Grace glared at him. "Of course, besides my sister."

"I don't know, but I do know that things weren't as happy at the Lakes' home as they wanted people to believe. The tension in that house was unbelievable. Everyone was angry with Crystal, but they tried playing the perfect little family. It was a complete sham. They could barely sit next to each other through that reunion."

Grace suddenly recalled Melodie's strange reaction whenever Crystal would touch her. "Do you mean Melodie or are you referring to someone else?"

"You saw it too, didn't you? All of that 'favorite sister' stuff at the table was completely phony. Melodie loathed Crystal. Crystal liked to pretend that everything was normal, but there were serious problems between them."

"So, Crystal was putting on a show of family solidarity during the reunion. Why?"

"She didn't like reality to intrude on her version of events. In her world everyone loved her. The truth was that she had a lot of enemies."

"Are you counting Tom among her enemies? They seemed pretty close at the reunion?"

Adam snorted. "Tom who? I never saw Tom. I've lived there the last month, and I think I've seen Tom maybe twice. Crystal would make excuses for him. 'Lawyer's work long hours,' she would say. You remember what Tom was like, don't you? He was a slacker. Back in high school, could you imagine him spending every waking moment at the office?"

Grace shook her head. Tom hadn't been a slacker, but she couldn't imagine him throwing himself into his work, either.

"The only reason he was putting in long hours was to stay away from Crystal."

"Are you sure he was at the office?"

"That's what I was wondering, too. Melodie and Tom seemed rather close." Adam wiggled his eyebrows.

"I thought you said you barely saw Tom?"

"I didn't, but I saw more of him leading up to the reunion. Crystal suddenly decided she wanted to be a part of the planning committee. She sort of interjected herself. They had a lot of meetings at the house. I got the feeling attendance was mandatory. It was horrible. Melodie wouldn't even look at her. Tom just drank. The only one that even tried to keep the peace was Diana."

Grace sighed. "It sounds like the police are going to have their hands full."

"No, they won't. Don't you see, Grace? They are going to try to pin this on me."

"Why, Adam? Why would they suspect you over someone else?"

Adam laughed bitterly. "Someone else? Like their buddy, the Assistant District Attorney?"

Grace noted once again that Adam deflected her questions. He seemed far more than willing to talk about everyone else's reasons for killing Crystal, than any he may have had. Not that she could blame him.

"I'm not kidding when I say they are going to try to pin this on me. They won't even look at Tom. I doubt they'll really consider Hope a suspect. But me? Tom's boss hates me."

"Why on earth would he hate you enough to try to blame you for Crystal's death?"

Adam looked uneasy. Shrugging his broad shoulders, he said, "Everyone's keeping secrets. I don't know for certain that Crystal and he were having an affair, but I wouldn't doubt it, either. Simpson was always over at their house. He was a regular fixture at dinner. He seemed fine with me at first, but then he started making snide comments and acting very aggressive. Wanting to know how long I was planning to stay around. It was bizarre, but I got the feeling he was protecting his territory. Crystal probably told him I was making the moves on her or bothering her, just to watch the resulting chaos. Now I think he has it in his mind that I'm the prime suspect. He sure won't look at his golden boy, Tom. You have to help me," Adam pleaded.

Grace lifted up her hands. "How? What do you want me to do?"

Adam reached out and ran his hands down her arms. "I need you to investigate. Find out who did this. I will pay you whatever you want." Taking hold of her hands, he said, "Just name your price."

Grace couldn't decide whether she wanted to laugh or cry. Why couldn't Beth have thought she was a dentist, or an astronaut, or even a magician? She could have at least had some help on that one. Anything, but a detective. "Adam, I'm sorry, I just can't help you," she said gently, laying her hand on his arm.

Adam stood up straighter and shrugged off her hand. Tilting his head back he said, "Fine, then I'll speak to your boss. If you won't help, maybe he will."

Grace didn't like the sudden change in attitude. Adam had clearly gotten used to getting his own way while in Hollywood. "He's in New York, and has no intention of coming back," she said coolly.

Adam grabbed her by the shoulders, and turned her around. "Grace, he's been talking to Melodie for the last ten minutes."

♈ ♈ ♈

Grace paced in front of the funeral home, periodically stopping to glare at the entrance. It was supposed to be so easy. Put him on the plane. Wave bye-bye. Gone. Back to New York. Safe. Where he couldn't get into trouble.

Grace looked at her watch. As soon as she discovered Kyle was back, she marched up to him and tapped him on the shoulder. Unfortunately, Melodie had wrapped herself around him and was sobbing uncontrollably. Grace told him she needed to speak to him outside, which, for some reason, made Melodie cry even harder. That had been ten minutes ago.

Grace was about to give up, and drag him out of the funeral home by his pretty blond hair when she saw him walk outside. Her heart dropped. He was wearing the exact same expression he had on his face when he told her he had accidentally wiped out the company's accounts.

"What did you do?" she demanded, as soon as he walked up to her.

Kyle immediately gave her a wide smile.

"Don't smile at me. That's not a human smile. Kyle, we are leaving. Where's your car?"

Kyle didn't answer. He simply pointed to a shiny ruby-red Camaro.

"A rental?" she asked hopefully.

Kyle shook his head. "I thought I should have something flashy." Kyle took a step back. "Really a detective of my caliber should have something . . . flashy." Kyle took another step back. And then another. "Grace, your eye's twitching. It's been doing that since I've met you. You really should get that checked out."

Grace's brain at some point had shut down. The only thing going through her mind was 'flashy'. "Flashy? Flashy?" she asked, her voice rising with every syllable.

"Yes, you need money to make money. People will be more likely to hire me if they think I am doing well in my profession."

"How were you able to afford a car like this?"

Kyle shrugged and took another step back. "I put a down payment on it."

Grace didn't want to ask, but knew she had no choice. "Where did you get the money, Kyle?" When it didn't look like he was going to answer, she took a step towards him.

"Melodie paid me a retaining fee. Grace, you don't have to worry. I will take care of everything."

Grace took a deep breath and very carefully chose her words. "Kyle, things are getting way too complicated. Let's just go home. Back to New York." Grace held out her hand. "I'll go with you. We'll return this car, return Melodie's money, and then we'll both go back."

"I can't return it. I stopped off to grab a bite to eat before I got here and some idiot already dinged it with his door." He walked to the passenger side and pointed to a small dent and scratch on the side of the door. He patted the car affectionately. "Can you believe that? I even parked her as far away as I could. But don't worry. I should be able to get her fixed. Adam just paid me another retaining fee," Kyle said smiling. "I've always liked him."

Kyle's smile faltered. He took another step back. "Grace, your eye's twitching again. You know how that freaks me out."

♈ ♈ ♈

Kyle watched as Grace walked into the ladies' bathroom. He hated seeing Grace so upset. He hated being the one to upset her, but he was convinced they should be involved in this investigation. After speaking to the police, he didn't have any faith that they would actually catch the real killer, and the way they were grilling him about Hope worried him. He didn't believe for a second that she killed Crystal, but the police just might. Hope and Tom had alibied each other. If they suspect Tom and his alibi fails, Hope's would as well. They could claim her as an accomplice and Grace would be devastated. Kyle shook his head. The only way to protect Hope and Grace was to discover who really killed Crystal.

Kyle shoved his hands in his pockets and fingered Adam's check. There was another reason to get involved. He needed money. So did Grace. This was a way to keep themselves solvent.

"Kyle, I've been looking for you," Melodie said, linking her arm with his.

"I've been looking for you, too. We need to talk about Crystal and who might have killed her."

Melodie's pretty eyes clouded. "Now? I don't think now is really appropriate."

"The more time we waste, the more chance the killer is going to get away. There's also a good chance that whoever did this is here today."

Wrapping her arm around his, Melodie leaned into his body. "After the funeral I will tell you whatever you want to know. I just can't right now. Not with her lying right here. It's just too painful," she said, turning her tear-filled eyes up to his.

Kyle looked down at her, trying to decide if he believed her. It hadn't escaped his notice that she only seemed upset about her sister's death when he was close enough to comfort her. Other times she just seemed frazzled. Right at the moment, however, he was pretty sure she was stalling. "I thought you wanted to know who did this."

"Of course I do," she said, wiping away a tear that had spilled over onto her cheek. At his disbelieving look, she added, "I hired you, didn't I?"

"Then help me do my job. Talk to me about Crystal."

Melodie grabbed his hand, led him to one of the sofas, and sat down. "I'm sorry. You're right. Please sit."

Kyle took the seat next to her. He sat still waiting for Melodie to start speaking, but when she did, it wasn't to him, but to another woman standing nearby. "Beth, you remember Kyle Drake, don't you?"

It seemed so easy in the movies. Kyle stood up and shook Beth's hand. If Melodie wouldn't talk, then maybe Beth would. "I'm so sorry for your loss. I understand you were good friends with Crystal?"

Beth nodded. "We all grew up with each other. Everyone's going to miss her."

Kyle felt Melodie slide her hand back into his and pull. "I loved my sister very much. It's just difficult for me to talk to you, because I have no idea what to say. She didn't have any enemies. That's why this came as a complete shock. I mean, I just can't believe someone would want to hurt her."

Tears began streaming down her cheeks, as she raised her arms up for a hug. Before Kyle could sit down next to her and give her the comfort she wanted, Beth quickly moved in and gave her a giant bear hug, rocking her back and forth. Kyle smiled when he saw Melodie stiffen and her eyes immediately dry up.

"Please don't cry," Beth sobbed. "You were a good sister. I'm so glad you two made up. Whenever my children fight, I always tell them they need to forgive—"

"Beth, please, you're hurting me," Melodie gasped. Beth pulled away, wiping her eyes.

Gently touching her throat, Melodie asked, "Where did you get the idea Crystal and I were fighting? I hope you didn't believe that silly rumor."

🏆 🏆 🏆

Grace looked at her hair in the bathroom mirror. No streaks of gray yet. Surprising. She expected to see a full head of gray hair when she walked into the bathroom. She shrugged. It's only a matter of time.

There is no way we're going to pull this off, she thought dejectedly. Maybe she could talk to Melodie and Adam. Explain that Kyle is an escaped lunatic. He's harmless. Beg their forgiveness, and then run back to New York. They're her friends. They'll understand. She nodded at her reflection. After the funeral, she decided.

🏆 🏆 🏆

Grace found Kyle sitting on one of the couches in the viewing room. On one side sat Beth, thrusting photo after photo in his face. On the other side sat Melodie, apparently now super glued to his hip.

"Ms. Holliday, are you feeling better?" Kyle asked concerned. "Here, sit down." Kyle attempted to stand and offer Grace his seat, however, Melodie quickly pulled him down.

"She can sit right next to me. Here, I'll make room for her." Melodie pushed herself closer to Kyle and smiled up at him, practically sliding into his lap.

Squeezing herself into the space provided, Grace asked, "Has anyone seen Tom? I want to offer my condolences."

"No," Melodie said, still staring up at Kyle, "but then there are several people missing. Tom's at work. Eric and Diana called and said they would be late. Steve is a no show, and I haven't seen your family yet," Melodie added, turning to Grace with an accusatory look.

Grace sighed. She and her parents had spent an hour trying to convince Hope to come to Crystal's funeral. It wasn't easy, and it was completely against Grace's better judgment. It was risky having Hope here. Hope wasn't really upset by Crystal's death, and she said she wasn't about to be a hypocrite and pretend otherwise. Grace tried to convince her that people would talk if she didn't come, but the only opinion that ever mattered to Hope was her own and possibly Thomas Lake's. It was only after convincing her that Melodie needed her support did Hope finally relent.

Grace looked over at Melodie, who was laying her head on Kyle's shoulder. How was she to know that Kyle was the only support Melodie needed? Still, after speaking to Adam, she worried that if Hope didn't appear people would wonder if guilt had kept her away.

Hopefully, Hope hadn't changed her mind. "They will be here," she insisted. "They're just running a little bit behind."

♔ ♔ ♔

"What do you mean you're not coming? Hope, I think it's very important that you be here," Grace whispered into her cell phone. Kyle watched as Grace's face drained of color. "Why? . . . I'll be right there." Grace sighed as she listened to her sister. "Fine. Just call me when it's over." She snapped the phone shut. "My family's at the police station. The police wanted to speak to Hope. She said to give Melodie her best."

Worried Kyle asked, "Have they arrested her?"

"No. They just want to ask some questions. Hope's insisting that her attorney be present first. It doesn't look like they're going to make it for the funeral. Let's not tell anyone. Hopefully, no one will ask where they are."

"I don't think they're going to miss anything. I've never seen a happier looking group of mourners, and I have been to a few wakes in my time," Kyle whispered.

Grace couldn't agree more. Adam was standing near the coffin flirting with a brunette who was giggling uncontrollably at whatever he was saying to her. Beth had cornered an older couple, Grace recognize as Mr. and Mrs. Murphy, the owners of the Rabbit Falls Saloon. She was busy showing them family photos. Grace watched as they politely nodded at each one. Various children were running through the room. No parents in sight. Eric Collins and Diana were the closest to Grace. When she leaned toward them, she could hear them making fun of the current crop of students. No one was crying. No one even looked sad. If it weren't for the coffin in the room, you wouldn't know anyone had died.

"It's rather ghoulish, isn't it?" Grace looked Kyle up and down. "Where's your new friend? I'm surprised you could tear yourself away."

Kyle smiled. "Do I detect a note of jealousy?"

"Do I detect a note of hope?" she countered.

Kyle patted her on the shoulder. "Don't worry. She is just a client. It would be completely unethical for anything to happen between Melodie and me. After all, I wouldn't want to violate my professional responsibility. I have a duty to behave with—"

Grace scoffed. "Professional responsibility? Honestly, do I need to remind you that . . ." she paused when she saw Tom enter the room, stopping every few feet to accept the condolences of the people around him. His eyes on Melodie, he walked by the coffin, barely giving it a passing glance, before reaching out and embracing her.

ΨΨΨ

"Kyle, can you give me a ride back home?" Grace asked, walking to his new car.

Nodding he asked, "Did you get a hold of Hope?"

"They're back home," Grace said, reaching the passenger side door. "She hasn't been charged with anything, but I'm worried."

Unlocking the car door, Kyle glanced across the car's roof. "Don't be. We'll figure this out."

"For the last time. We're not detectives."

Noticing Beth making a beeline for them, Kyle whispered, "Quiet! Here comes your friend."

Grace groaned. She completely forgot about Beth.

"Grace, did you bring your own car, or would you like me to drive?" Beth asked.

A sudden idea forming in her mind, Grace smiled at Kyle. Perhaps, he could be useful after all. "Oh Beth, I'm so sorry, but Mr. Drake needs me to work on something important tonight," she lied. "How about next week?"

"What?" Kyle smiled. "No, if you have other plans Ms. Holliday I wouldn't dream of interrupting them. You go on with your friend."

Realizing her chance of escaping was suddenly evaporating, Grace walked around the car to stand at Kyle's side. "But sir, you need my help."

Kyle smiled sweetly at her. "No, I insist." Evading Grace's hands, and more importantly her nails, he moved to the sidewalk to stand closer to Beth. "What do you two have planned? If you don't mind my asking?"

"Grace hasn't been home in such a long time that I wanted to show her all my family's videos."

Kyle quickly realized that now was his chance to get Beth alone. He had managed to corner her just before the funeral service, intent on finding out what Melodie and Crystal had been arguing about. At first, she had evaded his questions, insisting 'she wasn't a gossip'. She had just started to open up when Melodie interrupted them. All he was able to discover before the interruption was that the sisters absolutely weren't fighting, it was just a horrible, nasty rumor, but whatever it was, that didn't happen, occurred right around the time of Larry Baker's accident.

Taking Beth's hands in his, Kyle flashed her his most charming smile. "I would love to see your videos!"

Kyle looked from both Beth and Grace. Both stood staring at him, transfixed, their mouths opened in shock. Apparently, no one had ever asked to see these videos before.

Beth's face lit up in pleasure. "We're going to have so much fun, tonight."

CHAPTER ELEVEN

"I LOVE YOUR place, Beth. It's so . . . so . . . colorful," she said, trying to find some way to tactfully describe Beth's home. "You have so many interesting paintings."

"So many clowns," Kyle said, looking around in rapt horror. Every wall contained ten to fifteen paintings of clowns. In addition to the paintings, were the clown figurines and clown dolls. Big clowns, small clowns, happy clowns, incredibly scary, scary clowns. "Just so many clowns."

"Yes, aren't they wonderful? My husband draws the *Clown Family on Parade* comic strip. We love clowns. Every Halloween we all dress up as clowns. The kids just cry if I try to dress them up as anything else.

"Where are the kids?" Grace asked.

"At the circus?" Kyle whispered, then grimaced when Grace elbowed him in the stomach.

"I asked Mark to take them to the movies tonight," Beth said, taking out a large metal DVD carrying case from the storage ottoman. "They get so excited when I show the family movies. You should see their little faces. Now, where did I put Beatrix's movie case? I bet that little minx has hidden it again. She's so playful. Let me see if it's in her room."

Grace watched Beth bound up the stairs. Turning to Kyle, she asked, "Do you want to explain to me why you're here?"

"Beth let it slip that Melodie and Crystal were fighting about something."

"Old news. I knew about that hours ago," Grace said smugly.

"Do you know why?"

"No, do you?"

"No, but Beth does and we just need to get it out of her."

"How do you propose we do that?"

Kyle shrugged. "Bright lights? No food or water?" At Grace's expression, he added, "I'm only joking. It should be easy. I think she can't wait to talk."

"You do realize you're investigating your own client, don't you?"

"If we're going to keep your sister out of trouble, we need to know exactly what's been going on."

♛ ♛ ♛

Grace hadn't wanted to get involved. She still didn't, but she grudgingly had to admit that Kyle had a point. It was becoming painfully clear that the police considered Hope a suspect. If it took sitting through hours and hours of home movies to keep Hope safe then she'd do it. And the sooner they could get started, the sooner they could go home. With that in mind, Grace climbed the steps leading to the children's rooms.

She found Beth in the second room on the right, lying on her stomach, peering under her daughter's day bed. "Did you find it, yet?" Grace asked.

"Hmm. Maybe. I see something, but it's at the back of the bed."

Grace got on the floor, and peered under the bed. Now was as good a time as any to ask Beth what happened between Crystal and Melodie. Grace decided the best way to ask Beth, was simply to be direct.

"Beth, I spoke to Adam today. He said Melodie and Crystal were fighting. Was that true?"

Beth sat back on her heels and sighed. "Melodie says that it was just a rumor circling around town. That it's not true."

Realizing Beth just needed to hear that Grace understood, she said, "Of course. Rumors are rarely true, but if that rumor's going around, then it would be best if her friends heard about it from another friend."

That was all Beth needed to hear. Nodding enthusiastically, she leaned in conspiratorially. "That's what I think, too. It all started the day after Larry's funeral. I was there and they seemed okay then. Melodie was crying on Crystal's shoulder. There didn't seem to be any problem. Well, except for Larry being dead, of course. It was a lovely service. He looked so peaceful. Everyone was there. The Murphy's, Hendrix's—"

"When did you notice a problem between the two?" Grace interrupted, trying to keep Beth on track.

"The next day. I went over to see Melodie, and I found her on the front lawn, screaming at Crystal. Melodie told Crystal that she hated her."

"Did she say why?"

"I asked her what had happened, but Melodie wouldn't say. But I heard through the grapevine that Larry had been cheating with his secretary, and that Melodie was furious."

"Well, of course," Grace said, still wondering why Melodie would have been angry with Crystal.

"To tell you the truth, I was scared for Crystal. You know what a temper Melodie has, especially when it concerns someone she loves. Remember the artist she dated after graduation?"

Grace once again reminded Beth she left after graduation, and that she and Melodie had only kept up with each other sporadically through the years.

"Well, Larry and she broke up a month after graduation, and Melodie started dating David Hart. He was an artist the school hired to commemorate the school's centennial year. He's the one who painted that big mural near the front entrance."

Grace snapped her fingers. "I knew that name sounded familiar. I remember Melodie calling one night and telling me all about him, but the next time I spoke to her, she was telling me all about her wedding to Larry."

Beth nodded. "They weren't together for very long. Just for that summer after graduation. Melodie thought he was the cat's meow, let me tell you. I didn't think he was that handsome. I mean, he was okay looking. He was tall, had this long, stringy blond hair, and was really skinny. Not at all like Larry, but Melodie went crazy over him. She even bought him a car. Can you believe that? She had only known him for a few weeks, and she went out and bought him this really expensive car. It was beautiful. She must have spent a fortune. It had—"

"So, what happened between them?" she asked, trying to keep Beth from going off onto another tangent.

"He dropped her to date Sara Perkins. It was so sad." Beth reached out and grabbed Grace's arm. "Melodie completely lost it. I heard that she broke into his house and destroyed all of his paintings, then . . ." Beth looked over her shoulder and dropped her voice to a whisper, "she almost killed him. Not that I believe that. That's just a rumor."

"What happened?"

Beth shrugged. "I don't really know. No one does. All I know is that he left the very next day and moved back to California. It turned out okay in the end. Larry and she got back together. They got married a few months later. It was like a fairytale. Oh, you should have been there, Grace. She wanted you to be her maid of honor. All the girls wore pink satin—"

Grace shook her head and tried to bring the conversation back to Crystal. "If Larry was cheating with his secretary, why would Melodie be angry with Crystal? Or was Crystal sleeping with Larry, too?"

"No, of course not. Where would you get a crazy idea like that?"

"Then why was Melodie so mad at Crystal?" Grace asked in frustration.

"Because Crystal was the one who found out he was cheating. She didn't want to hurt Melodie, so she didn't tell her. I can understand Melodie being hurt, but I'm sure Crystal was only doing what she thought was right. I mean, how do you tell your sister that her husband's cheating?"

♆ ♆ ♆

Yawning, Grace stumbled to the car. The sun was just breaking over the mountains. "What time is it?"

Kyle looked at his watch. Narrowing his eyes, trying to focus on the time, he said, "I don't know. I think time has stopped." He leaned his head against the car. "So, are you going to tell me what the big secret is?"

Grace quickly outlined what she learned from Beth.

Raising his head, he said, "That's not much of a motive for killing Crystal. It's not as if Crystal was the one he was sleeping with. She probably didn't want to hurt Melodie."

Grace couldn't agree more. "Still, Melodie must have felt betrayed."

Shrugging, Kyle fished in his pocket for his keys.

Grace yawned again. "What's next on the agenda?"

"Well, I need to go back to motel and get some sleep," he said yawning.

"You still staying at the Cloverleaf?"

Kyle nodded. "I brought Abry back with me. He's probably wondering where I am. How about we go visit Tom Lake sometime this afternoon. He didn't seem to be very torn up at the funeral."

"I don't want to speak to him. Not after the way he treated my sister."

"Do you know why he left your sister and married Crystal?"

"I have no idea. One day, they were giggling over wedding plans. The next, he was acting as though she had the plague. Hope refused to speak to any of us about it. The name Tom was even stricken from our family's dialog. You talk to him."

Kyle shook his head. "You know him. He'll be more willing to talk to you."

"I'm not very comfortable speaking with Tom right now. We don't even have a license to act as private investigators. He could throw us in jail."

"Don't be so dramatic. It turns out that getting a private investigator's license is voluntary in Colorado. It's only necessary, if you want to call yourself a *licensed* private investigator, otherwise we're fine."

"Really?" she asked doubtfully. "Still, you've been telling everyone that you've been doing this for years. Not only that, but Kyle Drake isn't your real name. It's your stage name. You lied to the police, Kyle. That's a serious problem."

"Don't worry. I've taken care of everything."

"What do you mean you've taken care of everything?" she asked suspiciously.

Carefully looking around to make sure no one could overhear or see what he was doing, he took out his wallet and proudly handed her his New York private investigator's license. "What do you think?"

"About ten years in the state penitentiary, maybe five with good behavior. No. Who are we kidding? With you it would be the full ten."

"It's all perfectly legal. See, I finally had my name legally changed to Kyle Drake." Kyle took another document out of his coat pocket and thrust it into her hands.

"Oh, I'm sure your father's going to love that."

"He won't care. I've been performing under that name for years now. Ever since I struck out on my own and decided that I didn't want people comparing me to my father." He looked up reflectively. "That's the only idea of mine that my dad's ever whole-heartedly approved of."

"How were you able to do this so quickly?"

"I have friends in high places."

"You don't mean your cousin Felix, do you?" Grace rolled her eyes. "I thought he had been disbarred."

Kyle vehemently shook his head. "No, no. He hasn't been disbarred. For your information, Ms. Know-It-All, the disbarment hearing isn't 'til next month."

"None of this solves anything, Kyle. You made it seem that we had been investigators for years now. They're going to notice you just had all of this done since the reunion."

"Check the dates on the documents," Kyle said smugly.

Grace sighed and reluctantly checked the date of each document. They all had been backdated by three to five years.

"How much did you pay for this?"

"Not a dime. Felix did this pro bono. He also set up a web page for me. Kyle Drake Investigations. How does that sound? Impressive, isn't it?" he asked, clearly pleased with himself.

"Wonderful. If you think I'm going to carry around a fraudulent private investigator's license—"

"I didn't get you a fraudulent license. I thought about it, but if this falls apart—it won't—but if it does, I don't want you to get into trouble. As far as you know, I am who I say I am. You're just my lowly secretary. I discovered you working at the Straker Toy Company, and enlisted your help when I craftily figured out there was embezzlement afoot . . . or murder afoot . . . or whatever."

Grace's eyes narrowed. "Wait a minute. Secretary? When did I become your secretary? I was supposed to be your assistant or associate or whatever, remember?"

Sighing, Kyle rubbed his forehead. "Fine, you're my administrative assistant. Better?"

Grace shook her head. "Oddly enough, no."

"I knew you wouldn't go for the license thing, so secretary is the best I could do. I'm just going to tell everyone that I felt sorry for you the other night, and decided to go along with your completely innocent misrepresentation of your actual title at my agency. That way if—"

"When."

"*If* this comes crashing down, you won't be implicated. Happy?"

"Ecstatic," she said, thrusting the licenses back into his hand.

🏆 🏆 🏆

"For the last time Hope, being a size six is not a crime."

"It is when you stretch out a three hundred dollar cashmere sweater. My sweater," Hope snarled, holding up the offending item.

Grace snatched the sweater out of her sister's hand. "My sweater now. I should take your whole wardrobe after that stunt you pulled the other night. You promised you wouldn't say anything to Mom and Dad."

"I didn't say anything. I can't help it if they guessed."

"What did you do, play charades?" Grace felt Kyle's hand wrap around her upper arm and pull her towards him.

"Be nice. We need her to be cooperative," he whispered.

"Nice, to my own sister? That's against everything I stand for."

"Then let's go talk to Tom," Kyle said.

"Fine, I'll be nice," she whispered back. "Hope, if you don't sit down and talk to us, I'm going to tell Mom and Dad what really happened to Uncle Jessie's car fifteen years ago."

"You don't have to threaten me. I would be happy to talk to Mr. Drake."

Grace was taken aback by her sister's sudden change of attitude. "*Mr. Drake*? Just yesterday you were accusing him—"

"Yes, but I spoke to Melodie, and she explained that you were just his secretary. After I heard that, well, everything made sense. Really, Grace," Hope said shaking her head reproachfully.

"I'm sorry, Grace. I really felt that I should tell my client the truth," Kyle said, removing the sweater Grace was slowly twisting into a knot. "After all, you don't want me running around telling everyone you're a detective, do you?"

Quickly realizing Grace was beyond answering him, he turned to Hope, flashed his most charming smile, and led her to the window seat. "I'm so glad you want to talk. I'm afraid you may be in a lot of trouble."

"Don't be ridiculous. No one is going to believe that I killed Crystal. I'm world famous. She is or was insignificant. Why would I kill her?"

"For taking Tom away from you," he said.

Hope scoffed. "So, I wait until our ten year high school reunion? If I was going to kill her, it would have been ten years ago, not now," she turned to look at Grace. "Do you believe I killed her, too?"

Grace smirked, "No, but other people obviously do. What did the police want yesterday?"

"To waste my time. They were interested in my alibi."

"Yours or Tom's?" When she didn't answer, Kyle said, "Tell me about him."

"What do you want to know?"

"What is he like? What kind of man is he?"

"I have no idea." She sighed softly. "He used to be my best friend, but we haven't spoken in years." Hope turned her head away, blinking rapidly.

Grace sat down next to her sister. "What happened between you two? Hope, you need to tell us. Crystal has been murdered. The police consider you a suspect, so talk to us. At least, talk to me."

"I don't know what happened." Hope looked directly at her sister. "It's not that I didn't confide in you because I didn't want to, it was because I couldn't. I honestly have no idea what happened." Her voice hitched. "One minute we were happily planning our wedding. We were talking about college and our future. I was going to be a fashion designer, and he was going to become a veterinarian. He loved animals. Then after college we were going to move back here, and raise a family. We were even picking out baby names for our future children. If it was a girl, we were going to name her after me. Tom said, he couldn't think of a prettier name. If it was a boy, we were going to name him Jack." Smiling in remembrance, she turned to Kyle. "My middle name is Jacqueline. He loved that name, too."

"You've got to be kidding me," Grace said, rolling her eyes.

Kyle sensing this conversation was about to quickly deteriorate and deviate from where he wanted to go, jumped in. "A vet? How did he go from veterinarian to Assistant DA with aspirations to the Senate?"

"Crystal did that to him," Hope said bitterly. "His father was a lawyer, but Tom had no interest in the law. He said, he would never be an attorney, not after watching his parents' divorce, and his dad die of a stress induced heart attack."

"So, what went wrong?" Kyle asked.

"I have no idea. We had everything planned. We were going to attend college in the fall and marry on my birthday. Tom said he couldn't think of a more perfect day," Hope said smiling.

"Oh, neither can I," Grace said sarcastically.

Ignoring her sister, Hope continued, "One minute, he loved me and the next, he didn't."

Grace shook her head. "You two had been fighting the day before graduation, remember?"

"He didn't break up with me over that!" Hope stood up and walked towards the door.

"What was it about?" Kyle asked, attempting to keep Hope talking.

"After the honeymoon we were going to move into campus housing for couples. A few days before graduation we drove up there to take a look at the apartments. It was awful. Tom called it a rat's nest. He said, it wasn't good enough for me. He said, that I deserved better." Hope picked up a hairbrush and began brushing her hair. "I told him it was only for a few years. That we could make do until we were working and could afford a nice house. I was hoping we would save enough money to eventually buy the Moxley House."

"It's an old Victorian on Ferris Street," Grace added for Kyle's benefit.

"And our great grandparent's house." Hope placed the brush back down and pulled her hair into a ponytail. "I've always loved that old house. That's where we were going to raise our family. The next day Tom surprised me by taking me to the Moxley house. He said he had a great idea. We would buy the house now, and we would commute from there to the college." Hope groaned. "Over an hour away."

"Just out of high school? Where was he going to get the financing?" Kyle asked.

"That's what I wanted to know. Crystal, he said. Crystal's family, more specifically, would put up the money. I almost fainted when I heard how much the payments would be. I told him we couldn't afford it. He said that's where Sam would come in."

"Sam who?" Kyle asked.

"Sam Baxter, Tom's best friend," Grace answered. "Oh, I absolutely loved Sam. I had the biggest crush on him. Melodie and I would fight over who was going to eventually marry him. He was so cute. Tall, blond, athletic, smart—"

"And Crystal's boyfriend," Hope added, interrupting Grace's litany of Sam's best attributes. "Tom wanted to rent out one of the rooms to Sam. I told him, in no uncertain terms, that was not going to happen. I liked Sam, but I didn't want to start our married life with Sam in the next room. Especially knowing that Crystal would be in and out of the place visiting him. If Crystal's family put up the money and her boyfriend was paying rent, you'd better believe Crystal would treat our home as hers. I simply told Tom that it wasn't happening. We were going to stick with the original plan. Campus housing wasn't nice, but it was our only option. I would have rather slept in a car for four years, than have had Crystal walking in and out of our home as she pleased."

"How angry was Tom?" Kyle asked

"He wasn't really that angry. He was disappointed, but he said he understood. I saw him the next morning, and everything seemed fine. It was a normal day. Well, except for us graduating and Sam leaping off the bell tower. After that—"

Kyle sat back, "Wait, what happened to Sam?"

"Sam committed suicide," Hope said matter-of-factly.

"Yeah, it was awful," Grace added. "He had been pretty depressed for a while, ever since he got into a car accident and messed up his knee. He was our all-star quarterback. There was even talk of a full scholarship to Notre Dame, but all of that went away after the accident. We found out right after the graduation ceremony that he had jumped out of the bell tower behind the school."

Kyle raised an eyebrow. "When was the next time you spoke to Tom?"

Hope shook her head. "Except for earlier that morning, I didn't speak to Tom until Sam's funeral a couple of days later."

"That's not true. I saw you and Tom arguing right before commencement started," Grace said.

"It was nothing," Hope said, grounding out each word. "Anyway, I knew something was wrong. We had never gone that long without speaking before."

Realizing Hope wasn't going to elaborate, Kyle asked, "What happened at the funeral?"

"I couldn't get close to him. He was too busy comforting Crystal," she said bitterly. "He sat there rocking Crystal back and forth throughout the whole service. Once everyone got back to the reception, I finally dragged him away from her. He . . ." she hesitated, her voice breaking, "told me that he didn't love me. He told me to get out. He said, that since I had never liked Sam, that I didn't belong there."

"Did he blame you for Sam's suicide?" Kyle asked.

"How could he?" Hope asked surprised. "I had nothing to do with it."

"Could your messing up their living arrangements been the last straw, so to speak?" Kyle asked. At Hope's disbelieving look, he asked, "Then why the sudden personality switch after Sam's death?"

"I have no idea. I just know that he never wanted to speak to me again and he hasn't. Not one word since that horrible day. I tried to get him to talk to me at the reunion, but he just turned and walked away. Anyway, I left for Europe that summer and I never came back."

"And I left for college around the same time," Grace added.

Hope picked up the brush again and then angrily threw it on the bed. "Crystal was kind enough to send me an invitation to their wedding. They married on the same date Tom and I had chosen, using the wedding hall we had booked, and the honeymoon that we had planned. They even bought the house, my house."

Grace was bewildered. "I thought they've been living on Franklin Street since they were married?"

Hope shook her head, angrily. "Crystal's parents bought that gaudy mansion on Franklin Street and gave it to them as a wedding present. They never lived in the Moxley house, but they still own it. I tried buying it anonymously once, but they wouldn't let go of it."

🏆 🏆 🏆

"You don't really think that Tom broke up with Hope over Sam's suicide? Or that Sam killed himself because Hope wouldn't allow him to live at the Moxley house, do you?" Grace asked, following Kyle into the family den.

"Sam was his best friend, Tom must've cared for him. You said yourself that Sam had been depressed. Maybe he couldn't take it anymore. His dreams had been shattered. His one chance to remain close to his friend was cruelly taken away by your sister, so he jumped. Tom and Crystal both blame Hope for Sam's suicide. They make a horrible mistake and marry each other out of revenge, as a way to punish Hope. Why else pick her wedding date, hall and honeymoon? Obviously, they both blamed her for Sam's death. Now, they're trapped in a loveless marriage."

"So, you think he finally snapped and killed Crystal?"

"Why not? Ten years go by, and he sees Hope and realizes he made a terrible mistake letting her go, so he gets rid of the wife. He then alibi's the object of his affection and by extension himself. It's perfect. Case solved. That was so easy." Kyle flopped down on the sofa, picked up the remote control and started channel surfing.

"That's great, Sherlock. Very impressive, only problem is you have absolutely no proof, and I sincerely doubt Sam was so upset at the thought of not having to live with Hope that he chose to take his own life. Sam's living with them was probably Tom's idea or maybe even Crystal's, but I sincerely doubt it was Sam's. I just can't believe he would have wanted to live with

Hope." Having lived with her sister for the first eighteen years of her life, Grace found it hard to believe that anyone would willingly want to live with her.

"Well, at least I have a theory, what do you have?"

Grace took the remote away and turned off the TV. "As much as I hate doing this, I think we should talk to Tom."

CHAPTER TWELVE

KYLE PUT HIS new Camaro in park and glanced at the District Attorney sign prominently displayed in front of an old brick building adjacent to the sheriff's office and the County Water Commission.

"I saw a parking spot three blocks from here, are you sure you wouldn't prefer that one?" Grace asked.

"You were the one freaking out about the scratch on the door."

"I wasn't freaking out about the scratch. I was freaking out about everything else," Grace clarified as she shifted against the seat. "So, what's the plan?" At Kyle's confused look, she asked, "What do you plan on asking Tom?"

"Me?" he squeaked. "Coming here was your idea."

"You're the detective, buddy. I'm just the lowly secretary, remember?"

"But you know him," he said.

"But you are the great detective," she parried back.

Grace sighed with relief when Kyle finally unbuckled. To her surprise, instead of opening the car door and marching across the parking lot, Kyle twisted around and leaned over the back of the front seat.

"What are you doing?" she asked, as he brushed against her while reaching behind her seat.

"Getting help."

After a few grunts and groans, he finally turned back around, bringing with him several books.

"What do you have, the newest edition of *Detecting for Dummies?*"

"Very funny. I'll have you know, there is no such book, but I did find these," he said, proudly displaying five rather worn looking books.

Grace took the books from him and quickly scanned the titles. "Hmm, let's see, *Investigating in the 20th Century*, *Perspectives From the Front Seat—A Detective's Life*, *How to Become a Private-Eye in Six Easy Steps*, *Private Eyes in the Movies*, and *Opening Your Own Detective Agency in the Age of Aquarius.*"

At Grace's less than impressed look, Kyle said, "I didn't have much choice. This is all the library had."

"The library? Are you crazy? Why don't you just announce to everyone that you're a fake?"

"It's a library, not a chat room. They're not allowed to tell anyone what people check out."

"Who checked out the books to you?"

"The very nice librarian, why?" he asked warily.

"Let me guess, she's about fifty; wears a neon bright sweater; black pencil skirt; matching neon high-heels; bleach-blonde, curly hair, pulled back by a matching neon headband; and she called you sweetums?"

Grace took Kyle's silence as a yes. "That would be Mrs. Anderson. Wonderful lady, very friendly, very talkative, too. I once borrowed *What Every Girl Should Know About the Opposite Sex*. Oh, weeks of fun followed. It started with some rather crude offers from some of the boys in my class, and ended with my parents wanting to have a talk with me."

"It's okay . . . it's okay," he said. "If anyone asks, I'll just say I got them for you. Yes . . . yes, that should work," he said, nodding his head and picking up one of the books and flipping through the pages.

♈ ♈ ♈

"Okay, I think I should be good cop, and you should be bad cop," Kyle whispered into Grace's ear as they waited for Tom in the District Attorney's lobby.

"I don't think we should be taking our cues from a book that was published when disco was king."

"It had some good advice."

"Yeah, I especially liked the part that discussed how to best infiltrate hippie communes."

"Quiet, here he comes," he said, placing his hand in the small of her back and shoving her forward.

"Gracie," Tom said smiling, spreading his arms out wide. He quickly dropped them to his side when he realized she wasn't about to rush into his arms. "I'm surprised to see you here. What can I do for you?"

"I want to talk to you about Hope."

Grace watched as a shadow dropped across Tom's face. "Why, what has she done now?"

"What exactly does that mean? Look here, Tom Lake, if anyone has done anything, it's you."

Kyle jumped forward. "Ms. Holliday, I'm sure Mr. Lake didn't mean anything negative." Turning to Tom and doing his best good cop impersonation, he said, "She's usually so professional. I think being home is getting to her a little, but you know how Hope can be. She has a tendency to set everyone's nerves on edge."

Tom coldly smiled back at Kyle. "I know what you're after. Melodie told me she hired you, and I told her she made a mistake. We don't need you around here. Sheriff Bellamy will find out who murdered Crystal. You're just wasting your time and Melodie's money."

"What exactly are you doing here, Tom?" Grace asked.

"I work here," he said.

"I know that," she said, "but I don't think anyone would have blamed you if you took some time off."

"Time off? And do what? I can't help find who killed Crystal sitting at home. I want to be here when they bring whoever killed her in. Now, if you two are done cross examining me, I have some work to do." Tom abruptly turned away and walked down the hallway.

"Nice bad cop." Kyle whispered in Grace's ear. "I knew you would be a natural."

While Grace tried to decide whether that was a compliment or an insult, Kyle rushed to open the door for the incoming district attorney. "Mr. Simpson, is it?" Kyle reached out to shake the other man's hand. "It's so good to meet you. I have heard wonderful things about you."

"Oh, thank you. Have we met?" the older man asked.

"No, sir, but my friend here," Kyle said, taking hold of Grace's elbow and drawing her closer, "is good friends with Tom Lake."

Simpson's face suddenly relaxed. "Tom? Thank goodness. He needs a friend right now." James Simpson inspected her closely. "I think I remember you. You're Hope's sister, aren't you?"

Grace nodded her head, wondering how he knew Hope.

Simpson smiled and shook his head. "You probably don't remember me, but I was a good friend of Tom's father. In fact, you and your sister attended a pre-graduation bash at my lake cabin."

"The house on Paducah Lake? With the tennis court?" Grace asked. She still couldn't place the man before her, but she definitely remembered the lake house and the party Tom threw for his friends, right before graduation.

Nodding, Simpson suddenly changed subjects and asked, "I don't suppose you convinced him to go home have you?"

Grace and Kyle both shook their head.

"I have been trying for days to get him to rest, but he acts like the world will come to an end if he gets any sleep." James Simpson turned to Grace. "I remember seeing you at Crystal's funeral. You were speaking to Adam Phelps, weren't you?"

"Yes, he's an old friend of mine," Grace said.

"I absolutely love his movies. They're so moving, don't you think?" Kyle added.

Ignoring him, Simpson asked, "I don't suppose you know where he is, do you? Sheriff Bellamy has been looking for him."

"Does he have a warrant out for him?" Grace asked.

"No, but the sheriff has a few questions he would like to ask him."

"You can't seriously believe that Adam has anything to do with Crystal's death?"

Simpson sighed and looked upward before saying, "I suppose you believe he is completely innocent. That's the problem with celebrities. No one ever wants to believe that their favorite actor, singer, or even director is capable of committing any crime, just because they feel that they know him."

"Well, in this case, I do know him. I grew up with him. I trust him."

Kyle shook his head. "Well, I don't trust him. His movies really aren't that great. The last one was completely pretentious. I still can't believe he was nominated for an academy award."

Sensing a like mind, Simpson smiled, "It was horrible, wasn't it? I fell asleep half way through. It was the worst fifteen dollars I have ever spent at the movies in my life. I felt like leaving and asking for my money back."

Grace listened as they continued to debate the various merits—apparently there weren't any—of the other films up for nomination that year. The consensus was that, while awful, any of them were better than Adam's film.

When the academy award discussion somehow segued into a discussion on taxidermy, of which Kyle seemed to creepily know a great deal about, she decided it was time to tell Kyle she would meet him out at the car. Before she had a chance to interrupt, she spied Steve slip through the door and walk down the hallway toward Tom's office.

Recalling his argument with Melodie, Grace decided it couldn't hurt to ask him a few questions. Perhaps, she could find out what they had been arguing about the other day.

By the time she caught up to Steve he was standing in front of Tom's office door, staring up into Tom's scowling face.

Steve's face flushed. "Come on, Lake. I would think you'd be clamoring for my business. Don't you want this creep caught?"

"I'm going to tell you the same thing I told Drake. I don't need a detective. Sheriff Bellamy is investigating this case, and I have no doubt, he'll find the perpetrator—"

"Perpetrator? Case? Listen to you, you sound like a prosecutor. This was your wife. This isn't one of your regular *cases.*"

"I am aware of that," Tom snapped. Seeing Grace standing off to the side, he added, "Oh Gracie, you're still here. Make sure to tell your sister I said hi," he said, before slamming the door shut.

"Unbelievable," Steve muttered before turning to Grace. "What are you doing here?"

Grace shrugged her shoulders. "I just wanted to talk to Tom."

"Good luck. He's not the easy going guy he was in high school." Steve looked over her shoulder. "Hey, are you here with Kyle Drake? I was thinking he and I might be able to team up. I could use a good partner."

Over my dead body, she thought. "I think he would love that, but after all of this," she said, waving her hand around, "is over."

"So, he is investigating! Who hired him? Tom? No, probably not Tom. Melodie?"

Grace held up her hands. "I can't tell you that, Steve, I would get fired. He's very strict about that sort of thing. What about you? Are you working on Crystal's murder?"

Steve snorted. "Of course. The Assistant DA's wife gets whacked, you'd better believe I'm on top of it," he said puffing out his chest. "I didn't get to be where I am today by sitting on my can."

"Uh huh," Grace muttered, suppressing a sneeze as a whiff of stale cologne blew past her. "Who hired you?"

Steve shrugged. "I'm just interested in seeing justice done. Look, sweetie, why don't you tell Drake that I would be happy to offer my expertise?"

"And just why would you want to do that, pumpkin? I would think you wouldn't want the competition."

Steve smirked. "Purely professional courtesy. He's new to the area and these are my old stomping grounds. I think he would appreciate my help."

"He has me," Grace pointed out, barely concealing her irritation. "These are my old stomping grounds, too."

Steve raised his hands. "Hey, sugar, I don't want to step on anyone's toes. I just thought I would offer. Seeing as how I've already got some hot information, but hey, he's got you. I mean, you probably already know who killed Crystal."

Sensing he was about to walk away from her, she reluctantly asked, "And just how can you help?"

He shook his head. "Well, I am willing to help, but I don't give away anything for free. If he doesn't think he needs a partner, then, I thought, he might be interested in hiring me as a consultant."

"How about this, I'll tell you what I know, and you tell me what you know. If it's good, I'll pass it on to Mr. Drake. I'll even tell him where I got the information. Happy?"

He smiled slightly. "All right, you go first."

"The police suspect Adam."

Completely unimpressed, he said, "That's it? That's what you've been able to figure out? Oh, darling, your boss seriously needs me. I've known that for days now."

"Good for you, pudding. Do you believe Adam killed Crystal?"

"Adam's a liar, cheat, thief, plagiarist, conman—"

"You forgot cattle rustler."

"Well, if he ever films a western, I'm sure he'll commit that crime too, but I doubt he's a murderer. I mean, what could be in it for him? That's what I can't figure out. Why do they suspect him? Lots of people hated Crystal."

"That's rather harsh."

"It's true. Crystal got what she deserved. I'm sure Adam wasn't the only one who would've liked to see her dead."

"Does that include you? I was at Melodie's house the other day when you came by."

"Did she say anything to you?"

Grace briefly considered telling him the truth, but decided a little deception might be in order. "Melodie was my best friend. She often confides in me." There, not exactly a lie. "I would like to hear your side of the story."

Steve snorted. "What would be the point? You're her friend. You'll take her side, you always did. Besides, she wasn't even there. She has no idea what happened." Steve looked embarrassed. "Whatever. I'm wasting my breath. Did you tell Drake what Melodie said?"

Grace shook her head in bewilderment. "Still, I would rather hear it from you. Melodie can be rather, um . . ." she broke off not sure how to finish her sentence.

"Eh, do what you like. I'm sure you will, anyway," he said, turning to leave.

"Wait," she said grabbing his elbow. "We had a deal, remember? A little give and take. I told you what I knew."

Steve smirked, "It wasn't much."

"Still," she snapped, "if you want to be hired as a consultant, consider this your first interview."

Steve stared at her, considering. "Okay. Don't ever let it be said that I'm not a good sport. Three trophies are missing. They think she was killed with one of them. The murderer took out one of the trophies, hit Crystal over the back of the head, then—get this—stole two more. He or she then tried to make it look like an accident. My source said she was killed next to the trophy case. The killer moved the body to the bottom of the stairs and then broke the heel off one of her shoes. Trying to make it seem like she fell down the stairs when her heel broke."

"One of her heels was broken. Kyl—Mr. Drake said that one of the heels was loose. That's why Crystal tossed them into the trash."

"Yeah, but the killer didn't know that. The killer broke the heel on the wrong shoe. He or she then cleaned up the crime, badly according to my source."

"Which trophies are missing?"

"One of the cheerleading competitions—the one Hope won when she was captain of the squad—Adam's debate trophy, and the 1972 football championship trophy."

"Why three? It would have only taken one to kill her?"

Steve simply shrugged.

"Who told you this?"

"Hey, I can't reveal my source," he said smiling. "Actually, most of that information is already around town. You know how fast information flies around here. By the way, what was your boss doing picking up detective how-to-books this morning? Seriously, if he needs my—"

"They're for me," she said, while making a mental note to make Kyle pay later. "My boss thought it would be funny."

"That's rather cruel of him," he said sighing, clearly uncomfortable with what he was about to say. "I mean, it's all over town how you were passing yourself off as a detective when actually you're his secretary. I just thought you would want to know. You know, I don't blame you. If half those people could have gotten away with lying about their lives they would have done it, too."

🏆 🏆 🏆

Grace opened the car door and sank down in the soft leather. She needed time to think. Crystal murdered, three trophies missing, most of her close friends suspects. That was the problem. She knew these people. Grew up with them. It was difficult to believe that one of them could be a cold-blooded murderer.

It was even more difficult to believe that either Kyle or she would be able to figure out who did this. Their suspect list seemed to be growing by the minute. Crystal wasn't just disliked, people seemed to loath her. Grace thought back to what Crystal had been like as a teenager. Spoiled, arrogant, rude, and annoying, were the first words that came to mind. No one really liked Crystal, but other than Hope, Grace couldn't remember anyone actively hating her.

Grace turned around in her seat, and picked up one of the library books lying in the back seat. One of these things has to have some practical information in it, she thought, flipping through the pages.

Ten minutes later, she set the book down on the passenger seat. Absolutely useless. Still, it did have a few tips that would be worth trying. If only Kyle wasn't trying to pass himself off as some great detective, and worse, billing her friends in the process.

She laid her head on the steering wheel imagining a packed courtroom. Tom on one side. Her, Kyle, and more than likely Felix, on the other. Friends and family in the seats behind them, shaking their heads in disappointment. Words like fraud, obstruction of justice, and loser being bandied around. She could easily imagine Felix grandstanding, while Kyle pulls scarves out of his sleeves, smiling at the female jurors.

Grace snarled as she lifted her head up and looked across the parking lot. Kyle and Simpson were standing on the steps to the district attorney's office. Simpson was laughing at something Kyle was saying. Maybe she was worrying too much. After all, Kyle could be quite charming, when he wanted to be. Grace tapped her fingers against the steering wheel, considering. Having the District Attorney as a friend is probably a good thing and Kyle does have the requisite identification right now. Perhaps he won't look too closely into Kyle Drake Investigations.

With a sudden optimism, Grace took out her cell phone and called Adam. He had lived in Crystal's house for over a month; he had to know more than what he's been saying. He definitely had been acting suspicious before and after Crystal's murder. Once Adam answered, Grace quickly arranged a time to meet, and hung up.

Smiling, Grace looked back to the District Attorney's office door, just in time to watch Kyle fan out a deck of cards, accidentally dropping half the cards on the ground. Sighing, as her newfound optimism flew out the window, Grace laid her head back on the steering wheel.

♛ ♛ ♛

"Well? What did you and James Simpson have to talk about?" Grace asked.

"A lot. He's a very nice man. Very helpful. Absolutely hates your friend Adam. He's completely convinced Adam is guilty."

"That's great. You do remember that Adam is one of your clients, don't you?"

"Yes, I remember. It hasn't slipped my mind. In fact, I think we need to see him as soon as possible."

Grace explained that she just spoke to Adam and had made plans to meet with him at the local diner for dinner.

"Excellent! Did you tell him to bring a check?"

"No."

"Cash?" Kyle asked hopefully.

"I didn't call him so you could squeeze some more money out of him before he's arrested. He paid you to find out who killed Crystal, and that's what we are going to try to do."

"I know that. Why do you think I've been chatting up the District Attorney for the last thirty minutes? No help from you, I might add. Where did you run off to?"

Grace filled Kyle in on her talk with Steve.

Kyle let out a low whistle. "Three trophies were stolen? That's rather strange. You couldn't find out what he and Melodie were talking about?"

"I tried to trick the information out of him, but no luck. By the way, for some bizarre reason he really wants to work with you."

Kyle smiled, as he leaned his head against the headrest. "Naturally. Who wouldn't want to work with Kyle Drake Investigations."

"You're not falling for your own publicity, are you?" she asked nervously.

"Don't worry, I have my feet planted firmly on the ground." He tilted his head to the side as he looked at her thoughtfully. "I just have faith that we'll figure this out."

Grace sighed. "Seems like everyone I know hated Crystal, but no one's willing to say why."

"Not everyone hated her. James Simpson thought she was the greatest thing in the world. He called Tom and Crystal the most beautiful couple he had ever seen in his life."

"Did he say why he suspects Adam?"

"Crystal confided in him a few days before the reunion. She told him that she was afraid someone was going to try to hurt her. He tried to get her to tell him who she was afraid of, but she wouldn't say."

"Wonderful."

"The next day, James saw her and Adam arguing. He overheard Adam say that she had better not mess with him. He's convinced Adam killed her at the reunion. You add in Adam's missing trophy . . ." he said shrugging.

"So, he lays in wait for her and kills her with his old debate trophy? Why not his Oscar?" she asked sarcastically.

"Oh, be serious. It's a high school trophy case. It wouldn't have an Oscar in it."

"His isn't the only one that was taken. The killer may have taken Adam's to throw suspicion onto him."

Kyle snapped his fingers and grabbed Grace's arm, suddenly remembering the stolen flash drive. "Maybe we are going about this all wrong. What if she was simply in the wrong place at the wrong time? The trophies aren't the only thing that went missing that night. Diana told me that someone had stolen a flash drive, too."

"I don't know of a market for flash drives," Grace said. "Especially, not one worth killing for."

"Well, we have six hours until we have to meet Adam," Kyle said glancing at his watch. "What do you want to do in the meantime?"

"One of those books said the first thing an investigator should do is organize. So, let's create a timeline and a list of suspects. Maybe if we write everything down, things will become clearer. Do you have a piece of paper and a pencil?"

Kyle shook his head as he looked in the glove compartment. "I don't think . . . oh wait, yes I do," he said as he reached into his pocket and pulled out a piece of orange-colored paper.

Grace took the paper out of his hand and carefully unfolded it. In the center of the page were two phone numbers written in delicate script, and at the top was a small emblem of a blast hole drill in front of the rising sun. Larry Baker's company. "Where did you get this?"

"Melodie. She wrote her number on it for me, why?"

"On the day of the funeral, while we were at Crystal's house, I saw Melodie crumple up a piece of paper like this. I don't think she was very happy with what was written on it." Tapping her fingers on the steering wheel Grace added, "Perhaps, we should talk to both of our clients today."

CHAPTER THIRTEEN

GRACE READJUSTED HERSELF on Melodie's rich Italian leather sofa. For the last twenty minutes, the only information she or Kyle had succeeded in getting out of Melodie was that there was an "absolutely divine French restaurant which recently opened" that she had been "dying to try," her house was just "so big" and she was "so lonely," and that she had recently bought a silk nightie that she, unfortunately, was going to have to return because it "just didn't cover myself adequately."

She was kindly demonstrating—for Kyle—just how far the slit up the side went up her thigh, when Grace decided she had enough. "Melodie, I'm so sorry to hear about your underwear troubles. Next time, you should try the merchandise on at the store before you buy, or ask for help from one of the store clerks. Well, now that we have that problem solved, perhaps you can help solve one of ours. Why were you and your sister fighting? And don't bother saying that you weren't."

Melodie sat down next to Kyle. "We weren't fighting!"

"It's okay, you can tell us," Kyle said, slipping an arm around her shoulders. "We know it had something to do with your late husband."

Grace watched as Melodie crumbled beside Kyle. "We weren't fighting. At least we weren't when she died. We had come to an understanding, and I had decided to forgive her. I mean, you can't go through life hating your own sister. I won't say it was easy to forgive her, but I did," Melodie said as she burst into tears.

"Melodie, if you could just tell us what happened," Grace said gently.

Sniffling, Melodie looked up at Kyle. "It really isn't important. I forgave her. Please believe me."

Kyle held her closer. Looking over her head, he sent a questioning glance to Grace.

Realizing they were getting nowhere, Grace decided to change the subject. "What about Steve? I overheard you two arguing the other day. "

Melodie dried her eyes and leaned in closer to Kyle. "He's just a pest."

Grace scowled. "You said something about knowing what he was capable of. What did you mean?"

Melodie smiled ruefully. "Nothing. I was just irritated with him. You know what a nuisance he can be sometimes."

Kyle pulled away. "It would help to know what you two were arguing about."

Melodie reached out and pulled Kyle back. "Don't go." It was amazing to Grace, how in just a few days, Kyle had managed to thoroughly wrap Melodie around his little finger. Sighing, Melodie said, "Steve almost killed someone once."

"Who?" Grace and Kyle asked in unison.

"An old boyfriend of mine," she said reluctantly. "David Hart. Steve pushed him down a flight of stairs. David was okay, though. He didn't die. He left the very next day."

"Why did Steve try to kill him?" Grace asked.

"You know Steve," Melodie said, leaning back against Kyle's arm. "He's always been insanely jealous, but I doubt he had anything to do with Crystal's death. I was just frustrated that day. I shouldn't have taunted him."

♼ ♼ ♼

Grace sat down on the hard stone steps, wishing she hadn't insisted that Kyle and Melodie go on without her. Melodie had refused to say any more about Crystal, Steve, or David Hart after initially opening up, and it didn't take a genius to realize that the only person Melodie was interested in opening up to was Kyle. So, in the interest of gaining some information, Kyle offered to take one for the team and take Melodie to Chez Robere for lunch. Grace just hoped he could get her to open up about Melodie and Crystal's fight or at the very least why Steve hated Crystal so much.

Grace looked up and down the street. Jeff had promised he would be right on his way. She was going to have to get her own car. Grace was starting to miss New York's public transit system. Despite being mugged the year before, Grace could definitely say it was safer, more reliable, and far cleaner than riding with Jeff.

She was just about to call her brother again when she heard the sound of a car approaching. "About time, Jeff," she said standing up, only to sit back down when she realized it was Diana pulling into Melodie's drive way.

"Grace, what are you doing out here by yourself, sweetie?" Diana asked, as she walked up the front steps.

Grace explained that Melodie had left, and she was waiting for Jeff to pick her up.

"Oh, why didn't Melodie let you wait inside?" Diana asked perplexed.

"She was a bit distracted at the time," Grace said, remembering how Melodie had wrapped her arm around Kyle's, pushing and pulling him towards his car, once he had agreed to take her out.

Diana laughed. "I take it that Mr. Drake was here at the time. She hasn't been able to talk about anyone else since he arrived. Well, come wait inside."

Grace gratefully followed the other woman inside.

"Eric will be here soon," Diana putting down her purse and sitting on the sofa. "We're going to watch a movie at his place. You're welcome to come, if you like."

Thanking her, Grace sat down next to Diana, explaining that Jeff should be there at any moment.

"What happened to his home on Ferris Street?" Grace asked, curious as to why Eric was no longer living at the beautiful yellow Victorian.

"He gave that up," she said, tilting her head trying to remember, "about ten years ago. Right before you all graduated."

"I'm surprised he sold his house. Didn't his great-great grandfather build the place?"

"I was rather surprised myself. I wish he hadn't sold that house. I absolutely hate where he's living now."

"Is he still planning on retiring?"

Diana laughed as she pushed her auburn bangs out of her eyes. Her ruby ring flashing in the light. "No. He just says that every year. Crystal says that he'll be . . . I'm sorry," she said shaking her head. "I just can't get used to her being gone."

Grace nodded sympathetically.

"Grace, how is the investigation going? I just wanted to let you know that if there is anything I can do to help, please let me know."

"I don't suppose you know who would have wanted to hurt Crystal, do you?"

Diana sadly shook her head. "Besides Tom, you mean?"

"You accused him before."

"And I will again until someone listens to me. I told one of those deputies exactly what I saw that night and he just said 'is that all?'"

Grace leaned forward. "What did you see?"

Diana hesitated before carefully looking over her shoulder. "Right after Crystal's body was found, during all the commotion, I saw Tom walk out towards the parking lot carrying a small black duffle bag. Now why would he do that? His wife was just found murdered and the first thing he does is go to his car. Obviously, he must have been hiding something. I just wish the police had listened to me. They could have searched his car right then."

"Do you know what was in the bag?"

"I have no idea but he was acting suspicious." Diana shook her head. "Oh, I wish they had never gotten together, but she had been in love with him since they were children. Right from the beginning, she only had eyes for Tom."

"I remember her and Sam dating our senior year."

"Her one brief moment of happiness," she said, running a hand over eyes, fighting back tears. "I remember when she was thirteen, her running home, and telling us she was going to marry Tom Lake. Her mother and I just laughed. We thought it was your typical crush that would go away after a while. Then we hoped and prayed that it would. When Hope and Tom announced that they were going to get married after graduation, well, I was really worried about Crystal. She was just so heartbroken. One day Sam came into my office—it was after his accident—and I asked him if he wouldn't mind taking Crystal to the New Year's Eve dance at the Country Club. That's how it all began. Suddenly, she lost all interest in Thomas Lake. Sam became her world."

Diana stood up and walked over to Melodie's mini bar. She poured herself a drink, after offering one for Grace. "They were inseparable after that. At least until the accident."

"You mean his suicide?"

Diana grimaced and nodded her head. "Sorry, I still can't wrap my head around that. I still want to believe it was just a horrible accident. To think, none of us realized just how unhappy he had been. It still breaks my heart when I think about it."

"I really liked Sam."

"I did too. He was a much better man than Tom. If only he hadn't died. Things would have been so different. At least, Crystal would have been loved. Oh, I'm sorry, I'm crying again." Diana wiped away her tears. "I've been doing that a lot lately."

"Tom must have loved Crystal at some point. They seemed happy with each other during the reunion," Grace said, remembering how he held onto her and gently kissed her shoulder while up on the stage.

Diana sighed. "Tom is a good actor when he wants to be. The truth is he never loved anyone but himself. He certainly didn't love Crystal."

"If Tom didn't love her, then why do you think he married her?"

Diana looked at Grace with a mixture of pity and disbelief. "Money and connections, sweetie. That's why. I hate to be so crass, but that's what Tom was after. I'm sure he enjoyed your sister, but Tom was about to graduate, and he suddenly realized that Crystal and our family had far more to offer him than Hope ever could." Suddenly realizing how insulting she sounded, Diana turned bright red. "Grace, I'm sorry. I don't mean to sound so, so . . ."

"Elitist," Grace provided helpfully.

"No, I was going to say snooty. Don't get me wrong, we all love Hope. It's just our family has a certain history in this town."

Grace smiled, taking pity on the woman. "Like you said, you have money."

"Yes, to put it bluntly. Tom has always had big dreams. Do you know that he plans to be a state senator someday? I always felt bad about the way he treated your sister. Even before Sam died, Tom was trying to seduce Crystal, but by then Crystal was in love with Sam, and told him he was too late. Crystal told me, she had tried to warn Hope about Tom, but you know your sister."

Grace could just imagine what her sister's reaction was to that piece of news, especially coming from her arch nemesis.

"Anyway, Sam had her heart, but when he died . . . she was devastated and that gave Tom the perfect opportunity to slither in and take advantage. He was the first one at her side that night, all through the funeral, and basically ever since."

🏆 🏆 🏆

"I'll have a cheeseburger, fries . . . let me see," Grace said as she surveyed the menu, "oh, and a chocolate milkshake. Thanks." Grace handed the waitress her menu.

Adam fidgeted in his chair. "Nothing for me."

"Why aren't you eating?"

"I'm not hungry. Are you going to help me or not?" he whispered across the table.

Grace shook her head, convinced Adam had lost his mind. "Forget it, Adam. I'm not going to help you break into the high school," she whispered back.

"Why not? I thought detectives did this sort of thing all the time. Why do you think I handed your boss all that money?"

Grace wondered about that, too. "You forget. I am just a lowly secretary. I leave the breaking and entering to the professionals. You should have called my assistant."

"Who?"

"What? I don't . . . what?" Grace asked, suddenly realizing her mistake. "I mean, you should call someone else."

Adam lounged back in the booth. "You're the only one I trust. Besides, we aren't going to break anything. We're just going to take a look around." He grinned and tapped the table with his fingers. "Remember that time in junior high when we snuck into old Mr. McCollum's place. Remember how much fun that was."

"Hmm. I remember you, Hope, Tom, Sam, and Melodie sneaking into old McCollum's place, and me calling my parents and telling on all of you."

"That was you?" he said aghast.

Nodding her head vigorously, she said, "Yes. Maybe you should call Hope for help." Realizing that was a bad idea, she quickly said, "Actually, please don't."

"Please meet me tonight, at midnight, and whatever you do, don't tell your boss. You're the only one I can trust, Grace. I need you." Adam took her hands into his, softly rubbing his thumb across the back of her hand. His big hazel eyes pleading with her.

"Why should I? You haven't exactly been cooperative. I've asked a dozen questions since we sat down, and you have deflected each one. You're hiding something. If you trust me so much, then prove it. Tell me what you and Crystal were arguing about the night of the reunion."

"I promise, Grace, I will tell you everything," he said, glancing around the room as he stood up, "just not here." To Grace's surprise, he leaned down and kissed her. "See you at midnight."

♆ ♆ ♆

"Why am I doing this?" Grace asked herself for the hundredth time, as she paced in front of her old high school. She looked at her watch again, debating how much more time she should give Adam to show up. Five minutes more, she decided, and she was out of here.

She suddenly froze. She felt, more than heard, someone moving behind her. Turning, she softly called out Adam's name.

No answer. She peered into darkness, wishing she had told Kyle what she and Adam were going to be up to tonight.

She wasn't exactly afraid. This was her old high school after all. It had always been safe, well, except for a few nights ago.

Grace turned her head and looked across the parking lot toward Mrs. Partridge's house. Seeing the house lit up gave her some comfort when she had climbed out of her car and made her way to the front of the school, but now with her mind helpfully replaying all the horror movies she had ever seen, she was starting to become jumpy.

She knew she should have told someone where she was going and what she was going to do. Problem is she couldn't just say 'oh by the way, Adam and I are going to run by the high school and do a little breaking and entering. Don't tell.'

Kyle, she could have told. Unfortunately, he would have also wanted to tag along, and Adam wasn't going to go along with that. If she wanted to know what Adam knew, she was going to have to play by his rules, at least, for the time being.

Snap.

She felt her heart skip a beat. There was that sound again. She called out Adam's name, as she peered into the night. All she could make out were shadows.

A sudden breeze swept through, blowing her hair into her face and causing the trees to sway. Grace quickly reached up and pushed her hair back out of her face. One of the shadows had moved. The logic center of her brain tried to tell her it was simply a tree swaying in the breeze, casting shadows. The more primitive center told her to run.

Deciding Adam could take care of himself, Grace swiftly turned toward the parking lot only to come up against an immovable body. She shrieked and struck out with her fist, before realizing who it was that had come up behind her.

"Adam! You scared me half to death!" Grace said pushing him further away.

"Owww," he said, holding his nose. "I think it's broken. What is wrong with you?"

"Me? Why were you skulking around?" she asked angrily.

Adam gingerly pressed his fingers against his nose. "I haven't been skulking around. I just got here."

Grace turned to look behind her. The trees were still swaying, their shadows dancing around the ground. It must have been her imagination, she thought.

"Are you okay?" she asked, more out of politeness than any real concern.

"No! I think it's broken, Holliday," he said, carefully wiggling his nose with his fingers.

"Sorry. Come on. I'll drive you to the hospital," she said, taking a hold of his elbow and steering him toward the parking lot.

He planted his feet. "I'm not leaving here until we go through that school, room by room."

Realizing he wasn't about to leave, Grace threw up her hands, and walked to the school's steps, with Adam close on her heels.

Once she reached the glass doors, she pressed her gloved hands against the glass and looked inside. "Well, it looks like the coast is clear."

"Yep. We'd better get started."

"Okay." Grace stepped back to give Adam room to open the door. When he didn't rush to the door, she motioned for him to go ahead. To her surprise, he echoed her motion. She shook her head, pointed to the door and said, "Go on."

"Ladies first."

"Adam, at this rate we're going to be here all night. Would you open the door, so we can get this over with?"

"I don't know how to open the door. You're the professional, don't you have a lock pick or something."

She shook her head. "I'm a secretary, not a detective"

"Drake hasn't taught you how to do this?" he asked in disbelief. "I thought all detectives knew how to break into places."

"If you wanted the door open, you should have let me bring him along."

Exasperated Adam snapped, "Haven't you ever seen him unlock a door before?"

Grace nodded. "Of course, but he doesn't just wave his hands around, say alakazam, abracadabra, hocus pocus and poof the door magically opens." Actually, that is exactly what he does, but Adam didn't need to know that. "He has tools he uses to open the door, and I don't have them," she said, relieved that Adam's plan wasn't going to work. "Let's go home, Adam. We'll come back in the morning. We'll ask Mr. Collins for help. Maybe he can find whatever it is your looking for."

"There's no way I'm asking Collins." Adam turned around and jumped up on the stone railing.

"What are you doing?"

Grace watched, horrified, as he jumped up and caught the window's ledge, seven feet off the ground. She shook her head, as he hung there for a few minutes, desperately kicking at the wall and air. Finally finding his footing, he hoisted himself up to a standing position, grunting and panting as he did. Once he was facing the window, he carefully looked first to the right and then to the left.

"Adam, think about what you are doing." She groaned as she heard glass breaking. "I thought you said there would be no breaking."

♊ ♊ ♊

Sweat beaded Grace's face despite the cool interior of the school. Her mind kept replaying the image of Crystal's body at the bottom of the stairs. Suddenly, her old high school appeared dark and sinister.

"You are paying for that window, Adam."

"Would you stop nagging? Don't worry, I'll present them with a nice donation next week, now keep your voice down," he said, as they crept along the empty hallway. "We'll start with Collin's office." Adam motioned for Grace to follow him down the hallway.

"It might help, if you told me what we are looking for."

"We're looking for a black binder."

"Here? At a school?" she asked in disbelief. "Do you have any idea how many binders are in this school."

"No. Do you?"

"No, but I'm willing to bet, quite a lot."

"Don't worry, it's a special binder. It has Reunion written across the top."

"Why is this binder so important?"

"Let's find it first and then I will tell you why it's so important."

Grace was about to argue when she heard the sound of a door shut and footsteps approaching. She whirled around, swiftly running in the opposite direction, with Adam close on her heels.

Her goal was to make it to the stairwell, climb up the steps, and run down the hallway towards the library. She knew from past experience she could open up one of the windows in the science room and jump out without making too much noise.

Adam must have realized the same thing because he sprinted ahead of her, taking the stairs two at a time.

Grace took a second to look behind her. The footsteps were becoming louder and closer. Whoever it was coming down the hall knew they were there and was chasing them.

She had only spared a second to look behind her, but that was enough time for Adam to disappear from her view.

Grace ran up the stairs, trying not to imagine Crystal still lying at the bottom. She rounded the corner and ran down the hallway. The science room was only four doors down on the left.

The footsteps were getting closer. She didn't dare take time to look back.

She reached for the door.

Too late, she realized, as a strong hand clamped down on her shoulder and pushed her against the wall.

🏆 🏆 🏆

"Breaking and Entering, Criminal Trespass, Assault on a Police Officer," the dour looking police officer read out in a flat monotone.

"Assault on a police officer? Grace Lucille Holliday!" her mother, Jeannie Holliday exclaimed. Grace watched as her normally talkative mother was rendered speechless, her mouth opening and closing in shock.

"Mom, it's not as bad as it sounds," she said lamely. "I barely bit the guy. I didn't even break his skin."

Grace looked around the police waiting room. In addition to her shocked parents, overly amused siblings, and the bored police officers, were a very unhappy principal and a very happy Steve Mattingly, who apparently spends his days loitering around the police department.

"He should have announced himself! I was in fear of my life. Naturally, I reacted when he grabbed me from behind. Really, I think we should fight that one."

"Grace," Hope said.

Grace turned toward her smiling sister. "What?"

"Shut up," Hope said, patting Grace's shoulder and flouncing into the nearest chair.

Ignoring her sister's less than helpful advice, Grace continued to press her case. "I didn't break that window," she insisted. There, she thought, open with the truth, hopefully they'll believe the rest. "I was walking by the school …"

"Alone? At midnight?" her sister asked sarcastically.

"Yes! I used to do it in New York all the time."

"What?" her mother yelled.

"The door was open. I saw some kids running around. I went in to keep them from damaging the school. Once I was in there, I realized I was being stupid, and was just about to call the police to make a report, when I heard footsteps and got scared."

She looked around the room trying to judge everyone's reaction. Trouble was she didn't even believe herself. Unable to stop herself, she rambled on. "Kids today, you know in my day we had respect for authority—"

"Was Kyle Drake with you tonight?" her mother asked accusingly.

Before Grace could answer, Sheriff Bellamy said, "No. I spoke to the District Attorney a few minutes ago, and he verified Drake's whereabouts."

Interesting, Grace thought. "Do you normally call the District Attorney for a simple breaking and entering?"

Sheriff Bellamy tipped back his hat. "No, ma'am," he drawled slowly, "but considering the Assistant District Attorney's wife was just murdered a week ago, in that very building, we figured he might want to know. Now, what I would like to know is whether Drake put you up to breaking into the school?"

"No, I give you my word. He knew absolutely nothing about this." Good, she thought, end with the truth. "My story isn't going to change, so you can either book me or let me go."

To her and everyone else's surprise, Mr. Collins stepped forward. "No, please Sheriff, we don't want to press any charges. As you know, we have been having trouble with students breaking in at night, lately. Mrs. Partridge phoned me an hour ago to tell me she saw a couple of kids running around the school and thought they were up to no good. That's why I called the police. No, I believe Grace completely. She has always been very trustworthy."

"Unbelievable," Steve whispered, rolling his eyes. Grace couldn't help but agree. She was certain someone had been spying on her while she waited for Adam. It must have been the same kids Mrs. Partridge had seen.

Bellamy sighed loudly. "That's real nice of you, Eric, but there's still the matter of assault on one of my deputies, not to mention trespass. Now, Ms. Holliday, I know your boss has been hired to investigate Mrs. Lake's murder. I'm going to ask you again, what were you doing hanging around the high school this late at night?"

Grace was about to retell her fictitious story of the night's events when the door opened and Kyle walked in, followed closely by Melodie and James Simpson. On their entrance, all eyes swung to the door and stayed there. Melodie was decked out, wearing a red low-cut evening dress with a ruby and diamond choker. Both men were wearing tuxes, although Kyle, with his six-foot-one inch frame, broad shoulders, blond hair, and blue eyes was definitely the most noticeable of the trio.

Hope was the first to speak. "Where in the world did you three come from, and why didn't I get an invitation?"

"We were at the annual Harvest Ball at the Gold Rush Country Club," Melodie said. "It's a member's only event."

Grace looked at her watch. "This late?"

Melodie looked irritated. "It was just ending when Sheriff Bellamy called."

"Since when is he a member?" Hope asked, pointing to Kyle.

"Oh, I'm a prospective member," he said smiling. "I'm surprised you haven't been asked yet, Hope? I barely unpacked before they were begging me to join."

As fun as it was to see her sister at a loss for words, Grace decided it was time to bring everyone's attention back to her and her impeding imprisonment. "Excuse me! Do I get some kind of bail or something?"

"Could someone explain to me what is going on?" Kyle asked, clearly confused.

Grace, for the second time that night explained her side of the events. A quick look at Kyle's face told her that he didn't believe her any more than anyone else in the room, with the possible exception of Mr. Collins. She always did like Mr. Collins, such a sweet man, she thought, as she smiled at her lone ally in this horrible affair.

Sheriff Bellamy shook his head. "Okay, Ms. Holliday, perhaps some kids did break in tonight, but I don't believe for a second you just walked in there to clear them out. I think you decided to take advantage of the situation. When you found the school open, you went in there to do some investigating."

"Ms. Holliday!" Kyle said in a patently false outraged voice.

Bellamy continued, ignoring Kyle's outburst. "I can tell you, me and my deputies have been all over that school. We don't need some slick investigator from New York mucking things up," Bellamy said, turning to glare at Kyle. "Now, what I want to know is, did you put her up to this?"

"Absolutely not!"

"Sheriff, I can assure you Mr. Drake has been with Melodie and I all evening," James said. "If she did this it had to be on her own initiative."

"Yeah, I can see that," Steve chimed in. "She was probably trying to score points with her boss."

Mr. Collins tried to shush him, but Steve continued. "I mean, the night of the reunion, she made such a big deal out of her being a detective, and we all know she's just his secretary. She was telling all of these outrageous stories."

Grace scowled at Kyle.

"She clearly just wants attention." Steve looked over at Kyle, carefully gaging his reaction. Kyle, his face grave, glared back.

"It's kind of sad, actually," Steve said, looking down at his shoes. "Oh, hell, why don't we all just forget this night happened and let her go?"

"Thanks Steve," Grace said, through gritted teeth.

"Well, we don't need any amateur detectives mucking about, either," Bellamy shouted, pointing a thick finger at Kyle's chest. "You need to control your people."

"Sheriff, I assure you that this is not how I run Kyle Drake Investigations. I'm sure Ms. Holliday was only trying to help," Kyle said trying to smooth things over. The last thing he wanted was for Grace to be thrown into jail.

"Drake," Steve said, walking up and slapping a hand on Kyle's back, "I know it's hard to do, but sometimes it's best to let problem employees go. I can't tell you how many secretaries I've had to fire. You know, I'd be happy to help you out with anything you need here."

"She's just a little excitable," Kyle said reluctantly. "I'll have a talk with her."

Traitor, Grace thought. "Oh no. I completely understand, sir, if you need to let me go."

Grace sat back in her chair, amused, as he started to backtrack. "That's not necessary, Ms. Holliday. You're a good assistant. We just need to talk."

Melodie stepped forward and laid a hand on Kyle's shoulder, as she looked down at her. "Grace, you ought to be grateful Kyle is still willing to talk to you, and not fire you on the spot. A lot of people would love to work for a boss as kind and understanding."

To Grace's shock and horror, heads started nodding up and down in agreement. Apparently, there was a consensus forming among her family and friends that she was lucky Kyle was still willing to put up with her. Even the officers seemed to agree.

"Oh, I don't think grateful really captures my feelings on the subject."

"Honestly, Grace, I really think you should apologize," Melodie said, while winding her arm through Kyle's. "Did you know what she was planning on doing tonight, honey?"

Honey? Grace thought, as she glared up at Kyle.

"No, I thought she was staying in for the night."

She suddenly found her normally passive father towering over her, "You told us you were going to a late movie."

"It's the lying that really disturbs me," Kyle said, following her father to the corner of the room where her mother, James Simpson and Mr. Collins were quietly speaking to Sheriff Bellamy. Grace shifted over on the bench as Melodie sat down next to her.

"Grace, don't worry, I'll talk to Ky," Melodie said soothingly.

Ky? While processing this new bit of trivia, Grace continued glaring at Kyle's back.

"I know he seems upset now, but I'll calm him down. Don't worry. I won't let him fire you."

"Thanks. I can't tell you how worried I am about that," Grace said. Melodie not sensing the sarcasm smiled sweetly, gave Grace a hug, and walked over to speak to Hope who, Grace noticed, distraught over her twin's predicament was soothing herself by filing her nails.

Grace watched as Kyle sauntered over to her with a smug expression on his face.

"Yes. Hopefully, I will be able to keep this job. I don't know what I would do without it. I mean, where else can you find a fake job—" Panicking Kyle quickly pulled Grace out off the bench and dragged her into the hallway away from the rest of the group. "Fake boss. No pay. I don't know what I would do with the rest of my life without this job. Hopefully, I can pick up the pieces of my life . . ."

"Shh," he said, placing his hand over her mouth. Realizing they were alone, he removed his hand and smiled down at her. "What did you do? I thought you were just going to meet Adam for dinner and go home."

"Things changed," she said crossing her arms and glaring at her family and friends filing out of the waiting room and into the hallway. "What happened to you? I thought you and Melodie were just going to go to that French restaurant in town."

Kyle grinned sheepishly. "We ran into James Simpson after lunch, and he invited us to the country club ball. I tried to call you, but your phone just went to voicemail. You're not going to quit on me, are you?"

Grace raised her hand to her heart. "You mean I'm not fired?" she asked sarcastically. "Oh thank goodness. I was so worried."

"Oh, come on. What was I supposed to say? I've convinced Bellamy that you're just a tad bit overzealous. I told him that I'm going to keep a close eye on you. Thanks to James, he's agreeing not to bring charges. Please don't quit," he pleaded with her.

"I'm not going to quit. Not now. Everyone in that room thinks I'm an idiot. If it's the last thing I do, I'm going to find out who killed Crystal. I'm hoping its Steve, but whoever it is, just so you know, even if you figure it out first, I'm taking credit for it."

"Fine by me," he said, pleased she wasn't giving up.

"First thing tomorrow we are going to talk to Adam, and he is going to tell us everything he knows."

CHAPTER FOURTEEN

GRACE PULLED BACK the white lace curtains, hanging in her parent's living room, and looked out at the empty street. Kyle had promised he would pick her up early the next morning. She should have remembered that Kyle's definition of early was a few minutes before noon.

She let the curtain drop and considered asking her parents for the keys to their car. She could catch up with Kyle later. After the events of last night, she was ready to get started. Despite her best intentions to stay out of the police's way, she was failing miserably. Sometime between being arrested and her parents arriving at the sheriff's office, she had decided that she was deeply involved in this murder investigation, whether she wanted to be or not.

At least now, she and Kyle wouldn't be flying blind. They had a lead. If it could be called that. A nice six-foot, curly-headed, bad-boy director lead. Adam knows something and she was determined to drag it out of him, even if she had to pull every little curl out of his head.

She caught a glimpse of red peeking out through the lace curtains and pulled them back to get a clearer look. Finally, she thought, as Kyle pulled into the driveway.

"Nine o'clock, Gracie," her father warned, as she pulled the front door open.

Grace let out a long-suffering sigh. "Dad, I am too old to have a curfew." After her family had left the police station, she and her parents had spent the remainder of the night arguing about the new rules of the house, which, Grace felt, were very much like the old rules of the house.

"Gracie, I completely agree, but you heard your mother. You may not be afraid of her, but I am. I have plans to watch the championship game tonight and I don't want that interrupted. So do as your mother says."

"This is ridiculous. Hope didn't get home 'till one o'clock the night before; why don't you talk to her, too?"

"We didn't have to pick Hope up at the jail, remember?"

"Yeah, yeah," she muttered as she dashed out the door.

Noticing that Kyle had already moved to the passenger seat, Grace moved to the driver's side and sank down into the rich leather seat.

Feeling better than she had in a while, she threw the car in gear and backed out of the driveway.

She hadn't spent the morning sitting on her hands waiting for Kyle. She had spent a good three hours trying to track Adam down. Granted, two and half hours were spent talking, or rather, listening to Beth, but it wasn't completely unproductive, she was able to discover that Adam's Great Aunt Margaret was still alive and might know where he was currently staying and that the house next to Beth's was for rent. Apparently, Beth's next-door neighbor had suddenly packed up and moved out. According to Beth this was the third neighbor in just three years—something about the neighborhood just not agreeing with them—but Grace decided it couldn't hurt to take a look, once she had cornered Adam, that is.

Shortly after hanging up with Beth, Grace had a pleasant conversation with Adam's aunt, who was more than happy to give her directions to the family's old lake house where Adam was currently staying.

Grace smiled, as she imagined surprising Adam at his hiding place. Nothing like having a goal in life to make one feel useful, she thought. Granted, ringing Adam's treasonous neck wasn't really a life-long goal, but it would suffice for now.

It took Grace a few minutes before she realized that her cheery greeting hadn't been returned, nor had her usually talkative assistant made any noise whatsoever. She spared a few seconds to look at Kyle sitting next to her. His arms were folded across his chest, his mouth pursed together and his eyes were staring straight ahead. It's just going to be one of those days, she thought.

"Kyle, what's—"

"Why didn't you call me last night?" he said, before she could complete her question. "We are supposed to be working on this together. You know I would have dropped everything."

"Gee Kyle, I'm sorry that you weren't invited to go on a late-night crime spree! You'll just have to bring it up to our client when we see him."

"Is that where we're headed?"

Grace nodded and explained how she found the information. "We are not leaving until Adam spills his guts. I still cannot believe that he just left me there! What if that had been a homicidal maniac chasing us through the school? I could be dead right now. Dead!" she said, as she swerved around a slow moving car, prompting Kyle to reach out a hand, ready to grab the steering wheel if necessary. "You may have to act threatening."

"Well, considering how mad you are now, I think you would do a better job at that than I would."

"He's hiding something, and if we want to actually solve Crystal's murder and not just play detective we need to find out exactly what he knows."

"Speaking of playing detective, I wanted to let you know, James Simpson told me last night that he had me checked out."

Grace felt her heart sink into her chest. Seeing her expression, Kyle quickly assured her that everything checked out. "Allen gave us a glowing recommendation."

Disbelief warred with relief. "How did you do it?"

"Remember Allen's mandatory engagement party and the mystery of the strawberry punch?"

Grace nodded. It's hard to forget the engagement party from hell. Grace spent weeks living in dread of that party. The last thing she wanted was to spend her well-earned time off with people she could barely stand to be around during work. She intentionally arrived late and had already planned her escape, but to her surprise, her normally unhappy, desolate, miserable co-workers were happily partying and enjoying the night. Kyle appeared to be on his best behavior, preforming a magic trick for a few of the female staff. Nothing was on fire and several people were dancing.

Even the boss, Franklin Straker, who made Scrooge look like a hippie, had gotten into the spirit. Without warning, he jumped on the conference room desk, promised every employee the next week off and a thousand dollar bonus. It didn't stop there, once off the desk, he grabbed his new secretary around the waist and kissed her passionately. By the end of the night, he was passed out under the desk, wearing nothing but a wedding veil. It turned out to be one of the best office parties she had ever attended. That should have clued her in that something was very wrong.

The next morning, as she was enjoying her day off, she received a frantic call from work. An emergency staff meeting had been called. Turned out someone had spiked the punch, and Straker was not happy. He vowed to track down the culprit. To her knowledge, no one ever found out who the guilty party was.

"You know what happened?"

Kyle nodded. "Yes, and despite what you assumed, it wasn't me. It was Allen, and I have proof. I had taken a picture of Abry with a little top hat on, and it turned out Allen could be seen in the background pouring a bottle of vodka into the bowl."

"If you knew who did it, why didn't you say anything at the time?"

"Because of you. I was very hurt that you immediately suspected me. Here I was trying to be good, and not cause any trouble. And what do I get? You, accusing me of that heinous crime. I was angry and decided not to tell you." At Grace's disbelieving stare he added, "Plus, I didn't know what was in the picture until a few months ago and by that time everything had died down. Let's just say that Allen was very cooperative after I told him about that picture."

"You blackmailed him? If you were going to do that, why didn't you use that picture to save our jobs?" Grace could tell from Kyle's expression that hadn't occurred to him until now.

"Well, it's better to use it now. You don't want to go back to New York, do you?"

"I think we shouldn't talk for the rest of the trip."

"Don't you want to hear about my date with Melodie?"

"Date? I didn't know it was that serious?"

"Don't worry, it's not."

"I'm not worried, but I'm not particularly interested, either."

"Even about her and David Hart and what caused Steve to push him down a flight of stairs?"

Grace reluctantly admitted that she might be interested in that.

"Larry had broken up with her after graduation, so she decided to date Hart in order to make Larry jealous. Melodie said it was a huge mistake. All he wanted to talk about was his 'gift'. That's what he called his art. Apparently, he never would shut up about it."

"How did Steve get involved?"

"Well, she quickly got bored with Hart and decided to break it off. When she went to his studio, she found him in bed with another girl. She said she was so angry, she slapped him, he slapped her back, and then she ran off crying. She ran into Steve right after the fight and told him all about it. It was about a week later that she found out what happened to Hart. Crystal told her that Steve had tried to kill the guy."

"She didn't see it happen herself?"

"Nope, but Crystal must have."

Grace made a left onto an old dirt road. Within seconds they came upon a small dilapidated shack sitting next to the lake.

"This is it?" Kyle asked. "When was this place built?"

"I think in the '50s."

"1750s or the 1850s? This can't be right."

"I followed his aunt's directions," she said, opening the car door. Grace had to agree with Kyle. This didn't look like a place

Adam would ever set foot in, not unless he was planning on filming some type of backwoods horror movie.

They both reluctantly walked up to the little shack. Reaching the door first, Grace knocked. She watched as Kyle crossed over the porch to look into the only window.

"Do you see anything?

Kyle shook his head, as he took a step away from the window. "I saw a suitcase," he said, carefully leaning over the rickety railing. "I don't know—"

"Well, I do! He must be here," she said, banging on the door. "Adam open up!"

"Grace!"

"We know you're in there! You can't hide!"

"Grace!"

"What?" Grace turned around. Kyle was standing directly behind her, facing away from her with his hands up. She very carefully stood on her tiptoes to see over his shoulder. Adam was standing in front of them pointing a sawed-off shotgun at Kyle's chest.

Unimpressed, Grace pushed Kyle out of the way. "Adam, put that down."

"Hi Grace," Adam responded cheerfully while keeping the gun leveled at Kyle's chest.

"You're not going to shoot anyone, so put that down."

"Grace, maybe we shouldn't antagonize him," Kyle whispered.

"How did you two find me?"

"He's a detective or did you forget?" Grace asked, jerking a thumb back at Kyle.

"Did you tell anyone you were coming here?"

Kyle nodded his head. "Absolutely! Everyone, in fact."

"I told my family," Grace said.

"I told several of my friends and colleagues in New York."

"I got the directions from your aunt," Grace added.

"I even updated my Facebook status before we got out of the car. Plenty of people know, exactly, where we are and who we were going to be with, so if we don't show up . . ." Kyle added pointedly.

"Don't worry. I'm not going to hurt you. This is just for my protection," Adam said, nodding to the shotgun. "Why are you here?"

"I know where the binder is," Grace said, surprising both Adam and Kyle.

"Where is it?" Adam asked excitedly, taking the last few steps up to the porch.

"It's in the car," she said, pointing behind him.

Adam lowered the gun as he started to turn towards the car. Kyle took the opportunity to lunge forward. Grabbing the gun out of Adam's hand, he quickly unloaded and pocketed the shells.

To Grace's and Kyle's surprise, Adam didn't even seem to notice. He sprinted to the car, throwing the passenger door open and looking around the inside. "Grace, where's the binder?" he shouted over his shoulder. "Did you hide it under the seat?"

"No. Sorry Adam, I lied. I don't have the binder. Never did."

Adam slid out of the car, and sat heavily on the ground. He looked like a kid who had just been told Santa didn't exist. "Why would you do this to me?" he asked plaintively.

"You left me last night," Grace said, pointing out the many ways she could possibly been killed by a vicious serial killer prowling the empty Hogan High School halls.

Adam picked himself off the ground. "Oh, Grace, don't be so melodramatic. There isn't any serial killer or maniac or monster running around. You were perfectly safe. The only monster in town was killed last week."

"Would you mind explaining that," Kyle asked, motioning for the other man to walk into the shack.

"Can I have my gun back?"

Kyle smiled. "No, I think I'll hang onto it for a while."

"I'm paying you, remember?" Adam snarled, stomping through the door and sitting down at a dusty little table in the corner of the room.

"I'm starting to wonder why, Adam." Grace said sitting down opposite him. "You haven't been very cooperative."

"It was an impulse buy. I saw him at the funeral, and I thought he looked like he knew what he was doing."

Grace felt Kyle's hand brush against her back. She knew without looking back that he was pleased.

Adam leaned back in his chair, and propped his foot on the table. "Don't take this the wrong way, but I think I'm going to go in another direction. I did some checking on you, and no one seems to have ever heard of Kyle Drake Investigations. No offense Grace, but I think I want my money back."

Before Kyle could start hyperventilating, Grace stood up, leaned over, and pushed Adam's foot off the table. "That may work back in Hollywood, but don't forget you're back home, now. I know you, so drop the act. Considering, I was arrested last night because of you, I think we have earned that retainer. Now, for whatever reason, you've hired us to find Crystal's killer, and that's what we are going to do. If you don't start talking to us, I'm going to go to that nice Mr. Simpson, and tell him who was with me last night, and how interested you seem to be in a binder. In fact, I'll go one better, I'll tell Beth, and it will be all over town before lunch."

"Okay, okay," he said holding up his hands. "Geez, calm down. You don't have to pay me back."

Kyle patted Grace's shoulder as he sat in the remaining chair.

"Adam, spill it, or I'm going straight to the sheriff's office."

Kyle leaned forward. "Let me offer you some friendly advice. The DA is looking for any reason to put you away. I think he would love to know you were running around the crime scene last night, don't you?"

"Fine. It's not that I don't want to tell you, it's just that I don't want a lot of people to know, at least not yet."

"Know what?" Grace asked annoyed.

"Crystal was a blackmailer," Adam said. "She had a little group she was routinely blackmailing."

Kyle looked at Grace and mouthed 'told you so.'

"I had no intention of coming to this reunion," Adam admitted reluctantly, "until Crystal called me and proposed a business deal. She would sell me everyone's secrets, and I would turn it into a big screen movie. Sort of like *Peyton Place* only less respectable."

Grace shook her head. "Why would Crystal need money? Her family is loaded."

Adam shook his head. "Was loaded. They're all broke. Every one of them. Although, Diana might be a little better off than the others, at least for now. Melodie, on the other hand, barely had enough change to buy a sandwich."

Kyle shook his head. "She seems to be doing fine."

"Yeah, *now*. She just received a nice little payout from the insurance company a couple of days ago. You should have seen her last month. She had to borrow money from Diana just to feed herself."

"And the Lakes?" Grace asked.

"Even worse. They were heavily in debt and about to lose their house. Tom couldn't care less, but it was killing Crystal. She kept talking about starting fertility treatments and needing to come up with the money. Anyway, she was getting desperate. Her well of money had dried up."

Kyle leaned back in his chair. "Ah, so that's why she was now turning to you. How many people was she blackmailing?"

"Not many. Just a few people, actually. Her nearest and dearest and she was willing to sell their secrets to me."

Grace drummed her fingers on the table considering this new information. "Well, why didn't she? You were here for a month. If she had, you wouldn't still be here. So why didn't she?"

"She was holding out on me." Adam shrugged his shoulders. "We couldn't work out the details."

"Did she tell you anything?" Grace asked.

"She told me a few things. Nothing that scandalous. At least nothing worthy of turning into a screenplay. She told me Larry had—"

Kyle shook his head. "We already know Larry was cheating with his secretary, and Melodie was angry because Crystal knew and didn't tell her."

Adam laughed. "What? Where did you hear that?"

"Beth," both Grace and Kyle said in unison.

Adam looked at Grace and laughed. "Do you remember playing the telephone game when we were little? You whisper a secret in the ear of the person on your left, and then they do the same to the person on their left, and so on. The last person in line usually has a garbled up version of the original secret. Beth is always the last person in line. Why would you believe her?"

Grace glared at him. "No one else knew what had happened, and you wouldn't talk. What makes you think it's not true?"

"His secretary was Louise Perkins. She's eighty-two. Unless he was into octogenarians, I doubt they were spending their lunch hours at the no-tell motel." Adam, sensing he was making his audience angry, quickly added, "Beth had some of her information right. Larry was cheating, but it wasn't with his secretary."

"Fine," Grace said. "Please, enlighten us."

"Crystal ran through her inheritance pretty quickly after her parents died. When she ran out of money, she turned to her family. Unfortunately for her, Larry got tired of Crystal using their accounts as her own piggybank, so he finally cut her off. He told Melodie not to give her any more money. As you can imagine, Crystal wasn't too happy with that, so she set him up. She hired a prostitute to seduce him, and then hired a detective to discover the 'truth'. That's all it took. That was actually one of her favorite methods of coercion."

"So, she walked up to Larry and threatened to tell Melodie unless he paid up?" Kyle asked. "What was to keep him from strangling her on the spot?"

"Oh no, Crystal was far too clever for that. She would send an anonymous note with a copy of the pictures. She never let her victims know who was blackmailing them."

"I'm surprised Larry let himself be used like that," Grace said, remembering Larry's temper.

"Larry couldn't afford Melodie finding out. After all, Melodie was the one with the money and a pre-nup. After Crystal sent him the pictures, she slowly began bleeding him dry. Larry had to sell off property and even started embezzling from his own company to keep her quiet. He ended up taking a few loans from some rather unscrupulous people, if you get my meaning."

"You don't mean—" Kyle asked apprehensively.

"Oh, yes." Adam smiled. "It all came to a head about three months ago. The business was practically bankrupt, Crystal wanted more money, and his 'new' business partners wanted him to pay back what he borrowed. He finally had enough. Unfortunately, by that time, he had committed so many crimes trying to cover up the affair that he was in more trouble than from just an angry wife. So, when Larry stopped paying, Crystal sent an anonymous note to Melodie along with the pictures."

"How did Melodie react?"

Adam shook his head. "Not well. She called Crystal for help when she got the letter and pictures. When Larry didn't return home that night, they went into his office and found a note laying on his desk, attached to a two million dollar life insurance policy. It was your basic suicide apology note"

"Larry committed suicide? I thought his death was an accident?" Grace asked.

"That's the official version. Melodie destroyed the note. Can't collect insurance if there's a suicide."

"No one suspected?"

"No. Melodie went to her aunt and borrowed enough money to get the business back on track and pay off the loan sharks and then waited for the insurance check to arrive."

Kyle stood up and placed the unloaded shotgun over the mantle place. "How did Melodie find out that Crystal was behind it all?"

Adam shrugged. "Your guess is as good as mine, but I'm convinced she knew."

Grace pushed her hair back off her face. "All right, let's say you're right. Why would Melodie have anything to do with Crystal after—"

"After she drained her husband dry and caused him to commit suicide?" Adam finished for her.

"Because Crystal threatened to tell everyone," Kyle guessed.

Adam nodded. "If Larry committed suicide, then Melodie would lose all that nice insurance money. Over two million dollars. Melodie had to play nice with Crystal in order to keep the money. And the moment Melodie received that check; there was Crystal with her hand outstretched. Mel tried to resist, but Crystal reminded her what would happen if the insurance company found out the truth."

"And Crystal told you all of this?" Grace asked.

Adam smirked. "I think she was proud of herself. At times, she fancied herself some type of Machiavellian villain. A puppet master pulling the strings. Then if she started to feel guilty about what had happen, she would put the blame on everyone else. According to her, she hadn't really done anything wrong. She was a Hogan and had more of a right to Melodie's inheritance than Larry did. She said she didn't force Larry to cheat or to get into bed with the mob. She didn't force him to kill himself. As far as she was concerned, she was perfectly innocent. It was Larry's fault for being weak." Adam made a face. "She was a horrible person."

"You said that was one of her favorite methods of coercion. Who else did she set up that way?" Kyle asked.

"She tried to do the same thing with her Aunt Diana around the same time." He laughed at their shocked faces. "After all, Diana was a Hogan, too. She inherited a bunch of money and land from her parents when they died, just like Crystal and Melodie had. Crystal firmly believed that whatever money Melodie or Diana had should belong to her, as well. Share and share alike. So, she used the same method to blackmail her aunt. After all, it had worked so well with Larry."

"Did it?"

"Oh yeah. She found this gigolo and paid him to seduce her aunt. Then, just like with Larry, she sent an anonymous letter with pictures and threaten to tell Diana's husband. However, unlike Larry, Diana called her blackmailer's bluff. As soon as she got the letter and pictures, she went to her husband and confessed. Told him everything. Then she went to the police."

"Smart woman," Grace said.

"Hmm. Maybe not. Police never found out who sent the letter or took the pictures. And as for her husband . . . It would have been cheaper to pay the blackmail. Her husband filed for divorce the next day. She's been battling him in divorce court for the last six months. There was no pre-nup and he's trying to take everything."

"Did Diana know it was Crystal who sent the letter and the pictures?" Grace asked.

"I don't think so. I never noticed any tension between them. They seemed to get along with each other rather well. I'd bet anything Diana doesn't know, yet."

"What about Steve? Was Crystal blackmailing him for trying to kill David Hart?"

Adam hesitated. "Not that I know of, at least she never mentioned him. So, Steve tried to kill someone. That's interesting."

"You didn't know?" Grace asked.

Adam shook his head.

"Who else was Crystal blackmailing?" she asked.

"There's James Simpson."

Grace leaned forward. "What did she have on Simpson?"

"He's Tom's father, and he's the reason that Tom's parents divorced. He is terrified of Tom learning the truth. Crystal told me that she had been going easy on him. Only asking for little things. The old man was so grateful that he happily agreed to anything she asked. I don't even think he realized he was being blackmailed. If you ask me, I think she was looking to trade up, from the son to the father."

Grace and Kyle exchanged looks. "To be honest, Adam, this doesn't really sound like Academy Award winner material," Grace said sarcastically. "I mean, it's sleazy but . . ."

"You didn't need Crystal for any of this. You could have just used your imagination," Kyle said.

Adam smirked, "That's what I said. When she told me all of this, I told her to forget it. The only real story here was about the bored, rich, housewife, psycho, blackmailer, nut case—she wasn't too happy with that description—and I didn't think anything she had told me was worth forking over the amount of money that she wanted. That's when she started dropping hints about something big. Someone dangerous."

"Let me guess, she didn't tell you who." Kyle said.

Adam ran a hand through his curly hair and sighed in frustration. "I was so close. She was about to spill everything, but then she got all cagey on me. She wanted more money, up front, before she would say anything."

"Someone dangerous," Grace repeated. "How dangerous?"

"She hinted that she knew a murderer."

"Crystal tried to blackmail a murderer?" Kyle asked incredulously. "No wonder she was killed."

"She told me she never blackmailed this person. She was too afraid." Adam shook his head. "I don't believe it. Crystal was far too greedy. She had turned blackmail into a nice little part time job. I just don't believe she would let this one slide. The only thing I could figure is maybe this person didn't have any money, or it was someone she cared about or—"

"Or maybe, it was because she couldn't do it anonymously like with the others," Kyle said thoughtfully, remembering the conversation he had overheard at the reunion. "If she tried, the killer might have figured out it was her. It would have been too risky."

"Whether she was blackmailing this person or not, the killer obviously thought she was too big of a risk to keep around anymore." Grace sighed. "Did Crystal tell you who the victim was?"

Adam stood up and walked to the window. "Crystal hinted around that she saw someone push Sam off of the bell tower right before commencement. Someone we all know. That's the information I was trying to get from Crystal before she died, and that's why I need to get into that school."

Shocked, Grace said, "Sam committed suicide."

"Crystal gave me enough hints to make me believe he was murdered."

Grace was quiet for a few seconds. "And you think you're going to be able to find out who killed him by breaking into the school?"

"Crystal said she had proof. Evidence which she kept in a 'scrapbook', she called it. She said she would hand it over after the reunion for a nice, hefty sum I might add. I could do whatever I wanted with it, as long as I never mentioned Crystal's name."

"Why did she want to wait until after the reunion?" Grace asked.

"Crystal and her little games," Adam smirked. "She wouldn't say anything until I came up with more money. I finally had it, too. I called in a bunch of loans. I had to liquidate my house and a few stocks to get the amount she wanted. By the time the reunion came, I was all set to go, but then Crystal suddenly had a change of heart."

"What did she say?" Kyle asked.

Adam snorted. "She tried to tell me she had been lying. That none of it was true. Sam committed suicide. Larry didn't commit suicide. She said, she was just playing a game with me, but Crystal was not a good liar. I think Sam's murderer got to her that night and scared her. Suddenly, she didn't want to talk to me anymore. I had the money. I even took her to my car and showed it to her, but she didn't want it. If I can find that binder, then I'll know who murdered Sam and probably who murdered Crystal."

"What makes you think the murderer hasn't already destroyed it by now?" Grace asked.

Adam shrugged. "I don't think so. I think it's still out there somewhere. I've already checked Crystal's home, Melodie's, her aunt's, Tom's secret apartment no one knows about, even the district attorney's house, but I can't find where she hid the damn thing."

"Were you the one at Melodie's house the day after the reunion?" Kyle asked.

"Yeah, I saw you guys come up to the door and ran out the back."

Grace pushed her bangs off her face. "How did you get in?"

"Crystal had a set of keys. I swiped them after she died." Adam shrugged. "Anyway, I think it might be at the school."

"Why the school?" Kyle asked.

"You remember that binder she was carrying around that night. That's what we were arguing about. I'm not a hundred percent sure, but I think that binder was her little 'evidence scrapbook'. She insisted that it wasn't, but she wouldn't let me see it, either. She could have just been messing with me, but if it wasn't the scrapbook, why would she have been carrying the thing around the whole night? We need to go through the school again. It's the only place I haven't been able to completely search. And we need to hurry because I'm not the only one looking for it. When I broke into Simpson's house, I found someone in the bedroom."

"Did you see who it was?" Grace asked.

Adam shook his head. "It was too dark, and they were dressed all in black. They were wearing a mask, too."

"There's only one problem with your theory, Adam," she said. "Sam didn't have any enemies. He was one of the nicest guys I've ever known. Everyone at school loved him. He was 'Mr. Popular'. Who in the world would've wanted to kill him?"

"I have a few guesses."

"Such as?"

"I think it was either Tom or . . . Diana Collins," he admitted reluctantly. "I don't know for certain, but they're both at the top of my list."

"Tom was Sam's best friend," Grace pointed out slowly.

Adam shrugged. "So? Friends fight. I think he wanted Crystal for himself, and Sam was in the way. He was acting weird during graduation, and then you saw how quickly he moved on to Crystal once Sam was out of the way. Think about it. Crystal's dad had just inherited a pretty large estate from his father. I mean, they had always been well off, but they were rolling in it after that. Meanwhile, Tom's family was breaking apart. His mom ran off and gambled away the money. Then his dad had a heart attack. By the time we graduated, Tom was left with nothing but his parents' debts. I think Tom suddenly decided that he didn't want to live like a pauper anymore."

Kyle looked over at Grace. "I guess it's possible. The trouble between Hope and Tom began when he decided campus housing wasn't good enough for them both.

"See?" Adam said excitedly. "It fits. What if Crystal saw Tom kill Sam and helped him cover it up? I don't know, maybe he convinced her that he loved her, and it was an accident or something. Only he didn't love her. He was just after her money. Flash forward to today. Crystal realizes he was using her all along and decides to contact me. Only Tom finally realizes what she's up to at the reunion and kills her before she can tell me what she saw."

Grace looked over at Kyle, who was nodding his head in agreement. "Okay," she said, not completely convinced, "but you said that you also suspect Diana. Why would she kill Sam?"

"To keep him quiet. You remember what happened to Sarah Collins? The accident," he said, placing accident in air quotes.

"Sarah Collins?" Kyle asked, turning to Grace.

Grace shook her head. "Eric Collins' second wife. He had left Diana, for our English teacher, Sarah Scott, the year before."

"It was supposedly a freak accident," Adam said. "It happened during winter, right after a horrible ice storm. Sarah Collins left the school to go home, but when she opened up the door, an icicle fell right on top of her."

"It was ruled an accident," Grace said. "Diana had nothing to do with it. In fact, I remember Melodie telling me that Diana wasn't even at the school when it happened."

"Yes, it was ruled an accident," Adam confirmed. "Do you know why it was ruled an accident? Sam said he saw it happen. What if he lied? What if he saw Diana kill Sarah? What if he covered for her?"

"Sam was a good guy. He wouldn't have kept quiet like that," Grace argued.

"Sam changed after his accident. He wasn't the same boy scout we all grew up with. I think, it's possible, that he saw what happened and blackmailed her. Don't forget, Sam came into some money that winter."

"Yeah, because of his accident," she said. "It was insurance money."

"Really, are you so sure? I think he told Crystal what he saw. That's how she knew, and that's why she never said anything."

"Did Crystal say Sarah Collins was murdered?" Grace asked.

"No," he said slowly, "but remember how much Diana hated Sarah? Right before Christmas break, she threatened to kill her. We all heard her. Eric Collins had to get between them. She was absolutely crazy back then. She wouldn't take off her wedding ring, even after Eric had asked for it back."

"Yeah, he had a lot of nerve."

"It was his mother's ring."

"I don't care."

Adam rolled his eyes. "Fine. You remember how no one knew what to call her? One day she would want to be referred to as Mrs. Collins, the next day she would only answer to Ms. Hogan. She would then burst out into tears if anyone called Sarah, Mrs. Collins. The woman went nuts."

"Her husband abandoned her for her best friend. She had a reason to be emotional."

Adam pounded his hand on the table. "That's right. She had a reason to kill Sarah Collins. Sarah stole her husband. She got back at her by killing her. Sam saw her do it, so she had to kill him to keep him quiet. Then Crystal, because she was talking to me. I truly believe it's her . . . or Tom. It's got to be one of them."

Grace shook her head. "But you don't know, for certain, that Tom killed Sam because he wanted Crystal's fortune."

"Well, no," Adam admitted reluctantly.

"And you don't know for certain that Diana killed Sarah Collins and then killed Sam to cover up her crime."

"No."

"So, at this point, you're just guessing."

Adam slowly nodded.

"It could just as well be Melodie, for what happened with Larry," Grace said.

"Or Steve—" Kyle pointed out.

"Or any number of people at that reunion that night." Grace sighed. "There were over a hundred people there."

"No," Adam said vehemently. "It is definitely someone we all know. Crystal at least told me that much. If we could just find that binder we would know."

Still suspicious of Adam's intentions, Kyle asked, "What about you? What was she blackmailing you for?"

"Me?" Adam asked, pointing to his chest. "She wasn't blackmailing me."

Grace and Kyle exchanged disbelieving glances.

"I swear. She wasn't blackmailing me."

Grace sat back in her chair. "Why don't you tell us about the picture, Adam?"

Adam tried to look innocent. "What picture?"

"The one hanging in the high school hall way. The charcoal drawing that was ripped up."

Adam shrugged his shoulders. "I don't—"

"Don't bother lying. I know you had something to do with it. That wasn't a bruise on your head. It was charcoal dust," she guessed.

Adam made a face. "Yes, it was charcoal dust. I got it all over me. I didn't rip the drawing up though. I was trying to get the killer's attention, so I wrote 'who killed Sam?' on the drawing and I drew a little stick figure on the ground. The drawing wasn't that good anyway. The killer must have seen it and tore it up."

Kyle sighed. "What about the 'Most likely' boards—"

"I didn't touch those. Someone had already marked those up by the time I got there."

"I still don't understand why you felt you had to get the murderer's attention?" Grace asked. "What did you hope to accomplish."

"What was I supposed to do? Crystal wasn't talking. I thought if I let the killer know, someone else knew, then maybe he or she would make a mistake."

"You know that little stunt probably got Crystal killed," Kyle pointed out. "She had worked out a deal with the murderer to keep quiet. The killer probably saw that drawing and decided Crystal couldn't be trusted anymore."

Adam merely shrugged.

Appalled, Grace said, "I still want to know what Crystal had on you."

"Listen, I work in Hollywood. The moral code is dead and buried. What could she have on me that I wouldn't want to get out? After all, scandal sells baby, and that's why I want that scrapbook."

At their disgusted looks, Adam said, "Think of it this way. Not only can I use it for my next movie, but we can discover what really happened to Sam on the bell tower before graduation. If we're really lucky it might point us to Crystal's murderer, too."

CHAPTER FIFTEEN

GRACE PULLED OUT a chair and flipped through the *Rabbit Falls Gazette*, the town newspaper. She was waiting for Harper Price, the gazette's editor. Harper had been Sam's uncle and guardian after Sam's parents had died during Sam's junior year of school. If Adam was correct and Sam was murdered, Grace hoped, Harper would be able to help or at least answer some questions.

Her memories of the events surrounding Sam's death were hazy. She had been so preoccupied with her own graduation and then comforting her sister over losing Tom, that she hadn't paid much attention to Sam or even to his death. Like everyone else, she had just accepted that Sam had committed suicide. And as far as she knew, there had never been a question about it being anything else. Not even a rumor.

Of course, she thought, there was the chance that Adam was wrong or that Crystal had been lying to him. Grace put down the paper and sighed. Now instead of one murder, they were investigating two. She would have felt better if they were a little closer to solving the one before they embarked on another. Oh well, Adam may be right. One might lead to another.

"Sorry about that," Harper said, walking into the room and sitting down. "This whole town is going crazy. Seems everyone has a crackpot theory about who killed Crystal. So," he said, looking at her expectantly, "what's your crackpot theory?"

Grace smiled. "Don't get too excited. I don't know who, but I may know why?"

Harper stood up and walked over to his office door, closing it quietly. When he had settled back down, she offered Adam's theory.

"You think Sam was murdered?" he asked, the color draining from his face. Grace watched as a mixture of emotions passed over his face. "It's possible, I guess. Anything's possible. I know there was something bothering him. It's just that Sam was incredibly unhappy after . . . well, you know, after the accident. The suicide just made sense," he said, quietly. "But I don't think this has anything to do with Sarah Collins death. He liked Sarah Collins. She was his favorite teacher. If he saw someone kill her, he would have said something. There's no way Sam would have kept that quiet."

Grace couldn't agree more, but she had to press on. "Can you think of anyone who would want to kill him?"

"No. Everyone loved Sam." Harper picked up his pen. Twirling it slowly in his hand, he looked toward the door and back. His face was grim. "If I had to point my finger at anyone, it would be Adam."

"Adam? Why?"

"Adam's the only one that has a motive. That movie, the one that put him on the map, the one he won all of those awards for, he didn't write that all by himself. The whole idea was Sam's. After Sam died, Adam passed it off as his own. Not one mention of Sam."

Surprised Grace asked, "Why didn't you say anything?"

"I have no proof. It would be my word against his and frankly, the only person who would be upset was dead. Still, I can't see Adam as a killer." Harper slowly shook his head.

Grace agreed. If Adam had killed Sam, why would he clue them into the fact that Sam was murdered?

"Those last few months . . . Sam was just a different person after the accident. We weren't as close as we used to be. He was withdrawn and moody. Always disappearing. The suicide just seemed plausible. But if Sam was murdered, and Crystal knew about it . . ." He smirked. "In fact, I can see her keeping quiet and trying to blackmail the person. That seems exactly like something she would do."

Grace had already had this conversation with Kyle on the way back from Adam's lake shack. She couldn't believe Crystal could have been that money hungry, but then she would never have believed she would have blackmailed her own family, either. "See, that's the one part that bothers me. They were dating. She loved Sam—"

Harper snorted and threw the pen he had been playing with on the desk. "Crystal didn't love anyone but Crystal. Her whole world revolved around herself. I've never believed that she loved Sam. I still think she was just using him to make Tom jealous." Harper shrugged. "It must have worked too. She and Tom married right after Sam died. Actually," he said leaning back and staring at the ceiling, "if Sam was murdered, why are you so certain that Crystal saw it happen and blackmailed anyone? Now that I'm thinking about it, Crystal also had a motive to kill Sam."

"What makes you say that?"

"Sam didn't love her, either. He was seeing someone else on the side. Perhaps, Crystal found out and killed him in a jealous rage. Just because she didn't want him, doesn't mean she would have liked him going behind her back. Crystal was mean enough to kill for that reason alone. I remember Sam telling me how scary she could get when she flew into a rage. I think he may have been afraid of her."

♆ ♆ ♆

The sight of the mess Kyle made in the library caused Grace to sigh loudly, disturbing the elderly lady dozing in a nearby chair, a well-worn romance book lying on her lap.

Kyle looked up and smiled when he saw Grace approaching. The table where he sat was covered with an assortment of newspapers, microfiche, and books. He picked up the books sitting on the chair closest to him, making room for Grace. "Well, how did it go?" he asked, softly whispering in her ear.

Grace quickly and quietly outlined what she had learned from Harper, earning a succession of "shhs" from the lady behind her.

"Find anything, yet?" Grace asked in a low whisper, cringing when she heard the inevitable "shh" coming from the woman sitting behind her.

To Grace's surprise, Kyle nodded enthusiastically and motioned for her to follow him. Excited, Grace followed close on his heels. Her usual pessimism dampened by her curiosity.

Once they reached a back corner, devoid of other patrons, Kyle turned to her, smiling. "You're never going to believe it. I think Adam might have been telling the truth."

"Why? What did you find?" Grace asked, anticipation making her bounce on her toes.

"Nothing!"

Grace felt the excitement drain from her body, briefly wondering how quickly the library denizens would pounce on her if she screamed in frustration.

"No, really, absolutely nothing!" he repeated happily.

"And that's exciting, why?" Grace asked confused by his obvious pleasure.

"The newspaper articles surrounding Sam's death are missing. The microfiche copies for the weeks after graduation? Gone. The copies in archives? Gone, too! I haven't been able to find one article on Sam's suicide. Not one. Someone's stolen them. I think we may be onto something. Did Sam's uncle say who he had been cheating with?"

Grace shook her head. "He didn't know. Sam would change the subject whenever Harper would ask. Harper thought he was afraid of Crystal finding out."

♆ ♆ ♆

"What time do you want to meet tonight?" Kyle asked, as he opened the front door to Grace's house.

"Not so loud," she said. "I'm grounded, remember." Grace peered around the corner into the family room.

Jeff was sitting on the couch, a calculus book lying at his feet and a graphic novel on his lap.

"What are you doing?" she asked him, sneaking into the room.

"Studying. Did you have Mrs. Bailey when you were in school?" Grace shook her head. "You're lucky. I think she hates me. We have to do twenty problem sets before Monday," he whined.

"Poor baby," Grace said without an ounce of sympathy. "Where is everyone?"

"Mom and Dad are at the store, and Hope is out back with her old boyfriend."

"Tom?" Grace asked in surprise.

"Yep," Jeff said flipping another page.

Kyle spun around, accidentally knocking into her mother's curio cabinet. As he attempted to catch a vase which fell from the top, Grace ran past him, down the hall and out to the back.

She found Tom standing in the backyard, his back to the house. Grace looked around the yard, searching for her sister. Unless she was hiding under one of the lawn chairs, Tom was out here all alone. Grace cleared her throat to get his attention.

"Hope, I told you, I'm not here to speak to you," he snapped.

"Then who are you here to speak with?" Grace asked, glancing behind her as Kyle came through the door.

Tom turned around and glared at them. "You two. I heard you both were running around town, playing detective."

"Playing?" Kyle asked nervously.

"Yeah, playing. I don't know what you two are up to, but I want it to stop, right now. Sheriff Bellamy is in charge of this investigation. All you're going to do is confuse the issue and let the murderer get away. Grace, you're like my sister. I don't want—"

"Speaking of sisters, where is mine?"

"Upstairs. I didn't want to speak to her."

Grace crossed her arms, but before she could speak, Kyle stepped forward. "We've received information that your wife's death may have been connected to another murder."

At Tom's confused expression, Grace said, "Sam's."

Grace watched as Tom's normally handsome face went cold. "This is exactly what I'm talking about. Crystal was in the wrong place, at the wrong time. This has nothing to do with Sam. Crystal was murdered, and Sam committed suicide. There is absolutely nothing between the two events."

"Well, there's one thing. You," Grace pointed out.

"Yeah, there's me. Crystal, my wife, was brutally murdered by some stranger. Sam, my best friend, on the other hand, was upset the day of graduation and chose to end his life." Grace watched as Tom slipped his championship ring off his finger and shoved it back on.

"And you just stepped right in," Grace snapped.

"I went to Crystal to comfort her. She just lost someone she loved. We both did," Tom turned away, as he thrust his hands into his pockets. "That day I realized how much I loved her . . . how much I had always loved her. I'm sorry I hurt Hope. I didn't mean to, but something's are just not meant to be." Turning back around and walking to the door, he snarled, "Just stay out of it Grace, before someone else gets hurt."

"Well, that was interesting," Kyle said, when Tom was out of earshot. "Do you think he knows I'm not really a detective?" Kyle asked worried.

"No, if he did, we would be in jail," she answered, pushing open the back door and entering the house.

Grace needed to find her sister and make sure she was all right. She took the stairs two at a time and knocked on Hope's door. Without waiting for an answer, she opened the door. Hope was standing at the window, holding the drapery back. "Is he gone?"

"Yes. Are you okay?"

Hope let the drape slide back and walked to the mirrored vanity table with the royal-purple velvet chair their parents had spent a small fortune on for their sweet sixteen birthday. Grace had been happy with a simple bike. "What did he want?" Hope asked, picking up the pearl encrusted hairbrush.

Grace filled her sister in on their conversation, as well as everything Kyle and she had learned so far. "Perhaps, you should listen to him," Hope said, running the hairbrush through her hair. "Stay out of it. You're barking up the wrong tree. You don't seriously think Tom killed Sam?"

Grace decided it wasn't worth pointing out that was just one of many theories.

"Harper's right. It's not as if Crystal loved Sam, everyone knows she was just trying to make Tom jealous. It was so obvious. Tom had no reason to kill Sam. All he had to do was snap his fingers and Crystal would have come running."

"Do you know who Sam was seeing behind Crystal's back?"

Hope threw down the brush. "Sam and I weren't exactly best buddies."

"I should have asked Tom."

"He doesn't know." At Grace's questioning look, Hope added, "Tom told me back then that Sam was fooling around on Crystal, but it was a big secret. Sam wouldn't even tell him." Hope walked over to her closet and pulled out a green sundress. "Tom kept trying to figure it out. Like it was some sort of game. He even tried to follow him one day. He never found out who it was, though."

"Are you sure?"

Ignoring her, Hope held up a dress and asked, "What do you think of my new dress?"

Grace, not fooled by the sudden change of subject, ignored the question. "How upset was Sam that day on the tower?"

Hope blinked rapidly. "How should I know?"

"Hope, you told me right before graduation, you had just had it out with Sam on the bell tower, remember?"

"Oh that's right. I forgot I told you," Hope said shrugging. "You haven't told anyone, have you?"

"No, of course not."

"Not even your boss?"

Grace shook her head. "No, I haven't told a soul. What happened up there?"

"Nothing happened. When I left, he was standing up there, quite alive. Or do you believe I killed him, too?"

Grace ignored her sister's question. "What were you both doing at the tower?"

"I don't know what he was doing there, but I was on my way to the stadium when I saw him unlocking the tower door. I ran up to him to smooth things over about the house. He was Tom's best friend, after all, and I didn't want him to be upset."

"What happened?"

"Nothing. He said he understood and that it wasn't his idea in the first place. It was Crystal's. He told me to watch out for her because she was evil. She was after Tom, and nobody was going to stand in her way."

"Do you think he killed himself?"

Hope sat down on the bed next to Grace. "I don't know. I thought so at the time. I mean, he was acting so strange."

"How so?"

"He just seemed really depressed. After we talked, I told him we had better go because the ceremony was about to start, but he said he wasn't going. Then he hugged me and told me to tell Tom good-bye for him."

"Did you think he was going to kill himself?"

"Do you honestly believe I would have left if I thought he was going to jump out of the tower as soon as I walked out? I assumed he was just leaving town, but when they found his body a few hours later . . ."

When her sister didn't finish her thought, Grace asked, "What were you and Tom fighting about right before the graduation ceremony?"

"It was so silly. He was jealous. He said he saw Sam and me on the tower. He must have seen us hug. I tried to explain, but Tom was just being unreasonable and wouldn't listen. Then he started yelling at me about my bracelet."

"Your bracelet?"

"You know, the charm bracelet he gave me on my sixteenth birthday. It had been a family heirloom. I loved that bracelet."

"Whatever happened to it?"

Hope shrugged her shoulders. "I don't know. I remember putting it on that morning, but I haven't seen it since."

Perplexed, Grace asked, "Why was Tom yelling at you about the bracelet?"

"I don't know. He just kept asking me what had I done with it. Where was it? He was being completely unreasonable. I'd never seen him so angry before. Then I got angry. I told him that I wasn't going to allow him to treat me like this and that if he didn't like it he could go take a flying leap." At Grace's horrified expression, she quickly added, "I know. I know. Poor choice of words."

♀ ♀ ♀

Grace found Kyle, sitting at the kitchen table, attempting to explain what an indefinite integral was to an extremely disinterested Jeff. "I'm telling you, my teacher just hates me."

"Yes, Jeff, she went back in time and developed calculus just to punish you." Grace opened the refrigerator and pulled out the ice tea pitcher. By the time she had poured herself a large glass, Jeff had declared that math sucked and since he and his band, the *Dead Toad*, were going to make gazillions someday, he didn't need to waste his time, and left the room. Grace happily wished him good luck and sat down next to an amused Kyle.

"Discover anything interesting?" Kyle asked, reaching for her glass and taking a drink.

Grace took the drink from his hand and handed him an empty glass. "Not really." Grace didn't like keeping things from Kyle, but she wasn't about to betray her sister's confidence. "She didn't really want to talk," she hedged, hoping he wouldn't push for more information.

"Right. So, Hope was the last one to see Sam alive?"

Grace slammed down her glass. "You were eavesdropping!"

Completely unapologetic, Kyle nodded his head and said, "Yes, and good thing I did, or I would have no idea. The last one to see him alive," he repeated slowly.

"Except for the murderer," she immediately corrected. "If he was, actually, murdered."

"Of course," he said, readily agreeing with her. "Last one to see him alive. Just like with Crystal."

"Hope wasn't the last one to see Crystal alive. She was in the gym when Crystal was murdered."

"I was all over that gym looking for her. She wasn't there."

"She's small. Maybe you missed her," Grace said hopefully.

Kyle shook his head. "Tom wasn't in the gym, either. They both lied to the Sheriff that night."

"Whatever. It doesn't matter, because she didn't kill Crystal or Sam."

"Have you ever wondered why your sister didn't want anyone to know she had been in the tower?"

"She was afraid. She was seventeen years old, and she was scared people would talk. She was afraid they would say that she had been cheating on Tom with Sam, and that's why he left her."

"Maybe, that's the truth," Kyle said.

Grace shook her head. "I doubt it. Hope loved Tom. She would never have betrayed him."

"Maybe Tom just thought she did." Kyle shrugged. "Well, are you ready to go?"

Grace laid her head on the table.

"We have to go. We need to scope out the area before we break in tonight."

"How 'bout you break in, and I stay here."

Kyle quickly nixed that idea.

CHAPTER SIXTEEN

"GRACE, IT'S SO good to see you again." Eric Collins stood up and walked around his desk to clasp Grace's outstretched hand in both of his.

"Eric, I just wanted to say that I am so sorry about last night." Which was very true, Grace hadn't completely shed the mortification of being found out yet and according to Hope, she's the new talk of the town.

The only thing worse was knowing she was going to be breaking in again in only a few short hours. She would just have to trust that Kyle would have their escape route planned out, should everything fall apart. She could at least trust him not to leave her in the lurch if something went wrong.

"Grace, there's no need to apologize," he said, warmly as he led her to the chair across from his desk.

"I also wanted to thank you for last night. For defending me."

Eric waved a hand dismissing her comment. "I know what it's like to have everyone piling on top of you. You were always my best student, Grace. I knew you must have had a good reason to be here. Why were you here, by the way?"

Grace decided that it would be best to be as vague as possible. "It's the scene of the crime."

Eric smiled. "Sheriff Bellamy has been all through this school. Besides, school's in session. If there was anything here, I'm sure it's gone now."

"Would you mind if we took another look?"

"Not at all. During school hours," he said, wagging his finger at her. "I covered for you last night. I don't think I can do it again.

Then he did know, Grace thought. "Why did you cover for me?"

"Because I want Crystal's killer caught. I liked Crystal. Oh, I know, I'm probably the only one who did, but it's true. She wasn't all bad. We worked on several charities together in the last ten years. She was a huge help. What with her family's connections. Tom's too. She loved children. She used to go to the hospital every Sunday and read to the children there. It's a shame she didn't have any of her own." Eric's voice softly faded away in remembrance.

"To be honest, I didn't know her very well. She and Hope—"

Eric laughed. "I know. Hope and Crystal were like repelling magnets. If you only knew the amount of work that went into keeping those two apart for four years. I don't know that it mattered; they always seemed to search each other out. It got even worse after she started dating Tom's best friend. You know, I always suspected that they both secretly enjoyed the conflict."

"My sister may disagree with you there, especially with what happened with Tom."

"Yeah, I was rather surprised at that myself."

"It's a shame about Sam. I always imagined that they would have married right out of high school." Grace paused at his grimace. "You don't think so?"

He shook his head. "Sam confided in me that he didn't really love Crystal. I know Crystal had been talking about marriage, but Sam told me he was planning on joining the Army after graduation and had no plans of ever coming back."

As far as Grace knew, Sam was a broken man after the car accident. "But his injuries—"

"No, he was pretty much healed. Don't get me wrong, he still had some problems. He couldn't run as fast as he used to, but he was well enough to enlist."

"You were pretty close to him, weren't you?"

Eric shrugged. "I guess. I spent a lot of time tutoring him after the accident. The poor kid, even when he was at school, he spent most of it at the nurse's office, but he slowly got better. Each day I watched him get healthier and stronger. He spent so much time at our home trying to catch up with school work that Sarah was ready to adopt him. She thought the world of him."

"I don't think I ever told you how sorry I was to hear about your wife's death."

Eric closed his eyes. "Thank you."

Grace chewed her lower lip. She didn't want to go into Sarah's death with Eric, but felt that she had to at least see his reaction.

"What happened that day?"

"It was a horrible accident. We should have cancelled school. I wish we had." Eric shook his head. "Sarah was sick that morning. Flu, I think. She had been sick for over a week, but she wouldn't stay home. Anyway, she had gotten sick again and I told her to go home. That was the last time I saw her alive."

"Are you sure it was an accident?"

Eric's eyes flew up to meet hers. "Of—of—course," he stuttered. "Why would you think otherwise?"

"It's just such an unusual death."

"It's not that unusual," he said, his face reddening. "Icicles' are very sharp and very dangerous."

A knock sounded at the door. Eric looked past Grace towards the door. His face clouded. "Come in."

A bleach-blonde, overly made-up woman stuck her head in the door. "Oh, Eric, I'm sorry. I didn't know you were with someone." Grace's eyes focused in on the large unobstructed glass window right next to the door. "Should I come back later?" the woman asked, clearly expecting Grace to volunteer to leave.

Eric, polite as always, stood and gave out introductions, despite seemingly reluctant to do so. "Ms. Avery is our new English teacher."

Grace smiled and nodded politely. So this was Whatshername.

Ms. Avery did not return her greeting. Instead, she sized Grace up in a matter of seconds before batting her eyes at Eric. "I really need to speak to you about my class."

Eric's clear blue eyes narrowed. "All right, why don't we make an appointment for this afternoon?"

"I would really like to see you now," she said, twirling her hair around her fingers. "But if you would prefer, I could see you at your home, tonight."

"No," he said quickly. "This afternoon."

Whatshername, clearly not happy with being told no, glared at Grace before saying, "Fine. I'll be back at one," she said making it sound like a warning. Turning, she walked out of the room, leaving the door wide open.

Eric smiled at Grace and said, "Sorry about that," as he closed the door.

"She seems nice."

Eric frowned. "She's just a bit, how should I put it," he said, looking up searching for the right word, "persistent. Please don't say anything. Diana and I, we're . . . well, I made a mistake ten years ago, and I'm trying to correct it."

Grace held up her hand. "You don't have to explain."

Eric looked down at the desk. Tracing circles on the mahogany, he said, "I know. It's just that I don't want Diana to worry. I'm not the same man I was ten years ago. I've grown. We both have. I just don't want to make the same mistakes I did before."

"You mean, like leaving her for the English teacher?"

Still tracing circles on the desk, he said, "Don't get the wrong idea. I should never have betrayed Diana like I did, but I did love Sarah. Very much. Why do you think her death wasn't an accident?"

"I'm just curious about all strange deaths in the last ten years."

Eric looked up from the desk. "Is that why you're asking about Sam, too?"

Grace nodded.

"Grace, I assure you. My wife died accidentally."

"What about Sam? Do you really think he killed himself?"

"I don't know," he shrugged helplessly. "Some kids don't like change," he added weakly. "Crystal told me that he was very upset that morning. She never told me why."

"Did Crystal know about his plans to leave?"

"I'm not sure. I think he may have told Melodie. He and Melodie were very close. I hope she never told Crystal. It's bad enough knowing the man you love took his own life, but to know what he really thought of you. That's just too much. I hope she didn't know."

Grace suspected it wouldn't have made much difference to Crystal. She had to agree with Harper and Hope. Crystal had been using Sam to get to Tom.

"Grace, if you find out anything. No matter how small, about Sarah, please tell me immediately. I know it was an accident, but . . . please keep me informed."

🏆 🏆 🏆

"She's not going to know about this is she, dude?"

"No," Kyle said patiently, "Melodie won't know. I promise."

"I don't want that psycho anywhere near me. DeeDee's completely nuts. I mean a complete whack-job."

"Yes, David. I know. You keep saying that. Can you just tell me what happened?"

Kyle could hear the other man breathing hard through the phone. "All right, but you better not tell her about me. I have a good life now, and I don't need some lunatic messing things up. I have an art show coming up. People are going to finally see my gift."

Kyle leaned his head back against the wall. If he had to hear about this man's gift one more time, he was going to throw the phone out the window. "She won't know."

"Good. Well, it started off great. I thought she was kind of cool. I mean, she was hot and an artist, too. So, she recognized my gift right from the beginning."

Kyle suppressed a groan.

"Everything was good at the beginning, but then she started to get clingy. I couldn't walk down the street without her wanting to tag along. She wanted to talk every day. It was horrible."

"Sounds frightening. Tell me about the night you fell down the stairs."

"She completely went off the wall. I was in my studio entertaining another lady friend and Dee walked in. She went crazy. You know, we weren't exclusive, but she started ranting and raving about morals and how she was wasting her time. It was crazy, man. She even slapped me."

"Did you slap her?"

"Uh uh. No way. I never touched her. I told her to get out."

"Did Melodie leave?"

"Yeah, but I heard her outside running her mouth to that little weasely dude."

"Weasely dude?"

"Yeah, I don't know his name, but he was always following Dee around. He was like her little lap dog. Anyway, she ran off and he came running up, barking at me."

"Is that when you fell down the stairs?"

"I didn't fall! I was pushed. I broke my collarbone. It could have been my neck or worse my hands. What if I had lost my gift, dude?"

"That would have been a shame. So, is that when you almost died?"

"Uh uh. Not then. It happened later that night. I dropped my lady friend off and then came back to my studio. It was completely destroyed. Everything was gone. All my paintings had been ripped up. I heard something outside, so I thought I could catch whoever did that to my artwork. When I got outside, I felt someone push me. I went straight down, man. When I woke up, I called a friend to come and get me. He took me to the hospital."

"Did you call the police?"

"What do you think? Of course, I called the police. They wouldn't do anything, though. They said there wasn't enough evidence. Couldn't they see what happened to my art? The crazy lunatic ripped them up. Just shredded them. That had been some of my best work, too, man. I mean, isn't that evidence enough? I think she paid them off. Her family was a big deal in that town. Anyway, I got out of there, dude. I left the next day."

"Why do you think it was Melodie?"

"Who else could it have been? She was real mad that morning. You should have seen her."

Kyle tapped his pencil against his pad of paper, thinking. "Why couldn't it have been the weasely dude?"

"No. No way. It was her. Sometimes, she would get so mad . . . Just completely furious. Over nothing, too. No, it was her. I have bad luck when it comes to women. She's like the sixth girlfriend who's tried to kill me in the last ten years. I just attract psychos, dude."

🏆 🏆 🏆

Five hours later Grace and Kyle stood next to the school. Both had changed into the darkest clothes they had and were huddled behind a bush waiting for Adam to join them. Adam was late, again and Grace was about to give up on him, when she felt Kyle place a hand on her back. When she turned to look at him, he was holding a finger up to his lips. She peeked through the bushes and saw two deputies walking up the steps to the high school. One of them she recognized from the night before.

Grace and Kyle watched as one deputy, a large, portly man with a thick mustache, checked the door and shined a light through the window. The other one, the tall lanky one that she had bit the night before stood at the foot of the steps.

Grace ducked down when one of the deputies' flashlights passed over their bush.

"Don't worry, it will be okay," Kyle whispered reassuringly. "We won't get caught and if we do, it will still be okay."

"Really how do you figure that?" Grace asked, less than convinced.

"You see the big cop who looks like he stepped out of a bad '70s TV movie?"

"Yeah, what about him?"

Kyle nodded his blue eyes lightening up in mischief. "Well, I have a feeling he is open to a little bribery."

"Number one, that's illegal and number two, we don't have any money to bribe someone, even if we wanted to. You spent it all on that car and a new wardrobe."

"We might have just enough to convince him to put us in cells next to each other."

"Oddly enough Kyle, that's not making me feel much better."

"Shh," he whispered as the police officer in question walked by. They sat in silence until they heard the sound of car doors slam and saw the police drive away. "Well, your police force certainly does a thorough job around here."

"Lucky for us," she said. "Look, there's Adam."

"About time." Kyle stood up and motioned for Adam to join them next to the school.

"That was close," Adam said, as he approached. "You guys ready?"

"Just follow me." Kyle led them around the high school and to one of the side doors. "Now ladies and gentlemen, what I am about to show you—"

"Mr. Drake!" Grace said. "I have to get back home in a couple of hours, could you hurry this up."

"Right," Kyle said turning back to the door. "Abraca—"

"Sir!" Grace snapped.

"All right. All right. It's open," Kyle said, pushing open the door and turning on his flashlight.

"Okay, Adam, this is your show. Where do you want to begin?" Grace asked.

"Let's start with the administrative offices. I know Melodie was using one of the conference rooms when she was planning the reunion. Crystal might have hidden it in there. I'll start there. You two, take the other offices."

Kyle and Grace followed him to the offices with Kyle helpfully opening the doors.

They went from room to room, looking in drawers, on shelves and any other place that could possibly hold a binder. After about an hour, with Adam going back through each room, to double check, they met at the front desk.

"It's got to be here," Adam said. "Did you check this desk?"

"Yes, and so did you an hour ago. It's not here, Adam," Grace said, shinning the flashlight in his face.

"Maybe we're just missing it. Let's turn on the lights," he said, walking to the light switch.

"No!" Grace and Kyle shouted in unison.

"Someone will see the light and call the cops. It's just not here!" Grace said.

Frustrated, Adam threw his flashlight against the wall.

"You're paying for any damages, Adam," Grace warned.

"Yeah, yeah. I'll donate some more money for the dramatic arts. Happy? Look, let's split up. Grace, you take this floor, Drake—"

"No, absolutely not. Grace and I aren't splitting up." Kyle instinctively moved closer to Grace.

"It will go faster if we split up," Adam insisted.

Kyle, however, steadfastly refused to leave Grace's side. Giving up, Adam agreed to meet them back at the administrative offices in an hour. If they hadn't found it by then, they would go home and meet up the next day to discuss their next move.

"Come on." Kyle wrapped his fingers around Grace's upper arm and led her away from Adam. "Let's go to the library."

Grace nodded, leading him down the hallway to the library doors.

"By the way, Melodie called while you were changing, she asked if I could stay with her, tonight. She thinks someone has been in her house, and she wants me to stay with her for protection. She sounded scared."

"Oh, I just bet she is." Grace pushed against the library doors.

Locked.

"It's true." Kyle stepped in front of her and examined the lock. "Adam admitted breaking into her house, after all."

"Did you tell her that?"

"No. I just told her that we would both come by later tonight."

"I bet she felt much safer knowing I was coming by, too," Grace said sarcastically.

Kyle smiled as the door swung open. "Jealous?"

"No, not at all." Grace stepped through the threshold. "I just hope I'm invited to the wedding. Will she be going by Mrs. Dragovich or Mrs. Drake?"

"I told you, it's official now. My legal name is now Kyle Drake."

"You know, you better be careful Kyle, or you're going to find yourself tagged, bagged, and tied to the roof of her car." Grace looked around the room and its rows of books. "Why did you want to start here?"

"Adam said that she had the binder with her that night. We know it was with her most of the night, but when I saw her later on she didn't have it with her. She had just come from the library, so I think she may have hidden it in here."

Grace looked around. There must be thousands of books on the shelves. Finding this binder was going to be impossible.

"Think Grace. Pretend you're Crystal. You have evidence of all the horrible things your closest friends and family have done over the years in a binder and are planning on selling it later to a sleazy Hollywood screenwriter, where would you hide it?"

"At home."

"Grace, you're not playing," Kyle complained.

Grace walked to the reference desk and grabbed a layout of the library. What did she know about Crystal? She was vain, arrogant, selfish, entitled, and not very bright. A great combination of traits. Knowing Crystal, she would hide it in plain sight, convinced everyone else would be too stupid to find it. "Is there a section on true crime?" she asked aloud while scanning the library map. "Or maybe a local history section? If this scrapbook does contain the sins of the town, then she might have hidden it there."

She felt Kyle lean over her shoulder. "There!" Kyle pointed to a corner of the map, before turning and dashing to the back of the library. The map showed a small little room devoted to local and state history. Grace followed a bit more slowly, convinced it couldn't be this easy. By the time she caught up, Kyle had already picked the door lock and was pulling each book off the shelf. "You don't have to take apart the library," she scolded.

"She may have hidden it behind one of the books." Kyle cleared a section of the lower bookcase. "Shine your flashlight over here. There's something—"

"See anything?"

"Yeah," he said disappointedly. He blew out a breath and handed her a black binder. An empty black binder. Grace turned it over and ran her fingers over the label. Reunion was written in bold lettering.

"Well, this is just great. Let's keep looking. She must have taken information out and stuffed it somewhere. Do you see anything else back there?" she asked shining her light over the lower shelf.

Kyle pulled out a leather book and flipped through it. "No, it's just some family's genealogy history. I thought—" he paused to look closer at the back pages. Smiling, he stood up and hugged Grace. "We've got it. Look," he said thrusting the book into her hands. "Someone stuffed in newspaper clippings, pictures, and handwritten notes in the back."

"Isn't that typical for a genealogy record?"

"Guess who the book is about? Or rather, whose family?"

Grace turned to the title page. "The Ancestors and Descendants of Marshal Benton Hogan. Crystal's great-great-great grandfather." She flipped to the back of the book and pulled out a newspaper clipping dated the day she graduated. *'Tragedy at the Hogan High School Graduation.'* As she read the clipping, Kyle removed another piece of paper from the book.

"Whoa," he said in a whoosh. "I knew it."

Grace placed the clipping back in the book and moved to Kyle's side. In his hand were pages from a ledger. "She kept track of her blackmail payments?" she said in disbelief. "Hmm. Crystal was nothing if not organized. Come on, let's get out of here. This place is creepy." Grace took the ledger page out of Kyle's hand and stuffed it back into the book.

"All right, but let's not tell Adam that we found this just yet. At least, not until we can go through it ourselves."

Grace agreed, pushing the book back into his hands. "Take the book and go to the car. I'll find Adam and—" she stopped when the door to the local history room slammed shut.

Grace and Kyle looked at each other in stunned disbelief. Kyle handed Grace the book and crept up to the door.

"Maybe it was the wind," she whispered, looking around the windowless room.

Kyle turned and looked at her before placing his hand on the doorknob. "It's locked." At her panicked expression, he smiled and reached into his coat pocket. "Nothing to worry about."

"Nothing to worry about? We're trespassing, we're trying to catch a killer, and the door slammed shut just as we found a key piece of evidence. My years of horror movie watching have taught me that there is plenty to worry about." Grace turned in a circle, looking for an alternate way of escape, as Kyle slowly backed away from the door.

"What's wrong?" she asked, shinning her flashlight in his face. "Why do you look so pale? I thought you said there was nothing to worry about?"

"Bit of a problem," he said quietly.

"Do you smell something?" Grace turned her flashlight to the door, as smoke began to pour into the room from underneath the door. "It's all right. This is a school. I'm sure the fire trucks are on their way."

"Grace, I don't hear any alarms, do you?" he said, pulling a table over to the corner wall. Kyle jumped on the table and started to unscrew the vent above his head.

Remembering that Adam was still in the building, Grace began shouting his name, only stopping when flames began to engulf the wall. The sound of something falling to the floor caused her to look over her shoulder at Kyle.

Coughing, Grace looked from the vent to Kyle's shoulders. "That's too small to get through."

"No, it's not," he said, reaching out his hand and pulling her onto the table. Making a stirrup with his hands, he hoisted Grace up into the narrow vent. "Don't worry I'm right behind you," he shouted when she stopped.

It took less than a minute before she reached another vent. Using her hands, she pounded on the metal until it gave away and she less than gracefully dropped to the floor, coughing. She looked up just as Kyle's feet landed a few feet from her head. Turning Grace over, he picked her up in a fireman's hold and ran to the nearest exit.

Smoke filled the hallway.

Without warning, he fell to his knees only a few feet from the exit. Crawling they both tried to reach for the door. The last thing Grace remembered was Kyle pushing her closer to the door.

CHAPTER SEVENTEEN

THE FIRST THING Grace became aware of was the excruciating pain in her chest as she gulped in air. The second thing was someone gently caressing her forehead. The third thing was someone wrapping something tight around her arms, stomach, and legs. Carefully, she opened her eyes to see an EMT standing over her, strapping her body down on a stretcher and Diana telling her to calm down.

Pulling off the oxygen mask, she croaked out Kyle's name.

"I'm over here."

Relieved, Grace turned her head towards the sound of his voice to see him sitting a few feet away pressing an oxygen mask to his face. Melodie stood next to him, massaging his shoulders. Grace noticed Steve standing behind them, taking pictures of the smoldering building.

"Let me up," she demanded, trying to sit up. "I don't need to go to the hospital."

"Yes, you do and so do I," Kyle said standing up. He quickly jumped into the back of the waiting ambulance and motioned for the EMTs to move Grace into the ambulance.

Once Grace was settled, he turned to Melodie, who was trying to climb into the ambulance. "Would you do me a big favor? Would you go to my hotel and get me some clean clothes? Please, it's really important," he said, pressing his hotel key into her hand.

Once they were in the ambulance and on the way to the hospital, Grace asked how they survived.

Kyle quickly explained that Diana and Eric had pulled them out of the building and called 911.

"What were they doing there? At this time of night?"

"Apparently, some lady next door saw something suspicious and called Collins. He thought it might be us, so he and Diana decided to come over instead of calling the police. They were looking for us when they smelled the smoke and called for help."

Worried she asked, "Did Adam get out?"

Kyle snorted, "Did he get out? Yeah, he got out. Eric and Diana saw him running from the library only seconds before they smelled smoke. But you want to hear the really big news? His name was in the ledger."

♔ ♔ ♔

Grace shifted restlessly in the uncomfortable hospital waiting room chair as she waited for Kyle to finish the paperwork. Luckily, neither one of them was seriously hurt and the school had only suffered minor damages. Unfortunately, most of the damage occurred in the library, specifically in the local history room. Whatever information Crystal had hidden there was now lost.

Grace glanced at her watch again. It was now fifteen past three in the morning. They had spent the last three hours at the emergency room. Most of the time had been taken up by the Sheriff and his deputies interrogating them, while they sat in the ER.

To Bellamy's obvious disappointment, both Eric and Diana had covered for them. Despite Eric's earlier warning, he once again covered for Grace, going as far as telling Bellamy that he had personally given them permission to be at the school that night.

Bellamy did seem to cheer up when Kyle mentioned Adam's name and how they became locked in the library while a fire raged around them. Grace and Kyle listen patiently as Bellamy entertained himself at their expense. He seemed to enjoy scolding them about the dangers of being a detective and how a valuable piece of evidence was now lost. He was practically giddy when going over the many ways they could have died. Only after promising Bellamy that they would keep him informed of their every move from now on, did he finally leave.

"Honestly, Drake, if you had just called me, all of this could have been avoided."

Now if only Steve would leave, she thought.

"Now, don't you worry," Melodie said, stroking Kyle's hair. "I've moved your things out of that horrid hotel room and into one of my nice clean guest rooms. You'll be perfectly comfortable there."

Grace glared at Melodie's back. She could leave at any time, too.

"What you needed was a lookout," Steve said, for the fifth time since arriving at the ER.

Ignoring Steve, Kyle turned to Melodie, "Abry's with you?"

"Who?"

"My pet rabbit," he explained, signing the last form and handing it back to the nurse with a smile.

"Oh, that . . . precious thing . . . I mean, bunny," Melodie said shuddering. "I thought Grace could take it home with her."

Grace smirked, remembering Melodie's dislike of anything with four legs and fur.

"I mean, after all that you've been through tonight. I think you should just relax and let someone take care of you," she said, practically purring. "Grace loves animals. Don't you Gracie?" She threw Grace an encouraging look.

"I do. I do love animals, but after everything I've been through, tonight," Grace sighed dramatically, "I just don't think I'm up for it. Besides, Abry will love it at your house. He can hop his little heart out."

"Melodie, I really don't want to impose," Kyle said, holding up his hand as she started to object. "Besides, I paid for the room in advance."

"Oh, but I have this nice big room and to be perfectly honest, I'm afraid to stay by myself." Melodie leaned against Kyle's chest. "I mean, there's a killer loose."

"Hey, Melodie, I offer bodyguard services. I'm very reasonable." Steve reached into his pocket and pulled out a business card.

Ignoring Steve's card, Melodie linked her arm through Kyle's arm. "I've already hired someone, Steve," she said coldly.

Steve was undaunted. "After what happened tonight, I'm thinking he might need a bodyguard, too. Seriously, Drake, it wasn't very smart taking an amateur in with you," he said, jerking a thumb at Grace.

Too tired to protest, Grace leaned her head back against the wall, trying to stifle another yawn.

"He does have a point, honey," Melodie purred. "You two, together at this time of night . . . It doesn't seem like that was a very good idea.

Grace sleepily wondered what Melodie really objected to: their almost dying, at this time of night, or their being together, at this time of night. "What are you doing here Melodie? How did you even know about the fire?"

"Diana called me on her way to the school. She thought I might have been with Kyle," she said, laying her forehead against his arm. "I wish I had been. I could have helped. I definitely wouldn't have let you get locked up in that room."

Grace rolled her eyes. "And what about you, Steve?"

Steve smirked. "Listen to the detective over here. I don't have to answer any questions from you."

"How did you find out?" Kyle asked annoyed.

"Police radio," Steve said quickly. "All's I'm saying, is it's getting rather dangerous around here. Obviously, there's a vicious killer out. You need someone with some experience. No offense, Grace."

Kyle reached down to give Grace a hand up. "Nonsense. I wouldn't have found anything if it wasn't for Grace."

Steve snorted. "Look, Drake, you can play with the amateurs if you like, but when you want to play with the big boys, you give me a call," he said, handing Kyle his business card.

"What exactly are you doing here?" Kyle asked coldly.

"What do you mean?" Steve asked.

"No one's hired you? So, why are you here?"

"Because you obviously need my help. I've been watching you two running around town . . . You're completely lost. Grace can't help you, but I can."

Melodie let go of Kyle's arm and stepped between the two men. Facing Steve, she asked, "I have a much better question. How did you know to be here tonight? Hmm? Do you want to answer that one, Stevie?"

"I already told you. I have a police scanner."

Melodie shook her head. "No. You showed up before Aunt Diana called the police. Right about the same time I did. Quite the coincidence, don't you think?"

Steve pointed a stubby finger at Kyle. "You keep my number handy. You're going to need me," he snarled, throwing open the door and walking out into the night.

Kyle leaned down to whisper in Grace's ear. "What do you think about that?"

Before she could answer, Melodie clamped a hand around Kyle's bicep, pulling him towards her. "You will come stay with me tonight, won't you?" she asked, running a fingernail up his chest.

"Absolutely!" Grace answered her, taking Kyle's other arm. "We would be happy to stay with you, Mel. We'll have a slumber party, just like when we were kids."

Taken aback Melodie's smile grew tight. "Wonderful," Melodie said, sounding less than thrilled as Kyle and Grace followed her to her car.

♛ ♛ ♛

The drive to Melodie's house took less than ten minutes. Grace was almost asleep when they pulled into Melodie's garage. Stumbling out into the kitchen, she sank into the nearest chair, as Melodie went upstairs to make up an extra guest room. Kyle sat down next to her. "Well, do you think Adam's our killer?"

"I don't believe he set the fire. It's just not like Adam. Besides, why would he kill us? We don't know anything and if it weren't for him, we wouldn't have even been at the school in the first place."

"Maybe he didn't want us to see what was in the scrapbook. He just needed us to find it, so he could get rid of it and any witnesses. According to Crystal's ledger, he's been making regular payments to Crystal for the last ten years."

"That doesn't mean he killed Crystal. Why now? Why not ten years ago when she started blackmailing him?"

"Remember, him telling us that she tried to blackmail people anonymously. Maybe he didn't realize it was her until recently." Kyle shook his head. "Collins and Diana saw him running out of the library right before the fire."

"I just can't believe he would steal Sam's screenplay. Kill him. Pay the blackmail, for the screenplay, mind you, not the murder. Wait ten years. Kill Crystal. Hire us to find her killer. Then convince us that the murder he committed ten years before, that everyone assumed was a suicide, was actually a murder. Send us off looking for evidence that would incriminate him and then try to burn down the school and us when we find it."

"Yeah, I guess it doesn't really make much sense. I don't know, maybe he's gone crazy. Anyway, I guess . . . Adam wasn't the only one who could have set that fire."

Grace looked at him questioning.

"I spoke to Eric and asked him if he and Diana were together the whole time. He said, they were, except for about five minutes before the fire. Collins decided that they should split up and search different parts of the school. They did, but he ran into her in front of the library just before Adam came running out and the fire started. Either one of them could have tried to kill us. If Adam is right and Diana did kill Sarah Collins, she could have had plenty of time to set the fire."

Grace nodded her head. "Let's not forget that Melodie was there, too. The moment she found out we—or rather you— were there, she made a beeline for the school."

"With Steve probably right behind her." Kyle laid his head on the table. "Why would Melodie care about Crystal's scrapbook?"

"How much do you want to bet Crystal made a copy of Larry's suicide note?"

"Well, I guess that let's Tom off the hook. He's the only one who didn't know we were at the school."

Grace sighed, "We don't know that. For all we know, he could be following us."

"Who's following you? Steve?" Melodie stood in the doorway. Smiling, she tied the sash of her red silk dressing gown into a pretty bow at her waist, and slid into the chair next Kyle.

Grace laid her head down on the table. "Probably."

"The guest room is already made up, Grace," Melodie said. "You can go up there now if you would like."

Grace raised her head off her arms. Smiling she said, "I was just teasing, Mel. I called home from the hospital; they'll be expecting me soon."

"Oh, that's too bad." Melodie smiled sweetly at Kyle, as she scooted her chair closer. "I was really hoping you would stay, Grace. Oh well, too bad." Leaning into Kyle, she asked, "You can stay, can't you?"

Kyle sleepily looked towards Grace. He didn't really want to stay, but he was growing too tired to move.

"I would just feel so much safer if you were here," she said, her voice lowering another octave as she laid her hand on Kyle's arm.

Before Melodie could begin her great seduction act, Grace quickly changed the subject. "It's really not safe to be around either one of us. Someone did try to kill us tonight," she said, finding it strange that she would have to point this out to Melodie.

"I still don't understand why you were at the high school."

Kyle quickly explained that they were looking for the binder Crystal had been carrying around that night and asked her if she had noticed it.

Nodding her head, she said, "I saw it. I just figured it had something to do with the reunion. What do you think was in it?"

"Were not completely sure. We had just found it when we noticed the smoke," Grace said.

"Did you read any of it?" Melodie asked, slipping her hand into Kyle's.

Kyle shook his head, while trying to stifle another yawn.

"We think it may have something to do with Sam," Grace said.

Melodie's head turned sharply toward Grace. "Sam? Sam Baxter? What on earth does Sam have to do with anything?" she snapped.

Grace and Kyle exchanged glances.

"We're starting to think that maybe Sam was murdered, too," Grace said.

Melodie turned her head from Grace to Kyle and back again. "Sam committed suicide," she said sharply.

Grace shook her head. "Do you know anyone who would have wanted to kill Sam?"

Stunned, Melodie shook her head. "No. Everyone loved Sam."

"Do you know if he was seeing someone besides Crystal?" Kyle asked.

"Besides Crystal?" Melodie asked slowly.

"We think he may have been secretly meeting someone behind your sister's back. They might know what happened to him. Do you have any idea who it could be?"

"What could this possibly have to do with Crystal's death?" she asked coldly. "I'm paying you to find out who killed my sister, not about what happened to Sam."

Kyle glanced at Grace, before smiling broadly. "We haven't lost sight of that. Don't worry we're going to find out who killed your sister."

"We just think the two deaths might be connected," Grace added.

"I really don't see how," Melodie said as she pushed her chair back and stood up. "It's late—"

Not wanting to end the conversation and let Melodie run off, Grace changed the subject. "I was really sorry to hear about Larry, Mel."

"Thank you, but to be perfectly honest, it had been over for quite some time now." She smiled at Kyle. "We had a somewhat stormy relationship."

"What really happened between you and Crystal?" Grace asked.

Dragging her eyes away from Kyle's, Melodie said quickly, "I keep telling you. Nothing. We had a fight, but we got over it."

Kyle reached up and held her hand. "We know that she must have been difficult to live with at times."

Melodie looked at Grace and then Kyle before sighing. "She wasn't always bad, you know? It's just . . . in the last few years she got desperate. She started getting into debt. She ran through her inheritance. Tom just doesn't make a lot working for the state, but she was hoping that, eventually, he would run for office. He finally told her that it wasn't happening. She sort of became needier after that."

"Is that when she started to blackmail Larry," Kyle asked gently.

"You know about that?" When he nodded, Melodie sat back down and said, "I didn't find out about the blackmail until after Larry's . . . accident. I wish I had known. Larry might still be alive."

"Why do you say that?" Grace asked.

Melodie hesitated. "I found out about the affair, shortly after it happened. I should have confronted Larry right then, but I was so angry. I decided to put the screws to him. Scare him, a bit. Make him sweat before I asked for a divorce. Unfortunately, I didn't realize my own sister was putting the screws to him, too and bankrupting me in the process."

"How did you find out about your husband's affair?" Grace asked.

"Oh, you don't know? Crystal hired a detective to catch Larry cheating. She wasn't going to tell me, of course, but the detective couldn't wait to talk."

"Steve?" Grace guessed.

Melodie nodded. "She brought him back from Denver. He was more than happy to do it, too. Once he took the pictures, he ran right over to show them to me. I guess it was his way of getting back at Larry and probably me, too."

Grace stifled a yawn. "What do you mean?"

"Steve had asked me to marry him right before my freshman year at college. I, of course, told him no. I mean, Larry and I had just gotten back together, but Steve wouldn't take no for an answer. He kept harassing me. Showing up wherever I was. Sending me flowers. He was becoming even more of a nuisance than usual. He was even starting to bug Crystal, too. So she told Larry that Steve was dangerous. She even told him he had threatened to kill me. Well, you remember what Larry was like. He went ballistic." Melodie smiled fondly. "Larry wasn't that great of a boyfriend or a husband, but he was very protective. I always felt very safe around him."

"Did Steve threaten you?" Grace asked.

"No. Steve's a pain, but he would never hurt me. I think he still loves me." At their shocked expressions, she added quickly. "It was Crystal's idea. She's the one who actually told Larry that. I just . . . didn't disagree. I wasn't happy about it when I found out, but by then, the damage was already done." She shrugged her shoulder, causing the shoulder of her dressing gown to fall down her arm. "Anyway, like I said, Larry went crazy. He beat Steve up and told him if he came near me ever again, he'd kill him. Steve was terrified. Larry wasn't like David or any of the other guys I've ever dated."

At Kyle's questioning look, Grace added, "Larry was six-foot-four. Built like a house."

"Steve was at a slight disadvantage. He left the next day," Melodie said. "Now Larry's gone, Steve's back and I'm all alone."

"So, when Crystal asked him to investigate Larry, he jumped at the chance," Grace said.

"I'm sure he's following me," Melodie said, standing up and pulling back the kitchen curtain hanging by the table. "That's how he got to the school so fast."

"Was Crystal blackmailing Steve for what happened with David Hart?" Kyle asked.

"Not that I know of, but Crystal didn't share that part of her life with me," Melodie said bitterly.

A sudden thought occurred to Grace. "How did Larry feel about David Hart?"

Melodie smiled ruefully. "He hated him. He was so jealous when he found out I was dating him."

"Did he know that David had hit you?"

"Absolutely not. Larry would have killed him if he knew."

Grace looked down at the table. She was so tired, it was becoming difficult to think, but an idea just flashed through her mind. "How do you know that it wasn't Larry who pushed David down the stairs and destroyed his studio?"

Angry, Melodie shook her head. "I told you, Larry didn't know. Besides, Crystal told me that it was Steve that did that."

"Did she see Steve do it?"

Melodie said, "No. I don't think so, but she was pretty sure."

"We heard a rumor that you might have been the one to push him down the stairs," Kyle said gently.

Melodie looked from Kyle to Grace. "I didn't hurt anyone. I know what this is about. It's not about David Hart or Sam Baxter." Her voice grew shrill. "You think I had something to do with my sister's death, but I didn't!"

Kyle reached out and took her hand again. "Calm down. We're not accusing you of anything. We're just trying to sort everything out. I know you wouldn't do something like that."

Mollified, she lowered her voice. "Listen, I'll admit I was angry when I found out. I was very angry, but I eventually forgave her. She apologized. She begged my forgiveness and promised she would change. I had to forgive her. She was my sister, after all."

Remembering Melodie's strange behavior to Crystal at the reunion, Grace said, "You were still angry at her. I remember seeing you and her at the reunion. You could barely stand to sit next to her."

"True, but I didn't kill her. I made my displeasure known in other ways."

Kyle leaned closer. "How so?"

Melodie laughed bitterly. "Completely juvenile ways. Hope didn't win the Reunion Queen crown, you know. Crystal won. It was close, but I decided to help Hope stuff the ballot box . . . I just wanted to watch Crystal freak out. I regretted it the moment I did it." Laughing she added, "I still can't believe Crystal made us go through a recount."

"Did you also destroy the charcoal drawing and the 'most likely to' board?" Grace asked.

Melodie shook her head. "No. That wasn't me. You should talk to your sister about that. I saw her carrying around a big red marker at some point during the reunion. Just like the one used to deface the 'most likely to' board."

🏆 🏆 🏆

When Grace woke up, it was a quarter past noon. A persistent buzzing was coming from the nightstand. Groggily, she reached for the alarm clock, before realizing the buzzing was the vibration from her cell phone. She managed to open the phone before it transferred to voice mail.

"Hello?" she muttered sleepily, before turning her face back into her pillow.

"Grace?" She bolted up in bed, recognizing Adam's voice. "Grace, are you okay? I was so worried about you. What happened?"

Grace reached down beside the bed and shook Kyle awake. When they had reached Grace's home, Kyle had insisted on staying over. Grace wasn't sure if he was worried about her safety or his own, but too tired to argue, she let him sneak upstairs and sleep in her room. She fell asleep the moment she laid down on the bed and didn't realize he had slept on the floor until she had fallen over him on a late-night trip to the bathroom.

Grace turned on the speakerphone. "What happened? That's what we would like to know. What happened to you?"

"Grace, I was so worried about you."

"Knock it off, Adam," she said angrily. "You weren't worried about me. If you were, it wouldn't have taken you almost twelve hours to call."

"I didn't find out about the fire until I saw it on the news five minutes ago. I swear I had no idea that you were in any danger until just now. That's why I'm calling now."

"Why did you run away then?"

"I heard a noise. I thought it was the cops, so I took off. Please, tell me you're okay."

"I'm fine." She looked over at Kyle, whose handsome features were twisted into a scowl. "We're both fine."

"Thank God."

Softening Grace asked, "Are you—"

"Did you find anything last night?"

"Yes, we found Crystal's scrapbook. We even saw her ledger."

Adam gave a small yelp. "That's great! I knew I could count on you. That's wonderful, Grace! This is what I want you to do. You need—"

Grace smiled. It was almost worth losing a key piece of evidence, just so she could ruin his day. "Bad news, Adam."

"What?"

"Unfortunately, it's ashes."

"It burned . . . you lost it?" Disbelief and then anger colored his voice. "How could you possibly have let that happen? I can't believe this. I hired you—"

"Why did you hire us, Adam?"

"What do you mean?"

"You haven't really been helpful. You certainly haven't given us all the information."

"What are you talking about?"

"You told us you didn't have a motive for killing Crystal, but you did."

"Grace, we've already gone over this. Why would I kill Crystal? I needed her for my movie."

"Because she was blackmailing you. We found your name in her book. You've been paying her a small fortune for quite some time." When Adam didn't say anything, Grace continued, "I heard a rumor that you stole Sam's screenplay."

"Who told you that? No, wait. Let me guess. Steve told you that. Why would you believe him? He's a creep."

"I didn't hear that particular rumor from Steve."

"Whatever. I didn't kill Crystal. It's true that Sam and I discussed writing a screenplay together, but it was never more than that."

"Then why were you paying Crystal?"

"Crystal said she had proof that I plagiarized my screenplay. She said that she had Sam's handwritten notes, and that they were identical to my screenplay. I knew that she couldn't have though, because I'm the one who actually wrote the thing! I'm the one who fleshed it out! I'm the one who made it real! Not Sam! But, I couldn't take the chance, so I paid her, but I didn't kill her."

"That's the real reason you wanted the ledger, isn't it? Sam wasn't murdered. That was just your excuse, to get us to search for those notes?"

"No! Sam was murdered. I didn't lie to you about that. And I didn't need you to find the notes. I already have them. They were part of the deal Crystal and I struck with each other. She promised to hand over the notes during the reunion, along with the evidence of Sam's murder. She changed her mind on telling me who killed Sam, but she still handed over Sam's notes. I was right, too. She didn't have anything. It was just gibberish. So, you see, I didn't kill her. I didn't have to and I can prove it, too. I still have the notes, and you can see them for yourself."

Grace bit her lower lip, considering. She wanted to believe him. If he were telling the truth, why would he have killed Crystal? And if he wasn't telling the truth, why hire them to look for her killer? There was still one piece of the puzzle missing. "If you and Sam were working on a screenplay together, then you must have been seeing a lot of each other."

"Yeah, a little bit."

"I've been hearing rumors that Sam was seeing someone besides Crystal. Is that true?"

"I have no idea. Even if he was, so what?"

"Whoever that person is, they might know something. Like, why was Sam so upset the days before graduation? Why was Sam leaving town in such a hurry? Did she know he was planning to leave her? If so, how did she feel about that?"

"He was leaving town?"

"He wasn't even going to stay for the graduation ceremony. Here's a few more questions our mystery woman could help us with. What in the world was he doing on the bell tower? The place had been locked up and condemned. Students weren't allowed up there, so why was he there? And most importantly, if he didn't love Crystal, why was he keeping his affair a secret? What was he afraid of?"

"Why? Because, Crystal loved him. She would've killed—"

"Would she have? Crystal and he had dated, for what, five months by then. For the previous five years all Crystal wanted was Tom. The moment Sam dies, she's latched onto Tom again. Face it. She was just killing time until she could finally sink her claws into Tom Lake."

"Wait a second . . . you're right," Adam said slowly, "Crystal wouldn't have cared, would she? She was just using Sam to try to get close to Tom."

"Did you ever see Sam with another girl?"

"Nooo," he answered slowly, "but . . . I wonder . . . Grace, did you happen to see that memorial picture show they had at the reunion?"

"I saw bits and pieces, why?"

"I think I might know who he was seeing. I need to hang up—"

"Wait! Adam, what are you up to?"

"I need to talk to someone. In fact, if I'm right, I may know who can answer all of your questions." His voice rose in excitement. "I think you've solved it, Grace. I've had everything all mixed up. I was looking at this the wrong way."

"What are you talking about?"

"I've got to make a call. Once I know for certain—"

"Adam, don't do anything stupid."

"I'm not," he said excitedly. "I'm just going to make a call. I promise. I'll call you right back. Ten minutes, tops. I promise."

The line went dead.

Grace snapped the phone shut.

Kyle laid back down. "What do you think Adam meant when he said, he 'was looking at it the wrong way'?"

Grace shrugged. "I don't know. He was talking about the slideshow."

"The one on the stolen flash drive? I mentioned that days ago." Kyle pulled a pillow over his head. "I overheard Crystal say something about a picture during the reunion. Maybe he's on to something. What do you think? Should we call Bellamy?"

"No. Not yet. Let's wait until Adam calls back."

CHAPTER EIGHTEEN

GRACE OPENED HER cell phone and scrolled through the missed calls.

"Any news?" Kyle asked.

Grace shook her head and closed her phone. Two days had passed since they had spoken with Adam. "I wish he would call. I'm worried, Kyle."

"Don't be. I'm sure he's fine. He's probably holed up somewhere, sitting in front of a fire, sipping cognac."

"He said he was going to make a phone call, not go skiing."

"Whatever. Now come here and hold Abry," he demanded, thrusting the bunny in her arms and leading her to the old, creaky green motel chair. "I will be right back."

Grace lifted Abry up, nuzzling her face into his soft fur. "Who's a good bunny?" she asked, softly petting the rabbit.

A sudden shout and banging sound from the tiny closet caused Abry to leap out of her hands and hop under the bed. "It's okay, baby," she said, dropping to her knees and looking under the bed.

"Ow, no, it's not okay. The top of the closet fell on my head."

Grace sat back on her knees and smiled at Kyle, who was gingerly touching his head and peering at his reflection in the mirror, "I wasn't talking to you. Are you okay?"

"Yeah, I don't think it will scar."

"Well, that's a relief," she said, walking over and taking his head in her hands. She ran her fingers though his thick hair, momentarily forgetting that she was supposed to be checking for damage.

Deciding he was going to survive, she turned her attention to the three dry erase boards he had pulled out of the closet. "What's this?" she asked, picking up one of the boards.

"I read in one of those books that we should organize our thoughts, so I bought these boards."

"That's great." Looking at the empty board, she said, "I think this pretty much sums up what we know."

Kyle smiled and picked up a pack of brightly colored pens. "We know more than that. Here, I'll do the writing," he said, placing the boards on top of the dresser.

Grace watched as Kyle labeled one board SUSPECTS FOR CRYSTAL'S MURDER, one SUSPECTS FOR SAM'S MURDER, and one TIMELINE.

"All right, I'll play," she said, hopping onto Kyle's bed and leaning back against the headboard. "Let's see, we'll start with Crystal's murder. Our first suspect should be Tom. Police always suspect the spouse first, and we know that things weren't exactly happy between them."

"Then there's Adam," he said, writing Adam's name down.

"You mean our client?" Grace felt compelled to point out. "I still don't think Adam should be a suspect."

"Honestly, I think anyone who has ever met Crystal should be considered a suspect," Kyle said. "But he does have a motive. She *was* blackmailing him. And let's not forget, he hasn't brought us those notes. The ones that are supposed to prove that he no longer had any reason to kill her."

"He will," Grace said a little less confidently. "There's also, your new friend, Melodie."

"You mean our other client," Kyle asked, adding her name to the board.

"She was clearly angry with her sister the night of the reunion. She may have decided not to share Larry's life insurance money with her."

Kyle finished writing and looked at the board. "Who else was angry at Crystal?"

"Her Aunt Diana. Crystal was trying to come between Diana and Eric. I can't imagine Diana would have killed her over that, but who knows."

"There's also the chance that Melodie and Diana compared notes. Diana may have figured out it was Crystal that blackmailed her over the affair she had," he said, dutifully adding her name to the board.

Grace looked up at the ceiling. "Let's see . . . we also have Steve Mattingly. Supposedly, he tried to kill David Hart. If that's true, I'm sure Crystal would have blackmailed him, as well."

"According to David Hart, it was Melodie. There's something strange about the whole thing. If it was Steve, and Crystal was blackmailing people, then why, when she was passing everyone's secrets off to Adam, didn't she mention it to him?"

Grace pulled back her long red hair into a ponytail. "You know, we really only have Melodie's word that Crystal even said that. She could be lying to protect herself."

Kyle shrugged. "I can't see Melodie pushing someone down a flight of stairs. Can you?"

Grace shook her head. "Not really, but I could see Larry doing it. He had a horrible temper and was extremely jealous. If he found out that someone had hit Melodie, I could see him going after the guy. But then again, I could see Steve doing it, too."

"Who's next?"

Grace looked at the list of names. All of them had a reason for killing Crystal. "I think we're forgetting someone. James Simpson. Maybe he was afraid Crystal would talk to Tom about who his biological father really was."

"Maybe."

"You might as well put an X down. If Adam was right and Crystal knew who killed Sam, then that person would have the best motive for killing her."

Using a red marker, Kyle wrote *Mr./Ms. X* in the center of the board.

Grace looked over the board. "Well, that's it."

"There's one more," Kyle said, adding one more name to the board.

"Take my sister's name off the board!" Grace sputtered.

"No, it's my board, get your own," he said, looking proudly at his creation. "Well, what do you think?"

"It's very pretty and colorful," she said, looking at the list of suspects, each written out in a different neon color. "It doesn't really tell us who the killer is."

"If the same person who killed Crystal, also killed Sam, maybe we can find a connection," he said, moving to Sam's board.

Grace watched as he began filling out the board.

"I think we can put Tom down again." Kyle said, adding Tom's name to the board.

"I think Adam is wrong about that. Why would Tom kill Sam? I just don't believe Tom would have killed him over Crystal. He wouldn't have had to. Sam was leaving town, alone. And I don't care what Adam, Diana, Eric or Beth thought, if Tom had shown the slightest interest in Crystal, she would have happily left Sam in the dust."

"What if Hope was the mystery woman Sam was having an affair with?"

Grace scoffed. "Hope wasn't interested in Sam."

"Are you sure?" Kyle countered. "What was she doing on top of the bell tower, right before graduation?"

"I'm still trying to figure out what Sam was doing there, right before graduation. The bell tower had been condemned. No one was allowed to go up there."

"Even if she isn't Sam's mystery woman, my theory still holds up. Tom did see her and Sam on the tower that day. He knows Sam was seeing someone in secret and wouldn't tell him who. He sees Hope and Sam in an embrace. Platonic or not, Tom doesn't know that."

"So, he goes crazy and kills Sam?"

"Then to punish Hope, he marries her rival," Kyle said, picking up a green marker and circling Tom's name. "It would explain why he married Crystal on the day he and Hope were to be married."

"Our birthday, too."

"Then he went on the honeymoon Hope had planned."

"Don't forget, he also bought the house Hope had wanted." Grace sighed. "Very cruel."

"They definitely went out of their way to hurt Hope."

Grace had to admit it was possible. "But why kill Crystal? Why now?"

"She was tired of the way he was treating her, so she contacted Adam. She was going to ditch Tom for his father and let Tom swing."

Grace wasn't convinced. "Who else do we have?"

Kyle looked between the two boards trying to find a connection. "What about Diana? We know Sam witnessed Sarah Collins death. If Diana did kill Sarah, then Sam had to have seen it."

"But why wouldn't he have said something?"

"Maybe he felt sorry for her. Maybe she paid him a lot of money to keep quiet." Kyle shrugged. "I don't know. Sam may have had second thoughts and wanted to confess, so Diana killed him. Crystal somehow finds out and covers for her . . ."

"But years go by . . . Crystal's desperate for money and calls Adam."

"Diana freaks out and kills her."

"It's possible," Grace said. "She hated Sarah Collins. Eric, too. Who else is a suspect?"

"Well, we can add Adam in again, since he stole Sam's idea for a screenplay. I can't believe anyone would kill for that story. Did you see it? It was absolutely the most boring film I have ever seen in my life. Which is strange, I usually love movies about mimes."

Grace made a mental note to never let Kyle pick out any movies they watch in the future. "The only problem with Adam as a suspect is, why would he hire us? Why would he tell us about Sam? We wouldn't even be looking at his death if it weren't for

Adam. If all he wanted was for us to find the binder he could have made up any story."

"He may have told us that just to confuse us."

"He's done a good job, then."

Kyle shook his head. "I'm serious. He could have killed Crystal and then made up this story about Sam."

"You mean send us on a false trail."

Kyle nodded. "There is a chance that Sam really did commit suicide."

"It's possible. Any other suspects?"

"What about Crystal?" Kyle asked. "She has a motive, too."

"Crystal?"

"We can't really let her go. She was dating Sam. If she found out that he was cheating and planning on leaving her, she may have decided to kill him."

"I truly, don't think she would have cared."

"Melodie was about to break up with David Hart when she found him in bed with another woman. She still cared enough to slap him and possibly push him down the stairs. Crystal sounds like she was just as vindictive. Even if she didn't want Sam, she may not have wanted anyone else to have him."

"If Crystal killed Sam, then who killed her?"

Kyle pointed to the other board. "Any of those people could have murdered her. They all had motives. Or maybe it was someone who loved Sam and had just found out Crystal had killed him. She may have killed Crystal out of revenge. If so, we're back to Ms. X."

Grace shook her head and crawled closer to the end of the bed. "Crystal was a blackmailer, not a murderer. She found something out about someone, and she squeezed. That's why she died. If this *is* related to Sam's death, then we can assume she knew who killed him and was blackmailing them for it."

"Or they thought she was going to talk."

"Right. We just need to find out who wanted Sam dead. If it's not related, then we're back to square one."

"I'm still putting her down." Kyle stood back and examined the boards. "If the two murders are related, then I guess that lets

James Simpson, Steve Mattingly, and Melodie Baker off the hook. They're the only ones without a motive for killing Sam. Can you think of anyone else?"

"And we're back to Ms. X," Grace added. "Adam seemed pretty sure he knew who it was when we spoke to him the other day."

Kyle looked over his shoulder. "Yeah, he was going to call back, too. It's been more than ten minutes."

"You may have been right about the flash drive. It could be connected to Crystal's death. I wish I had paid more attention to it." Grace sighed. "The picture had to have been of Sam and our Ms. X. Otherwise, why would Adam have gotten so excited?"

"I think he struck out, and that's why he hasn't called."

"He did say that he had it all wrong. What could he have meant?"

Kyle shrugged. "He suspected Diana had killed Sarah Collins and then killed Sam."

"He also suspected Tom, too." Grace bit her lower lip. "Let's say, Harper and Hope were right. Sam was seeing someone in secret, for whatever reason. But Sam suddenly decides he doesn't want to be with her anymore. He tells her, he's leaving her. She may have gotten so angry that she pushed him from the tower. Although, she may have done it accidentally, too. The tower wasn't safe. One kid went up there in our freshman year and fell down the stairs. He broke both of his legs. They locked it up tight after that."

"Why didn't they tear it down?"

"They finally did after Sam died." Grace focused in on Tom's name at the top. "You may be right about another thing, too. A jealous lover could have killed Sam. Whoever that person is, may have seen Sam and his girl together and killed Sam out of jealousy. It doesn't necessarily have to be Tom and Hope. That may be why Sam kept the affair a secret, too. Whoever he was seeing may have been married or with someone else."

Kyle picked up a red marker and started scribbling on the board. "The only problem with that theory is we don't really know who he was seeing. We don't even know if they're male or female. I do like your idea of our Ms. X being the killer. It's just a shame we don't know who that could be."

"Whose name are you writing, then?" Grace asked, peering around his shoulder. "Take my sister's name off there!"

"No! Get your own board."

🏆 🏆 🏆

Two hours later, Grace was still sitting in Kyle's hotel room arguing with him over their suspect list. The three boards were now complete, with suspects, motives, alibis, or lack thereof, diagrams, arrows, stars and even a crude drawing of the bell tower. The boards were starting to resemble a colorful Roshak test. Realizing that they were no closer to discovering who killed Sam and Crystal, Grace started to suggest getting a bite to eat when her phone rang. Not recognizing the number, she decided to let it go through to voice mail. Seconds later, her phone rang again.

Incapable of not answering a ringing phone, Kyle answered it for her. "Guess who," he said, handing the phone back to her. Recognizing the voice on the other end Grace asked, "Can you not tell time? Do you not know how long ten minutes—?"

"Grace, I need your help," Adam said. "I can't talk now. Can you meet me at my aunt's lake house?"

"Why?"

"Because, I know who was in the picture with Sam."

"You found the picture?"

"It's going to be great, Grace. I'm going to record the whole thing, and I want you to be a part of it."

"It's nice that you thought of me, but—"

"Of course I did. I need someone to operate the camera. Bring Drake with you. He can help me set the lights up."

Before she could ask any more questions, Adam hung up.

🏆 🏆 🏆

Kyle drove the Camaro into a small clearing near the shack. The sun had just set in the distance.

"Why did you park here?" Grace asked, opening the car's door and stepping out into a foot of mud.

"I don't trust Adam. You remember the last time we were here? We were greeted with a sawed-off shotgun. Let's just scope the area out first before we walk up to the door."

After scraping off the mud on her shoe with the help of the Camaro's door, Grace carefully made her way around the car to Kyle's side. "I hope you have a flashlight."

"The moon's out. We'll be fine," he said, before nearly tripping over a small branch.

Walking through the woods, they quietly made their way to the old shack. As Grace hopped over a small thicket, she heard a car pass along the road. She could just see it tail lights as it disappeared around the curve in the road.

Kyle looked over his shoulder, towards the empty road. "I wonder if that was Adam."

Shrugging, Grace passed him. She could just make out the shack past a tall grouping of trees. High weeds and thorny bushes blocked any path that might have once existed to the shack. "He left a light on, at least," she said, as she carefully attempted to navigate around a particularly thorny bush.

Kyle grabbed her arm and pulled her back, until they were standing directly behind a tree.

"What's wrong?" she asked, shivering as the wind rustled the leaves around them.

"The door's open," he whispered uneasily. "Let's wait a few minutes and see what happens."

Nodding, Grace slid down the trunk of the tree, moving closer to Kyle as lightening flashed across the sky.

"We're going to get drenched," she said, peering around the trunk of the tree she was hiding behind. The wind rattled the dilapidated shutters still fixed to the building, and whistled through the trees. Caught by the wind, the door swung the rest of the way open and slammed against the wall. Grace and Kyle kept their eyes on the door, waiting for Adam to come out and close it.

Five minutes passed before Kyle whispered for her to stay there while he checked the shack.

Grace tried to dissuade him from leaving her, but he paid no attention, only stopping at the sound of thunder directly overhead, followed by a quick flash of lightning.

Deciding it wasn't exactly safe sitting by a tree in the middle of a thunderstorm, Grace quickly followed him through the woods.

By the time he reached the front steps, she had caught up with him. They slowly made their way up the steps and to the door. Thunder cracked overhead, followed by a sudden downpour. Grace seized Kyle's arm. The darkness, the storm and the utter stillness of the cabin was combining to make her jittery.

Kyle grabbed her hand. They both peered into the room.

Adam had redecorated the one room cabin since they had last been there. A video camera and equipment were spread out around the room. A stack of cash sat on the table located in the center of the room. The corners of the room were set up with lights, the kind normally found on a movie set. A packed suitcase sat on the twin bed in the corner. A muddy shovel sat under the bed. Next to the bed was a bulletin board decorated with pictures.

Notably missing was Adam.

Grace walked over to the bulletin board. No pictures of Sam. All the pictures pinned to the board were from the reunion. Crystal and Tom dancing. Hope being crowned. Crystal being crowned. A group shot of everyone sitting at the table. A shot of Grace tripping over that hideous gown.

Grace sucked in a breath as she looked back at Kyle counting the money at the table. Carefully, she yanked the last picture off the wall, quickly stuffing it in her purse.

"What are you doing?" Kyle asked from the table, a handful of bills in his hand.

"Nothing," she said walking towards the table. "What are you doing?"

Kyle's gaze moved back to the money. He carefully placed the ones in his hand back onto the table. "Nothing."

"Did you count it?"

Kyle nodded his head. "Over five thousand."

Grace whistled. "Wonder why he left it out?" she asked, picking up a notepad lying beside the money.

Grace read the notation aloud. "Duffle bag—buried after reunion—next to the fountain—Moxley house—Where's Hope's wrap?"

"Hope's wrap?" Kyle asked confused.

"I had forgotten all about that. Hope lost her wrap that night. She complained about losing it all night at the hospital. She wanted me to ask the police to find it, but I told her that I thought that might be in poor taste," she said, turning the paper over. "I wonder what Hope's wrap has to do with this."

Kyle walked to the back of the cabin and looked out the window. The rain was coming down hard, making it difficult to see anything out the window. "Something's not right here. Where is he? What man in his right mind would leave the door wide open with four thousand dollars just sitting on the table?"

"Five thousand."

"Nope, I'm pretty sure I said four thousand," he said pulling back the curtain.

"Put it back."

"We have expenses. Do you know how much all of this driving around is costing me? Besides, he only paid a retainer. He still owes us."

Suddenly, the sky lit up with lightning. Kyle could just make out a car and a figure sitting in the driver's seat behind a grouping of trees. "There he is. He's out back. Sitting in his car," he said, feeling Grace standing behind him.

"Are you sure it's him?" she asked, trying to peer into the darkness.

Kyle nodded. "I think so. Why would he just be sitting there?"

Grace shrugged. "Maybe he doesn't know it's us and is scared. Come on." Grace picked up a flashlight sitting on the kitchen counter. Turning it on, she dashed out the front door and around the side.

Kyle moved closer to the window. "Are you sure you want to go out there? Grace?" he called out, when he didn't get a response. Realizing she had already left he turned around and raced after her.

Grace reached the car first. The first thing she noticed was that the windows were down. Heart pounding, she walked up to the driver-side door. Shining her flashlight into the interior, she could see Adam slumped over the wheel.

CHAPTER NINETEEN

IT WAS AN hour before a squad car came barreling around the corner and screeched to a halt besides the shack. The rain had slowed to a small drizzle, as Grace and Kyle sat underneath the porch waiting for the police to arrive.

Sheriff Bellamy jumped out of the car and headed to the back of the shack. When Grace would have followed, a deputy motioned for her to sit back down. While the deputy was taking their statement, an ambulance and another police car arrived.

Once Adam's body had been taken away, Bellamy came rambling from around the corner of the shack. His boots made slapping sounds through the mud as he made his way to the porch. Pausing only long enough to glare at them, he stomped past them and opened the door to the cabin, trailing mud behind him.

Grace watched as he threw his hat on the table, pulled out a chair and sat down counting the money.

Unable to sit still any longer, Grace snapped, "What are you doing? Why aren't you checking for fingerprints?"

"Now, why would I want to do that, Ms. Holliday?" he drawled, as he divided the money up into piles. "See, that's the problem with civilians." Looking at Kyle, he asked, "You saw the body, didn't you? I'm sure you can explain it to your secretary, why I'm not worried about fingerprints."

Kyle looked back at Grace, not sure what to say, "Yes, of course. Well, because . . . well, I'll explain it to her later." He ended lamely. "She's been through a lot, you know."

"Why don't you explain it to me right now, Sheriff? You like to show off. So explain to me why you're not interested in finding out who killed Adam."

Bellamy sighed dramatically before looking over at his deputy, who was trying to hide a smile.

"Ms. Holliday, we don't collect fingerprints for an obvious suicide," he explained patiently. "Not everything is a murder."

"Suicide?" she asked, incredulously.

Bellamy nodded. "I just spoke to the ME. That's a medical examiner, by the way. He thinks it's a suicide and frankly, so do I." He held up his hand to prevent her from arguing. "He knew we were closing in on him. He couldn't take the stress, so he shot himself. Case closed. So, you see, no need for fingerprints."

"Where's the suicide note?"

Bellamy sighed and picked up the notepad lying on the table and waved it at her.

Grace protested. "That's not a suicide note."

"Looks like he buried something on the Moxley property. I think he had a guilty conscience. Don't worry, we'll see what he buried, but I'm willing to bet it's our missing murder weapon."

"Sheriff, did you find a picture of Sam Baxter, anywhere near Adam?" Grace asked.

Bellamy simply stared at her.

"If you find Sam's picture could I have it, please?" Grace asked, as nicely as possible.

"We didn't find any pictures in the car or on the suspect."

Feeling a sudden headache coming on, Grace laid her head on her arms.

🏆 🏆 🏆

It was twenty after nine the next morning when Grace arrived at Melodie's home. Kyle had wanted to come with her, but she quickly nixed that idea. Grace had noticed a disturbing inclination in her old friend to ignore everything but Kyle when he was anywhere within a fifty-foot radius. At first, Grace and Kyle thought that Melodie's interest in him would prove beneficial in uncovering more information, but surprisingly, Melodie had proved quite adept in steering their conversations away from her sister and her tragic death. So far, the only secret that Kyle had been able to uncover was that Steve attacked David Hart—although they still weren't sure about that one— and Melodie stuffed the ballot for Hope. Grace reasoned that if they wanted answers, it was best if Grace spoke to Melodie alone.

Walking up Melodie's stone steps to her front door, Grace now felt certain that the key had to be in one of the pictures used in the slideshow. Despite what Bellamy believed, Grace was positive that Adam did not kill himself. By looking for the pictures used in the slideshow, he had somehow gotten too close to the killer. If she could get her hands on the pictures used that night, she was convinced that she would be able to figure out who killed Adam, Crystal, and maybe Sam. She waited impatiently for Melodie to answer the door.

As soon as the door opened, Grace asked Melodie for the pictures used in the slideshow.

Melodie looked over Grace's shoulder, towards the car parked in her driveway. "Are you alone?"

Grace nodded, explaining that Kyle had somewhere he had to be, but he really needed to see the slideshow.

Melodie sighed. "He's avoiding me, isn't he?" she asked, leading Grace through the hallway and into a well-furnished office, dimly lit by a small tiffany lamp.

"No, not at all," Grace said, not wanting to make Melodie angry.

"Did you say something to him about me?"

Taken aback, Grace simply shook her head, wondering why Melodie was suddenly suspicious.

"What exactly is your relationship with Ky?" Melodie asked, bending over the massive mahogany desk in the center of the room.

Irritated, Grace tilted her head. Lost between wanting to ask whether it was such a hardship to pronounce what is at best a two syllable name, that it absolutely must be shortened and trying to come up with a description of her and Kyle's relationship, which was becoming more complicated by the minute, she decided to stay strictly on the reason she was visiting Melodie without sounding too condescending. "*Ky* just sent me here to look at the pictures. I'm his assistant, remember? This is what assistants do." There, not condescending at all.

Melodie, sensing Grace's anger, laughed. "I knew it. You like him, don't you? I've seen the way you look at him. You probably didn't think I noticed, but the day we buried Crystal, I saw how intensely you were watching him."

Grace hid her smile. She was watching Kyle all right, but not for the reasons Melodie thought.

"Look Grace, we used to be friends, so let me give you some advice—"

"Used to be?" Grace asked in stunned surprised. "I thought we still were."

"Of course we are. That's why I want to help you, before you embarrass yourself," Melodie said sweetly, sitting down behind the desk.

Grace made herself comfortable in one of the large wingback chairs facing the desk. This ought to be interesting, she thought bitterly. If she didn't know better, she would say Crystal was sitting before her. She had never realized quite how alike the two sisters were. "Go on. Just exactly how am I embarrassing myself?"

Melodie leaned over the desk, a picture of friendly concern. "Grace, he is just not right for you. For one, you work for him. Office relationships never work out. Didn't anyone ever tell you that you should never date the boss?"

On that point Grace had to agree, but she wasn't about to give in just yet. "Melodie, I assure you. I am not dating my boss, but even if I were, it really isn't anyone's business."

"Number two. Kyle just travels in a different world than you do. He's sophisticated, cultured, urbane. Were you aware that he is descended from royalty?" she whispered as if sharing a deep dark secret.

Royalty? Showing remarkable restraint, in not laughing in her face, Grace said, "Fascinating. What does that have to do with anything?"

"He needs someone who is worldly. You're from . . . well, you're from here."

"So are you."

Deftly ignoring Grace's retort, Melodie continued. "Number three. And don't take this the wrong way—"

"How could I?" Grace asked sarcastically.

"He needs someone his own age."

"I'm only three years older than him and besides, you're five months older than me."

"I meant spiritually. You're just so serious sometimes and while that's a good thing, it just isn't right for him. He and I have a connection. We have the same interests, the same likes and dislikes, the same background, the same—"

"You're descended from royalty, too?"

"My point is," Melodie continued testily, "He and I just make more sense together, and you're just going to get hurt if you try to come between us."

Sitting up straighter in her chair, Grace asked, "Are you threatening me?"

"No. Of course not," Melodie said shaking her head. "I'm just warning you. Grace, you're my friend and I don't want to see you hurt. I want you to be happy for us."

"Us? Melodie, you just met him. You barely know him."

"I know enough. Did you know he spends his days writing poetry?"

"Did you know he spends his evenings making rabbits disappear?"

"What?"

"Nothing. I just think you're moving a little too fast."

Her face turning red, Melodie asked, "Why? Did he say something to you? Is that why he didn't call me back yesterday?"

Tired of this argument, Grace glanced at her watch. Twenty to ten. "Melodie, he really needs to see those pictures. Do you have them or not?" she asked, speaking slowly.

Sitting back, Melodie took out a key and unlocked one of the desk drawers. Reaching into the drawer, she pulled out an expanding folder. The top of the folder had been marked 'Remembrance Pictures'. Holding up the folder, she turned it upside down, spilling its contents onto the desk. Pictures, a draft invitation, and some handwritten notes lay on the desk between the two women.

"Weren't the pictures placed on a disk?"

Melodie nodded her head. "Yes, but they're gone."

"Where?"

Melodie raised an eyebrow. "I don't know. If I knew, they wouldn't be missing."

When it was clear Melodie wasn't going to elaborate, Grace asked, "Didn't you have a copy or a backup?"

Melodie shrugged her shoulders. "That was Crystal's job."

Leaning forward, Grace picked up several photos. "Are these all of the pictures that were used?"

"I have no idea. Crystal is the one who set up the slideshow."

"Crystal really never struck me as the sentimental type. Did she say why she wanted to handle that part of the reunion?"

"I thought she was doing it to be nice. To spare me from having to remember Larry's death. She said she didn't want me to be depressed before the big event. Anyway, I know these are some of the photos she used," she said, picking up one picture, one thumb lovingly caressing the image. "Here's one of Larry, right before graduation. I remember seeing it in the slideshow that night."

Grace took the picture. The picture showed a smiling Larry sitting in class. From the looks of the class, Grace thought it was probably Mr. Collins' History class. She could just make out Melodie and Tom in the background.

Picking up the remaining pictures, Grace carefully examined each photo in turn. Most of the photos were of Larry and a couple of teachers who had died in the last few years. None of Sam.

"This can't be all," Grace said. "Are you sure that's all that was in that folder?"

"Yes, I'm sure," Melodie said testily, picking up the folder and setting it down on the floor.

"I know I saw a couple of pictures of Sam that night. There must be more. Can I see the folder?"

Grace thought Melodie was about to say no, when she suddenly reached down and handed the folder over. Taking the folder, Grace opened the lid. There were four compartments in the folder. Grace carefully opened each one, checking to make sure that they didn't miss anything. In the last compartment, Grace discovered a small picture stuck in the corner of the expanding folder. Holding her breath, she pulled it out.

Sam. Finally, she thought. It must have been taken after his accident. Sam was sitting in a wheelchair, with both legs in a cast. Tom, Melodie, and Crystal were standing behind him, smiling. Grace flipped the picture over. Written on the back were their names and the date. November 1, 2001. Grace turned it over again. If there was a clue here, she was missing it.

"Do you remember where this was taken?" Grace asked, handing Melodie the picture.

Melodie shook her head. "I'm not sure. It doesn't look like it was taken at his house. I don't even remember posing for it," she said, tossing the picture back on the desk.

"There has to be more. Are you sure there's not another folder somewhere?"

Melodie shook her head. "All of the reunion material is here."

"What about at Crystal's house?"

"No, I brought that here, too. Everything is in this drawer. You're welcome to see it if you want," she said, reaching into the drawer and pulling out more folders.

Grace went through each folder, carefully turning over each piece of paper. Other than the ones in the expanding folder, there were no other pictures to be found. Frustrated, Grace sat back in her chair.

Melodie stood up. "Well, that's it. That's everything."

"Do you remember seeing any of the pictures that night?"

"No, I was busy, Grace. I spent most of the night trying to keep Crystal and Hope away from each other."

"You took a break to stuff the ballot box, didn't you? I just thought you might have seen the pictures, since they were a part of the reunion."

"Afraid not," Melodie said, "that was Crystal's—"

"Job," Grace said, finishing Melodie's sentence. "Yes, I know. I think you've mention that a few times. Someone had to have seen the pictures."

"Why are you still investigating?" she asked perplexed. "The sheriff's office called me this morning. They found the murder weapon right where Adam said he buried them. Clearly, Adam killed my sister."

Grace quickly filled Melodie in on what happened last night. "That was *not* a suicide note, and it definitely wasn't a confession. I believe Adam found out who killed Crystal and possibly Sam. We need to see those pictures."

"You went with Kyle to the lake? Just exactly how much time do you two spend together?"

Ignoring the question, Grace asked, "Where's the list of alumni who attended the reunion?"

Melodie reluctantly handed her two sheets of paper. Quickly perusing the list, Grace counted over hundred names. Groaning, she dug through her purse, until she found her cell phone.

"What in the world are you doing?" Melodie asked in disbelief.

"I'm calling everyone who was there that night," she said matter-of-factly. "I need, um, I mean, Mr. Drake needs to know if anyone saw the slideshow that played last night. You want to help?"

Standing, Melodie threw Grace a disgusted look. "I think that's what I'm paying you for," she said, as she walked towards the door. Before leaving, she reluctantly added that she would fix lunch.

♈ ♈ ♈

Kyle picked up his iced tea and enjoyed the cool autumn breeze, as he sat waiting for James Simpson to return to their table at the country club. He could get used to this, he decided.

"Well, it's all taken care of Kyle." James pulled out a chair and sat down.

"That quickly?"

"Yep, you can consider yourself a full fledge member. Your references were impeccable," he said, helping himself to a buttered roll.

Kyle smiled. Felix came through and here Grace thought he was just an ambulance chaser.

"All you need now is to open up an office, and you'll be in business."

"Excellent! I can't tell you how refreshing this is. You know, in my experience, the authorities don't necessarily enjoy a private investigator hanging around, poking their noses in police business." Kyle's experience, of course being what he had seen on television and at the movies.

"To tell you the truth, Tom has had some reservations, but I think it's just the stress he's been under."

Kyle nodded sympathetically.

"I have the information you asked for, by the way." James passed a folder across the table. "The coroner was convinced Sarah Collins' death was an accident. If you find out any information that would indicate otherwise, I'd be interested in hearing it."

Kyle picked up the folder and leafed through the coroner's report. "She had been threatened just a month before."

"Diana Collins." James nodded. "The sheriff at the time was John Anderson. Wonderful man. Best sheriff this town ever had. He heard about the threat and launched a full investigation.

His report is after the coroner's. Diana Collins had an alibi. Air tight."

"Those can be faked."

"Not this one. She had slipped on a sheet of ice the morning Sarah died. She was still at the Emergency Room being treated for a concussion when the icicle fell on Sarah. An ER doctor and three nurses provided affidavits to the effect."

Kyle frowned. Well, that eliminates one suspect, he thought. He tested the weight of the folder. Pretty large for an open-and-shut case. "Did they have any other suspects?"

James hesitated. "Not really. The sheriff thought her husband may have killed her, but," he said, shaking his head, "he had an alibi, too."

Kyle looked up. "Eric was a suspect?"

James nodded. "He had a motive. She was pregnant when she died and there was a rumor that the baby wasn't his."

"Really?" Kyle leaned forward. "Who was she having an affair with?"

"The sheriff couldn't substantiate the rumor, but what was significant was that Eric Collins apparently believed it. According to a neighbor of theirs, Eric and Sarah had a huge fight the week before she died. Eric had basically accused her of sleeping with all the men in a five mile radius."

"But you have no idea who she was sleeping with?"

"Anderson thought it was with the principal at the time. Hank Cooper. He wasn't sure. Cooper denied it."

"You said Eric had an alibi?"

James smiled. "An excellent one. He was tutoring Tom at the time. Tom swore he was with Collins from the moment Sarah Collins left, to the time Sam came running in to get help. Anderson didn't really believe him, which is ridiculous. Why would Tom lie about something like that? Anyway, after Tom—" James paused as he reached for the buzzing cell phone in his pocket.

"Hello," he said, answering his phone.

Kyle watched as a multitude of expressions passed over Simpson's face. First surprise, disbelief, and finally anger. "He can't do that! Tom, don't worry. Does he have a warrant? . . . Just relax, I'll be right there," he said his voice rising in anger.

"Bellamy, that stupid son—" he said, stopping himself and smiling as a couple of elderly voters passed by.

"What has he done?" Kyle asked.

James leaned forward. "I don't know how he got elected. He is completely incompetent. Tom caught him and his deputies trying to search his house on Franklin Street."

"Did he have a search warrant?"

James laughed bitterly. "No. He didn't have a warrant for Tom's house on Ferris, either, but that didn't stop him. He is such an incompetent fool. Our sheriff's office could use some help. You should see some of the evidence he brings me. Tom and I have had to dismiss more of his cases than we've had to try. Tom told him to get off his property and don't come back without a warrant. However, he just found out that Judge Rawson is seriously considering giving them the warrant. Bellamy's just doing this out of revenge. He's out to get my office."

Kyle sat back in his chair. "What do they hope to find?"

"Adam left a note describing where he buried the murder weapon. They followed the instructions but—" he stopped speaking when a waitress came up and refilled his glass.

As soon as she left, Kyle said, "So, they think Adam is the killer."

"You would think so, but no." Simpson shook his head. "They're not so sure Adam killed Crystal anymore. Apparently, they didn't find the trophies where the note said they were supposed to be. Instead, they found evidence of someone else digging around the fountain. They now think that Adam wasn't the one who buried the murder weapon. They think he was trying to find it, and the note was actually an anonymous tip, he had received."

"But I thought they had found all three trophies in a duffle bag this morning."

James nodded. "Bellamy tore apart the yard. They didn't find them near the fountain where the note said they were buried, but they found them somewhere else on the property. They also found a couple of purple silk threads inside the duffle bag. They're hoping they can find more of these threads somewhere at Tom's home, so they're trying to get a warrant for his house on Franklin Street now. I don't know how Judge Rawson can seriously issue a search warrant. Absolutely ridiculous," he said in disgust. "Tom had nothing to do with Crystal's death. It's obvious Adam killed Crystal."

"You still think Adam is the killer?"

"Don't you?"

Kyle quickly outlined their theory about Sam's death.

"I can't believe this has anything to do with Sam Baxter. As far as I know that was a suicide. Now the stolen flash drive and the slideshow? Perhaps, but I don't know what you could hope to learn now. I doubt Bellamy has even thought about investigating the theft. Anyway, I have to go. I want to be there when Bellamy conducts his search," he said, rising from the table.

♛ ♛ ♛

Grace stood rubbing her neck, trying to release the tension of sitting in one place holding a phone to her ear for over three hours.

A third of those contacted didn't even know there was a slideshow playing. Another third was completely unaware that Sam had died and another third of the class asked, "Sam who?"

But it wasn't a total loss. One person remembered seeing the slideshow and had made a special point to videotape it. Unfortunately, that person was Beth. Having noticed Beth's videotaping skills at the reunion, Grace didn't hold out too much hope that the video would be clear, in focus and actually pointing at the pictures and not Beth's feet or her own chest. Still, Grace didn't feel like she would be able to rest until she had at least seen the pictures. There had to be some connection. There had to be a reason the flash drive was stolen, and Crystal was killed,

Grace thought, as she left the office and walked towards Melodie's kitchen.

Melodie and Diana were sitting at the table, glaring at one another. "I had nothing to do with it," Diana was saying as Grace walked into the kitchen.

Sensing the tension, Grace asked, "I'm sorry, am I intruding?"

"Grace, I didn't know you were here," Diana said warmly.

"Have you had any luck?" Melodie asked, still glaring at her aunt.

Deciding not to join them at the table, Grace stood by the kitchen island. "Yes, as a matter of fact, Beth said she purposely recorded the slideshow. You remember, she was going around recording everything that night."

Finally turning to look at Grace, Melodie laughed. "You'll be lucky if she remembered to turn the thing on."

Seeing Diana's look of confusion Grace explained what she was looking for and why, before asking if she had seen the pictures Crystal had used for the slideshow.

Diana slowly nodded. "I don't see how they could help. There were only a couple of shots of Sam. His yearbook photo. There was one of him and Crystal. I remember it was their prom photo. There was one of him as a little boy with a train set, I think. A couple of him in his football uniform. A couple of school photos. That was about it. I don't remember seeing anything unusual."

"Grace, I think you're wasting your time," Melodie said pouring more sugar in her tea. "Even if you saw it, what could you possibly learn?"

"I won't know until I see it," Grace explained, reasonably.

"Wait," Diana said excitedly. "There were a couple of pictures of Sam by the lake. It looked like it was taken at James Simpson's lake house."

"Was there anyone with him?"

"Um, Tom was in one of them."

"Of course, you would mention that one," Melodie said testily. "I remember that one, too. In fact, I'm the one who took that picture of them. Trust me, it wasn't anything special."

"What were they doing?" Grace asked.

"What do you think?" Melodie snapped. "They were standing and smiling at the camera. That's it." Sighing audibly, she added. "Honestly, Grace, you are on a wild goose chase. Why don't you go find Kyle and tell him I need to see him, immediately? Please."

"You call him and tell him yourself. I'm going to go to Beth's house and watch the video. Do me a favor. If you get a hold of him, tell him where I am."

"Isn't Beth at work?" Diana asked. "I thought she works at the comic book store part time nowadays."

"She said she'd leave a key under the mat. Can one of you give me a ride there?"

Melodie turned to her aunt. "Eric is coming by to pick you up in few minutes, isn't he?"

Diana nodded and smiled at Grace. "We can drop you off."

"I don't want to impose," Grace said, wishing once more she owned a car or, at the very least, a bike. She was getting tired of depending on the kindness of anyone with a car.

Speaking for her aunt, Melodie said, "Nonsense. They were going out anyway."

CHAPTER TWENTY

KYLE WALKED THE dirty hallway, searching for room 108. When Steve Mattingly called and asked Kyle to meet him at Steve's brand new office, Kyle didn't really expect to find Steve's office in a large high rise with a downstairs security guard, but he never expected to find it in a rundown office building with loose flooring, bad lightening, and graffiti, either. If this dilapidated building isn't already condemned, it should be, Kyle thought miserably, as he watched a small mouse scurry across the floor. The only thing keeping him from turning around and leaving was the fact that Steve had something important to tell him. Kyle hoped that the *something* was about Crystal's death and not just another job pitch.

Turning another corner, Kyle finally found room 108. Taped to the door was a piece of notebook paper, with the words *Mattingly Private Investigations – No case is too small* printed in red ink.

Smiling, Kyle gently pushed the door open. To his surprise, a large cavernous dance studio, complete with wall mirrors and mounted ballet bars, lay behind the old, wooden, double doors. Shaking his head, he walked past the threshold. The studio was virtually empty, but at the far end of the room, he could just make out an old desk, an antiquated hutch, and a couple of rickety lawn chairs. Quietly, shutting the door, Kyle began the trek to the back of the room. The sound of his new boots, hitting the hardwood floors, echoed throughout the room.

Steve sat facing the hutch, furiously typing away at the desktop computer. Hearing footsteps behind him, Steve called out, "Just have a seat. I'll be right with you."

Kyle looked down at the dirty green lawn chair facing the desk. Reaching out, he gingerly, pulled the lawn chair back and sat down, only to quickly jump up, when the cheap, plastic chair legs' began to buckle. "Thanks. I think I'll stand."

Steve stopped typing and turned around. A small grin spread over his face. "Well, look who it is. Just the person I wanted to see."

Kyle felt a shiver go down his spine. It wasn't so much what Steve said as how he said it. "I got your message. What's so urgent that you had to see me right now?"

"I'm considering expanding my business. How does Mattingly and Drake sound to you?"

"Crowded. I'm flattered, but I like to work alone," he said, turning around and walking to the door.

"You know, you're a real interesting guy. Big time detective from New York, comes to our small little town, investigating the crime of the year. Hobnobbing with our town elites. Besides the murder, you're all this town has to talk about."

Turning around, Kyle shrugged. "I think everyone would be better served if we focused our attention on finding Crystal's murderer."

"I'm more interested in you, personally. You know what's strange. I can't really find anything on Kyle Drake, the big time detective. Funny, you think I would."

Feeling his heart speed up, Kyle said, "I like to keep a low profile."

Steve smiled. "Oh, I'm sure. You know, the night of the reunion, I remembered you telling us about some of your more exciting cases. You were kind of vague on who your clients were."

"I'm sorry." Kyle shook his head. "I'm not really at liberty to divulge—"

"And I wouldn't expect you to. Not a professional like you. But I distinctly remembered you mentioning how you investigated a murder of a magician's assistant last Halloween. It only took a couple of minutes to discover the victim's name." He looked down at his notes. "Lily Straker. So, just out of professional curiosity, you understand, I decided to call the victim's husband. He wasn't available, but I was able to speak to his son-in-law, Allen," Steve said, fumbling through his notes, "here it is, Allen Madison, Vice President of the Straker Toy Company."

Kyle smoothed his features. He had been on stage enough times to learn to hide his emotions from his audience. "What did he have to say?"

"He was rather reluctant to talk to me but he did confirm that you are a detective and that you were hired to find Lily Straker's killer."

Kyle smiled. "There you go."

Steve scrunched up his face. "Yeah . . . here's the problem. You work at this type of job long enough you start to learn pretty quickly if someone is lying to you. Madison was very vague, and frankly, he sounded like he couldn't wait to get off the phone."

"Well, don't take it personally, that's just the way he is."

"Now, Jackie King, on the other hand, was very friendly."

Kyle felt his heart sink into his chest.

"You remember Jackie, don't you?" Steve asked, leaning back in his chair. "She definitely remembered you. But here's the interesting thing, she seemed rather confused when I told her you were a detective. In fact, she laughed. She thought I was joking. We didn't get to talk for long, but before she hung up, I did find out something pretty interesting. According to Jackie, Kyle Drake, isn't your real name. She said it's your stage name."

Kyle thought quickly. "I'm afraid she's a bit confused. I was undercover."

Steve shook his head. "No. No," he said slowly, "Jackie seemed rather certain that you are, in fact, Aleksis Dragovich. She also hinted that Grace was fooling around with the boss which I thought was rather strange. Grace didn't seem like that type of woman."

Kyle smirked. Apparently, Grace was going to have to have another talk with Jackie.

"Anyway, once I hung up with her, I discovered that Aleksis Dragovich is a stage magician. Unfortunately, not nearly as good as his famous father, who by the way, really wants to talk to you."

Kyle blanched. "You called—"

"Why, yes I did. Just before you came in. He didn't sound too happy with what I had to say. You know, you don't sound Russian at all."

"I'm not. My father is." Kyle closed his eyes. To be honest, he didn't expect this to last this long. Opening his eyes, he decided to do as much damage control as possible for Grace's sake. "Grace doesn't know. She really thinks I'm a detective."

"How did you two meet?"

"She was working as a designer at the toy company. I wasn't hired as a detective, but I really was there investigating Lily Straker's death. After it was over, I lied to Grace and told her that I was a detective and that I was only pretending to be a magician. That it was part of my cover." Kyle shrugged. "She bought it and I eventually convinced her to come work with me. I guess, I was trying to impress her." Kyle looked back to the door. "Have you told the police?"

"The police? Why would I talk to them? This is just between the two of us."

Kyle looked at the man sitting across the desk. Realization dawning, he asked, "How much do you want?"

"I don't want money."

At Kyle's disbelieving look, he added, "I want to be your partner. You are setting yourself up pretty well here. Meeting all our esteemed town leaders. I hear you're already ensconced at the Gold Rush Country Club. The only way I can get into that place is if I take a job as a golf caddie and even then I probably couldn't pass the background check. Look, I just want us to work together. I see no reason why we can't help each other out."

Considering, Kyle asked. "What do you want?"

"First off, we'll team up. I personally like Mattingly and Drake, but I'm flexible. I'm no fool. I see you. You're handsome, charming, educated. You're the whole package. You walk into the room and everyone's head turns. You're our draw. With your natural abilities, you'll be able to pull in the wealthier clients. So, I'm okay with calling us Drake and Mattingly Investigations, as long as I take part in some of the glory."

Kyle felt queasy. "What else?"

"Secondly, we'll use this office."

Kyle looked around the dance studio and smiled. "This isn't exactly what I have in mind."

"Really, pretty boy? You got the capital to get us something nicer?" Steve asked. "Yeah, I don't think so. I'm betting you've already blown through whatever you've gotten from Adam and Melodie, but that's okay, because I'm looking towards the future. Don't worry, with the right clients, we'll be able to upgrade in a year or two."

"Anything else?" Kyle snapped.

"Third, Grace has to go," Steve said.

"Not an option."

"Now, don't get upset. I can see you're a loyal guy. I admire that. Really, I do. And don't get me wrong. I like Grace. I always have. She was actually one of the nicer ones in school. That's why I don't want to see her get hurt."

"What do you mean by that?" Kyle asked worriedly.

"What do you think? She almost died in the fire the other day. You too. This is a dangerous business. Me? I can take care of myself. And you look like you can handle yourself in a fight. Grace, on the other hand. She could get hurt."

"Your concern is touching, but she's tougher than she looks."

"I'm not just talking about getting hurt physically. I mean emotionally, too. She likes you. I can tell. What is she going to do when she finds out you're a complete fraud? She's going to be devastated. Worse, she's going to turn you in. This is something you probably don't know about Grace. She is a stickler for rules.

If she finds out that you're a fake, she will run to the police. You can bank on that. She'll blow everything out of the water."

Kyle felt like laughing. "I think I can handle her."

"It's too risky. There's too big of a chance that you'll screw up and say something. She's actually pretty sharp, you know. I'm surprised she hasn't already suspected something. She's probably just hung up on your looks. That won't last. Once she finds out. She'll kill you."

"I'll take my chances."

"Fine. She might as well find out early. Do you want to call and confess, or do you want me to do it?" Steve picked up the phone and held it out.

Kyle took the phone and placed it back in the cradle. "How about a new deal? When I find out who killed these people, I'll make sure you share in the credit. Think of it as free publicity."

"You're still investigating, then? Surprising. Sheriff Bo Bo thinks he has this all wrapped up. As of this morning, the official police statement is that Adam killed Crystal and then offed himself because the police were closing in on him."

"Do you believe that?"

Steve snorted. "No. Adam was an egotist. There is no way he would have killed himself in some rinky-dink shack in the middle of nowhere. He certainly wouldn't have left a simple little note. The man thought he was the next Cecil B. DeMille. If he had tried to kill himself, he would have made a gigantic production out of it. Who do you think killed Crystal and Adam?"

"You mean beside yourself."

Steve leaned back in his chair and laugh. "Why would I kill either one of them?

"Crystal was blackmailing you and you obviously hated Adam."

"Blackmailing me? For what?"

"You attacked that artist Melodie dated after graduation. I heard that you almost killed him."

"That's a lie," Steve said calmly.

"You didn't push him down a flight of stairs? You didn't destroy his paintings?"

"I didn't push him down and I didn't destroy anything. I saw Melodie run out of his studio one day, crying. She was hysterical. The jerk was still cursing at her from his door, so I went over there and told him to knock it off. I'll admit, I did threaten him. I told him that if he didn't leave her alone, he would be sorry. I was trying to protect her. Not that she appreciated it. She's always had horrible taste in men. But I didn't try to kill him."

"Someone pushed Hart down a flight of stairs and broke his collarbone. If it wasn't you, then who?"

Steve's face turned red. "Larry Baker. I never understood what Melodie saw in him. He was a violent, alcoholic, jealous thug. He's the one who pushed Hart."

"There's a problem with your theory. Larry didn't know what had happened between Melodie and David. She said she never told him."

"She didn't . . . but I did. I ran into Larry right after I confronted Hart. I told Larry what happened. He was furious," Steve smiled in remembrance. "It was the first time Larry ever thanked me. I found Hart lying at the bottom of those stairs not more than ten minutes later. Larry was just getting in his car and driving away."

Kyle leaned against the mirrored wall. He still wasn't convinced. It was easy to put the blame on a dead guy, but he had to admit Steve wasn't saying anything Grace hadn't already suspected.

"Do you know that Crystal told Melodie that you were the one who attacked David?"

Steve frowned. "I'm not surprised. Crystal was afraid Melodie was falling in love with me. Melodie and I have a rather odd relationship. She's only ever been nice to me when others aren't around to see. I think she's embarrassed to admit that she actually likes me. Anyway, after I stood up to Hart, she started treating me nicer. I think she liked how I told that creep off. Crystal saw that Melodie was warming up to me and wasn't happy about it. I wasn't good enough for her sister. A Harper marrying a Mattingly? She couldn't have that."

Feeling slightly sorry for the other man, Kyle said, "I didn't know you two were an item at one time."

"We went on a couple of dates, but then a week later, she turned cold and started dating Larry again. I guess that's when Crystal told her I was the dangerous dude who almost killed her ex." Steve leaned back in his chair and chuckled. "I'm actually surprised that Melodie didn't come running to me after that. She likes dangerous guys. After that description, I should've been peeling her off me."

"Why did you leave town?"

"Larry Baker told me that if I didn't leave Melodie alone he would kill me."

"And you believed him?"

"Absolutely."

"Then why did you come back?"

"Crystal hired me. It was nothing major," he said waving a hand, dismissively.

"Let me guess, she hired you to take pictures of Larry and a prostitute, didn't she?"

"Melodie told you that?" Steve sighed. "All right. Yes. Crystal paid quite a lot, too. It wasn't as if I enjoyed it. Well, maybe a little. I hated Larry." Steve looked Kyle in the eye. "I know what you're thinking, but you're wrong. I didn't push Hart. Crystal was not blackmailing me. And I've never killed anyone. It's not me, pretty boy. Who else do you have?"

Running his hand through his hair, Kyle sighed. "Pretty much all of your friends. In fact, there are only a few that aren't on our suspect list."

"I hear Grace has been at Melodie's house all morning, burning up her phone, calling practically everyone who was there that night. She's been asking about that stupid flash drive and whether they saw the slideshow. Why? What is she looking for?"

"She is just following up on some loose ends."

"Melodie told me that you suspect Sam was murdered. Is that true?"

"Did you see the slideshow?"

"Yeah, of course I did, but I didn't see anything that would point to who killed Crystal or him. They were just your normal everyday pictures. Certainly nothing to kill for. Has Grace found any copies, yet?"

Before arriving at Steve's office, Kyle had finally reached Grace, who told him about Beth's video. "Maybe. A few," Kyle hedged.

"Where is she right now?"

Kyle turned away.

"Come on. I could have gone straight to the police and told them you've been lying to everyone if I wanted to. I came to you first because I want to work with you. I want you to trust me. I want us to be friends," Steve implored.

"We can be friends when you're not a suspect."

Steve sighed. Turning back to his desk, he picked up his phone and dialed. "Melodie? . . . Wait! Don't hang up. I just want to know if Grace is there. . . . No? . . . She's at Beth's?" Smiling, Steve turned towards Kyle. "Chasing a wild goose, you don't say? I need—" Making a face Steve placed the receiver back into its cradle. "She and her sister have or had the worst manners of anyone I've ever known. In case you didn't know, Grace is at Beth's."

"Why do you even need me?" Kyle asked, frustrated. "You obviously can do quite well by yourself."

"I can't do everything. I'm persona non grata among many of the elites in town. We can be allies, though. I help you, and you help me."

"Fine. Tell me about the pictures."

"It's a waste of time."

"I don't have anywhere else to be."

Steve began ticking off the pictures on his hand. "There was one of him as a kid, a couple of him playing football, a prom picture of him and Crystal, one of him outside, one of him at the lake. Like I said, absolutely none of them worth dying over. Now my turn. Let's suppose Sam was murdered. Who do you think did it?"

"We don't know at this point, but," Kyle hesitated unsure of how much information he wanted to give the other man, "one of our suspects—one out of many you understand—is Eric Collins."

"Why would he have killed Sam?"

"I heard a rumor that Collins may have killed his wife. Sam may have witnessed her murder. If that's true, then it's possible Sam was blackmailing Eric. I've been told that Sam came into some money that year." Kyle decided not to mention Eric's alibi, since he was still trying to figure how Tom was involved. Did Eric pay off Sam and Tom to keep them both quiet?

Steve sat quietly for a moment absorbing this new bit of information. "The money? It came from the insurance company."

"Are you sure?"

"No, but I can't see Sam blackmailing Collins. Crystal would, but I doubt Sam would have. Sam was a boy scout. If Collins had killed his wife, Sam wouldn't have been able to keep quiet."

"Maybe that's why he was killed. One theory is that he wanted to tell the police what he saw."

"Maybe," he said, sounding unconvinced. "All right, you said one suspect out of many. Who else do you have?"

"Actually, I should be asking you that question. He was your friend. Did he have any enemies?"

Steve shook his head. "No. Absolutely no one. Everyone loved him. Well, except for Hope, but she didn't hate him. She just tolerated him."

Kyle hated asking, but he had to know what Steve would say. "Do you think she could have killed him?"

"I don't think so. I mean, she could have done it. He was pretty weak after the accident, and if the bell tower's ledge was low enough . . . I mean, physically it's possible that she could have pushed him over, but I can't see it. It's Hope. She might have mussed her hair or broken a fingernail and right before graduation pictures? No. No way. Do you have other suspects?"

"Hmm. Maybe. But I have a question for you. Why aren't you at Tom's place right now?"

"Why would I be?"

Glancing down at his wristwatch, Kyle said, "Because Sheriff Bellamy is getting a search warrant and should be there by now."

Within seconds, Kyle found himself alone in the office.

♕   ♕   ♕

Sitting in Beth's basement/entertainment room, Grace watched as the sun finally disappeared behind the trees in Beth's backyard. When she had arrived at Beth's home, she had high hopes that she would be able to quickly start the video and fast forward to the point Beth had recorded the memorial slideshow. Believing it wouldn't take more than twenty minutes tops, she had called her family and told them she would be home, long before the sun set. That turned out to be a hopelessly foolish prediction. It had taken thirty minutes and two phone calls to Beth just to find where she had placed the video and another forty minutes, turning all the pictures of clowns, figurines of clowns and most importantly the stuffed clown dolls around and facing the wall, before she could even think of getting started. Grace had never been afraid of clowns. Had never thought twice about clowns, but sitting in Beth's furnished basement, completely alone, surrounded by nothing but clowns, began to unnerve her.

Once she had turned the last clown picture around and was comfortably sitting on Beth's couch, Grace hit the fast forward button. Having fast forward through the video twice she came to the unhappy realization she was going to have to sit through all four hours.

She was halfway through when her cell phone rang.

"About time you called me back, Kyle. I've been calling for the last hour," she complained. "Where have you been?"

"Sorry. My dad needed to talk to me about something. Any luck?"

"None, but I have . . ." she paused in order to glance at her watch, "two hours left. So, did Steve have any information about Crystal's murder?"

"Not really."

"Well, unless something turns up on this video, I think we're stuck."

"How's it going?"

Groaning she said, "Dreadful. I don't understand how my sister—my flesh and blood—could have let me walk out of the house in that getup."

"It wasn't that bad," he said soothingly.

Grace cringed. "Kyle, I'm looking at myself right now. It's far worse on camera." Grace cringed as Beth caught Grace from behind, tripping over her dress. She fast forwarded the tape until she was finally, mercifully, out of the frame. "I'm 'accidentally' destroying this tape as soon as I'm done."

"Don't do that. I want to see it."

Grace groaned at the sound of a door opening upstairs.

"What?"

"Beth's home. I was hoping to have this done by the time she came home." When Beth had reminded Grace of the videotape, she had offered to watch it with Grace later that night. She had suggested making it a girls' video night. Still reeling from the last girls' video night with Beth, Grace firmly insisted on watching it alone and immediately. Unfortunately, it looked like she was going to have company.

"Were you aware that Crystal had filed for divorce from Tom three months ago? She and Tom went on a cruise for their anniversary. They returned three days early, and she filed for divorce as soon as she got off the ship. She stopped the divorce proceedings a month later. Right after that they began seeing a doctor about fertility issues."

"Where did you hear that?"

"Steve has a computer file on Crystal. As well as, all of Crystal's families and friends. I'm looking through it right now. You should see the file he has on Melodie. We are talking detailed. Pages and pages of information. He has a folder with over a hundred pictures of her. I think he may be a little obsessed with your friend."

"How did you get into his computer? Kyle, he's going to call the police if he catches you," she said worriedly.

Kyle snorted. "Relax. Steve and I are good friends now. He's not going to call the police."

"Why do you sound so strange? What's going on?" she demanded, suddenly suspicious.

"Nothing. Would you stop worrying? This is weird. Crystal had been trying to keep Diana and Eric apart."

"Diana and I caught them arguing at the reunion. She was warning Eric to stay away from her aunt," Grace pointed out. "Does it say anything else about them?" she asked, getting up off the couch and walking upstairs and into Beth's kitchen. Seeing it empty, she opened the door to the garage. Empty as well. Checking the back door and walking through the hallway to the front door she found both locked.

"Let's see." Grace could hear the sound of Kyle's fingers on the keyboard. "Crystal tried to set up Collins with an English teacher at the school, but Collins didn't want anything to do with her."

"I got the same feeling that day at the school. He looked like he couldn't wait to get her out the door. Although, they did seem friendly when they went out the night after the reunion. I hope he and Diana can work it out. She was so in love with him. I felt so bad for her when he left her for her best friend."

"Oh, I haven't had a chance to tell you. I got the file on Sarah Collins' death investigation from James Simpson. Diana has an alibi."

"Good."

"It's pretty solid, but Eric Collins, on the other hand, was the police's most likely suspect. Unfortunately for them, someone corroborated his whereabouts at the time of his wife's death. Guess who provided him with an alibi?"

"I have no idea."

"Tom. The sheriff didn't really believe him, but couldn't come up with any other evidence."

"What was Eric's motive?"

"Sarah was having an affair. They couldn't figure out with who."

"Interesting." Grace looked around the kitchen. Clowns could be found in every corner. Their glass eyes shown in the light. She just couldn't shake the feeling that she was being watched. "Kyle, when are you going to get here?" Feeling unsettled, Grace turned around and let out a small shriek, dropping her cell phone in the process. Heart beating fast, she bent down to retrieve the phone.

"What happened?" Kyle asked worriedly.

"I hate this house. I thought someone was behind me, so I turned around really fast and ran right into this big stuffed clown." Grace looked at its huge stuffed face with one eye missing. "It's the creepiest thing I've ever seen. Funny, this place wasn't so scary when Beth was here," she said, suddenly wishing she had taken Beth up on her offer.

"Isn't Beth there?"

"No, I thought she was. She should be here any minute though," Grace said, walking back downstairs and into the basement. "Anything else?"

"There's a file on Adam," Kyle said. "When are—"

Grace looked toward the ceiling. "I think . . ." she started to say before tilting her head to the side. Straining to listen, she heard nothing but the sound of a car passing on the street. She shook her head. "Sorry. This place is getting on my nerves. Anything else?"

"You know, I can be there in less than fifteen minutes."

Feeling guilty and a little foolish at her nervousness, she forced a laugh. "Don't be silly. I'm perfectly fine, besides, Beth and her family will be here in a few minutes," she said, more to reassure herself than him at the moment. "Keep reading."

"Well, this is interesting. I opened up the file on Adam. Turns out Steve knew Adam and Crystal were working on a deal to make a movie about what she knew. Quote, Adam is looking for Crystal's scrapbook, too, unquote. Following that is a list of times and dates. It looks like he had been following Adam.

According to the date and time here, he was following Adam the night you and he broke into the school."

"No wonder he got to the police station so quickly."

"I wonder why he didn't let Bellamy know Adam had been there, too. Oh . . ."

"What?"

"I think I just found the smoking gun. Listen to this, Steve followed Tom after the reunion. Apparently, Tom didn't go straight home. He went to the Moxley house first. He was there all night. Hey, have you heard the latest? That's where they found the murder weapon. They found all three trophies buried in a duffle bag in the back yard. They also found three purple silk strands on the murder weapon. They're trying to connect them to Tom right now."

"Diana told the police that night that she saw Tom carry a black duffle bag to his car," Grace said reflectively.

"And Steve watched him go straight to the Moxley House after the reunion."

"How much you want to bet that Tom has Hope's missing wrap, too."

Excitedly Kyle said, "That's it! That's where those three strands came from. Tom must have killed Crystal and wiped down the murder weapon with Hope's wrap. He then buried the weapons in the back yard. I wonder if Bellamy's found any more evidence, yet."

"We're still missing something. If Tom killed Crystal, then who killed Sam?" she asked softly.

"I don't know, but I think we should talk to the police. I wonder why Steve hasn't said anything to them . . . Grace? . . . Are you still there?"

Grace tilted her head. "That's got to be Beth this time. I just heard a door shut," she said, walking up the steps. She pushed open the door to the kitchen. "Beth?"

Sudden darkness caused her to freeze. There was just enough light from the window to see the door slowly open the rest of the way. The next instant a dark figure darted out of the garage, hurtling straight for her.

Reflexively, Grace threw up her hand as her attacker pushed her back. Unbalanced and with nothing behind her, she toppled down the stairs.

CHAPTER TWENTY-ONE

SOMEONE WAS CRYING. Her brain sluggishly processed this bit of information as she slowly struggled to open her eyes. Basic awareness came next. She was lying on her stomach. The ground beneath her was hard and cold. She could feel someone gently stroking her hair, whispering her name. Kyle, she thought. Next, came pain, hitting her hard, causing her suck in a breath and open her eyes.

She jerked back, causing pain to shoot through her body.

Surrounding her were four of the most frightening faces she had ever seen. Heart thudding, she tried to sit up, but strong hands held her down.

Their voices were set in a high-pitched wail. Their faces were twisted and ravaged: white and cakey, with huge red bulbous noses, gigantic mouths, and frightful multicolored hair. Battling through the pain, it took her mind a few moments to realize she was looking at the very worried and upset faces of Beth and her children; for some bizarre reason, all dressed up as clowns.

Finally remembering where she was, she tried to lift her head, only to have the hand softly stroking her hair, tighten and hold her still.

"Grace, please don't move. The ambulance will be here in just a minute," Kyle whispered, sounding suspiciously close to tears.

Closing her eyes, Grace reflexively tested her muscles. Except for the excruciating pain in her arm, she seemed to be all in one piece.

Opening her eyes again, she found herself face to face with Beth, who was still sobbing her heart out.

Trying to get some semblance of order, Kyle begged Beth to take the kids upstairs. Four pairs of large red feet stomped past Grace's head and disappeared from view.

Realizing that the night was literally turning into a three-ring circus, Grace again struggled to sit up, only to have Kyle push her back down and order her not to move.

"Kyle? The video."

"What?" he asked, lying down next to her.

"Is it still here?"

Disbelief crossed his face. "I don't know or care. Just stay still. The ambulance is on its way."

After a few minutes of argument, Kyle stood up and crossed the room to check the video recorder, giving Grace enough time to finally have her way and sit up.

"I think my arm's broken," she said, carefully holding it against her chest.

"I told you to sit still," he snapped. Frustrated, Kyle turned back around and shook his head. "Who ever tried to kill you, took the video with them."

♆ ♆ ♆

Kyle sat on the leather sofa in the living room, glaring at the women seated a few feet away in the dining room. Silently cursing the emergency system in this town, he checked his watch again. Twenty minutes had passed since he made the call to nine-one-one. Twenty minutes and no sign of an ambulance. Twenty minutes of pure torture.

Despite his better judgment, Grace had insisted in coming upstairs. She then insisted on not being treated like an invalid. Kyle tried arguing with her. Tried convincing her to lie down in one of the spare bedrooms until the ambulance came, but Grace would have none of it.

Happy that Grace wasn't dead, Beth surprisingly took her side. She quickly ushered Grace into the hallway bathroom to help her clean up. They emerged three minutes later with Grace's arm in a makeshift sling and sat down at the table where Beth related the harrowing experience of finding Grace at the bottom of the basement steps. Neither Kyle nor Grace asked where the family had been, or why they were dressed like clowns. Kyle wasn't sure he wanted to know.

"It was just so scary! Coming home and finding you like that." Beth said, draping another quilt over Grace's shoulders. "I just can't believe it."

Grace nodded her head. "Neither can I. Was anything else stolen?"

Beth shook her head. "Not that I can tell. It seems it was just the video. It's just so strange that they would take that video. But the weirdest part is that they turned all of my pictures and dolls to the wall. Why would the killer do something like that?"

Adopting a completely innocent expression, Grace shook her head and shrugged her uninjured shoulder. "Weird."

"I think we are dealing with someone really disturbed," Beth said, her multicolored wig bobbing up and down. "A true sicko."

Hearing the siren, Kyle breathed a sigh of relief, while Beth, still in costume, rushed out of the house to greet the ambulance.

Mark sat in the armchair next to the sofa. Taking the green wig off his head, he looked Kyle in the eye and pointed to his wife. Using his other hand, he pointed his index finger towards his temple as he made a twirling motion.

Kyle nodded his head. "I hear you, buddy."

♈ ♈ ♈

Grace stirred. She was lying on her side facing the hospital door. The clock on the table next to her said seven twenty a.m. She closed her eyes. Everything was quiet. Her parents must have gone to the cafeteria for breakfast. She had gotten very little sleep, what with family, police, doctors, and nurses traipsing in and out of the room all night. All because of a broken wrist, a little bump on the head and some minor dizziness. She had tried to convince her parents to go home, but after Bellamy had refused to provide police protection, they had insisted on taking turns keeping watch. Turning over on her back, she yawned, and sleepily wondered when they were going to be back and more importantly if they were going to bring her something to eat.

As she lay back, pondering her breakfast options, the door quietly opened. Without opening her eyes, she asked if they brought her any coffee or a donut, at the very least.

"Sorry, I didn't come bearing gifts."

Grace's eyes flew open. Tom had walked the rest of the way in and was standing beside her bed. Worried, she asked, "Where's my family? What have you done with them?"

Tom smirked. "Relax. They're fine. Your mom went to change clothes and your dad just left to get some coffee. He asked me to watch over you for a few minutes."

Stunned, Grace sank back down. She was seriously going to have to have a talk with her dad on what his definition of 'keeping watch' actually meant.

"I told you to stay out of this, Grace. You're lucky you just have a broken arm and a knock on the head. You could have died."

"I thought you would be in jail, by now," she said, reaching a hand down to grab the call button.

"Why? Because of that search warrant?" he smirked. "They spent all afternoon searching and didn't turn up anything. They're not going to find anything, either."

Pressing the call button, she asked, "Someone saw you carry a black duffle bag out of the high school. Someone else saw you go straight to the Moxley house later that night. The same place where they found the murder weapon hidden inside a black duffle bag. I think even Bellamy can connect the dots."

He laughed. "Unfortunately, it's not going to do them any good. It's just such a shame they didn't have a warrant when they dug up my back yard. Ever heard of the fruit of the poisonous tree? Since they searched my property without a warrant, they won't be able to introduce the murder weapon or say where they found it. Without that, they don't really have anything tying me to the murder. And that duffle bag *someone* says she saw me carry out? Well, it could have contained anything. I had helped my wife plan the reunion. Crystal brought a lot of stuff to the high school that night. No one can prove that the duffle bag contained anything other than extra party favors, and balloons. Not that I'm admitting to carrying any such duffle bag, you understand."

"What about Hope's wrap? That's what you used to wipe off the trophies, isn't it? They haven't found that yet. Once they do—"

He leaned over her. "They're not going to find Hope's wrap."

"Why Tom? Why did you do it?" Grace still couldn't believe that the boy she had grown up with, that she so easily would have accepted into her family, could have turned into such a monster.

"Have you ever wondered why I cut off all ties with Hope? Have you ever wondered why I married Crystal, Grace?

"It wasn't for love, was it?"

Tom laughed bitterly. "As a matter of fact, it was. I'm going to give you some very good advice Grace, and I want you to take it. Leave. Go back to New York and if you love your sister, if you value her safety, take her with you. Leave, before you both get hurt."

Their heads swung around as the door opened and Hope walked in.

"Well, speak of the devil," he said, smiling as he turned to leave.

Before Tom could walk out the door, Grace asked, "What about Sam? Did he really commit suicide?"

Tom reached out to gently caress Hope's cheek. "Ask your sister. She should know. She tends to have a bad habit of being in the wrong place at the wrong time."

♈ ♈ ♈

Grace sat at the table trying not to notice the creepy clown painting hanging in Beth's 1950s retro kitchen. Everywhere she stood, the clown's dead eyes watched her. It was a completely unnerving feeling. Especially, after the night before.

Suddenly, a coffee cup in the shape of a clown head was thrust into her good hand. Grace looked up as Beth sat down across from her. Beth was her last hope.

"Beth, do you remember—"

"Are you excited? I bet you're excited! Oh, it's just like a fairytale!" she said, accidentally spilling her coffee on the table.

Grace reached for a napkin to prevent the coffee from spilling over the edge of the table. Oblivious, Beth continued, "I'm just so happy for her! Aren't you?"

"Who are you talking about?" Grace asked in confusion. As far as she knows none of her friends or acquaintances had anything to be particularly happy about.

"Don't be coy! I want all the details," she said excitedly. At Grace's confused look, Beth added, "I'm talking about Kyle Drake and Melodie, of course. I saw them at the country club the other day. They make such a beautiful couple.'

At Grace's less than enthusiastic expression, Beth asked, "Aren't you happy they found each other?"

"Oh yes, I can't begin to describe how happy I am," Grace said, trying to keep the sarcasm out of her voice or at least sound less sarcastic. After her near death experience, she had made a vow to be a little less sarcastic. It was wasted on Beth anyway, since she never seemed to notice. Unfortunately, it was getting harder and harder to keep her vow.

"See, I knew you would be happy for her. Some people in town are saying it's too soon. I can understand their point. I mean, Larry only died a couple of months ago, but if two people love each other . . . I just don't think time should stand in the way. Do you think they may get married soon?"

Grace choked on her coffee. "If they do, I hope they name their first born after me," Grace said, deciding some resolutions were made to be broken.

The next ten minutes was spent listening to Beth discuss possible wedding venues, whether Melodie would wear white again, Melodie's first wedding, Beth's wedding and finally why Grace wasn't married yet, before Grace finally was able to focus Beth's attention onto the subject of the slideshow, and if she had seen any of the pictures of Sam.

"Let me see . . ." she said, tapping her forehead with her finger. "There were a couple of Sam playing football. One of him when he was five; I think he was playing with a train set. I bought a train set for my boys a few years ago. They were so cute. I think the older toys—"

"Beth, the pictures," Grace insisted, desperately attempting to refocus the other woman's thoughts.

"Oh yes, there were a couple of school pictures. I always hated my school pictures . . ."

Grace decided to make herself comfortable. The best thing to do in these circumstances was to just let Beth talk. Eventually, Beth would get back on track. Grace took a peek outside.

It was pretty outside. Much prettier than the clown painting hanging behind Beth's head, staring at her. Grace glanced back at Beth, who had launched into a description of how her mother used to style her hair before picture day.

Ten minutes passed with little comment from Grace except the occasional "hmm" and "oh." She started to take another drink, when Beth's last words registered in Grace's mind.

"I mean, I think it was in really poor taste. I don't know why Crystal used that picture of Sam in the slideshow," she said, clucking her tongue and shaking her head. "Personally, I would have chosen a nicer photo of him. I have a really nice one that was taken in our junior year—oh here, let me go find it," she said standing up.

Grace grabbed Beth's hand and brought her back down. "What was wrong with the picture, exactly?"

"Well, I just don't think they should have used it. I mean, that's where he died."

Containing her excitement, Grace pressed for more details.

"It was just a picture of Sam standing up at the top of the bell tower," Beth explained.

"Could you tell when it was taken?"

"No, but it must have been taken right after his car accident."

"How do you know that?"

"He was covered in bruises. From his neck all the way down."

Grace repeated the words back in her mind. "From his neck down? Didn't he have any clothes on?" she asked.

"I couldn't tell. The picture was from his waist up. He had a blanket wrapped around his shoulders."

"Anything else? Try to remember, Beth." Grace asked, hoping someone else might be included in the picture.

"Oh, is this about your investigation? This is so exciting. Did Mr. Drake send you to talk to me?" Beth asked, jumping up and down in her seat.

"Beth! The picture. What was in the picture?"

"Okay. Let me see," Beth said suddenly excited. "The picture was taken in the bell tower. Sam was standing up. He was right next to the bell. He wasn't wearing a shirt, but he did have a red blanket wrapped around his shoulders. Um, you could see the school in the background. Oh, what else…" she said trying to remember. "Oh, I know, um, it was so cold outside. You could see his breath in the picture."

"What was he doing? I mean, was he smiling? Frowning?"

"Well, you know how when you try to take someone's picture, and they don't want their picture taken, how they cover their face with their hands?"

Grace nodded.

"My kids do that all the time. You should see my photo album—"

"I would love to, but let's focus, Beth. What else can you tell me about the picture?"

"Well, that's what he was doing. He was covering his face with his hand. He seemed to be laughing or crying. I'm not sure which. I think he may have been crying. Oh, oh, I know what you are looking for," waiving her hands around excitedly. "He had something in his other hand."

"What was it?"

Beth scrunched up her face. "I don't know. I just remember one hand was in front of his face, and another was holding something. It kind of looked like someone was pushing him back, and he was holding their wrist. It must have been the person who was taking the picture because it was directly in front of the camera."

Excited Grace asked, "Are you sure it wasn't taken at graduation?"

"No. It definitely wasn't at graduation. The picture was taken during the winter. I could see snow and icicles in the background. It looked like a winter wonderland behind him. Remember how hot it was during graduation? I remember, Hope saying it was so hot she wasn't going to wear anything under her gown. I wore a handmade outfit. Remember?" she asked, pushing herself from the table. "It's upstairs. I bet I can still fit in it. Do you want to see?"

Grabbing Beth's hand to keep her from leaving, Grace asked excitedly, "Could you tell who it was that was pushing him?"

"No," at Grace's crestfallen expression, she added, "but why don't you ask Melodie? She was standing right next to me when I was recording the slideshow. I think she agreed with me. It just wasn't right to include that picture."

"Why? What did she say?"

"Oh, she didn't say anything, but I could tell by her expression that she was really mad though."

♈ ♈ ♈

"That's it?" Kyle asked. "Why would anyone care about that picture?"

"Well, it is of Sam on the Bell Tower, apparently being pushed," Grace pointed out.

"Yeah, unfortunately, several months before he fell. Since, it doesn't show the other person's face, it doesn't really help. Besides, I doubt the murderer was putting in a practice run and taking a picture at the same time."

"No, of course not! But what was Sam doing out on the Bell Tower in the middle of winter? How did he get up there? Who was he with? What were they doing up there? If you can't see the other person's face, then what could be so damaging that he would kill to keep us from finding the picture?"

Kyle shrugged, "So, what's next?"

Grace shook her head, as she threw her purse onto the motel's bed. "I have no idea. I thought for sure it would have some sort of clue."

"Maybe Beth left something out?"

Grace admitted that it was possible, but without the picture, they were no closer to solving Sam's murder than they were before.

"Why are you so certain that Tom didn't kill them both?"

"He doesn't really have a motive to kill Sam." When Kyle started to interrupt, she said, "I know what you think, he saw Hope and Sam hug and flew into a jealous rage, but Tom's just not the jealous type. I've never known him to rage at anything, either. I still think there's more to this. There has to be another reason why Sam died. Where are your dry erase boards?" she asked, taking off her coat and laying it across the table.

Kyle rolled off the bed and onto his knees. Peering under the bed, he said, "There you are. I had wondered where you had hopped off to. You were supposed to be in your home," he said, coming back up with Abry in his arms and explaining he had stashed the boards under the bed.

Grace picked up Abry's still locked rabbit cage. "You should have named that rabbit, Houdini. You know, he's a better escape artist than you."

"What have you done to yourself?" Kyle asked, still speaking to the bunny.

Curious, Grace walked over to where Kyle was still kneeling. Bending down she ran her good hand over the bunny's fur. "He's got little pink and blue spots all over his fur."

"Green too," Kyle said, holding out a green bunny foot for Grace's inspection.

Realization dawned on them both at the same time. "The boards!"

Kyle groaned as he bent down and looked under the bed. Within minutes, he had all three boards out and displayed on the bed. The suspect boards were a mess of colorful bunny tracks. "They sort of resemble an abstract art painting. Who knew Abry was so talented?"

Grace only took a passing glance at what remained of the suspect boards, feeling like she knew the suspects intimately at this point and could recite them in her sleep. Instead, she dragged the timeline board away from the other two, and with Kyle's help, propped it against the pillows. Luckily, there were only a few bunny tracks, obscuring Kyle's work.

TIMELINE

2001

May 20th Sam's accident.

July 24th Sam is released from the hospital.

Summer, fall, and winter – Sam works on a screenplay with Adam.

December 15th Christmas Party – Tom asks Hope to marry him.

2002

January 1st New Year's Party – Crystal and Sam start dating.

January 15th Sarah Collins dies when an icicle falls on her head. Witnessed by Sam. Eric is alibied by Tom.

May 9th Hope tells Tom, she doesn't want Sam to live with them.

May 10th Graduation Day.

9:30-9:40 Hope and Sam meet in the tower. Witnessed by Tom.

10:00 Hope and Tom argue.

10:30 Commencement Starts.

11:45 Crystal finds Sam's body – news spreads across school.

May 12th Sam's funeral'; Tom breaks up with Hope.

May 20th Hope leaves for Europe; Grace leaves for college.

June – July David Hart arrives. He and Melodie begin dating. Someone pushes him down the stairs (Suspects: Melodie, Steve or Larry).

June 22nd Crystal and Tom marry.

August Larry runs Steve out of town.

2012

February Larry cheats – Steve investigates; Crystal begins blackmailing Larry; tries to blackmail Diana.

June 25th Crystal files for divorce.

July 2nd Larry commits suicide.

July 15th Crystal contacts Adam.

July 20th Crystal stops the divorce proceedings; Tom and Crystal reconcile.

August 1st – Adam arrives in town.

August 25th Reunion – Slideshow is stolen – Crystal fights with Adam – Adam defaces the Bird's eye view from the Bell Tower' drawing – 'Most likely to' boards were defaced (more than likely by Hope) - Crystal is murdered – three trophies are taken.

September 1st Adam is murdered.

Grace's mind focused on the last entry. It was still strange to think that several of her childhood friends were dead. She felt her eyes well up with tears as she remembered playing with Sam,

Crystal, Larry, and Adam in her backyard when she was a little girl.

Kyle came around the bed and stood next to her, still holding Abry in his arms.

"Grace, we need to talk," he said, blowing out the breath he was holding.

"Uh oh. That sounds ominous."

"It is, actually," he said, moving the board to the side and sitting down on the bed. "I haven't had a chance to tell you what Steve said to me yesterday."

Grace looked down at Kyle. "What's wrong?"

"Steve made a couple of good points. We really don't know what we're doing here."

Grace smirked. "Since when did that bother you? Besides, we know more than Steve."

Kyle reached out and gently took her uninjured hand. "I don't know about that. He is a professional."

Grace scoffed. "A professional? Please. He's about as professional as we are."

"He's been at this far longer than we have."

"Yes, and he's no closer to solving these murders than we are."

"I'm just saying things are getting kind of dangerous. I'm worried. I don't want anything to happen to you."

Grace smiled. "Don't worry. I doubt the killer will be coming after me. After all, he or she got what she wanted. Without that picture, we're no closer to solving Sam's murder."

"I guess not."

At Kyle's pensive expression, she asked, "Did Steve say anything else?"

"Well, he did make me an offer. He wants to become my partner."

Grace laughed. "How did he react when you told him no?"

Kyle looked down at Abry. "Surprisingly well," he said softly.

"I have a feeling that if we could just see that picture for ourselves, we would know who killed Sam."

Grace reached out and ran her good hand through Abry's new colorful fur, feeling slightly calmer as she petted the bunny. "How are we going to get all of these spots out?"

"Here take Abry," Kyle said. Grace happily cuddled the Abry next to her chest, as Kyle walked to the table and began rummaging through her purse.

"I promise you, I don't have any bunny shampoo in my purse."

"No, but you have these." Kyle held up the keys to the Camaro. "Let's go talk to Melodie again. Maybe if we describe the picture to her it would spark something. I mean, there has to be something on it that points to the murderer. At the very least, we can find out why she was so angry when she saw the picture. You know, she's starting to worry me. She calls me a dozen times a day. Is she always this…" Kyle paused, searching for the right word, "intense?"

Grace stood next to the bed, staring down at the dry erase boards.

"Grace?"

When she didn't answer him, he walked over to her and ran his hand down her back. "Grace, are you okay?"

"Did David Hart happen to mention when he came to town?"

"Um, June 2002. About a month after you all graduated."

Grace smiled. "That's what I thought. I think it's time to talk to Sheriff Bellamy. I've got a pretty good idea who killed Sam."

🏆 🏆 🏆

Sheriff Bellamy led them out into the hallway. Clapping a hand on Kyle's back, he gently pushed him towards the door. "Come back when you actually have something close to evidence."

Grace followed Kyle into the hallway. She had spent the last hour, carefully explaining to Bellamy who killed Sam and why. To her surprise, he actually listened before telling them it was a nice theory, but without any evidence, it wasn't worth investigating. Unfortunately, he then went into excruciating detail on what constitutes good evidence and what doesn't. Only after their eyes had glazed over, and they were sufficiently schooled, did the sheriff take pity and let them go with a promise, that if they could prove their "little theory," then he would be more than happy to arrest the perpetrator.

Passing Kyle and Bellamy, Grace paused only long enough to wave to Tom and Melodie, who were just coming out of Tom's office.

Before she could reach the door, she felt Kyle's hand close on her arm. "I need to talk to you."

"Hi Kyle," Melodie called, running up to him and wrapping her arms around his neck. "Just the person I wanted to see. What are you doing here?"

Kyle shrugged. "Not much. You?"

"I was just visiting, Tom. I needed to talk to him about Crystal's estate. How about lunch?"

Feeling Grace pull away, Kyle tightened his grip. "I can't right now."

"Oh no, here comes Steve. Please say yes," she said, pouting.

Sighing, he looked from Grace to Melodie. "I can't, Melodie. I agreed to meet Steve for lunch today."

"*Steve?*" both women said at the same time.

"Hey ladies. Are my ears burning?"

Melodie and Grace groaned.

"You ready, Drake?"

"Yeah, just give me a second. Grace, I really need to speak to you, now. Could you just follow me for a second?"

Grace followed him to a corner of the room. Once she was next to him, she looked over her shoulder. "What's going on? Why are you going to lunch with Steve?" she whispered.

"Grace. I've been trying to tell you all day," he said. "I've decided to go into business with Steve."

"What?" she shouted. "Are you crazy?"

"Would you lower your voice, please?" he said, looking over his shoulder. Melodie, Steve, Tom, and Bellamy were awkwardly standing off to the side, pretending they couldn't hear every word they were saying. "They can hear you."

"I don't care if they do. I'm not working with Steve Mattingly."

Kyle sighed, running his hand through his hair. "You don't have to."

"What do you mean by that?"

"Just what I said. I'm working with Steve now. You're not a part of this."

"I don't believe this? You're firing me?" Grace laughed. "You're the one that dragged me into this. If you remember, I wanted nothing to do with your investigation."

"I know. I shouldn't have gotten you involved. I'm sorry. I hope we still can be friends." He looked over at Steve and waved. "Look, I have to go. Bye Grace." He reluctantly turned away and took a step towards Steve and Melodie, who were openly staring at them.

Grace pulled him back around. "Listen to me. What's happened? Are you angry with me or something?"

Kyle shook his head. "No, not at all. I just don't need your help anymore. Please, don't take it personally. This is purely a business decision. If you need a reference—"

"A reference?" she repeated slowly. "A reference? You must be kidding. Why are you doing this? We are so close to catching the killer."

"No," he said, crossing his arms, "we aren't. Didn't you just hear the sheriff? You have absolutely no evidence."

"But I've been thinking and I'm pretty sure I know where we can find the picture. If you would just listen—"

"No, Grace. I'm not listening to you anymore. I told you Bellamy wouldn't believe you, but you insisted on coming here and talking to him anyway. Just stay out of it," he said harshly.

CHAPTER TWENTY-TWO

"I HAVE THE picture of Sam on the bell tower, and I know you killed him. I'm willing to part with it for a price. One hundred thousand dollars. Meet me at Adam's cabin and you can have it." Grace smirked. "Why would I hand over the picture to Kyle Drake? You must not have heard. I no longer work for him . . . Don't worry, this isn't a trap. You bring me the money and you can have the picture. If you don't, then I'll go to the police. I'll look like a hero. Albeit a very poor hero. I'd much rather be one hundred thousand dollars richer—"

Listening carefully, Grace said, "Oh, I think they'd believe me. Once they see that picture, they'd have to take me seriously." Turning off her phone, Grace smiled at Kyle, who was busy shaking the dirt out of his hair.

"Do you really think this is going to work?"

Grace placed the phone on the table. "We'll know soon." Worriedly, she chewed at her bottom lip. "I just wish the sheriff was here."

"Why, you need another lecture on police procedure?"

"He had a point." They didn't really have any proof. All the evidence that could be collected was long gone. All they had was conjecture. They were guessing. Baring a full confession, Sam's death would remain a suicide.

Kyle propped his feet onto the table. His normally cheerful features were grim. "Relax. I'll be right here. What could possibly go wrong?"

"Everything." Grace looked around at the shack. Kyle had spent the last few hours rearranging the shack for "maximum effect." "I still don't know why you wanted to do it here?"

"I needed room to work, and we needed someplace safe."

"We're miles from anyone," she pointed out. "Besides, it wasn't too safe for Adam. He tried the same thing not too long ago and look what happened to him."

"I meant safe for our guest. We don't want to advertise that we're setting a trap. Hopefully, our little performance worked." Kyle ran a hand over his face and rubbed his eyes. "It's not too late. We could always back out and go home."

"Now you're starting to sound scared," she accused.

"Terrified," he admitted cheerfully. "You should be, too."

"Don't worry. I have something Adam didn't," she said, amused by his questioning expression. "You."

"True."

🏆 🏆 🏆

Yawning, Grace threw down the deck of cards and rubbed the back of her neck. Stretching, she stood up and looked out the window. Five hours had passed since the phone call. Five of the most boring and terrifying hours of her life. She was just about to call it quits and go home, when she saw the headlights of a car bounce along the dirt road.

Heart pounding, she unlocked the door, turned off the lights and backed into the room. Standing on the chair sitting in the middle of the room, she reached up and removed the overhead light bulb. Hopping off the chair, she moved it to the side and got back into position. Wiping her sweating palms on her jeans, she told herself to relax.

"Grace?" Diana called out. "Are you here?"

"I'm over here, Diana."

"Where? Why do you have the lights off?"

Grace flipped a switch and one of Adam's movie lights came on. Pointing straight at Diana. Blinding her.

Diana threw up her hands to shield her eyes. "Grace this is ridiculous. I can't see you."

"Good. Considering what happened to Adam, I think that's a good idea, don't you?"

"Sweetie, I don't understand what you're talking about. You said you had my picture. What picture were you talking about?" she asked, straining her eyes, looking for Grace.

"You know what picture."

Diana smirked. "You're going to have to be more specific than that. Describe it or I walk," she said, all pretense gone.

Using what Grace learned from Beth, Grace described the picture as best as she could.

Diana shook her head in disbelief. "Where's Drake?"

"I told you on the phone that he fired me earlier today. I was surprised that you hadn't heard."

"No, I had heard. Melodie told me this afternoon. I'm just surprised. You should have left things alone Grace. Did you show Drake the picture before you came here?"

"Don't worry. This is just between you and me. You give me the money, and I'll return the picture to you. There's no reason why my ex-employer should know anything about this."

Diana reached into her bag and pulled out several large stacks of cash. She took a few steps toward the sound of Grace's voice.

"No. Place them on the kitchen counter behind you, please."

Diana stopped, and glared into the darkness for several seconds, before turning around and slamming the money onto the counter.

"Is that all of it?"

Diana nodded. "I'm surprised at you Grace. I would expect this sort of thing from your sister, but not you. You should be ashamed of yourself."

"You're questioning my morality? That's rich, since you murdered not only Sam and Adam, but I'm betting, your own niece, too. Besides, I was fired today, I need the cash."

"I never said I killed Sam or Adam or," she said her voice cracking "Crystal. It's crazy. Why would I kill anyone?"

"Then why did you bring me a stack of money?"

"I just want the picture, Grace. I didn't have anything to do with their deaths. It was Tom. He's crazy, you know. He wanted Crystal and Sam was in the way. I tried to tell you—"

Grace ignored her. "You were in love with Sam."

"What an imagination you have. Sam was a student."

"You spent a lot of time with him after his accident. Eric told me he was often at your office. You helped him recover. Sam was handsome, smart, kind. I'm sure it was easy to fall in love with him. After all, you weren't that much older. Your husband had left you for another woman. You were vulnerable. Sam was broken. He needed you. It was so easy to take advantage."

Diana shook her head vehemently. "It wasn't like that. I saw Tom kill him. I was terrified."

"You had to keep the relationship secret. He may have just turned eighteen, but he was still a student. You couldn't risk the scandal. You used to meet in the bell tower, didn't you? That was your secret place."

"Why won't you believe me? I'm telling you, it was Tom—"

Grace ignored the interruption. "No Diana, it was you. Only school personnel had keys to get into the tower. That's how I figured out it was you. It was so simple. How did Sam get a key to the tower? How was the murderer able to unlock the trophy case? The killer needed a key and only school personnel had a key. Out of all of our suspects, only you and Eric work at the school. Then, there was the picture of Sam on the bell tower, taken right around the time of that horrible ice storm. At first, I thought he was covered in bruises, but then I realized, that wasn't right. His accident occurred in the summer before our senior year, so he couldn't still be covered in bruises. Then I thought, if they weren't bruises, what else could they be? That's when I remembered the charcoal drawing of the school. According to the plaque, it was drawn during the winter of 2002. He wasn't covered in bruises. He was covered in charcoal dust.

All this time, I thought the DH stood for David Hart, but he didn't show up until the summer after graduation and then he left a few months later. The DH had to be someone else. You must have been going by your maiden name the day you drew the picture. You're a very good artist, Diana. I was really impressed with the oil painting you did of Crystal."

Diana simply shook her head, her voice soft. "Crystal and Sam were in love—"

"No, they weren't. Those few moments in the bell tower or in your office weren't enough. You needed an excuse to see him all the time. That's how Crystal got involved. How much did you pay her to pretend to date Sam?"

Diana took a few steps into the shack. Squinting against the light, she peered into the darkness behind the light. She smirked. "I'm impressed, Grace. You've got one thing wrong. I didn't pay her. I told her I would help her keep Tom and Hope apart. I didn't, but Crystal didn't know that. I actually liked your sister."

Grace pressed on. "Everything was going so well, wasn't it? You were in love and were planning on moving with him to the east coast after graduation. You had it all planned but then graduation came and you found out that he didn't feel the same about you. That's the day you found out that he didn't love you."

"That's not true. He loved me."

"No, Diana." Grace sighed dramatically. "Sam was going to leave you."

"No!"

"He didn't love you. He was planning to leave, without you. You couldn't take it. Another man that you loved, walking out on you. So, you pushed him out of the tower."

"That's not true. He loved me. It was an accident."

"Was it? He told Eric he was leaving. Is that what he told you when you met him up in the tower? You must have been so angry. So angry, you pushed him, and he fell."

"It was an accident!"

"Crystal knew you had been up in the tower when Sam died. She covered up for you. I bet she helped you clean everything up before Sam's body was found. Didn't she?"

Diana took a step closer.

"She loved you. She wanted to protect you."

Diana laughed mercilessly. "She didn't do it for me. She did it for Tom."

Grace shook her head in confusion. She knew Tom had to be involved somehow, but she still had no clue how. "Why did she help you for Tom?"

"Tom was such a fool. Crystal told me that she and Tom were in the parking lot when Hope was in the tower having her little heart to heart with Sam. They apparently saw them hug each other."

"Where were you?"

"I was below, waiting for your sister to finally leave. Crystal, ever the opportunist, immediately tried to convince Tom that Hope was cheating on him. While they were arguing in the parking lot, Hope finally left and I . . . went up the stairs . . ." Diana trailed off.

"Tom and Crystal saw you push Sam off the tower," Grace guessed, still trying to figure out why Tom would have lied to protect Diana.

Diana laughed again. A strained, angry type of laugh. "Crystal saw it happen, but Tom's back was turned. He still thought it was Hope in the tower. As soon as she saw Sam fall, she ran to the tower, with Tom close behind. They found . . . him lying there, with Hope's bracelet in his hand. It must have fallen off when they hugged."

"So, Tom thought Hope had killed Sam?"

Diana laughed again, as if it was the funniest thing she had ever heard. "Can you believe that? Crystal told him she saw Hope push Sam, and he believed her. She grabbed the bracelet and then started to run. Tom caught up to her and begged her not to tell. He was willing to promise anything to save Hope. That's all Crystal needed to hear."

Dumbstruck, Grace asked, "That's why Tom married Crystal? To protect, Hope?"

Diana nodded. "He's such an idiot. Crystal promised not to say anything if he would drop Hope and marry her. Why she wanted him is beyond me. I told her it would never work, but I was wrong. Every time he stepped out of line, she would threaten to send Hope's bloody bracelet to the police, as well as a statement as to what she saw. I never understood why he would put up with Crystal just to protect Hope. He finally cracked a few months ago on their anniversary. He refused to do something Crystal wanted, so Crystal decided to divorce him. She told him she was going to the police, too. He panicked. You should have seen him. Begging her not to tell. That he would do whatever she wanted. I kept thinking he would eventually kill her, but no such luck. He's so pathetic."

"Is that why you killed Crystal? Because she threatened to go to the police?"

"She wasn't going to the police. She just said that to try to get Tom to jump back in line. No, she would never have called the police. She decided to call Adam, instead. She was desperate for money. She was going to tell him everything, but it wasn't going to be the lie she had told Tom. No, I knew she was going to tell the truth. She was going to sell me out," she said bitterly. "Can you believe it? She was going to betray her own aunt."

"Why would she tell Adam the truth? You were safe as long as she had Tom. If she told the world that you killed Sam, then Tom would leave her."

Diana glared at Grace in utter disappointment. "It wouldn't have lasted much longer," she said patronizingly. "She was growing tired of the way Tom treated her. And Tom couldn't keep up the charade any longer. I knew when she took him back, it wasn't going to last. He couldn't even bother hiding his contempt of her. She started spending more and more time with Simpson. I could tell that she was setting herself up to be the next Mrs. Simpson. No, she wouldn't have been with Tom much longer. Why would she want him, when she could have James Simpson? Someone who actually liked her. Crystal was such an idiot. She spent ten years trying to get Tom to stop loving Hope and to fall in love with her. Nothing worked. So, when she finally filed for divorce, and called Adam, I knew she was eventually going to betray me."

"But she changed her mind. You didn't have to kill her. She had decided not to tell Adam what she knew. She remained loyal to you."

"Loyal," Diana scoffed. "Did you know that she tried to blackmail me before? Not for the murder, but for something else. She would never have dared try to blackmail me for the murder. She knew what I was capable of."

Grace nodded her head before realizing that the other woman couldn't see her. "She set you up to have an affair. I'm surprised you didn't kill her then."

Diana vigorously shook her head. "I wanted to, but I couldn't do it. She had no idea that I knew. Melodie had told me what Crystal had done to Larry. It didn't take a genius to figure out she must have been the one to set me up, too." She sighed softly. "I realized Crystal couldn't be trusted anymore, but I still didn't want to kill her. She was my niece and I loved her. Then after I returned home, and when Eric and I began to reconcile, she tried to warn him away from me."

"Why?"

"She liked him. She was afraid that I was going to hurt him. Like, I'm some sort of crazy psycho. I wouldn't have hurt, Eric. If I wanted to kill him, I would have done it all long time ago."

"But you killed Sam."

"I told you," she yelled. "It was an accident. He said he was leaving, and that I couldn't come with him. I was angry and I slapped him. He lost his balance and fell. I swear it was an accident."

"What happened to Crystal wasn't an accident."

"No," she admitted softly. "I finally had to do something. She stole that picture of Sam. The only picture I ever kept of him. Then she put it on the slideshow for everyone to see. Then she wrote all over my charcoal drawing. Telling the whole world that Sam didn't commit suicide. She even had the gall to act like she didn't do it."

"But she didn't," Grace insisted. "Adam's the one who wrote that message on the drawing."

Diana ignored her. "If someone had seen that . . . Luckily, I found it in time and was able to destroy it. I kept hoping she would change. I kept giving her chance after chance, but she left me no choice."

"Did Adam leave you no choice?"

Diana laughed again. "He thought he was so clever. He figured out that Sam and I were . . . together. He thought . . ." She started laughing hysterically. "He thought . . ."

Grace gripped the side of her chair. It suddenly occurred to her Diana was becoming unhinged.

Grace couldn't take it anymore. "He thought you killed Sarah Collins."

Diana nodded her head. Taking a deep breath, she regained her composure. "At first, but I finally convinced him that I had nothing to do with her death. I even showed him the affidavits of the doctors at the ER. You should have seen his face. It was so sad. He was so disappointed. He thought he had it all figured out. Well, I didn't want him to walk away disappointed, not when he was so close. So, I told him that I knew who had killed Sam." Diana started giggling again.

"Let me guess. You tried to blame Tom."

Diana nodded. "I told him that Tom killed Sam, so that he could have Crystal all to himself. It was so easy to convince him. I even sent him an anonymous note about where Tom buried those trophies. I was certain that he had buried them around the fountain. Adam even asked for my help in prosecuting Tom. Can you believe it? I told him no. I was far too terrified of Tom," she said giggling. "He said not to worry. He even said he would pay me for my story." Diana leaned against the door. "Pay me. Like I wanted his money. I was more than happy to talk about Tom, but I wasn't about to talk about me and Sam."

"Why did Tom steal the trophies?"

Diana placed her hand on the door and shook her head. "Why do you think? I had used Hope's trophy to kill Crystal. I wasn't trying to implicate your sister, you understand. I've always liked Hope. I just knew Tom would bend over backwards to cover up the crime if he thought Hope was the murderer." Diana snickered. "And he did. Luckily, he was the first one to find her body. I had covered it with Hope's wrap. It was so funny. You should have seen him. Rushing around trying to hide evidence. I tried to tell the police that I saw him hiding a duffle bag that night, but they didn't care. If they had just looked in his car, they would have found Hope's wrap, the trophies, everything. He would have been blamed and then I wouldn't have had anything to worry about." Diana turned around and locked the door.

Grace felt a chill run down her spine. "I made a copy of that picture. If anything happens to me it will be sent to the police."

"I don't think you have the picture, Grace." Diana reached into her purse and pulled out a gun. Aiming at the light she pulled the trigger. Sparks flew throughout the cabin, before sending the room into compete darkness.

"That was really clever about the charcoal. I never even worried about that. I mean, who would have made that connection. Tell you what Grace, I won't kill you if you can describe the picture in detail. And in case you're wondering, there's just enough light behind you to make you out."

Grace leaned back against her chair.

"Come on Grace, at least guess. No?" she said, as she took aim. "All right, I'll give you a hint. You can just make out my left hand in the picture. What am I wearing on my left hand?"

Realization dawning, Grace shouted, "Your ring! You can see your ruby engagement ring in the picture."

"Oh, very good Grace! But I'm so sorry! Time's out! Bye bye Grace," she said, pulling the trigger.

Grace fell to the ground at the first hail of gunfire. The sound of breaking glass could be heard over the shots. Diana had fired four times before finally realizing something was wrong. Walking to the center of the room, she discovered shards of mirror fragments, instead of a bloody and dead Grace.

Grace pressed a remote control button, turning on a small tape recorder in the corner of the room. The sound of furniture falling and scuffling could be heard through the speakers.

Turning, Diana began firing aimlessly toward the sound until she ran out of bullets.

As soon as Grace heard the telltale click, she screamed for Kyle. The last two lamps came on, nearly blinding Grace.

Blinking rapidly at the sudden light, Grace opened the door to the closet she had been hiding in and ran forward just as Kyle came barreling in from outside. They both reached Diana at the same time. While Kyle held Diana in a bear hug, Grace wrestled the gun away.

Diana looked wildly from one to the other. "But I heard you!" she sputtered. "I saw you! You were right in front of me!"

EPILOGUE

"I KNEW THERE had to be a good explanation!" Hope said, smugly. "Of course, he still loved me. I've been saying that for years."

"Uh huh," Grace muttered, half listening, as she folded the newspaper in two. Her sister had been unbearable since hearing Diana's confession the night before. Every sentence had been a repeat of how wonderful Tom was, how brave Tom was, how much Tom loves her, ad nauseum.

"I should have made him talk to me. But of course he couldn't, not without endangering me and he would never do that."

Grace rolled her eyes.

"I called him the moment Diana started rattling on about how Crystal had tricked him."

Grace smiled at the memory. Everything had worked so well. Kyle had set up the laptop's webcam to capture Diana's confession. Jeff had been recruited and was recording everything back at home. It worked like a charm. Well, except for the actual video. Turned out the video was too dark for anyone to actually see anything, but they could hear what was being said, which was the important part.

Unbeknownst to Grace and Kyle, they had quite the audience. Jeff, unable to keep any kind of secret for more than a few minutes, told Hope, who then informed their parents. Even the sheriff had been watching. The moment Grace's siblings ratted her out and told their parents, they all rushed to Bellamy's office and forced him to watch. From what Grace had been told, he spent most of the time laughing, but the moment Diana started talking, he hopped into his squad car and rushed to the cabin. He arrived just moments after Grace had taken Diana's gun away and Kyle had pushed her into a chair. They've been quite the heroes ever since. Well, not to everyone, Grace thought, looking up from the want ads.

"Poor boy," Hope said, preening at herself in her compact mirror. "How he must have suffered all this time. Can you imagine?"

Grace nodded, "I'm sure it's nothing to what I'm experiencing right now."

If Hope heard the insult, she ignored it; instead, she focused on how she and Tom could now pick up where they had left off ten years ago.

"Except, he's going to jail. He's going to be disbarred."

Hope angrily slammed her compact down. "That is ridiculous. He should get a medal."

"For what?"

"For doing the right thing!"

"He hid evidence. He interfered with not one, but two crime scenes."

Hope scoffed. "So? He was protecting me."

"He thought you were a murderer. Doesn't that disturb you, just a little?"

Hope shook her head. "I spoke to him last night. He never thought I murdered Sam or Crystal. Not for one minute. He was convinced that someone was trying to frame me. He did all that," Hope said waiving her hand, "other stuff to protect me. I would like to point out, that if he hadn't, I could have ended up in jail. Some fool might have actually believed I had killed Sam . . . or *her*," she said sneering. "Of course, I don't know how anyone could actually believe I could do such a thing, but he just couldn't take the chance. Crystal had my bracelet. It was covered in Sam's blood. If she had sent it to the police and then told them that she saw me push Sam . . . I could have gone to jail. Poor Tom. He would have been devastated."

"Hey, look, the saloon is looking for a waitress. I could do that," Grace said, circling the ad with a red magic marker. When her sister didn't say anything, Grace looked up.

"I just want to thank you, Grace," Hope said, reaching out to grip her sister's uninjured hand. If it wasn't for you and Kyle, Tom would still be avoiding me."

Grace felt a warm glow spread across her face.

"I take back every bad thing I said, when Jeff told me what you were doing. Even though, I agreed with everything Sheriff Bellamy said at the time, I take it all back. You're not incompetent or foolish or a complete embarrassment to the family."

"Thanks, that means a lot," Grace said, not completely sure if her sister was apologizing or not.

"I mean, at least you had a professional with you like Kyle. He seems like he knows what he's doing. But then again," Hope said tightening her grip, "if you had left well enough alone, Tom wouldn't be going to jail. And since Crystal was dead, he could have come back to me once everything settled down."

Grace started to bristle. "What is this Hope? Are you thanking me or not?"

Hope smiled, as she patted Grace's hand. "Oh well, you did the best you could."

Grace removed her hand. "Thanks and I truly hope they offer conjugal visits wherever Tom ends up."

"Funny," she said, glaring at Grace, "I *was* trying to be nice."

"Yes, I know. That's what makes it so sad."

Hope opened her mouth to say something, but closed it when the doorbell chimed.

Both sisters continued to sit at the table as the door chime rang, neither one willing to give up their position to answer the door. Only after Grace pointed out it could be Tom, did Hope give up and leave the kitchen.

Smiling at her small victory, Grace went back to the want ads. "Oh! The horse ranch needs a helping hand . . . with a college degree. Wonderful," she said, tearing it out and applying it to the pile. "Looks like my degree in business is going to come in handy."

"Where are your parents?" Kyle asked, as he slowly walked into the kitchen. He looked around the room, making sure she was alone, before sitting across from her.

"They're out."

Kyle visibly relaxed. Grace nodded sympathetically. Her parents were less than happy when they found out what was going on last night. Even less, when Diana started shooting the cabin up. Kyle had tried to explain how Grace was not in any real danger. Using mirrors, darkness and a few magic tricks—which he had refused to explain to anyone—he had set up the room to misdirect Diana's attention. While it appeared that Grace was in the center of the room, in actuality, she was safely hidden away. Everyone was impressed, everyone except her mom and dad.

Looking at the want ad page spread across the table, Kyle grimaced. "What are you doing?"

"I'm doing what you should be doing. Looking for a job."

Leaning over the table, Kyle smiled. "I have a job. Did you see everyone's faces last night? They ate everything I said up." Kyle was nothing if not a good showman. "Even Bellamy. I was slapped on the back so hard, they left bruises."

"You're forgetting one thing. Money. We both need money. Did Melodie pay you the rest of the money she had promised?"

Kyle looked down at the table. "No. She says she has to save up to help her aunt. Apparently, Diana is already pleading insanity."

Grace figured as much. "Did Melodie say anything about the bell tower picture?"

"She admitted she saw the picture at the reunion. It was exactly as Beth described it, except she said you could clearly see Diana's hand and her ruby ring. Melodie said she had no idea, until she saw the picture that Diana and Sam were a couple."

"So, she was hiding the picture from me."

Kyle nodded. "She wants to apologize to you. She knew what you were looking for, but she couldn't help you without betraying her aunt's secret. She said she didn't start suspecting

Diana had murdered Crystal and was trying to frame Tom, until just recently. She was too afraid to say anything."

Grace promised to call her as she handed the want ads to Kyle, who informed her there was new advanced technology out there called a computer and the internet, which she could use to find jobs. "Besides, I keep telling you, we have a job. The clients are going to come pouring in. See," he said, turning the paper over to the front page and pointing to the front headline, "there we are. *Local Murders Solved by Drake and Mattingly Investigations*."

Grace pointed to the picture under the headline, showing a smiling Steve Mattingly shaking Sheriff Bellamy's hand. "Remind me again why you gave him credit for solving the case?"

Kyle looked sheepish. "I had to give him something. He was threatening to tell everyone that I was fake. It's just a temporary arrangement. Besides, what could it hurt?"

Dubious, Grace smoothed out the paper. "I need money, Kyle. Right now. So do you."

Kyle grinned smugly, waiving a check in front of her. "Don't worry. We have a new client."

"Who?"

"It's a real simple case."

"Who?"

"We already know all of the particulars."

"Who?"

"She just wrote us a check for over a thousand dollars, up front."

"Who?"

"Your sister. She wants us to prove Tom's innocence."

Sighing, Grace refolded the paper. "The comic book store needs a bookkeeper. That sounds like a winner," she said, circling it in red and adding a big red star in the corner.

The End

Thank you for reading Deadly Reunion! I hope you enjoyed my book. If you did enjoy it and if you have time, please consider posting a review at www.amazon.com or visiting my blog at www.elisabethcrabtree.wordpress.com. I would love to hear from you.

Thank you!

Made in the USA
San Bernardino, CA
21 February 2014